The
VIRGIN

Look for Tiffany Reisz's next installment
in The Original Sinners: The White Years
coming soon from MIRA Books

TIFFANY REISZ

The VIRGIN

MIRA

Recycling programs for this product may not exist in your area.

ISBN-13: 978-0-7783-1797-5

The Virgin

For questions and comments about the quality of this book, please contact us at CustomerService@Harlequin.com.

www.MIRABooks.com

Printed in U.S.A.

First printing: April 2015
10 9 8 7 6 5 4 3 2 1

Dedicated to Dr. Mark Lucas, who told me I could write.

So I did.

1

"IT WAS A DARK AND STORMY NIGHT," NORA SAID AS she came to stand next to Søren at the window. She gazed out on the summer storm tearing up the Scottish sky.

"Please tell me that isn't the first line to your next book."

"Oh, but it's such a good first line. Classic even." She tucked her hand into his and watched the light show with him. Wind and rain lashed the trees and the moors. A flash of lightning set the night afire for a split second and the hills revealed their colors before fading into black again. "How about this—'It was a dark and stormy night in the castle, and a woman named Nora was determined to seduce her priest.'"

Søren smiled slightly.

"An improvement. A minor improvement."

"Everyone's a critic." Nora squeezed his hand, and he lifted it to his lips for a kiss. He'd arrived this morning but she'd been so busy with her work here that they hadn't had more than five minutes together. At last the day was done, her work was over until tomorrow, and they could hold hands and simply be.

"Do I want to know what you're thinking?" Nora asked him.

"Merely watching the storm," he said, but she could tell he had something on his mind, on his heart. They both did.

Tomorrow was the big day… Everything between her and

Søren would change tomorrow. It was happening finally and there was no going back.

"Are you nervous about tomorrow?" she asked.

"Should I be?"

"I am," she admitted. "Big day for us."

"I'm at peace," he said. "Although I will admit the peace is hard-won."

"We've waited a long time to do this."

"It's time now," he said. "We've waited long enough."

A clap of thunder interrupted their conversation and together they peered into the storm outside the oriel window.

"What are you thinking?" Nora asked.

"Thinking about Job, chapter thirty-eight," he said. "It's every priest's dream to have God come and speak to him face-to-face. Even if it is to tell him how little he knows about the world. Storms always remind me of those verses. God says, 'Have you ever given orders to the morning, or shown the dawn its place?'"

Nora looked up at the sky. "'Can you raise your voice to the clouds / and cover yourself with a flood of water? / Do you send lightning bolts on their way? / Do they report to you / Here we are.'"

"It's comforting to know God is so powerful. Comforting to know we aren't," Søren said.

Perhaps only a priest could find comfort in his powerlessness. Perhaps only Søren.

"Are you coming to bed?" she asked Søren.

"Not yet. I won't be ready to sleep for hours."

In Scotland, it was nine-thirty. In New Orleans, where they'd been living for the past two years, it was half past three in the afternoon.

"Who said anything about sleeping?" she asked.

Søren arched his eyebrow.

"Well, in that case…" Søren turned from the window and

cupped her face with his hands. He kissed her on the lips, softly at first, a slight kiss meant to arouse and torment. Ever so slowly he deepened the kiss. As much as she wanted to, Nora didn't rush the moment. She'd been away from him for five weeks—four weeks spent with Nico at his vineyard and another week here in Scotland making the final preparations for tomorrow. Leaving Søren for any extended period of time was much like this kiss—a torture and a tease. Being away from him hurt, always. But the reunion at the end of the separation made every second apart worth the price.

He took her hands in his and brought them up and around his neck. His arms encircled her back and he drew her to him, deepening the kiss. The heat of his body warmed her to the core. She kissed his lips, his chin, his ear and his neck. He'd abandoned his collar for traveling and tonight wore only black trousers, black jacket and a white button-down shirt open at the neck. She pressed her lips into the hollow of his throat, a hollow made for her kisses.

And the moment when the kiss was perfect, everything she wanted and needed from him, she heard from behind her a small cough.

"Ms. Sutherlin?"

"God fucking dammit." Nora growled the words, and dropped her head to the center of Søren's chest.

"Eleanor, you're scaring the waitstaff," Søren said.

She turned and faced the interrupter, a young woman holding a bouquet of flowers. Her name might be Bonnie, or maybe she was just "bonnie" in the Scottish sense of pretty. Nora didn't know and didn't care.

"Miss, you've signed the nondisclosure agreement, haven't you?" Nora asked. Kingsley was treating tomorrow like a celebrity wedding with ironclad nondisclosure agreements for everyone even remotely involved. Even she'd had to sign one.

"Yes, ma'am?" The girl made everything she said into a question.

"Good. This man is a Catholic priest. We've been sleeping together since I was twenty. I'm sure you can imagine it's not easy being the mistress of a Catholic priest. We don't get to spend nearly the amount of time together we'd like to. In fact, I haven't seen him in five weeks. Admittedly that's because I was sleeping with someone else most of the time, but that's neither here nor there. As you can see, my priest here is possibly the most handsome man in the world, although I am admittedly biased. He's also kinky, well-hung and you've just interrupted the kiss I've been waiting for all day. So please tell me this interruption is more important than that kiss was."

"Your dress is here. We hung it in your room. You told me to tell you when it arrived and to interrupt you no matter what you were doing even if you were, as you said, 'blowing the pope.' Also, these arrived for you earlier today. They were accidentally put away with the wedding flowers," the girl said, passing the bouquet to Nora.

"Oh." Nora tapped her foot on the stone floor. "How nice."

"Eleanor…" Søren made her name into a threat.

"And sorry about the, you know, well-hung priest rant there," Nora said. "Pre-wedding jitters."

"It's fine, ma'am," the girl who was either bonnie or Bonnie said. "If he was kissing me, I'd be bloody pissed off to be interrupted, too. Catholic priest?"

"No comment," Søren said.

"We had a priest like you when I was a girl," she said. "We called him Father What-A-Waste. Glad you're not going to waste."

The girl bobbed a slightly sarcastic curtsy and sauntered off.

"Is it weird I kind of want to fuck her now?" Nora asked. "Castles makes me so horny."

"Little One?"

"Yes, sir?" She turned back to face him.

"Who are your flowers from?"

"No idea," she said. She looked through the small but exquisite posy of white roses, pink hydrangeas and green Cymbidium orchids until she found the small ivory card. She opened it up and read aloud,

"Dear Mistress,
I'm sorry I have to miss your wedding tomorrow but I never attend weddings where I'm not allowed to kiss the bride. Think of me during the ceremony—and on the wedding night. Love, Your Nico"

"Very kind of him," Søren said, smiling.

"He's a smart-ass like his father," Nora said. She tucked the card back into the envelope. "Now, where were we?"

"Here, I think," Søren said as he brought his arms around her waist and pulled her to him. He dropped gentle but hungry kisses along her neck.

"Oh yes, that's where we were."

"It's been too long since I've had the pleasure of beating you and putting you in your place." He whispered the words in her ear, and she shivered. "Do you even remember your place?"

"Underneath you, my sir," she said. "Or wherever you tell me it is."

"Very good answer."

He tapped her under the chin and she smiled. She did so love to please him. Collaring Nico two years ago and making him her property had been the best thing she could have done for her relationship with Søren. At the time she and Nico became lovers, she'd been running on pure instinct and grief and need. She'd gone to Nico searching for something she was missing and found it with him. Once she had a submissive of her own, her own personal property collared and owned, she

fully grasped Søren's love for her. Owning Nico had filled up
a void in her that not even Søren's love—boundless as it was—
could fill. She hadn't cleaned up her act, hadn't reformed. She
hadn't turned over a new leaf. Nora Sutherlin did not turn over
leaves—new or otherwise. But for the past two years she'd had
only two lovers—Søren and Nico—and wanted and needed
no one else in her bed or her heart. It might be the closest she
would ever get to monogamy.

Kingsley was already taking bets on how long it would last.

Søren took her by the hand and led her down the long ancient hallway. Portraits of noble Scotsmen, dead for centuries,
followed their progress as they walked the faded crimson car-
pet and took a set of stone stairs to the next floor. Lightning
created mad shadows in the castle. A suit of armor seemed to
move with one flash of light. A portrait of a young noblewoman
with pre-Raphaelite hair winked at Nora. The long-dead princess must have guessed what Nora and Søren had planned. Her
smile was one of approval. Envy even. Nora didn't blame the
lady. Who wouldn't want a night in Søren's bed?

The wink reminded Nora of someone she knew long ago.
And the castle reminded her of somewhere she'd once run
away to and hidden herself. The abbey. Her mother's abbey.
The gray stone walls, the wandering hallways and the portraits
like icons. The sound of her feet on the stone floors brought to
mind that year she'd lived in her mother's convent. Not quite
a full year but close enough. Close enough that she thought of
it always as "that year."

She pushed thoughts of the past away. The present was a far
more pleasant moment. Through an arched wooden door they
entered their bedroom. The fire in the fireplace was dead, but
no matter. Linen sheets and silk pillows invited them to the
bed. They needed only each other for warmth now.

Søren left her standing by the bed as he lit the bedside oil
lamp for light and the candles on the fireplace mantel for am-

bience. Nora slipped out of her shoes and let her feet sink into the soft woven rug that covered the stone floor. She put her flowers in the ice bucket, which made for a perfect makeshift vase. Displaying them on the table by the bed might be a little too much even for Søren so she set them on the fireplace mantel instead.

"We've never made love in a castle before, have we?" Nora asked as she turned from arranging her flowers to gaze around the room. She walked from the great stone fireplace to the hanging blue-and-red tapestries on the wall adorned with unicorns, dragons and knights.

"Belgium," Søren said as he strode to the bed, carrying a box in one hand and something long, thin and wrapped in fabric in the other. He snapped his fingers and she jogged to his side.

Nora smiled at the memory of a long-ago journey through Europe they'd taken together. An anniversary gift from Kingsley.

"We'll always have Belgium. And what was her name?"

"Odette." Søren opened the box that held her collar.

"Oh yes. That was it. She was fun, wasn't she?" While in Belgium, she and Søren had toured a little brewery and had met a beautiful Swiss translator named Odette. During the tasting, Odette had flirted shamelessly with them both—she and Søren had dueled over who knew more languages. Søren won, but just barely. After the tour, Odette had come back with them to their hotel room in a renovated castle. Nora had been young then, only twenty-four, and had never been that intimate with a woman. Søren hadn't touched Odette, but he'd certainly enjoyed watching the two of them together that night.

"You're smiling, Little One." Søren brought her collar around her neck and locked it on. While his fingers were at her throat he toyed with the necklace she wore always these days. It had three charms on it—two rings engraved with the words *Everything* and *Forever* and a small silver locket Nico had given her as a token of his adoration. They made a gentle clinking sound like tiny wind chimes when she moved.

"Good memories," she said. "So many good memories I've forgotten some of them."

"Speaking of memories, I have a gift for you. A gift in memory of something."

"You don't have to give me anything," she said, keeping her eyes low, respectful, submissive.

"I know," he said with that touch of arrogance she'd always loved and loathed in equal measure. "But it was time I gave you this."

He held up the bundle still covered in its fabric wrapping.

"What is it?"

"You'll find out. But you have to earn your gift first."

"It's not a gift if I have to earn it," she reminded him.

"Then we'll call it a 'prize.'"

"How do I earn my prize?"

"Trial by fire."

"You are in a mood tonight, aren't you?" she asked. "Sir?"

"Do you accept the challenge?" he asked, his eyebrow cocked, his smile tight but amused. She was thirty-eight years old, and she had loved Søren since she was fifteen…and yet…after all this time he could still scare the shit out of her.

God, she loved him.

"Yes, sir," she said. "I want my prize."

Søren cupped her face again, kissed her lips again.

"I already have my prize." He kissed her on the forehead.

She stood unmoving and made no protest as Søren stripped her naked. He unbuttoned her blouse and slid it off her arms. Under her shirt she wore a black corset, which he took an unnecessary amount of time unlacing. The more eager she was to have him inside her, the longer he took getting there. Her own fault for falling in love with a sadist, not that she regretted it. He unzipped her leather skirt and pushed it over her hips and down her legs. His fingers on her bare skin as he unhooked her stockings set her to shivering, even more when he tickled the bottoms of her feet as he pulled them off.

If she hadn't loved Søren before, she would fall in love with him again for looking at her thirty-eight-year-old body with the same desire that had once gazed on her naked seventeen-year-old form. She'd never suffered from a lack of self-esteem and had, more than once—rightly—been accused of being egotistical. A woman who took money from men for the privilege of letting them worship her had to have more than her fair share of confidence. But finding herself so much closer to forty than thirty had taken a little getting used to. Time had only increased Søren's beauty. The gray in his hair could barely be distinguished from the blond. The years had sharpened his features, scraped off the rough edges, and sculpted him into a man worthy of all the respect and love she had to give him. She had an older man to adore and a younger man who adored her.

Life was good.

"Someone's quiet," Søren said as he lifted her off her feet and laid her onto the bed on her back. The linen sheets tickled her, made her aware of every nerve in her body. "Are you nervous?"

"I was thinking about tomorrow."

"'Do not worry about tomorrow for tomorrow will worry about itself,'" Søren said.

"Yes, Father Stearns. I've read Matthew, too."

Søren set a basin on the nightstand by the bed and soaked a small white towel in the water.

"Good. Now stop worrying and hold still while I set you on fire."

Nora held still.

Fire-play wasn't so much about pain as it was fear. Fear and its mirror twin—trust. She closed her eyes while Søren painted her stomach with an ice-cold gel that smelled of rubbing alcohol. He took each of her wrists and buckled them one by one to the headboard with leather cuffs.

Søren lifted the candle off the bedside table and moved it slowly up and down her body six inches or less from her skin. When he inflicted his sadism on her, he did so intently, with respect for the act and respect for her willingness to serve him. Playing with fire was dangerous and it was rare when Søren asked her to submit to this sort of edge-play. She knew him. When anxious, troubled or under stress, he centered himself with sadism. He could pretend he wasn't worried about tomorrow, but she knew better. It was on his mind as much as hers.

Outside the castle, the storm battered the windows and the walls. But the eye of the storm was their bed. All was quiet if not calm. Søren brought the flame to the edge of the S and at once it flared into life.

Eleanor breathed in and didn't exhale. She could see the fire, smell the bitter smoke, but strangely could not feel it. The fluid formed a barrier between the fire and her body. As if the fire was a tongue lapping at her skin. But it did scare her and it was real fear. Real fire meant real fear. Real fear meant Søren was burning in his own fire. His breaths were shallow with barely controlled desire. His eyes were all pupil now, black as night, and in the inky depths she could see the fire reflected. Not once did he look away from the flame and neither did she.

Søren stripped himself of his clothes even as he watched the fire burn itself out on her.

He wrote on her with the gel again, set it alight again and watched her burn again.

When the fire was nearly but not entirely out, Søren straddled her hips and stretched out on top of her, using his own body to snuff out the last of the fire. He was aroused, brutally hard, and she felt his erection pressing against her thighs. She opened her legs wide for him and pushed her hips into his. He entered her fully, sliding through her wetness all the way to the core of her. Nora pulled against the bonds on her wrists, moaned and exhaled as he pulled out and thrust into her again.

This was bliss. How she had missed him these weeks she'd been in Europe. She loved Nico, loved the days and especially the nights she spent with him at his vineyard. The rest of her time was Søren's. Nico's one true love was his vineyard, and the vineyard was a demanding and possessive mistress. And Nora's one true love was Søren, who was a demanding and possessive master. She and Nico understood each other perfectly. She was a Dominant herself, and when she had Nico on his knees in front of her, his lips on her ankles, her welts on his back, that was Nora. But Nora was only one half of her.

"My Little One," Søren said into her ear as he moved inside her, filling her. "My Eleanor."

And Eleanor was the other half.

He kissed her breasts, sucking deep on the hard tips, and massaged her clitoris until the room filled with the sounds of her cries of pleasure, her cries for release. He didn't let her come yet. He ordered her not to come. An impossible command. He was inside her, thick and heavy, pushing hard and deep. She spread her legs wider, dug her heels into the bed and breathed into her stomach as she staved off her building climax.

"Tell me you love me and I might let you come," Søren said, punctuating the command with a rough thrust that made her flinch with both pain and pleasure.

"I love you, my sir, with all my heart."

"Tell me you want me."

"I want no one in the world as much as I want you. I love your body, your cock. I want you to come inside me. Please..."

"Tell me a secret you've never told me, and I'll consider letting you come."

"I fucked a nun at my mother's convent," Nora said, and Søren stopped moving. He pushed himself up and stared down at her.

"What?" she said, batting her eyelashes up at him in feigned innocence. "You asked."

"Lesson learned." He lowered himself onto her again and kissed her once more. The kiss was wild now, as wild as the night. He bit her lips, pushed his tongue into her mouth as he rammed into her with ruthless unforgiving thrusts. It was exactly what she needed. Her back arched and the muscles in her back coiled tight as a spring. She felt the ecstasy drawing together, pooling in her stomach. Then she rose and rose, higher and higher until she reached that throbbing peak and her body went still and stayed that way for one long perfect moment.

With a final cry, she came with a shudder that racked her entire body. She crashed back to earth with a thousand flutters of her inner muscles that left her shaking underneath Søren. He ignored her climax as he sought his own, thrusting into her faster and harder until he released at last, filling her with his heat.

Still coupled together Nora wrapped her legs around his back and relaxed her breathing. She loved this moment when she could feel the wild racing of his heart against hers. Bliss suffused her, peace and contentment. And then Søren spoke.

"You fucked a nun at your mother's convent."

"This is what you get for making me earn an orgasm by telling you a secret. It was the first thing that popped into my head."

Søren pulled out of her and looked down at her again. Then he laughed, a bright big laugh, big as the castle. Even as he unlocked her wrists from the bed and chafed her hands that had grown cool while in bondage, he still laughed.

"I will never reach the end of you," Søren said. "Every time I think I've seen it all, you lead me to a hidden door and open it."

"In my defense," Nora said, "she was beautiful, and I hadn't had sex in a very long time."

"When was this?" he asked as he slid off the bed and pulled

his trousers back on. He didn't bother with his shirt and that was fine by her.

"That year," she said, and didn't have to say anything else. Søren knew what "that year" was, what it meant. They didn't talk about that year, *never* talked about that year. In fact, they did their best to pretend that year never happened.

"I see."

"I'm sorry," she said. "I didn't mean to bring it up. I have no blood in my brain when you're inside me."

"I'm not angry." Søren poured water into a porcelain basin and brought it to the bedside table. He dipped a white cloth into the water. With it he wiped the residue of candle wax off her body.

"I would have told you if you'd asked," she said as Søren rinsed the cloth in the basin. She opened her legs for him and now he cleaned the semen off her vulva and inner thighs. "You never asked," she reminded him.

"That was a hard year for all of us," he said.

"I never asked you what you did while I was gone."

"Suffered," he said, meeting her eyes.

"Now I remember why I didn't ask."

"It sounds as if you didn't suffer the entire time you were gone."

"You know me. If I'm not having sex, I go a little crazy."

"What's your excuse the rest of the time then?" he asked and she play-punched him in the arm. He captured her by the wrists and kissed her again, entirely against her will. Well, mostly against. Partly. She pretended it was against her will anyway.

After he released her arms, she clambered out of the bed and found her suitcase. The castle was full of guests now, and all day she'd been working, answering questions, making decisions, putting all the finishing touches into place. If someone came knocking on her door—a distinct possibility—she should probably have some clothes on before she answered it.

She slipped into a pair of black-and-white silk pajama pants and a matching lacy camisole top. She kept her collar on for no reason other than she'd missed it. From Nico she'd learned the fine art of starting a fire in a fireplace, and she went to work stacking her kindling.

"So do I get my prize?" she asked.

Before she could answer, the door flew open, the rusty hinges screaming in protest. Kingsley rushed in and slammed the door behind him.

"What the hell?" she said, standing up.

"You have to hide me," Kingsley said, out of breath from running. "She's after me."

"Who? Céleste?" Nora asked. Kingsley and his daughter had been playing hide-and-seek all day in the castle.

"Juliette," Kingsley said. He looked at Søren and said, "Take off your pants if you want me to live."

"You've tried that line before," Søren reminded him. "It didn't work the last time you tried it, either."

"I'm a dead man then," Kingsley said, barring the door behind him.

"Why do you need Søren to take his pants off?" Nora asked. "I mean, other than the usual reason."

Kingsley pointed down at himself.

"That's why," he said.

Nora looked at him. He wore a black shirt and had his hair pulled back in a ponytail. His feet were bare; he looked like a pirate or a rogue or both and none of this was unusual. Except for one thing. Every man in the wedding party had already been given their formal wear.

So instead of his usual clothes, Kingsley wore a kilt.

"Juliette has a kilt fetish?" Nora asked, now understanding Kingsley's panic.

"A newly discovered kilt fetish," Kingsley said. "She's had me three times yesterday and three times today already—"

"You're her Dominant," Søren reminded him. "Satisfying her needs is your job."

Kingsley ignored him. "She's hunting me down for a fourth. I'm a man, not a machine. I feel violated, used…"

"You're being melodramatic. You know you love it," Søren said.

"Why does she keep calling me Connor in bed?" Kingsley asked.

"This explains why she's always trying to make me watch *Highlander* with her," Nora said as she stood up in front of the fireplace.

Nora looked at Søren and awaited his verdict.

"Please don't make me go," Kingsley said in a pleading tone. "I swear it'll break off if she gets her hands on me again."

Søren delivered his judgment.

"Throw him out."

"You heard the man," Nora said as she strode to the door, her feet tingling on the cold stone floor. "The priest has spoken."

"I'll be dead by morning," Kingsley said, pressing his back to the door.

"We'll miss you very much." Nora reached past him for the door bar. "I have my collar on. I have to follow orders."

"I'll beg for my life. How's that?" Kingsley looked straight at Søren.

"Beg then," Søren said as he dug through his suitcase and pulled out a T-shirt. He was a cruel man and putting on clothes was the most sadistic of all the many cruelties he inflicted on his lovers. "I'd like to hear this."

"He's in a mood," Nora said to Kingsley. "I had to beg for my orgasm."

"I can beg. I'll beg."

Nora crossed her arms and waited. She hoped Kingsley would find a way to earn his way into staying. She'd missed him too these past few weeks she'd been gone.

"*S'il vous plaît, mon ami, mon amour, mon coeur, mon maître, mon monstre*, I will do anything if you let me stay. Anything at all."

"Anything?" Søren repeated. "Define *anything*."

Kingsley looked at Nora then he crooked his finger at Søren. Søren sighed and walked over to Kingsley, who cupped his face and whispered something. Nora strained to hear what Kingsley said to Søren, but his voice was too low and his French too rapid. But whatever he said must have been good. Søren's eyes widened.

Søren met her eyes. "He can stay."

"*Merci, mon amant.*" Kingsley took Søren's face in his hands and kissed him first on each cheek and then on the mouth. Nora rolled her eyes. "You have saved me. Bless you."

Kingsley released Søren, walked to the fireplace and warmed his feet and hands. It was spring in Scotland and the castle was drafty. She almost felt sorry for all the men running around in kilts. Their pain. Her gain.

"It's good you're here anyway," Nora said as she returned to her suitcase. "I have something from Nico for you."

She pulled a bottle of wine out of her suitcase and a small envelope.

"'Rosanella Petite Syrah, 2004,'" Kingsley read the label aloud. "I have such a good son."

"He says it's the best vintage so far. He sent six bottles with me."

"We'll save it for the reception tomorrow then." Kingsley opened the envelope and pulled out a sheet of paper. Nora peeked over Kingsley's shoulder. Reading French wasn't her strong suit but even she knew enough to recognize the words *With love from your son, Nico*. Kingsley grinned at the note before folding it again and slipping it into his sporran. "He's inviting us all to the vineyard's one-hundred-year anniversary fête this fall. He says it wouldn't be a real celebration without me, Juliette and Céleste there."

"You better go then," Nora said. "You wouldn't want to ruin his party." Her relationship with Nico hadn't been easy for Kingsley to accept at first. He'd never been angry with her, not really, but he'd struggled as they all had, herself included. But after some time, some talking, Kingsley had given them his blessing. While Kingsley had loved his son from the moment he knew of his existence, Nico rebelled at the idea of accepting any man but the man who'd raised him as his father. But Nora had served as a bridge between father and son, and step by step, story by story she'd led Nico by the hand to Kingsley's side. Kingsley had Juliette as his submissive, Søren as his Dominant. He didn't need Nora in his bed anymore for either purpose. What Kingsley needed far more was his son's love, and that Nora had given him.

"Thank you for this," Kingsley said, folding up the invitation and tucking it back in the envelope. She knew he wasn't thanking her simply for delivering the mail.

"My pleasure," Nora said, and kissed him on the cheek.

"So what will we do tonight?" Kingsley asked as he left the heat of the fireplace and walked to the window. Outside the storm continued its assault on the castle. "Tell ghost stories? It's a good night for it."

"Perhaps Eleanor would be willing to tell us about the time she, and I quote, 'fucked a nun' at her mother's convent," Søren said, sitting on the bed and stacking a large red pillow behind his back.

"You fucked a nun at your mother's convent?" Kingsley asked, turning back to stare at her askance. "When did that happen?"

"That year," Nora said, and Kingsley winced. He knew what she meant, as well.

"And you never told me?" Kingsley asked.

"How is me sleeping with a nun any of your business?"

"Because it's *you* sleeping with a *nun*," Kingsley said with dramatic emphasis. "That is the very definition of my business. I need to know what she looked like, her name, if she had small breasts or large. Do you have pictures of her and you together? And can you tell me exactly what you did with her in detail while I take notes?"

"I could," Nora said. "I'm not going to."

"I could order you to," Søren said, and Nora groaned.

"You're as bad as he is," she said, pointing a finger at Kingsley. "You're perverts, the both of you. *J'accuse.*"

Kingsley nodded. *"J'accepte."*

"That was a really hard year for all of us," Nora said. "And it was twelve years ago. Can you give me one good reason why we should dredge all of that up tonight?"

"I can," Kingsley said. "Because you fucked a nun. *C'est la raison.*"

Nora put a hand to her forehead. "Dear Lord, save me from these men tonight."

"I would like to know," Søren said, and the room went still and solemn with the tenor of his words. "Neither of you ever told me what happened that year you both were gone."

"Maybe because you don't want to know," Nora said as she walked to the bed and crawled into it on the side opposite Søren. She pulled a pillow to her stomach and sat cross-legged. "You weren't our favorite person that year, after all."

"I wasn't my favorite person that year, either," Søren said, bending his leg to rest his arm on his knee. Kingsley came to the bed and stretched out at the foot, lying on his side to face them. "You both had disappeared on me and when you came back, everything had changed."

"I met Juliette," Kingsley said. "That's what I did that year."

"You've never told me how," Søren said. "And you—" he looked at Nora "—never told me why you came back."

"Do you really want to know?" she asked, meeting his eyes.

"We're happy now, all of us." She glanced at Kingsley and back at Søren.

"Ignorance is a poor excuse for bliss," Søren said, looking pointedly at her. "Tell me what happened."

Nora turned her head and looked into Kingsley's dark brown eyes. They stared at each other for a long quiet moment. She'd never told Kingsley what had happened when she'd left Søren. And Kingsley had never told her. In her more honest moments she'd admit she was curious what Kingsley did in that time and why he'd left when she had.

"That sounded like an order," Nora said to Kingsley.

"It was," Kingsley said, as accustomed to following Søren's orders now as she.

"Who starts?" she asked him.

"You left first," Kingsley said to Nora. The playfulness had left his demeanor. She saw the dark light of secrets in his eyes.

"You left after me, though. Why?"

"You don't know?" Kingsley said.

"No. I was afraid to ask," Nora confessed. "I thought…I thought all kinds of things that year. I think I went a little crazy for a while. But I guess you would too if you were trapped in a convent surrounded by nuns with nothing but your thoughts to keep you company."

"And a nun in your bed," Kingsley reminded her.

"And yes, there was a nun in my bed," Nora said with a sigh.

"This is my favorite story already," Kingsley said. "Go on."

Nora took a breath, got comfortable with the sheets and pillow.

"Well…" she began. "It was a dark and stormy night…"

"Eleanor," Søren said.

"It was," she said. "I'm not making that up. That night we fought, it was dark and stormy, remember?"

Søren nodded. "I remember. Go on."

Nora closed her eyes, let herself drift back to that night, that terrible night and that year, that dark and stormy year.

She was twenty-six years old.

Søren had just returned home from Rome.

And she was in the worst pain of her life.

"It was a dark and stormy night," Nora began again, opening her eyes to look at Søren. He returned her gaze with placid, waiting curiosity. "And I was leaving you. Forever."

2

2003
New York City

THIS IS NOT A DRILL.

This is not a drill.

Elle repeated those words in her mind as she wove between the dawn-weary commuters at Penn Station.

This is not a drill.

She wanted to walk faster, but she couldn't. Pausing by a trash can, she held the wire rim of it with both hands and breathed through her nose. A cramp twisted in her stomach and nausea hit her like a bus. The sickness passed quickly. Five hours since she last threw up. Her nausea ebbed. Her panic crested.

This is not a drill.

Standing up straight she strode forward again, tucking a loose strand of black hair under the Mets cap she'd bought at a gift shop. She didn't watch baseball often, although Griffin had taken her to a few games this season. He would never have forgiven her if she'd bought a Yankees hat. Then again, she would probably never see him again so what did it matter?

But still, it mattered.

Every few steps, temptation whispered to her, telling her to turn around, look around… She wasn't paranoid. But what was it Joseph Heller had said? It's not paranoia if they're really out to get you? By now Kingsley had surely sent the troops out looking for her, and this was the first place they'd look. It might have been a mistake coming here. This had been the plan though, the only plan she had.

This is not a drill.

Twice a year, every year, Kingsley had run her through the drill.

"There are five possible scenarios that would force you to run," Kingsley had warned her each time they'd run through the drill. "I want you to be ready."

The first time she'd been twenty years old. She and Søren had been lovers for only a few months. That was reason number one for the drill, scenario number one.

"He's a priest, *chérie*, and you're his lover now. You get caught in bed with him, and your world will explode. If that happens, the best thing you can do for him is run," Kingsley had said, his tone solemn and sober. He meant it.

"I'm not running away from Søren," she'd said. "Not now. Not ever. Especially not when he needs me the most."

"Your willingness to martyr yourself will only make things worse. Journalists are sharks, and the last thing we need is a feeding frenzy. This isn't an option, Elle. This is an order. From him and from me. Scenario number one—if you and *le prêtre* get caught, you run."

An order was an order. Søren had told her to do whatever Kingsley told her to do. Everything within her had rebelled at the idea of running away if and when she and Søren were caught, but she belonged to him—she'd sworn to obey him. Because of that vow, her decisions were not hers to make. Søren had decreed it—if the outside world found out about them, she would leave town. Immediately.

But that's not why she was here now hiding her hair under a baseball cap and walking as fast as the pain and the nausea would allow.

Scenario number two scared her more than the possibility of scenario number one.

"I know dangerous people, Elle, and they might kill me someday. They might take me captive. It's happened before," Kingsley had said, and she recalled the scars on his body, his chest and his wrists. "You two are the most important people in the world to me and that means they'll come after you two if they want to hurt me. If something happens to me, if anything happens to me, you go. You and Søren both. Together. Apart. I don't care. You go."

He'd meant it, and by now she knew how true those words were. He already had four bullet wounds on his body from four other attempts on his life. He had an in with every Mafia family in New York. He had reams of blackmail material on every politician in the tristate area. He could get the Prime Minister of Canada on the phone with one call, US senators, and billionaire CEOs. He knew too much and that made him a target. Elle had been Kingsley's lover since she was twenty years old—Kingsley's and Søren's. She knew much of what Kingsley knew and that made her a target, too.

But scenario two was not why she left, either.

Scenario three seemed unlikely, but Kingsley insisted on preparing her for it. If Søren died for any reason—motorcycle accident, sudden illness or foul play, she would need to get out of town. Fast. The rectory wasn't private property. It belonged to the church and the moment he was gone, his home would be flooded with the grieving and the curious. Even worse, a new priest would arrive to take over the church. Søren's personal effects would be gone through, his private life uncovered. It might happen before Kingsley could get someone to clean the house out. Even now, a large trunk sat at the foot of his bed. If anyone unlocked it, opened it and pulled the stacks of linens aside, they would find floggers, whips, canes and—most damning of all—photographs. They were of her, of course. A famous burlesque photographer who frequented Kingsley's clubs had been dying to photograph her since he first saw her. *The black hair, the curves, those eyes*, he'd said. According to him, she was Bettie Page reborn. She'd posed for a nude photo spread for him and given Søren the pictures for his thirty-seventh birthday. They were beautiful pictures—black-and-white, tasteful, not pornographic. But undeniably erotic. They were signed "As Always Beloved, Your Eleanor," and they sat in that steamer trunk anyone with a crowbar could open. A priest hiding naked pictures of a woman wouldn't be much of a scandal. But a priest hiding naked pictures of his lover, who also attended his church and had since she was born, would ruin his legacy and possibly her life.

Søren was the healthiest man she knew, however. And he was careful on his Ducati. And who would murder a priest? He had no enemies as far as she knew. She pitied anyone who would go up against Søren. She'd merely nodded at Kingsley when he told her she would need to run if something happened to Søren. It would never happen. And she was right. Nothing bad had happened to Søren.

So that's not why she'd left.

Scenario number four had also seemed preposterous when Kingsley had been training her for this moment.

"You could get pregnant," Kingsley had said. "Try not to do that. But if it happens, leave town before you start to show."

"I'm not going to get pregnant," she'd said, rolling her eyes. Nothing was going to get in the way of her life with Søren. Not a scandal, not the press, not the church and definitely not a kid.

And then it had happened. But it wasn't Søren's and it wasn't why she left. Not entirely.

Finally Elle found a bank of rental lockers and pulled out her keys. Locker number 1312 was three up and four over. She unlocked it and pulled out a black leather duffel bag.

Twelve times she and Kingsley had run through the drill.

Twice a year for six years. She was required to go the station, get the duffel bag and make it to one of Kingsley's safe houses in less than twelve hours. Now at twenty-six years old, Elle, for the first time in six years, realized how right Kingsley had been. She wished she'd paid more attention to his warnings.

"Scenario number five..." Kingsley had paused before speaking again. That pause had scared her.

"Scenario number five," Kingsley began again. "If Søren crosses a line, loses control, goes too far and—"

"No," she'd answered him the first time they'd run through this drill. "That won't happen."

"It might happen. It can happen. And you need to be ready for it."

"I know him, King. He loves me. He won't lose control with me."

With more compassion than she expected Kingsley to have left in his scarred heart, he'd cupped her face and forced her to meet his eyes.

"He hurt me so much after our first time together, I vomited on the ground after he was done with me. I passed blood for three days. My body wasn't bruised. My body was a bruise."

"You liked it."

Kingsley smiled at her, a smile that scared her. "You won't."

"He was seventeen then. He's an adult now—"

"He's more dangerous today than he was back then. He's better trained, but don't mistake well trained for tame. He is anything but tame."

"He's not like that anymore."

"I told you the first night you and I spoke that your shepherd was a wolf. He is a wolf on a leash and that leash might break someday. When that happens, you take care of yourself. I'll take care of him."

"It won't happen." She'd whispered the lie, and it had been a lie because it had already happened. She hadn't told Kingsley about that morning in the shower when the wolf had come off the leash. She'd wanted to, tried to…but the words never quite made out of her mouth. Shame was a foreign concept to her until that morning.

But surely Søren would never do it again.

Elle didn't take the time to unzip the duffel bag and check its contents. She already knew what was in it.

A passport.

Five thousand dollars cash.

Credit cards that Kingsley could track to find her if she couldn't get to any of his safe houses.

Three changes of clothes and toiletries.

A can of mace on a key chain.

A Swiss Army knife.

A wig to change her appearance.

Keys to the safe houses—one in Canada, one in Maine, one in Seattle.

A mobile phone and charger.

Beneath the duffel bag sat a black permanent marker. The marker was there for one reason only.

"I might be out of the country when it happens," Kingsley had said, the "it" being whatever scenario had occurred that meant Elle would need to flee.

"Write a number inside the locker so I know why you went. And know this…if it's number five, don't go to any of the safe houses."

"Why not?" she'd asked.

"Because whether I want to or not, I'll help him find you if he asks. And if I'm helping him find you, I'll find you."

She'd shivered then, because he was telling the truth. Søren had Kingsley's loyalty and his love. Even if Kingsley believed she was fleeing for the right reasons, he wouldn't be able to stop himself from helping Søren find her.

"What do I do?" she'd ask. "If I can't go to a safe house, where do I go?"

"I can't tell you that. You're as smart as he is. Use your brain. Find somewhere he can't follow. And whatever you do, don't tell me."

This was not a drill.

This was real.

Elle uncapped the marker. Inside the door of the locker she scrawled her message.

5.

3

ELLE STARED AT THE NUMBER SHE'D DRAWN ON THE metal door and knew what it meant—she had to go somewhere Kingsley couldn't find her.

Could she live with that? Never seeing Kingsley again? She would have to, wouldn't she? If she wanted to leave Søren she had to leave Kingsley, too. From inside her purse Elle pulled out a six-inch length of intricately carved bone. A beautiful thing, or it had been once. She held it in her hand for a second longer than necessary. Kingsley would know what it was the moment he saw it. He would know what it was, and he would know what had happened.

And he would know it was her way of saying goodbye.

It hurt to let go of it, but there was no reason to keep it, right? She had the other two pieces in her purse. This third piece was for Kingsley. She laid it inside the locker, slammed it shut and walked away.

Use your brain, Kingsley had said. Go where Søren wouldn't expect her to go. Go where Søren couldn't follow.

She had three ideas. One she dismissed out of hand. As furious as she was at Søren right now, she would not bring his family into this by showing up on his mother's doorstep in Copenhagen. The other two options were both bad, but one was worse than the other.

With the credit card from the bag, she bought a bus ticket to Philadelphia. Then she walked to another counter and with cash bought a bus ticket to New Hampshire. She threw the one she'd bought with the credit card into a garbage bin. The one she bought with cash she shoved into her pocket. She doubted the ruse would throw Kingsley off her track, but she had to try.

Kingsley had taught her how to flee from the press, from the church, even from Søren. But she wasn't sure how to get away from Kingsley. He could track like a bloodhound. He had eyes and ears everywhere. She needed someone who would be on her side, not Kingsley's. She needed someone who cared more about her than him. Or, more importantly, she needed someone who owed her a favor.

And only one man owed her a favor.

She got on the bus and found a seat near the back. Bus— when was the last time she'd sat on a bus? Maybe high school? Her senior year. Most days she walked to school, but if she was running late she took the bus. One morning she'd overslept because of Kingsley. The day before had been her eighteenth birthday, and he'd taken her to her first S and M club. She hadn't played, only watched while couples and trios had engaged in acts she'd only read about and dreamed about. Kingsley had asked her if she liked what she saw, if anything intrigued her, if there was anything she wanted to do.

"All of it," she'd answered.

She'd stayed out so late with him, she'd slept through her alarm the next morning and had taken the bus to school.

That wasn't right, was it? That wasn't normal. High school seniors shouldn't be oversleeping because they were at kink clubs with notorious underground figures the night before, right? How had it seemed so normal at the time? Why had it seemed so right? Where was her mother in all this? Pretending Elle didn't exist, more or less. They'd become strangers to each other, roommates at most. What if her mother had found out about her daughter's secret life when she was still in high school? Why had her mom not stopped her and said, "What are you doing with these people, Ellie?" If her mother, if anyone had asked that question she would have answered, "Because these people are my people." She was one of them.

But now she wasn't one of them anymore.

So who was she?

She pondered that question for the next two hours, only stopping when another stomach cramp hit her. She doubled over and rested her head on the back of the seat in front of her. Only June nineteenth but it was already as hot as August. The bus was air-conditioned—barely—and the stifling air added to her misery.

"Carsick?" an older man asked her. He was black with gray hair and sat on the seat opposite hers. He had a face like the grandfather you wished you'd had growing up. She nodded her head and squeezed her eyes shut tight.

"Hang in there. You want some crackers?"

The mention of food sent her stomach rumbling. Without answering him she raced to the bathroom at the back of the bus and vomited hard into the toilet. She prayed no one had heard her getting sick. People would remember a young white woman in a Mets cap on a Concord bus puking her guts out. But she couldn't worry about that yet. When she was done being sick, she rinsed her mouth out and splashed cold water on her face. Then she pulled her pants down and checked her bleeding. It was heavy and thick. She tried to feel sad, feel remorse or regret. Instead, she felt only relief. She held on to that relief as she made her way back to her seat.

She closed her eyes and leaned her head back. The man in the seat next to her patted her clammy hand and she opened her eyes. He placed three saltines in her palm. For the rest of the trip she nibbled on her crackers. In her weakened state and on her empty stomach, they tasted like manna from heaven.

"Thank you," she said. He reached out and patted her shoulder. A kind, grandfatherly touch. She ached so much for human warmth right now she wanted to sit next to him and lean against him. When another cramp slammed into her back, she grabbed his hand and squeezed it.

"It's all right," the man said in a low voice. "We're almost there. I get carsick too sometimes. Especially if I try to read. You're gonna make it."

She smiled so he knew she heard him, but didn't tell him the truth. She wasn't carsick. Elle Schreiber did not get carsick. Any car, any kind, she could drive it. She'd been driving since she was twelve years old. She could hot-wire a car in under fifteen seconds. She could shift like a race car driver. She felt more at home in a car than she did anywhere else on earth—except for Søren's bed. Carsick was the last thing she was.

When the pain passed, she lifted her head and rested back against the seat. For a few minutes all she did was breathe. Long breaths. Slow breaths. Breaths that filled her lungs and emptied her mind. At first she didn't realize what she was doing. Then she remembered.

"Little One, take deep breaths when you're on the cross. Deep full breaths. Fill your lungs and empty your mind. When I beat you, it's for us, for our pleasure—yours and mine. Don't be afraid. Never be afraid of me."

"Never ever, sir," she'd whispered back to him.

But now she was afraid.

"You running away from home, young lady?" the man in the seat next to her asked. She could hear the joking tone in his voice.

"I don't run," Elle said. "It's not running away from home if you're not running, right?"

"That's a good point. Visiting friends or family here?"

"A friend," she said. "I think he's a friend. I hope he is."

"Why wouldn't he be?"

"I broke his heart once," she said, smiling again.

"You look like a heartbreaker." The man nodded sagely and Elle laughed.

"I don't mean to be. I never mean to hurt anybody," she said. "But I do."

They'd been joking the way strangers packed into a crowded elevator or jostled about on an airplane joked. But what she'd said was too true and too somber, and he gave her a look of curiosity and compassion.

"A little girl like you couldn't hurt a fly," he said kindly.

Elle looked up and took a breath. If he only knew.

"I could hurt a fly," she whispered.

After six hours and two bus changes, she finally arrived in New Hampshire. She wasn't done with her journey yet. At the station she followed a young woman to a parking lot and offered her a hundred dollars to drive her forty miles. The woman seemed skeptical at first, but Elle held up the money. That did the trick.

Elle sat in the backseat of the beat-up Ford Thunderbird. The front seat was taken up by a child's car seat, and Elle was happy to sit in the back and not look at it. She thought about asking the woman where the kid was, but she didn't want to talk, especially about children. She apologized for her lack of conversation. Still recovering from car sickness, Elle said. The woman turned on the radio to cover the silence, and Elle kept her eyes closed all the way there.

A little after one in the afternoon, she arrived at her destination. Elle almost wept with relief at the sight of the long curving driveway she remembered so well, the columns, the stairs, the rows of windows in this old Colonial mansion.

The woman seemed stunned that this house, this mansion, was her destination.

"Old friend," Elle said by way of explanation. "I hope."

She paid the woman her one hundred dollars from the cash in her duffel bag. Five thousand dollars wouldn't last very long, but a deal was a deal.

The relief Elle felt faded as she walked up the long, curving cobblestone driveway to the house. Her back spasmed with every few steps and the heavy duffel bag dug into her shoulder. The blazing sun followed her every step. She took off the Mets cap and ran her hands through her sweat-drenched hair. As she walked, she wondered…would he take her in? Would he help her? She'd broken his heart, yes, but she'd also helped him when he needed her most.

Elle rang the doorbell and waited.

As rich as he was, no one would have begrudged him a housekeeper or a butler. But it was the master of the house who opened the door. His blue eyes widened as he looked at her and took in her paleness, her exhaustion and her fear.

"Oh my God…Eleanor. What did he do to you?" he asked.

Elle almost laughed. If she'd had the energy, she would have.

"Don't ask, Daniel," she said as she walked past him into the house. "Just don't ask."

4

DANIEL GAVE HER TEA AND PUT HER IN THE DOWN-stairs guest room. The entire time she was in his presence she stared at the gold band on his left hand.

"Where are Anya and the baby?" Elle asked. She hadn't seen either when Daniel brought her into the house.

"Upstairs in the nursery. Marius has the flu. We're taking shifts. She's on the day shift. I take the night shift so she can sleep." He smiled and she saw the contentment on his handsome face.

"God, you're so married."

"I am. Again," he said and smiled.

"Enjoying it? Being married again? Being a dad?" Elle asked as she pulled the blanket to her stomach.

"You show up on my doorstep with no warning and nothing but a bag and the clothes on your back and you want to talk about me right now?" Daniel pulled a chair up to the bed. It was barely two o'clock in the afternoon, but Daniel had seen right away that all she needed right now was rest. "Eleanor, please—"

"Elle," she said.

"What?"

"I told him the day I met him that I went by Elle. Not Eleanor. My whole life my mom called me Elle or Ellie. That's who I am. But he called me Eleanor anyway. He calls me Eleanor. I prefer Elle."

Daniel looked at her, rubbed his hands together.

"Elle," he said. "Please tell me what's happening. Can you do that for me?"

"You don't want to know." She tried to smile. She hoped he appreciated the effort that took her.

Daniel met her eyes, and she held the gaze. Back when he was a regular player in Kingsley's world, his blue-eyed Dominant glare was the stuff of legend. His late wife, Maggie, had even named it—The Ouch, she called it with equal parts fear and affection. When he gave her that look she knew she'd be saying "ouch" the next day, maybe the next week. But it wasn't the infamous Ouch he gave her now. Instead, he looked at her steadily with curiosity and compassion. And pity.

She hated pity.

"I'm fine," she said. "I needed to get away for a few days."

"You didn't come here because you needed to get away for a few days. You go to the Hamptons to get away for a few days."

"You go to the Hamptons to get away for a few days because you're rich. Normal people do not go to the Hamptons."

"Elle." Daniel met her eyes. "You're the most famous submissive in the entire city of New York. You're owned by a Catholic priest, and you're sleeping with the King of the Underground. You are not normal people."

"I am now," she said. "Trying to be anyway."

"How did you get here?"

"Kingsley's driver dropped me off."

"Kingsley drives a beat-up Ford Thunderbird now?"

If she had had the strength to give Daniel The Ouch, she would have.

"I have security cameras," he said. "I saw someone drop you off. It wasn't King."

"No, it wasn't."

"Does King know where you are?"

She shook her head.

"Tell me what happened."

"You don't want to know," she repeated. "Just don't tell anyone I'm here, okay?"

"I think I do want to know. Remember, I've known Søren for years. Not only do I know him, I like him. We're friends. If I can know him and still like him, I think I can handle anything you tell me."

"Maybe you can handle hearing it. I don't know if I can handle saying it."

Daniel moved from his chair to the bed. She tensed immediately and he seemed to sense it.

"I'm not going to touch you if you don't want me to," he said, raising his hands in surrender.

"You're married, you have a kid and I'm—" she paused to find a suitable lie and decided on a half-truth instead "—not feeling well."

He reached his hand out but didn't touch her with it, only waited. Slowly Elle leaned forward the three necessary inches and rested her face against the palm of his hand.

"You don't have a fever," he said.

"No."

"I don't see any bruises on your arms or your neck."

"Søren didn't beat me up or rape me," she said, annoyed that he would even think something like that had happened.

Daniel nodded.

"But he did hurt you."

"You didn't put a question mark at the end of that sentence."

"I told you, I've known him for years. It wasn't a question."

"Yes," she admitted finally, closing her eyes. "He hurt me."

"Kingsley?"

She shook her head. "This isn't his fault," she said, rolling over onto her side. "This is my fault."

"I refuse to believe that," Daniel said. "But you have to give me something here. If Anya left me, ran away, I would be so sick with worry I wouldn't be able to breathe. Søren pisses me off too sometimes, and I consider him a friend, but I have never doubted his love for you. Unless you have a very good reason to scare him like this, you need to go home."

"I can't go home."

"Tell me why you left him or I'm calling Kingsley right now."

Elle weighed her options. She could tell him the whole truth, which would hurt more than the pain she was currently in. She could lie and come up with a suitable story he would believe to explain why she left. Or she could tell him a half-truth, just enough truth to get him to stop asking questions.

She went with option three.

"Do you remember that thing you told me?" she asked.

"I told you a lot of things."

"I told you I was happy, content. You said that I should enjoy my contentment because someday something would happen and it would be gone."

He nodded. "I remember."

"It happened."

"What happened?"

"Søren ordered me to marry him," she said.

Daniel looked at her and looked at her and looked at her, and finally he spoke.

"Get some sleep. We'll talk more tomorrow. Do you need anything?"

"You have any other sheets?" she asked, her face warming.

"Are you cold?"

"No," she said, pushing the blankets. A red stain had formed underneath her. "I'm bleeding."

It took ten minutes of begging and pleading to convince Daniel not to call an ambulance. This was just part of the process, she told him. Nothing to worry about. She was fine. A little blood never killed any woman...

Even after calming him down Daniel still seemed dubious and worried. He stayed in the bathroom with her while she took a quick hot bath. He kept his back to her to give her privacy although he'd seen her naked before. Once upon a time she'd been his lover. They'd fucked in this very bathroom. Down the hall was the library where he'd bent her over his desk and taken her from behind. In the living room by the fireplace, he'd fisted her and given her one of the better orgasms of her life. In the bed he now shared with his wife, he'd fucked her more times than she could remember. But now that felt like a lifetime ago. Had it only been two years ago she'd last been with him? So much had happened in those two years. He'd fallen in love with someone who wasn't her, got remarried, had a son. And her? What had she done since then?

Elle got out when the water turned pink, and she drained the tub before Daniel could see it.

He ordered her to eat to some soup and then ordered her into bed. There was nothing at all erotic about any of these orders.

"You really are a dad now, aren't you?" she asked.

"Don't get any ideas. I don't do the Daddy-Dom thing," he said, pulling the covers up to her chest.

"Could have fooled me," she said.

"Don't flirt. Anya's the jealous type." He winked at her so she would know he was kidding. Not that he needed to tell her. She'd known Anya before he did. Knowing Anya, she would worry Elle would catch the flu from Marius, not that she would sleep with her husband. For the first time in Elle's adult life, sex was the last thing on her mind.

He kissed her on the forehead once and on the lips twice.

She smiled up at him.

"Get some rest, Elle," he said.

"It's not even night yet."

"I don't care. You're exhausted. Sleep."

"Is that an order?"

He smiled down at her. "If I gave you that kind of order, would you obey me?"

"No."

"Then no, it wasn't an order."

He caressed her cheek with the back of his hand. A fatherly touch. She didn't remember him ever touching her like that. Becoming a parent had changed him, changed him for the better. But she knew that didn't happen with every man. Her own father was proof. Her father, Søren's father, her mother...

Her mother.

"Good night, Elle," Daniel whispered, and she saw his reluctance to leave her alone.

"Good night, Daniel." He started to leave. She stopped him with a question. "Daniel—what am I going to do?"

Daniel turned around in the doorway and looked back at her.

"If you took orders from me, which you don't, but if you did...I'd order you to go back to Søren and marry him."

Elle rolled onto her side and gazed at Daniel through the dark.

"Now I remember why I left you," she said.

"Because I wanted to take care of you?"

"Because you don't know me at all."

The smile faded from Daniel's face.

"Rest," he said, and shut the door behind him.

It wasn't an order, but Elle followed it anyway. She slept an hour or two and when she woke up, there was a terrifying moment when she couldn't remember how she'd got here. But the moment passed, and she remembered.

What was she going to do? No Søren. No Kingsley. No town house. Jesus, she didn't have a real job. She had a little less than five thousand dollars to her name, a college degree in English literature and almost no work experience other than a few years at a bookstore. What was she going to put on a résumé? That she gave good blow jobs and could take a beating better than any masochist in New York?

She sat up in bed and buried her face in her hands. Panic threatened to overwhelm her. Slowly she breathed, slowly she calmed herself. She would not cry. She could not cry. If she started crying over Søren, she'd never stop. And if she cried, that would mean it was real, that she had left him and that she was never going back.

When she was calm again she whispered into the quiet of her room, "What am I gonna do?"

No one answered, not even her.

Wincing as her sore muscles protested the movement, Elle got out of bed. She walked down the hall to the bathroom where she'd stored her duffel bag. On the way back to bed she noticed a light on in Daniel's library. Wasn't he supposed to be on the night shift taking care of Marius?

She crept to the half-open door and heard him speaking to someone. She saw no one else in the room and then noticed he had a small mobile phone to his ear.

"She's not well," Daniel said. "Let her stay here a couple days until she feels better. Than you can come get her."

Elle froze.

"Not tonight, King. She's not in good shape. Mentally or physically. Let her rest. We'll take care of her."

Rage welled up in Elle. She took one step forward and then stopped. Kingsley had warned if she had to flee, she'd have to be smart about it. She'd been stupid before but she wasn't going to be stupid again. She crept back to the bathroom, grabbed her duffel bag and got dressed. As quietly as she could, she left the house. She didn't leave a note, didn't lambast him with accusations and recriminations. She didn't call him a traitor or

an asshole or an arrogant piece of shit who thought he knew
what was better for her than she did. She did something much
worse and much better at the same time.

She stole his car.

Thankfully Daniel wasn't some rich dipshit who drove a
flashy Maserati or a Ferrari to show off his money. Daniel had
a classic black Mercedes-Benz sedan. Nothing that would at-
tract any unnecessary attention. She took the keys right off the
rack in the kitchen. She coasted out of the driveway with the
lights off and resisted the urge to squeal the tires as a final fuck
you and fare thee well.

He wouldn't call the police. That wasn't Daniel's style. And
he wouldn't have to. She'd dump the car somewhere the cops
would find it, and it would be returned to him in one piece.

More or less.

After ten minutes on the road the adrenaline rush faded and
the reality that she was alone again with nowhere to go set in.
No...not nowhere to go. She had lots of places to go. Unfortunately there was nowhere she could go where Kingsley wouldn't
find her eventually. Especially now that she'd stolen a regis-
tered car. Wherever she dumped the car, that's where Kingsley
would start looking, and he would find her in a matter of hours.

Which left only one option. She would have to go somewhere Kingsley and Søren couldn't follow her. Even if he
knew where she was, it would be somewhere he couldn't enter.
She thought about getting herself arrested and sent to prison.
Seemed a better option than her only other choice.

Then again, she'd faced prison once before and Kingsley and
Søren had got her out of going then. He would do it again if
she was foolish enough to get herself arrested. Kingsley took
care of things. That's how it worked. She needed a ride somewhere? Kingsley's driver would take her wherever she wanted
to go. If she needed a vacation, Kingsley would send her and
Søren to Europe. If she got injured during kink, he'd send her

to his doctor, who knew how to keep his mouth shut. If she got pregnant…well, he took care of that, too, didn't he? Whether he wanted to or not.

Kingsley…she kept her mind on him. If she thought about Søren, really thought about him, she'd turn the car around and drive straight back to Connecticut. Instead, she focused her mind on Kingsley. Was he okay? She hadn't seen him in a few days. He hadn't offered to go with her to the doctor. He'd made the appointment for her, had the car take her. But he wasn't there when she left, wasn't home when she got back. If she'd asked him to come with her, he would have. She knew that. That he hadn't volunteered was proof that he didn't want to face it any more than she did. So she didn't ask him. She went alone and didn't make him more a part of it than he already was. Kingsley was more dark knight than white knight, but whatever his sins, he had one bright, pure and beautiful hope—that he would be a father someday. She wasn't going to make him stand there and watch her put an end to that dream.

"King…I'm sorry," she whispered as she reached a crossroads. If she drove south, she'd be in Manhattan in four hours.

Or…

Elle pulled the car over on the side of the road.

She had to do it, right? What other choice did she have except to go back? And that was no choice at all. Because if she went back she'd be admitting defeat. If she went back she would be walking straight into a different sort of prison.

Even now, her heart raced at the thought of Kingsley tracking her down and bringing her home. That wasn't right. She should be able to leave if she wanted to leave. She should be able to go if she wanted to go without fearing someone was following her. That's how it worked in the real world, right? Women got sick of the lives they were leading and they could do things like move out and move on and start over without an ex-assassin for the French government dragging her home by her hair.

Right?

Was it too late for her to be part of the normal world? If it wasn't, did she really want to go there? She didn't know the answer to either question. But she did know the longer she sat in the car, the sooner Kingsley would find her. It was nine o'clock now. The summer sun had finally set. By sunrise, Daniel would notice she—and his Benz—had disappeared. He'd call Kingsley, and Kingsley would start the search for her. She needed to be somewhere safe by morning, somewhere no one could follow.

That left only one option.

She was twenty-six years old.

She was the ex-lover of a Catholic priest.

She was recovering from an abortion.

Might as well go all in.

Goodbye, men. Goodbye, sex.

She headed west to her mother's convent.

She didn't look back.

5

KINGSLEY STOOD IN FRONT OF LOCKER 1312 BUT DIDN'T open it. He couldn't open it. Not yet. The last thing he wanted to do was open it and have every one of his fears confirmed.

At four that morning, Søren had called him looking for Elle. She wasn't answering her phone. When Kingsley had gone to her room and found her bed made and empty, he'd known exactly what happened. Kingsley had seen this day coming since the night he'd met her. She'd finally done it. She'd left Søren.

But why? Søren wouldn't tell him anything, only that they'd fought and Elle had driven off in Kingsley's BMW, which she drove whenever she went to Søren's. They'd argued. She'd driven away. Nothing new there. They'd fought before. All couples did. But this time was different and the empty bed proved it. She hadn't come home last night.

So where the fuck was she?

He took out his keys and opened the locker.

Kingsley stared at the hastily scrawled number five on the inside of the locker. He closed his eyes and took a breath. In between the intake of air and the outtake he whispered a word to himself.

"Fuck."

Then he saw it. Far more damning than the number inside the locker was the six-inch length of carved bone he pulled out of it.

Kingsley held it in the palm of his hand, stared at it and knew how it had got here, knew why she'd left it.

"This is why I left him," it told him. If she'd been here he would have replied, "Good."

Kingsley shoved it into his back pocket and slammed the locker door shut.

"You son of a bitch." Kingsley swore under his breath. If Søren had been here, he would have said it to his face. Kingsley was thirty-eight years old and had known Søren since he was sixteen. Søren had beaten him, brutalized him and used him. He'd married Kingsley's sister, which had precipitated her death. And never in all those years since they'd met had Kingsley felt this level of rage, of abject fury at the man he considered his truest friend and the only man he'd ever loved. Swear at him? If Søren had been here right now, Kingsley might have killed him.

And yet, he knew most of that rage was anger at himself. This was his fault, his doing. Kingsley never should have let her face Søren alone. He shouldn't have let her face any of it alone. If he needed any further proof he wasn't ready to be a father, it was this—he'd made her a doctor's appointment and then abandoned her. He'd left the city for two days, lain low in Boston and done more drinking than he'd done in years. And Elle? She'd thanked him for making the appointment. That was all. "Thanks, King, I'll take it from here." And there'd been a pause, as if she'd been waiting for him to say, "I'll go with you" or "Let me help you" or even "How are you?" He hadn't said it, hadn't said anything, and she hadn't asked him to come with her, to be with her during it all. Kingsley knew she thought she was doing him a favor by going alone, but in the end all that it had done was make him feel like shit.

He leaned back against the row of lockers. In scenarios one through four she'd been instructed to write the name of her destination inside the locker—Canada, Maine, Seattle, somewhere else if that's what she wanted. But in scenario five, she'd only write the number and disappear. And so she had. If he had any doubts about her determination to run away, they'd dissolved when he'd got the phone call from Daniel.

She's here, King. And she's not in good shape.

Kingsley was already on his way to the door when Daniel cautioned him to wait a day or two to let Elle calm down and rest. It was a smart idea even though Kingsley rebelled at the idea of leaving her alone another minute. But she wasn't alone. Daniel had loved her once and still cared for her. Anya adored her for bringing her and Daniel together. The house was beautiful, idyllic. She would calm down out there, recover, and when Kingsley showed up in a day or two, she'd be less likely to put up a fight about coming home.

But an hour later, the second call had come.

She's gone, King. And she stole my fucking car.

Kingsley had hung up and stared at the phone in his hand. Then he laughed. A sad tired laugh with no joy in it at all, but still, he laughed. Because of course. Of course she'd stolen Daniel's car and driven away in the night. He should have seen that coming.

Once upon a time, he and Søren had made an idle wish to someday have a girl who was wilder than him and Søren put together.

Be careful what you wish for.

In the back of his mind he wished Sam were here. He could use a sane and rational voice of comfort right now. She was always good at helping in a crisis. But Sam had left him six years ago shortly after that first night he and Søren had topped Elle together. Sam had met someone, fallen in love, but even that might not have broken up their partnership. Except Elle had quickly become the most important woman in Kingsley's life. She brought Søren back to Kingsley's bed, something Sam could never do. The first time Sam had seen Elle walking around the house in one of Kingsley's shirts, that was it.

Sam wasn't angry, wasn't hurt. She just knew it was time for them both to move on. Sam told him she loved him and then gave her two weeks' notice and started packing for LA.

His sister was dead because of his love for Søren.

His Sam was gone to California because of his love for Elle.

His Elle was gone because of his love for his stupid foolish dream to have children, a dream he put before her.

They were all gone. Maybe they were on to something.

Kingsley thought about going back home, but he couldn't face Søren right now. Søren was nearly catatonic with shock when they'd last spoken. "You'll find her," was all Søren had said to him before the first phone call from Daniel had come. They'd been sitting in the music room, Søren at the piano but not playing.

Kingsley had nodded. "I'll find her."

He wanted to ask Søren "Why did she leave?" but he also didn't want to ask it. Søren might tell him, and the last thing Kingsley needed was to hear what fate Kingsley had abandoned Elle to. Søren out of control was a sight as rare as a volcano erupting and nearly as terrifying.

It would be easy to find her. She'd stolen Daniel's car. All he had to do was call a few contacts in the police department with a description of the vehicle. In a few hours they'd know which direction she'd gone. From there they could extrapolate her likeliest destination. If she used one of the credit cards, they could pinpoint her whereabouts precisely. A quick jaunt on an airplane to wherever she'd gone and by tomorrow night she'd be back in Manhattan whether she wanted to be or not.

He could find her. Easily. Søren had asked him to find her, and he couldn't tell Søren no. He wasn't strong enough to tell him no, and he would fail her again as he'd failed himself. Over and over in his head he cursed himself. He'd gotten her pregnant and then abandoned her to deal with it on her own. Then she'd faced Søren on her own. And Kingsley had the shard of carved bone in his back pocket to prove that conversation had not gone well. He'd never met a stronger woman in his life, a woman as free and as fearless as she. If she said Søren had crossed a line with her, Kingsley believed her.

Kingsley owed her. She'd fled somewhere—he didn't know where but he assumed she'd picked a place she felt safe. What right did he have taking her away from there if that's where she wanted to be? But he would do it, and he would do it for Søren, and he would do it because she'd become such a part of his life he couldn't imagine waking another morning to find her gone.

If Kingsley went back to the town house right now he'd call all his contacts and find her. Søren would be sitting there, waiting, depending on Kingsley to find her.

But.

But if he didn't go back to his town house…

Kingsley pulled his mobile phone out of his jacket and dialed a number.

"Don't speak," Kingsley said before his assistant could say a word.

Silence was his answer. Good.

"Answer the next question I ask you only with a yes or a no. You understand?" Kingsley asked.

"Yes," Calliope said. Her voice was calm, controlled. She betrayed nothing. He'd trained her well.

"Is he there?"

"No."

"No?" Kingsley repeated. "Good. Now you can talk. Did he tell you where he went?"

"No," Calliope said. "He told me to tell you he had an idea

where she might be. Then he got on his motorcycle and drove away."

Kingsley's brow furrowed as he leaned back against the lockers.

"He's not going to get her back," Kingsley said.

"Are you going to find her then?"

Kingsley didn't answer. He had a decision to make. Calliope made it for him.

"She wouldn't leave him without a good reason, right?" she asked. "She wouldn't leave him unless she had to. I know her. I know how much she loves him."

"So do I," Kingsley said.

"Did he hurt her? Like in the bad way?" Calliope asked, her voice awash in fear and confusion. Kingsley could sympathize.

Kingsley didn't answer.

"King?"

He had a decision to make. He made it now.

"I need you to do something for me."

"Anything," she said.

"I need you to move into the town house. Someone needs to take care of the dogs. Can you do that for me?"

"I practically live here anyway. Dad's not going to be thrilled, but I'm eighteen. Not much he can do about it. Sure. Anything you need."

"You can have any room that isn't mine or isn't hers. There's ten grand in cash in my bottom desk drawer. The combination is—"

"I know the combination."

"How?"

"You hired me because I'm the sort of girl who knows combinations, remember?"

"Good point." He almost laughed. He did know how to pick an assistant.

"Shut the house down. Close it. Cancel all the parties. Cancel everything, even the newspaper."

"Are you going somewhere?" she asked.

"Yes. I have to leave the country. Don't tell him I'm going. I'm not going to tell you where I'm going so you don't have to lie when he asks you. The truth is, I don't know where I'm going, and I don't know when I'm coming back. But you can handle things while I'm gone. Yes?"

"I can, yes," she said again. This time he heard a tight note of fear in her voice. But she was smart, savvy. She was also barely eighteen years old, but he wouldn't have hired her if he didn't trust her judgment.

"I'm going now. I'll call when I can. It won't be for a week or two. But everything's fine. You believe that?"

Calliope answered, "No."

He cared about her too much to make her believe the lie.

"Me neither," he said. "Be a good girl. I'll call when I can. Take care of the kids for me."

"I'll walk them every day," she said. "And pet them all the time."

"*Merci.*"

"Come home soon."

Kingsley hung up and tucked his phone away again.

Once more he fished his keys out of his pocket. He turned back to the lockers. Underneath the one set up for Elle was another locker. He opened it, pulled out a leather duffel and checked it for a passport and money.

For you, Elle, he said to himself as he walked through the bus station and out onto Forty-Second Street. *I'm doing this for you.* Or was he?

He hailed a cab and ordered the driver to take him to the airport.

Well, it was about time he fulfilled a long-held dream of his. After all, his dream of being a father was dead. But he had other dreams, dreams about seeing parts of the world he hadn't seen yet. If he didn't go now, would he ever?

"Which airline?" the Caribbean-accented cab driver asked him.

"I don't know."

"You don't know?" the driver repeated.

Kingsley leaned forward. "If you had all the money in the world and could use it to go anywhere you wanted, where would you go?"

"All the money, sir?" the driver asked. "I'd go everywhere."

"Everywhere?"

"Everywhere," the driver repeated. "And then I'd go home."

"Where's home?" Kingsley asked him. The accent was like music in his ears—French but not French, warm as white sand under the sun.

"Haiti, sir," the driver said.

Haiti. Well, Kingsley had always wanted to go to Haiti. A tropical island, a long history with France. Maybe he would go there. Or maybe he'd do what his driver suggested. Maybe he'd go everywhere. He'd leave today and travel the world. Elle would have one less person to run from, one less man to fear.

And if Søren wanted to get his Little One back badly enough…

The bastard could do it himself.

6

Upstate New York

IN THE LAST MINUTES BEFORE MIDNIGHT, ELLE ARRIVED
at the Abbey of the Sisters of Saint Monica. It stood before her,
a two-hundred-year-old stone edifice rising up three stories
from the deep green earth. Spotlights shone on it, illuminating
the high gray walls and the cobblestone path that led from the
winding driveway to its hulking wooden front door. She knew
more about this abbey than any laywoman should. Briefly she'd
lived with her mother after graduating college in the hopes of
repairing their fractured relationship. Her mother had let her
move in for reasons unknown. Perhaps she'd harbored the same
hopes. Reconciliation was a sacrament to Catholics, after all.

It was on the first day back under her mother's roof that Elle
found a white folder embossed with the initials SSM on the front.
S and M Elle understood. But no, this was SSM—The Sisters of
St. Monica. That place had been a foreign country to her. Soon
she discovered her mother was in complete earnest about fulfilling her teenage dream to become a nun, a dream derailed when
a one-night fling with a handsome older boy ended in a pregnancy, a shotgun wedding and a quickie divorce soon thereafter.

Now William "Billy" Schreiber was dead and buried and no
one mourned him. Elle was an adult. And now Margaret Kohl

was Sister Mary John of The Sisters of Saint Monica, a small order that consisted of five abbeys around the world, less than five hundred women in total. Their charism, according to the literature Elle had read, was to serve Christ like true brides—with love and devotion, and to pray for His church unceasingly until it found salvation, as Saint. Monica, mother of Saint Augustine, had prayed unceasingly for her son's salvation.

The nighttime air was still warm with the day's heat, but Elle had put on the black jacket she'd found in the duffel bag. She had no idea what to wear that would be appropriate for a convent, but she guessed the less skin she showed, the better. Under the jacket she wore a plain white T-shirt and dark jeans. At least in her black-and-white clothes she'd match the sisters in their black-and-white habits.

She left the car parked at a gas station a mile away and had walked the rest of the way here. The car would sit and sit and sit until the owner called the police and reported it. The police would run the tags and call Daniel, who would likely say he'd lent it to a friend who forgot where he'd parked it. The police would be dubious, but would say no problem, hang up and Daniel would retrieve his car.

For that moment when owner and car were reunited, Elle had left a little note in the glove compartment for him.

Dear Daniel,
I lied. I didn't leave Søren because he asked me to marry him. I left because of what he did after I said no. If you'd been there, you would never have ratted me out to King. I hope you never have a daughter someday.
Love, Elle.
P.S. Fuck you.
P.P.S. Nice car. I dented the fender on purpose. And the driver's side door. And the passenger side.
P.P.P.S. And the hood.

★ ★ ★

At midnight she crossed the threshold and entered the convent. Silence reigned inside the heavy stone structure. She could hear her own breathing, her own heart beating. She breathed like a wounded runner who'd had to crawl to the finish line. But she wasn't done crawling yet. Not until she was behind the inner door. Only behind that door would she be safe. Only behind that door could she rest.

Like every monastery, the convent employed a doorkeeper. Søren had told her about the original doorkeeper for the Jesuit order, Brother Alphonsus Rodríguez, who joined the Jesuits after the death of his wife and his three children. According to Søren, Brother Alphonsus treated every person who knocked on the door of the Jesuit school where he was stationed as if it were God Himself at the door. He worked as nothing more than a porter, a glorified doorman for forty years. In 1888, the world's most devoted doorman became a saint.

Elle didn't feel like God as she walked to the porter's window. She didn't feel like the Devil, either. She felt tired and scared, and she wanted more than anything to wake up in her own bed at Kingsley's to find the past week had been nothing but a dream, nothing but a nightmare. She'd wake up and find Søren next to her in bed, and she'd roll over and stretch out on his chest, press her ear to his heart and listen to it beating. He would stir and wake and stroke her hair and her bruised back until she fell asleep again. When she woke up for the day he would be long gone with only the stains on the sheets, the welts on her body and the scent of winter on his pillow to prove he'd been there.

That was the Søren she knew and loved. She had no idea who this new Søren was, the one she'd met two nights ago. But she was relieved to know she'd put several hundred miles between them. And yet, several hundred miles wouldn't be enough. Nothing would be enough until she was behind that door in front of her, the door with a simple brass plaque that read, No Men Beyond This Point. No men allowed. Not even priests.

She rang the bell and said a prayer to Saint Monica, praying her earthly daughters would take her in and shelter her.

A wooden panel at a window that reminded her of an old-fashioned bank teller's was pushed aside and a woman in large glasses peered out at her.

"Welcome, child. Can we help you?" she asked, her tone kind and curious.

"My mother is here. Sister Mary John," Elle said, her voice wavering against her will. "I need to talk to her."

"Is it an emergency, or can it wait until morning? Now is the Great Silence and nearly everyone is sleeping."

That question utterly flummoxed her. Emergency? Nothing was burning down at the moment...except her entire life. Did that count as an emergency?

Yes. Yes it did.

"Someone's trying to find me, and this is probably the first place he'll look."

The sister's eyes widened farther behind her glasses.

"Is this person dangerous?"

"Very," Elle said.

"I'll find her for you."

"Thank you," Elle said with profound gratitude.

She closed the wooden panel at the window but she reappeared in seconds at the door.

"Come inside here," the sister said, ushering her in. "It's against protocol, but if someone's coming after you, you should wait here."

Elle could have kissed the woman for her compassion. The elderly nun trundled off down a long dimly lit hallway leaving Elle by the door. Even after the sister disappeared, Elle could hear the sound of her rosary beads and orthopedic shoes echoing off the stone floors and polished wood walls.

She leaned back against the door and closed her eyes. When she was a teenager, a closed door between her and Søren had been a challenge, a hurdle and a game. If she sat outside his office door and did her homework, it was only a matter of time before the door opened. He would step out, take a seat by her on the bench and go over her homework with her. She never would have survived precalculus without him. When the work was done and she put her things away, Søren would retreat back into his office, shutting the door behind him, and she would sit there staring at the door and loving him with all her heart and dreaming of the life they would have together when he let her behind all his locked doors.

But never in any of those girlhood dreams had she ever dreamed of this moment. She never dreamed she'd be grateful for the door behind her and the sign on it barring men from entering. She never dreamed she'd be relieved Søren couldn't get to her. She'd spent the past ten years of her life trying to get to him. Would she spend the rest of her life trying to get away?

"Ellie?"

Elle looked up and saw a woman in white coming toward her. White habit, white veil and a ghostly white face.

"Mom?"

"Of course it's your mother."

"Sorry, I didn't…" She didn't recognize her own mother. Gone was her mother's long black hair so like her own. Gone were the khaki skirt she lived in and the navy cardigans and her ubiquitous white Keds. Elle hadn't come to her mother's entrance ceremony. She would have if her mother had asked, but by then Elle had moved out and they'd stopped speaking. Elle had forgotten that part, that whole not speaking to each other thing. Hopefully her mother had forgotten it, too.

"What on earth are you doing here?" her mother demanded.

"That nun let me in here behind the door."

"No, what are you doing here? At the abbey?"

"Oh…long story."

"Long story?" her mother repeated. "Long story? I haven't seen or heard from you in two years—"

"You called me a whore, Mom. Did you really think I wanted to keep having that conversation with you?"

Her mother's spine stiffened visibly.

"That was wrong of me. I was worried about you, and I took what I'd learned about you…badly."

"Is that an apology?"

"It is."

"I'm sorry, too," Elle said, meaning it. Right now she was sorry for everything.

"Forgive me?"

"Yes. No. Maybe."

"Maybe?" her mother said.

"I'll forgive you for everything you said to me. And if you remember accurately, calling me a 'whore' was just the beginning of that discussion."

"I overreacted. I had my reasons for overreacting."

"I know you did," she said, although she'd had no sympathy for her mother at the time. Everything had been okay between them until one night Søren had driven her home on the back of his motorcycle. Her mother was supposed to be out late at a church function but had got ill and come home early. One glance out the window and she'd seen her daughter kissing a Catholic priest. Elle had been so angry after her mother had called her a "priest's whore" she'd spilled everything. The sex. The kink. And if her mother dared speak a word of it, Elle would never speak to her again as long as she lived.

The next day Elle had moved out.

"Mom, I need your help with something."

"How can I help you?" she asked, sounding both concerned and suspicious.

"I need to stay here for a while."

She shook her head.

"That's not possible. Only sisters are allowed in the abbey. You shouldn't even be behind this door."

"Maybe they can make an exception for me. I can work."

"Work? How? We do all our own work here. We cook our own food, clean, farm, everything. We don't hire outside help."

"But I can help. You don't have to hire me. I'll work for free."

"No, Ellie. I don't know what you're into or who you're in trouble with again—"

"I'm not running from the cops. I'm twenty-six years old. I'm not running away from home, either. I need a place to stay for a while, a safe place."

"So you didn't steal any cars this time?"

"No," she said. "Well, one. But that was more like borrowing. And he'll get it back."

"Elle, I don't have time for your games. I have work to do. I have a life here and you're not a part of it. You can't be. You can come to Mass here at the chapel. We can visit once a week. But this is a sacred place, a sanctuary."

"I need sanctuary."

"Why? Because you got arrested again?"

"No, Mom. Because I left him."

Silence.

Total silence.

A great silence even. A silence so loud it echoed off the floors like footsteps. Finally her mother exhaled and crossed herself. Tears shone in her eyes and she whispered, *Benedicta excels Mater Dei, Maria sanctissima.* Elle didn't know much Latin, but she knew a prayer of thanks to the Virgin Mary when she heard it.

Before she knew it, her mother had wrapped her up in her arms and Elle's neck was wet with tears. Not her tears but her mother's. Elle closed her eyes and breathed in the faint, clean scent of talcum powder. Some things were still the same about her mother. The clothes, the hair, even her name…that was all different. But at least her mother smelled the same.

"You can stay, baby," she whispered. "I'll make them let you stay."

"Thank you." She wanted to cry too but the tears wouldn't come. She wouldn't let them. Tears were not welcome here. Elle couldn't remember the last time her mother had hugged her, had held her like this. Years. It was almost worth it to leave Søren for this one hug alone.

"You really did leave him?" her mother asked again.

"I did," Elle said.

"For good?" her mother asked.

Elle nodded against her mother's shoulder.

"Forever."

7

ELLE'S MOTHER ESCORTED HER DOWN HALLWAY AFTER hallway. From the outside, the abbey looked like a gray stone square—three stories high and likely as long as it was wide. The inside, however, was labyrinthine. Every few feet they turned a corner, then another. Winding hallways, unmarked doors. On the walls were crucifixes, icons, shrines, image after image of Saint Monica in various poses, in various mediums. In one mosaic Saint Monica held her son Saint Augustine in her arms. Elle glanced at it only a moment, glanced away quickly.

"Where are we going?" she asked her mother, who hadn't released her hand this entire time.

"I'm going to the Chapel of Perpetual Adoration. Mother Prioress is there tonight. We'll need to get her permission to let you stay."

"Will she give it?"

"She doesn't like outsiders in the abbey."

"Is that a no?"

"No, but start praying anyway," her mother said, and Elle did as she was told.

Elle had a good sense of direction, but by the time they arrived at the chapel, she knew she'd never find her way back to the front door without help. Good. The front door was the gateway to the outside world. It was the last place she wanted to go.

They walked under a polished wooden archway and into an open seating area that looked like nothing more than a living room. She saw bookshelves, baskets of knitting and chairs of all types.

"Here. Wait for me in the library," her mother said. "I'll be back soon."

Elle took a seat in a cane-back chair that had probably been here since the convent was founded in 1856. It creaked under her weight but held her. A few minutes passed. Elle relaxed into the chair. For two days now she'd been coasting on the fumes of her fury. Now a deep exhaustion set into her body. She wanted to close her eyes and sleep. Sleep for a year, sleep for the rest of her life.

She looked to her right and saw a stack of magazines on a small table. *Catholic Digest. Inside the Vatican.* The *Catholic Times.* The front page of one of the magazines blared the headline Why God Demands Priestly Celibacy.

"What the fuck am I doing here?" Elle asked herself out loud. No one answered. No one had to. Elle knew what the fuck she was doing there.

Because she had nowhere else to go.

"This is your Eleanor?"

Elle stood up immediately. In the doorway loomed a woman who must have been almost six feet tall. She wore round glasses and a black habit with an elaborate rosary hanging down her side.

"Ellie, this is Mother Prioress. Mother Prioress, my only child."

Mother Prioress looked Elle up and down.

"Why are you here?" Mother Prioress asked. She had a slight accent, vaguely Irish, but time in America had washed most of it out.

"I was just asking myself the same thing," she said, deciding to try honesty.

"She left her lover," her mother said.

"How is this our concern?" Mother Prioress asked.

"Because he beats her."

"Mom, he—"

Her mother raised a hand to silence her. Elle closed her mouth.

"I'm very sorry to hear that. But isn't that a matter for the police?" Mother Prioress asked.

"He's in a position of power," her mother answered for Elle. "And he has dangerous friends."

Elle couldn't argue with either of those assertions. Søren *was* in a position of power. And he *did* have dangerous friends. She knew that because they were her dangerous friends, too.

"Are you certain she's telling the truth?" Mother Prioress asked Elle's mother. Elle was about five seconds away from losing the last vestiges of her self-control. "Isn't this the daughter who you said has had run-ins with the law?"

"That was over ten years ago, Mother Prioress. And I'm certain she's telling the truth."

"We don't let outsiders stay within the walls," Mother Prioress said. "That's against our rules."

"What of the rule of Saint Benedict?" her mother asked the prioress. "'Let all guests who arrive be received like Christ, for He is going to say I came as a guest, and you received Me.'"

Mother Prioress nodded. "Yes, and when Christ arrived to visit His disciples after the resurrection, He did not hesitate to prove Himself. Do you have any proof your accusations against this man are true?"

Elle looked her mother in the eye. She knew what she needed to do but was loath to do it. Everything within her rebelled at the lie she needed to tell. Søren was no saint and neither was she. But to blame him for a crime he hadn't committed felt like blasphemy. Søren had sinned against her, yes. Sinned so that she never wanted to lay eyes on him again. But leaving him and lying about him were two different things. And yet…

She turned around and lifted the back of her shirt. Without even having to look she knew what her mother and the Prioress saw. Five nights ago Kingsley had flogged her before fucking her, flogged her for an hour. Flogged her, then caned her. Flogged, caned her, whipped her, spanked her. And now her back boasted the fading welts and bruises from that long and beautiful night.

"Jesus, Mary and Joseph," the Prioress said, and the Irish accent came out in full force. Elle pulled her shirt back down. She'd always loved her bruises and welts, cherished them. Kingsley had kissed them after giving them to her. She knew he'd been especially bruising simply to goad Søren, whose return from Rome was imminent that week. The welts were Kingsley's way of saying, "Look how much fun we had without you."

"Only sisters and retreatants are allowed on the grounds," Mother Prioress said. "We have our own rules to follow."

"I can be a retreatant," Elle said. "I have some money. What does a week-long retreat here cost?"

"One hundred dollars."

A hotel room would cost her fifty a night, at least. "I can pay it," Elle said.

"I suppose," Mother Prioress said. "But this is highly unusual."

"I'll work, too. I'll be useful. Please. I can't…I can't go back out there yet."

Something in Elle's voice must have gotten through to Mother Prioress. The fear, the desperation. Or maybe it was the money. Who knew? Elle didn't care as long as they let her stay.

"If she works, she can stay," Mother Prioress said at last. "We'll consider it a special sort of retreat. No longer than a year, however. We work here. We pray here. We serve each other here. We, none of us, are in hiding."

Elle turned around and faced them. She was too ashamed of herself to meet their eyes. Not ashamed of the bruises on her back. Ashamed that she'd lied.

"Thank you," Elle said. "I'll work."

"You will." Mother Prioress took a step forward and looked down into her face. "You'll work and you'll behave. The sisters here have made great sacrifices to be part of this community. They are here to love and serve God, worship Him and pray for His people. This is good and holy work and they are not to be disturbed, bothered, interrupted or interfered with in any way."

"I understand," Elle said.

"You had a lover in the outside world. You will keep that information to yourself. We have all taken vows of chastity. Consider yourself under one, as well. You say you aren't safe outside our walls. Then you will remain inside our walls as long as you are a resident here. You will bring no one else inside our walls."

"No one."

"Keep you head down. Stay out of trouble. Work hard. If you harm any of the women here, you will be expelled. Immediately."

Elle nodded her understanding.

"I don't..." she began, and paused. Something had lodged in her throat. She swallowed it down. "I don't want to hurt anybody. Ever."

"Yes." Mother Prioress gave her the first smile she'd seen on the woman's face yet. "Yes, I believe that." She turned to Elle's mother. "Take her to the infirmary. I'll send someone to prepare a room for her."

"Thank you, Mother Prioress," Elle's mother said. Tears of gratitude were shining in her eyes. "Thank you."

Elle took her mother's hand and together they started from the room.

"Eleanor?" the Prioress said.

"Elle."

The Prioress gave her a tight smile. "Elle."

"Yes?"

"You will do as you are told here. I certainly hope you're capable of following orders."

Elle smiled. "Trust me. If I know how to do anything, it's follow orders."

Her mother tugged her hand and led her from the room.

"I don't need the infirmary, Mom," Elle said.

"You have to call me Sister John or Sister in front of others. And yes, you need the infirmary."

"It's bruises and welts. They'll be gone in a few more days."

"You look like you were mugged."

"Nobody gets flogged during a mugging, Mom. And if they did, I'd walk around bad neighborhoods more often."

"This isn't a joke."

"It wasn't even him who did it." Him. Søren. Although her mother didn't know that name. She knew him as Father Marcus Stearns. But Elle couldn't call him Marcus Stearns in case one of the other sisters had heard of him. So "him" it was.

"Do I want to know who did that to you?"

"My friend Kingsley."

"You have an interesting definition of friend."

"Maybe a better definition," Elle said. "It was consensual. You know I like this stuff."

"And you know I hate that you like it. And I hate him for making you like it."

"He didn't make me like it, Mom. And he didn't rape me. And he didn't seduce me."

"You were fifteen when you met him. He groomed you."

"I was also fifteen when I first tried to get him in bed. I

came pre-groomed." She couldn't believe they were having this fight again. "If you really thought he was a danger to children, you would have called the bishop. But you know as well as I do that he isn't."

"The church has enough scandals. I wasn't about to create a new one."

"Two consenting adults shouldn't be a scandal."

"Ellie, that man is—"

"Mom, you can hate him if you want to hate him. But at least hate him for the right reasons."

"Hate him for the right reasons?" Her mother stood up and came over to her. "I thought I was. But you tell me then. What are the right reasons to hate the priest who seduced and beat my daughter?"

"Hate him because I hate him."

"I can't do that."

"Why not?" Elle asked, meeting her mother's eyes.

"Because you might stop hating him. And then I would have to stop, too."

Elle looked away from her mother's beseeching eyes.

"What did he do to you, baby?" her mother whispered. "What did he do to make you come to me after all this time?"

"I don't want to talk about it," Elle said as they neared a bright white room, no doubt the infirmary or whatever passed for it in this aging edifice.

"You should talk to someone. A professional who can help you."

"I don't need counseling. I'm as sane as you are." If not saner. After all, she wasn't the one walking around in a wedding dress telling the world Jesus was her husband.

"You could talk to someone here. Sister Margaret is a trained psychologist. And once a week, Father Antonio—"

Elle turned her head and stared at her mother. "You think I'm going to talk to a priest about this?"

"Well…" her mother began. "Perhaps Sister Margaret then."

If she'd had the energy for it, Elle would have laughed. But she didn't so she didn't and in silence they walked into the infirmary.

Her mother left her sitting in a chair while she went to fetch another one of the sisters. Twenty minutes later, a nun who looked about her mother's age—no more than fifty definitely—entered the infirmary and gave Elle a once-over. Her mother introduced the woman as Sister Aquinas. She wore a white apron over her black habit and her sleeves were pinned up to expose her forearms. Sister Aquinas pointed to a bed behind a white curtain and told Elle to wait there.

"I'll go check on your room and make sure you have everything you need," her mother said, taking Elle's duffel bag from her. "I'll be back. Don't worry. You're in good hands with Sister Aquinas."

"Okay," Elle said, too relieved to have a place to stay for the time being to worry about anything much at the moment. "I'll see you soon."

Her mother kissed her on the forehead.

"Thank you." The two words came out of Elle's mouth entirely of their own volition.

"You're thanking me?" Her mother sounded utterly baffled.

"Well, you got them to let me stay here. I know we haven't gotten along the past few years…ten years."

"Twenty-six years," her mother said, but she said it kindly.

She paused to laugh. "Okay, twenty-six years. But yeah, I appreciate it, Mom. Sister John, I mean. Sorry."

Her mother cupped her face and looked her in the eyes.

"Every morning for the past three years I've woken up and prayed the same prayer. Do you want to know what that prayer is?"

"What?" Elle asked, even though she was certain she didn't want to know.

"Dear God, please don't let today be the day he finally kills her."

Once more her mother kissed her on the forehead and then hurried away before Elle could say another word.

Something turned in Elle's heart, turned like a knob on a telescope. For the first time, Elle looked through the eyepiece of her mother's heart, and now, this moment, the light had come into focus and Elle saw what her mother saw—a daughter she didn't understand in love with a powerful, dangerous man twice her size who couldn't make love to her without hurting her first. And every day she feared he would go too far and kill her only child. Every time her mother looked at Elle, that's what she saw. For one second, Elle saw it, too.

"Behind the curtain," Sister Aquinas said. "I'll be right there."

Dazed by her vision, Elle did as told, walking behind the curtain and sitting numbly on the hospital cot.

Sister Aquinas came around with a towel in her hand. She tossed it on the side table and put her hands on either side of Elle's neck.

"How are you feeling?" she asked.

"Oh...I'm fine," Elle said.

"Are you sure about that? Your eyes are bloodshot. Are you on drugs?"

"Nothing illegal. I had some nausea."

"Have you been vomiting?"

"A few times."

"Are you pregnant?"

"Not since Monday night."

Sister Aquinas blinked at her. But it was only one blink, one pause.

"Miscarriage?"

"No."

"I see." Sister Aquinas took a long breath. "Surgical or medical?"

"Medical."

"Miferprex?" Sister Aquinas asked.

"Yes."

"When?"

"First pills on Monday. Second pill on Wednesday."

"Today's Friday," Sister Aquinas said. "So five days then." She was speaking to herself. "Have you been to a doctor since Wednesday?"

"No."

"How severe was the bleeding?"

"Heavy. Very heavy."

"It's lighter now?"

"Much."

"Did you take anything else?" Sister Aquinas pulled out a scope and looked in Elle's ears.

"Nothing else."

"They should have given you Tylenol and Compazine."

"I had a prescription for them," Elle said. "But I was too sick to go get them filled."

"You didn't have anyone to help you? The father?"

"No."

Sister Aquinas sighed heavily. "It's times like this I remember why I became a nun."

Elle laughed. "Because you hate men?"

"No. I never wanted to go through anything alone again."

"Thank you for being nice about this," Elle said.

"I'm a doctor. Just because I don't agree with a certain medical procedure, it doesn't mean I didn't learn about it in medical school."

"You're a doctor? I thought you were a nun."

"I'm both. I have some painkillers here. I can give you something for your nausea if you still need it."

"I think I'm done puking."

"You'll probably bleed for a few weeks. That's normal. But I want you to come back here in a week. We can do a sonogram."

Elle stared at her wide-eyed.

"You can do that here? You get a lot of knocked-up nuns in here?"

Sister Aquinas smiled. "Kidney stones. I see a lot of those."

"I see." Elle rolled back onto the cot while Sister Aquinas prodded her stomach. "I'm going to be okay, aren't I?"

"Okay? Physically, yes. You'll be fine. Emotionally and spiritually? That's between you and God. But if any place can help you get right with God, it's here."

"I don't regret it," Elle said, and she meant every word.

"Pride is a sin, young lady."

"Put it on my tab."

"God sees the heart," was all Sister Aquinas said to that.

Sister Aquinas continued her perfunctory examination. She made no further comment about Elle's choice or her spiritual state. But when Elle took her shirt off, Sister Aquinas froze. It was only for an instant, and unlike Mother Prioress, no Catholic oaths were released.

"It's not as bad as it looks," Elle said. "Only welts and bruises."

"Did the man who got you pregnant do this to you?"

"Yes," Elle said. It wasn't a lie. Søren had been in Rome ten weeks, and Kingsley had been her only lover in that time. No doubt who the father was.

Sister Aquinas placed her hand gently on the top of Elle's head. It felt like a blessing although what she'd done to deserve a blessing, Elle didn't know.

"God sees the heart," Sister Aquinas said again. This time it didn't sound like a platitude. This time it sounded like an apology.

Sister Aquinas applied some sort of cream to her bruised back and gave her a week's supply of a mild painkiller. Elle accepted the pills with gratitude. It would be nice to be out of pain again. Even better than drugs, Sister Aquinas brought her a tray of food. Last night's leftovers warmed up, but Elle ate every single bite of it.

"Feeling better?" Sister Aquinas asked when she came for the tray.

"Much better. Almost human."

"Good. We like humans around here," she said with a smile. "Sister Mary John will be back soon. Lie down and get some rest."

Rest sounded heavenly. And rest was heavenly. The pillow under her head felt like a cloud. The plain white cotton sheets might as well have been silk. She was safe, safe at last. And now, now she could finally sleep.

Elle closed her eyes.

Then she heard a noise.

She sat straight up in the cot, her heart hammering against her chest.

Seemingly of its own volition, her body forced her onto her feet, her feet forced her forward. Her steps brought her to the window in the infirmary. It was well after 2:00 a.m. and all was dark for miles around. Elle could see the moon and the stars and the slight reflection of them both on the rolling hills, the fields and forests that surrounded the abbey. She saw nothing else. But she didn't have to see it. She heard it.

"What is that?" Sister Aquinas asked, coming to stand next to her. "Is that a car out there?"

"No," Elle said, her voice hollow and scared. "It's a motor-cycle."

"How can you tell?"

"I know cars," she said. "And I know motorcycles. That's a 1992 907 I.E. Ducati. Black."

Sister Aquinas laughed. "You know the color?"

"That's the only year they came in black."

The nun narrowed her eyes and peered out onto the black night.

"Someone you know?" she asked, looking at Elle with a curious light in her eyes.

Elle took a step back away from the window.

Then another step.

Then another. She shook her head.

"No."

8

2015
Scotland

"I DIDN'T KNOW," KINGSLEY SAID, AND NORA TURNED to look at him.

"What didn't you know?" she asked.

"I didn't know it was that hard for you." Kingsley's back rested against a bedpost at the foot of the bed and his eyes searched her face. "I didn't know about the pain."

"It was fine after a couple days. Bad cramps, that's all. Women are used to that." She shrugged it off. The past was past. She still remembered the pain, but there was no reason for Kingsley to know how well she remembered it.

"We should have been more careful, you and I," Kingsley said.

"We were fluid-bonded. It's what we do. That's the risk we take," Nora said. "I don't blame you. Or myself. Not anymore. Accidents happen, right?"

"I'm sorry you went through that alone," Kingsley said. "I should have said that a long time ago."

She smiled at him, grateful for the words. "You wanted kids and I knew it. It would have been too sadistic, even for me, to make you hold my hand during the whole process."

"I thought…" Kingsley began and stopped.

"Go on," Søren said. "We're talking about it finally. Talk."

"I thought I'd lost my only chance to be a father," Kingsley admitted. "I convinced myself of that, which is why I wasn't there for you the way I should have been."

"You did the best you could." Nora stretched out her leg and touched her bare toes to Kingsley's. "We both did."

"I didn't," Søren said.

"You were in Rome." She turned to look at him. "You couldn't have done anything."

"Somewhere along the way I did something wrong. If I hadn't, you wouldn't have been scared to tell me," Søren said.

"I wasn't scared to tell you," Nora said, not entirely truthfully. "I didn't want to drag you into this. And I didn't need to talk to anyone about it. As soon as I knew, I knew what I wanted to do. No reason to talk to you about it."

"Except you belonged to me, and you were going through a difficult time," he said. "I would have liked to have been there."

"And I would have liked my privacy," she said.

Søren took her hand and kissed the back of it. His way of saying "You win this round."

"That was you, wasn't it?" Nora asked. "The motorcycle I heard?"

"It was." He gave her a penetrating stare as if trying to see the woman she'd once been and reconciling her with the woman in front of him.

"Why did you come to me there?" she asked.

"I had to," he said simply. "If there was any chance, any chance at all I could speak to you or even see you, I had to take it."

"How did you know where I went?" she asked. "I was gone one day and by the next night, you'd found me."

"I knew where you would go because you did what I would have done in your place," Søren said. "If I were scared and in pain and on the run."

"You would have gone to a convent?" she asked, smiling at the idea.

Søren smiled. "No. To my mother."

"I would have loved to have gone to your mom's house," Nora said as she glanced at Kingsley who watched them both with quiet intensity. It had been her first instinct to leave the country and hide out at Gisela's house in Denmark. She'd rejected it out of hand.

"She would have taken you in," Søren said. "You know how much she loved you. It didn't matter I was a priest. She considered us married."

"I know. And I know she would have taken good care of me," Nora said, recalling in an instant a thousand memories of Søren's mother. Her Æbleskiver pancakes she'd made in winter. Listening to her and Søren playing piano together. The long talks she and Nora had while Søren was outside playing with his nieces. Nora sensed Gisela wanted Søren to leave the priesthood, get married and have children, but she never said a word about it. His mother respected their life together, their choices, even with all the risks they took. And Nora always loved her for not trying to change either of them.

"You might have been happier with my mother than you were with yours," Søren said, knowing how fraught her relationship with her own mother had been. Fraught until the day Nora's mother died over two years ago.

"Probably. But I loved your mom too much to make her pick sides between her only son and me. That wouldn't have been fair to her," Nora said.

"Considering how I behaved that night, it's safe to say she would have sided with you," Søren said. Nora wondered how her life could have changed if she'd chosen to run to Søren's mother instead of her own. That year at her mother's convent had changed everything, and if she'd gone to Gisela's she probably would have returned to Søren as his submissive in a week. "He sided with you against me." Søren nodded toward Kingsley.

"You can't blame me," Kingsley said without any hint of contrition. "You fucked up, and I wanted to rip your heart out with my bare hands. It feels good to say that out loud."

Nora laughed, and shockingly so did Søren.

"I wasn't very happy with you, either," Søren said. "You left without a word. Didn't tell anyone where you went, not even Calliope."

"That was the point," Kingsley said, rolling onto his back. "How could anyone tell you where I went if I didn't even know where I was going? I got to the airport and bought a ticket for the next international flight out."

"Where did you go?" Nora asked.

"Greece," Kingsley said. "Then Japan. I spent a month in Hong Kong, a month in New Zealand. New Zealand gave me island fever. I went to the Philippines next, and after that, the French Caribbean."

"Meanwhile I'm in upstate New York in a convent. Next time I split town, I'm going to your travel agency, King," she said.

"No more leaving," Søren said. Nora crawled across the bed and kissed him.

"Never again, I promise," she said, meaning every word. They kissed again, Søren's hand resting lightly on the side of her neck, pressing into her collar so she could feel it against her throat. She hadn't wanted to talk about that year ever, but now that they'd opened Pandora's box, she felt better, as if the last and final wall between the three of them was tumbling down at last. They should have talked this out years ago. She and Kingsley hadn't ever talked about the pregnancy they'd ended, but Søren was right as he usually was. Ignorance wasn't bliss. Ignorance was cowardice.

"Stop kissing him," Kingsley said. "Get to the nun-fucking already."

Nora turned her head and glared at Kingsley.

"I'll tell you about my first night with Juliette if you tell me about your nun. It's a good story," Kingsley said. "Deal?"

"Fair trade," Nora said, and held out her hand. Kingsley shook it. "But my nun didn't show up for about eight months. Let's see, I got there in June. It was almost spring when I saw her the first time."

"That's when I met Juliette, too. February in Haiti on the beach. I don't remember the day of the week, but I know it was Valentine's Day. Someone told me that." He laughed at something and didn't tell them what.

"You start," Nora said as she slid over Søren and got out of bed. "I'm opening the wine."

"We're saving that for the reception," Kingsley reminded her.

"If this storm doesn't stop, we'll all drown by morning and all that wine will have gone to waste."

"You make a good point, Elle," Kingsley said. "I'll have a big glass. I'll get in trouble with Jules for hiding from her. I might as well get in trouble with her for drinking, as well."

"Why would she be mad at you for drinking?" Nora asked.

Kingsley grinned broadly. "Because she can't have alcohol again for seven more months."

Nora almost dropped the wine bottle.

"Juliette's pregnant?" Nora asked.

Kingsley raised his finger to his lips. "Only you two know now."

Nora ran to Kingsley and embraced him. "You slut," she said, planting a kiss on both cheeks.

"She wanted two," Kingsley said. "And *le prêtre* doesn't look a bit surprised."

"I'm trying to look surprised," Søren said with a sly smile.

"You knew?" Nora asked.

"Juliette and I were working on something together recently. She got light-headed and almost fainted. She told me why she wasn't feeling well in exchange for me not calling an ambulance for her."

"And you didn't tell me?" Nora asked, grabbing him by the front of his shirt and pointing at his nose. "You jerk."

"I'm a priest. Keeping secrets is my job," he reminded her, taking her hands off his shirt and kissing them. He looked from her to Kingsley. "I'm very happy for you. And relieved you finally said something so I could tell you that."

"Are you happy?" Nora asked Kingsley, already knowing the answer.

"Is the pope Catholic?" Kingsley asked.

"Pope Francis is a Jesuit," Søren said.

"And Catholic," Kingsley said.

"Being a Jesuit takes precedence," Søren said.

Nora sighed. "Typical. So typical."

Søren got out of bed and stood in front of Kingsley. He grasped the back of Kingsley's neck, bent down and kissed him. Nora went back for the wine and let them have their moment of privacy. She opened the Syrah and poured three steep glasses. She brought one to Kingsley, one to Søren and kept one for herself.

"When are you telling Nico he's going to be a brother again?" Nora asked as she slid back onto the bed, careful not to spill any wine on the sheets. They'd already pushed their luck with fire-play and very wet sex. If she got her deposit back on this room, it would be a miracle.

"Soon," Kingsley said. "Now that you both know, I'll call him tomorrow. You think he'll be happy?"

"Thrilled and relieved," Nora said. "The more kids you have, the less pressure he feels to have them. He's already made Céleste the legal heir to his vineyard. But don't tell her that. She's only three, but I can see her attempting a coup."

"I'm relieved I won't have to worry about being a grandfather anytime soon," Kingsley said with a wink at her. He pushed a pillow behind his back, stretched out his legs and crossed them at the ankles. He had the legs of a professional soccer player, which the kilt displayed to marvelous affect. No wonder Juliette with her fetish and her pregnancy hormones had been all over him the past two days.

"No chance of that from me," Nora said. "Cheers to the good Doctor Hélène Faber." She and Kingsley clinked glasses, which was likely the first time in history two people had ever toasted to a woman's sterilization procedure before. Then again, no two people in history had Kingsley and Nora's history. With everything they'd put each other through, they'd had two choices—hate each other or love each other. They were so much alike, hating each other would have been like hating themselves. And both of them were rather too self-important for that sort of nonsense.

So they picked love.

"I have you to thank for my children," Kingsley said, pointing his wineglass at her. "All two and one-third of them."

"And why is that?"

"I would never have known about Nico if it wasn't for you. I would never have met Juliette if you hadn't left him." He pointed at Søren.

"Then shouldn't I get some credit here?" Søren asked.

"*Oui,* you get all the credit for being such an enormous asshole neither of us wanted to see you for a full year."

"Thank you," Søren said, saluting with his wineglass. "Credit where credit is due."

"Did you know Juliette would be the mother of your children when you met her?" Nora asked.

"The opposite," Kingsley said. "I thought she'd be a terrible mother when I saw her. In my defense, she was assaulting children. In her defense, they deserved it."

"No wonder Juliette wouldn't tell me about when you all met," Nora said, pulling the sheets up around her again. She pressed close to Søren, relishing his warmth and his nearness.

"Juliette," Kingsley began, and his voice changed subtly as he spoke. He sounded far away and Nora wondered what he was remembering and why it hurt so much. "She was in a difficult position back then. Trapped, you could say."

"So what did you do?" Nora asked, as eager to hear Kingsley's story of that year as they were to hear hers.

"I did what I always do when I meet a beautiful woman," Kingsley said with a shrug. "I fucked her."

9

2004
Haiti

KINGSLEY WOKE UP THAT MORNING AND DECIDED TO fuck the first girl who'd let him. Luckily there was a girl conveniently located in his bed. Who she was he didn't quite remember, but it didn't really matter. She was there by his invitation and her choice. Names, dates, places—the rest was irrelevant.

Last night—that's when he'd met her. He'd gone to a bar last night, drunk a few gallons of rum…or something. He'd met a waitress who spoke no traditional French and a little English. He spoke English and enough Creole to have her sitting on his lap by the third drink and home with him after the sixth. Home wasn't anything more than a shack on the beach furnished with a bed and a well-stocked bar, but that hadn't deterred her from spending the night with him and on him. Gorgeous girl. Coffee-colored skin and eyes, short curly hair that formed a halo around her face, lips like candy he clearly remembered biting.

And any minute now he'd remember her name. He rolled onto his side, spooned against her back and kissed the tip of her shoulder. Her name—it started with an *S*. He wanted to say Sabrina but that wasn't quite it. She stretched out in her sleep and pushed back against him. Fuck it. He didn't even remember his own name this morning.

She rolled onto her stomach as Kingsley ran his hand down

her back. She had the soft smooth skin of a woman who spent her days naked on the sand.

"Bon maten," she murmured as he nibbled the back of her neck that smelled lightly of citrus. Without taking his mouth off her body, he reached over the bed, pulled out a condom and rolled it on. No more accidents. No more mistakes. No more mornings like that one he'd had last year when he saw with his own eyes the consequences of his carelessness.

He pushed the thought out of his mind as he moved on top of the girl.

"Oui?" he asked. *"Non?"*

"Wi," she said, Haitian Creole for yes and gave him a smile that also said yes.

He laughed in her ear, nudged her thighs apart with his knees and settled into her with a few slow thrusts. She was still wet and open inside from the sex they'd had a few hours earlier. Wet and warm and he groaned from the pleasure of it. It had been a long time since he'd let himself have vanilla sex. It felt like a vacation—lazy, easy, self-indulgent.

But he wasn't complaining and neither was Sabatina.

Sabatina—that was her name.

Kingsley rolled his hips against hers, keeping the pace slow and easy. Her mouth opened under his, inviting his tongue in for a dozen more kisses, a dozen more bites. She tasted like white wine and pears. Lowering his head, he took a nipple into his mouth and sucked deeply while she arched underneath him. He pushed deep and her hips rose off the bed to welcome him into her. Last night...he could barely remember fucking her, although he knew he'd enjoyed it and so had she. Still, it felt like the first time with her so he took his time, relishing each push and the pleasant pressure it gave him in his stomach, thighs and back.

Her mouth curled into a smile of intoxication. She murmured softly in Creole. He didn't understand a word of it, but the tone was definitely encouraging. He licked and kissed his way from one breast to the other. Still he moved in her, harder and deeper. She reached her arms up to wrap them around his neck. Out of pure instinct he grabbed her arms and pressed her wrists down into the bed on either side of her head and bore down on her with a brutal thrust. She gasped and cried out. Kingsley froze.

"Don't stop," she said in her heavily accented English. He put more weight onto her wrists, more power into his thrusts and fucked her six inches into the mattress. Spread out beneath him, she received everything he gave her without protest and with enthusiasm. He released one of her wrists and yanked her leg around his back. When he pulled out, he pulled out all the way to the tip. When he thrust back in, it was with every inch at once as far as he could go. A deep pulsing resonated inside his thighs and hips all the way to his cock. He couldn't hold out much longer, but thankfully neither could she. He increased his pace and was rewarded with the lusty cry of her orgasm and the subsequent contractions of her vagina around him.

He dug his fingers into her flesh and let himself come at last. The relief as he collapsed on her body was profound. He wanted to close his eyes, fall asleep inside her and not wake up for days. Instead, he pulled out and lay on his side facing her.

"You liked that?" he asked.

"Non," she said, smiling broadly. "I loved it. But…"

"No buts," he said. "You stay. I'll find breakfast."

"I can't." She rolled up and stretched her neck left to right. From the floor she picked up her dress and pulled it on over her head. "I have to go."

"You have to work?"

"Babysit," she said. "Maman has to work today." She kissed him quick and hard before sliding off the bed. She shoved her feet into her sandals and tied a ribbon in her hair to tame it. "But I can come back tomorrow night."

"You should," he said. "I'll be here."

"For how long?" she asked.

"I don't know," he said. "Until they kick me off the island."

"This is Haiti. You spend money here, you can stay forever."

"Maybe I will." His money wasn't running out anytime soon. And the thought of returning to New York now, in winter, with no one to welcome him home but a brokenhearted priest?

"Good. I never fucked a white man before."

"Is that why you came back here with me?"

"Wi," she said with a wink.

Kingsley laughed. "I feel so used."

"You want me to come back and use you again?"

"Why not?" he asked.

"I don't know." She stared at him through narrowed eyes. "You were talking about another girl in your sleep last night."

"I was? Who?" Kingsley hadn't talked in his sleep in years as far as he knew. Not since that year after he moved to Manhattan and was still recovering from his gunshot wound.

"You never said her name. It was 'she.' Who is she?"

"I must have been dreaming. I know a lot of girls. They all have names."

Sabatina grinned. "I'll use you again tonight maybe. Come back to the club if you want. I can be your Valentine's Day date."

"It's Valentine's Day?"

"You didn't know?"

"I don't remember what year it is."

Laughing, she bent over and kissed him once more.

"It's 2004. Valentine's Day. Now I have to get home before Maman kills me."

"You live with your parents?" Kingsley asked.

She nodded as she bent to tie the laces of her sandals.

"How old are you?" he asked.

"Eighteen," she said, standing up straight again.

Kingsley's stomach flipped a few times. Eighteen? She was only eighteen? His last girlfriend had been twenty-seven. Somewhere deep in his psyche, his conscience reminded him it still existed.

"I have a rule. I don't fuck women under twenty-five."

"Then you broke your rule." She laughed again. "It's good. I like older men."

She ran a hand through his hair once, and after one more kiss, a kiss he didn't return, she left him.

Somewhere he had a watch but he didn't bother checking it. All he did was grab a towel, wrap it around his waist and walk out to the ocean. It must have been early. It looked early. But the temperature had to be in the eighties already. No one else was on his stretch of beach yet so he dropped his towel and dived naked into the clear waters. He swam out a hundred yards and rested on his back in the water. When was the last time he'd taken an actual bath or shower? He couldn't remember. Who needed a porcelain bathtub when he had the ocean fifty feet from his front door?

As he floated under the morning sun, he tried to forget he'd fucked a girl twenty-one years his junior last night. Twenty-one years. He was old enough to be her father and then some. Then again, he'd lost his virginity when he was twelve or thirteen... twelve maybe. Thirteen? Whichever it was, by that math he couldn't fuck anyone more than thirteen years younger than him. That was Elle's age...twenty-six. For a minute he let himself think about her, something he'd been trying to avoid for months. Where had she landed? Had she given up and gone back to Søren? He doubted it. Once a week he called back to his office and spoke to Calliope. No news from her yet. The house was quiet. The city was quiet. The dogs were content and his clubs were thriving in the hands of their capable managers. Everyone missed him, Calliope said. But no one needed him.

And no one back at the house had seen or heard from Elle

or Søren since Kingsley had left the country in June. Either they were tucked tenderly in Søren's bed making up for all that happened between them, or she was still gone and he was still searching. Kingsley refused to admit that he cared which one it was. His part in their domestic drama was done. They were adults. They didn't need him around to solve their problems for them.

Yet...

Still...

He couldn't stop wondering.

Reluctantly he swam toward the shore and grabbed his towel off the sand. He didn't dry off with it. No need in this heat. He'd be mostly dry by the time he reached his beach hut. Back inside, he drank a bottle of water and pulled on a pair of tattered khaki pants and a white shirt. He didn't bother buttoning it. He put on a pair of sunglasses and walked back out into the heat of the day in search of food and alcohol and anything else that would get him through the day.

A hut on another patch of beach half a mile away sold fish and fruit to visitors. He might eat there. He might keep walking. Didn't really matter. He wasn't going to starve. And he had no schedule to keep. If he was honest with himself, he'd admit he was bored. Bored in Paradise. But after five weeks of sleeping on a beach, bathing on a beach, walking on a beach, eating on a beach, having sex on a beach...he'd kill for the sight of a skyscraper or a mansion or a television broadcasting a French football match. He had no idea how *Les Bleus* were doing this season. As long as they were beating Denmark he could sleep at night. When he called home next time, he'd ask Calliope to check the scores for him. Even in Paradise, a man had needs.

Kingsley turned a corner and smelled fish frying in the near distance. Instead of awakening his appetite, it made his stomach tighten. After all he drank last night, he wasn't quite ready for solid food yet. Maybe in an hour or two he could eat. For now he would wander and not care where his feet took him.

He started caring very quickly where his feet took him when he realized they had taken him into a heavily touristed area. He would have been happy to go his entire stay in Haiti without setting eyes on any white Americans. So far he'd done fairly well staying away from happy families and/or businessmen trying to find a new way to exploit Haiti's beauty and resources. Yet everywhere he looked, he saw white faces squinting behind fashionable sunglasses, teenage girls in tiny bikinis, little boys building and destroying each other's sand castles, and bored mothers and bored fathers trying to pretend they weren't annoyed when their children interrupted their naps or their reading.

How did people go through life being so bored and so boring without killing themselves? *Never be boring* was the one and only commandment he followed. All the other commandments he considered mere suggestions.

He hated to admit that maybe if he stayed here in Haiti he would turn boring, too. Sleeping with an eighteen-year-old girl by mistake had been the only not-boring thing he'd done in weeks.

Bored and boring. He did the same things every day, walked the same paths, saw the same faces give or take a few minor variations. He'd caused no trouble, started no fights, blackmailed no politicians and engaged in only the most minor and unimpressive of sexual peccadilloes. If things didn't get more interesting fast, he'd be forced to go back to Manhattan to find a reason not to shoot himself in the head.

Good thing he hadn't packed his gun.

A few women and even more teenage girls gave him appreciative stares as he wove through the path of their chaises longues and beach chairs. He saw the rapacious looks in their eyes, their knowing smiles at each other. American women in foreign countries were more ravenous than a pack of sharks in a feeding frenzy. Could they not get laid back in the suburbs where they came from? He glanced at the men with them and rolled his eyes behind his sunglasses. No wonder they were staring at him. They really should have left their excess baggage back home.

He passed through a cluster of torchwood and palm trees. Off the path now, the ground grew rockier. He didn't care. This morning he'd remembered to put on shoes before heading out. Shoes were pleasantly optional on the beach in the morning. And if he wasn't going to wear boots, he'd rather wear nothing at all.

Boots. He did miss his boots. He missed his boots and his bed. The beach hut wasn't bad but the bed was no bigger than a full-size. He could only fit two people in it. After island hopping from New Zealand to the Philippines, he'd come to Haiti five weeks ago, rented a hut and settled down. But perhaps it was time to go home. Calliope asked him every week when he was coming home. He still didn't have an answer for her. If Elle was still on the run, he'd given her an eight-month head start to hide. And perhaps Søren had gotten the hint that Kingsley wouldn't do his dirty work for him this time. Kingsley turned around. He'd make a call. See what the flight options were for the week. Maybe it was time to go back. Or at least go somewhere else. Martinique? St. Croix? Miami? Manhattan? He would miss Haiti. After all it was beautiful, peaceful, restful.

And boring.

Kingsley heard a scream.

He whipped around, all senses on high alert. The scream had been loud, high-pitched and pained. He raced a few steps deeper into the trees and saw a boy—pasty white and still wearing his baby fat despite being twelve or thirteen—squealing in agony. Another boy next to him dropped a coconut-sized rock on the ground.

"Pick on someone your own size," Kingsley heard a woman yell at the boy in a strong French accent.

Then a rock whipped through the air and hit the boy again on the back of his Ludacris T-shirt.

"Crazy bitch," the boy shouted. The woman picked up another rock and threw it at him, hitting him in the thigh.

"Tu n'es qu'une merde, tu ne sais à rien," she shouted.

"You're psycho," his friend yelled, and he picked up a rock as big as a fist. The woman had thrown rocks the size of walnuts which would leave nothing but bruises. This boy was out for blood.

"Do it," she said. "You murdering little bastards."

Kingsley stepped between the woman and the boys.

"I wouldn't do that if I were you," Kingsley said in English to the boy with the big rock.

The boys took one look at him and made their first smart decision in their young lives.

"Come on. Let's go," the other, smaller boy shouted at his friend. The older boy dropped his huge rock and ran off as fast as his pale, hairless legs could carry him.

"Casse-toi," came the woman's voice again. She cursed in French but switched back to English when she saw him standing there. She must have assumed he was American. How insulting. "I should have killed them."

She bent down and picked up a soccer ball.

"You forgot your ball," the woman shouted, this time in English. "Want it back?"

She made as if she would throw it at them. Kingsley stopped her.

"I'll take it," Kingsley said. He grabbed the ball out of her hands, dropped it on the sand and kicked it with the perfect blend of force and precision. A hundred feet away, the ball hit the older boy in the back of the legs and sent him tumbling to his knees. He scrambled up and ran off again.

Kingsley looked at the woman. She looked at him.

"You have good aim," she said.

"You're not the first woman who's told me that." He waited. The woman got the joke. He could see that in her eyes. She did not, however, find it funny. She turned from him and knelt on the ground.

"What were they doing?" Kingsley asked her.

"Killing babies."

Kingsley looked down and saw a bird's nest on the ground, eggs shattered and oozing on the sand. A small bird with yellow on its wingtips danced in distress around the branches of a flowering bush. The woman studying the broken nest had dark skin and large black eyes. She looked much closer to twenty-eight than eighteen, thank God. Her long straight hair was pulled back in an elegant high ponytail. She wore a white ankle-length skirt and a white halter top that left her flat and muscled stomach bare. She was tall, too. Almost as tall as he. Her eyes were full of fury and her hands had balled into fists. She had the bearing of Cleopatra, the face of Venus and the wrath of God. And whoever she was, she'd attempted to stone two boys to death for the crime of throwing rocks at a bird's nest.

"Little monsters. Look what they've done."

"Do you want me to kill them for you?" Kingsley asked, almost sincere in his offer. He could hardly imagine a good man growing up out of the sort of boy who'd crush bird eggs for pleasure. "I didn't pack my gun, but I can use my hands. I can drown them and make it look like an accident. *Oui? Non?*"

Her dark eyes flashed in his direction.

"Are you mocking me?"

"Not at all," he said. *Pas du tout.* If this woman had asked him to bring him the heads of those boys to her on a platter, he would have done it.

"No," she said. "Let them go. They're in God's hands. We all are."

It could have been a platitude—*in God's hands*—but the way she said it made it sound like a fearful threat.

The woman knelt in the sand in front of the bush that the boys had attacked with their rocks. She studied the scene of carnage—the shattered eggs, the broken nest.

"Men destroy everything," she said, talking to herself. "Why do they have to destroy everything?"

Carefully, as if the nest was made of glass, the woman lifted it off the ground and tucked it into a tree. Then she bent down again and covered the broken eggs with sand. She did so quietly, reverently, as if performing a sacred burial ritual. The mother bird flitted down to the sand, looking for her lost babies.

"Try again, *Maman*," the woman said to the little bird. "Try again for me."

He looked at her face, and saw tears on it. Tears over a broken nest and a baby bird.

Fuck Manhattan. And fuck the entire world.

Haiti had just got very interesting.

10

"BEWARE THE IDES OF MARCH" READ THE NOTE KINGSley had slipped under her bedroom door. "Don't drink any alcohol today. Dress in your finest and wait for me by the Rolls at ten."

Eleanor supposed this note was Kingsley's version of a birthday card? Card and invitation. She hadn't planned on a big party for her twenty-sixth birthday. Sounded like Kingsley had planned one for her.

When evening turned to night and the city turned on its lights and switched off its inhibitions, Kingsley put her in the back of his Rolls-Royce. He had a smile on his face, a secret little smile. Something told her she was about to get her birthday present.

"You know I've had sex in the back of a Rolls-Royce," she reminded him. "So don't even ask."

She'd had sex with him in the back of a Rolls-Royce so many times she'd lost count. Luckily it was a limousine-style Rolls that kept the backseats separated from the driver by a partition and a thick black curtain.

"I know you've had sex in the back of the Rolls-Royce. But not with him."

"Him who?" Eleanor asked.

The car pulled over. The door opened.

A young man of about twenty-three years old with dark spiky hair, a handsome face and a dirty grin got into the car.

"Happy birthday, beautiful," he said.

"Oh my God. Griffin." Eleanor threw herself into Griffin's arms, and he pulled her so close to him it almost hurt. "When did you get back?"

"Two nights ago."

"And you didn't call me?" she asked, feigning irritation.

"Surprise," he said, grinning.

She sat on this lap and wrapped her arms around him. Griffin…she loved this kid. Had it only been eight months ago when Kingsley had first summoned Griffin to the town house and shown him the ropes? She'd been in the ropes that night as Kingsley beat her and fucked her, all as part of a demonstration showing Griffin what kink in action had looked like. He'd taken to the scene like a duck to water, but old habits had died hard. Kingsley had caught him snorting coke in one of the town house bathrooms one day and stone drunk the next day. Kingsley had enough demons of his own, he'd said, without inviting Griffin's demons over for tea. So Kingsley had laid down the ultimatum—go to rehab and get clean or…get out. Griffin had gone to rehab.

And now he was back.

"God, I missed you," she said as she pressed her face against his warm strong neck and inhaled cedar and suede. Griffin always smelled as if he'd just stepped out of a shower.

"Good," he said, taking her by the upper arms and positioning her on his lap. "Because I'm your birthday present."

He smiled ear-to-ear, a wide dirty grin that Griffin had perfected. Women and men both fell for that grin all the time. She was no exception. But until tonight he'd been off-limits for anything but friendship.

"Are you serious?" She looked back at Kingsley. "Søren's okay with this?"

"He is," Kingsley said. "But if you don't believe me, you can ask him."

The car pulled over again. The door opened again.

And Søren got inside.

She was off Griffin's lap and in Søren's arms in an instant.

"I appreciate the enthusiasm," Søren whispered in her ear. "But is it for me? Or for him?"

"Always for you," she said, kissing him on the mouth. "I can't believe you..."

"This is what you requested for your birthday, wasn't it?" Søren asked, a slight smile at the edge of his lips.

"I was joking. Sort of. I didn't think you'd say yes." Now she understood why Kingsley wouldn't let her drink. Griffin was two days fresh out of rehab. No reason to tempt fate by letting him taste alcohol on her lips.

Søren had teased her about her crush on Griffin, the new Dominant Kingsley had found. She'd sworn up and down her feelings for Griffin were of the purest sort of friendship. Although she wouldn't mind getting fucked by Griffin, of course. It would make a lovely birthday present, she'd said to Søren. She'd been joking obviously. Sort of. Not entirely.

"I pay the most attention when you pretend you're joking," Søren said, proving once and for all that he knew her better than anyone.

"I love you, sir."

He kissed her back, kissed her deep, and at the moment when she thought the kiss would go on forever, Søren gripped her by the back of the neck, unbuttoned the top button on her blouse and said, "Who's first?"

That's when Eleanor knew Griffin wasn't her only birthday present that night. All three of them were.

The silence that follows such a question is pregnant with

possibility. And in those few seconds, the various possible scenarios flashed through Eleanor's mind. Søren shared her with Kingsley all the time. Kingsley even had permission to be with her when Søren wasn't there. And once Søren had ordered her to spend a week at a mansion in New Hampshire with a man named Daniel. But she was one woman in the back of a Rolls-Royce and three different men were about to fuck her.

Happy birthday to her.

"I've been in rehab for the past month. If I don't fuck soon, I will literally die," Griffin said.

"Well, we can't have that," Søren intoned smoothly. He unbuttoned another button on her white sheer blouse. "Eleanor's fond of you, Griffin. I think she'd be most heartbroken if something happened to you."

"I would, Griff. You're my favorite rookie."

He glared at her, his handsome brow furrowing in playful disgust. "I should spank you for calling me that."

"You should," Søren said. "She won't learn to respect your authority any other way."

"Come here, bad girl." Griffin tapped his lap. "I have a present to deliver."

"One moment." Søren reached into the pocket of his black overcoat. "First things first."

He wrapped her collar around her neck and locked it into place. She leaned back against his chest and closed her eyes.

Søren put his mouth at her ear and whispered, "Even with them you're with me. Remember that."

"I remember, sir," she whispered back.

"You want this?" he asked, even softer now.

"Yes, sir."

"Happy birthday, Little One."

He kissed her neck where the leather of her white collar met her skin and she shivered in pleasure. Fear radiated through her body as Søren transferred her from his lap to Griffin's. But he was there, Søren was. Watching, guarding, protecting her. Nothing to be afraid of. Tonight was for her pleasure only.

Griffin had never kissed her before. And before he did now, she saw him glance at Søren for permission. Søren nodded and Griffin pressed his lips to hers. She opened her mouth, sensing his nervousness at performing for a crowd, this crowd especially. Kingsley and Søren sat on the back bench seat. She and Griffin were on the front one that sat behind the curtained wall separating them from the driver. No two men in the Underground were more feared and respected than Søren and Kingsley. And now Griffin was going to fuck her while they watched. If he could get it up under such circumstances, she'd be impressed. He shifted her on his lap and she felt his erection pressing hard against her bottom.

Count her impressed.

Griffin deepened the kiss while Eleanor unbuttoned his shirt. She touched his broad muscular shoulders and biceps as he bit and nipped at her lips. For a moment she forgot she had an audience until Griffin threw her onto her back in a quick show of power and dominance. She gasped in surprise. From the back of the Rolls, Kingsley and Søren applauded.

"Good show," Kingsley said. "Nice technique."

"It's not easy to catch her off guard," Søren agreed.

"Are you two going to comment the entire time?" Griffin asked, looking up from her.

"Of course," Kingsley said, reaching into a black satchel next to his booted legs. "I'm the French judge. He's the Danish judge."

Kingsley handed Søren a set of cards with the numbers one through ten on them.

Score cards.

"You've got to be kidding me," Griffin said, groaning and burying his face against her chest.

"Be glad Mistress Irina isn't here, Griffin." Kingsley shuffled casually through his cards. "No one ever impresses the Russian judge."

Eleanor reached up and touched Griffin's face. He met her eyes and she met his. He had rich hazel eyes, sweet and soulful, like a child's almost.

"Make me feel good," she said in a voice low enough only Griffin could hear it. "Please, Mr. Griffin. It's my birthday."

"For you, anything," he said back. He sat up and yanked her across his lap. She'd thought the threat of a spanking had been only that. A threat. But he wrenched her skirt up to her hips, pulled her white panties down to her knees, and hit her hard enough she flinched.

"God damn," she said, shocked by the force of the hit. She braced for a second slap, but instead he worked a single finger into her vagina from behind. She dug her hands into the leather of the seats as Griffin pushed his finger deeper into her. Very quickly she grew wet from the touch and Griffin pushed a second, then a third finger into her. With both hands he spread her open wide, exposing her to the view of everyone in the back of the car. It was a humiliation, a violation. She loved every second of it.

When he judged her wet enough, Griffin grabbed her by the shoulder and brought her to a sitting position on her knees. From the speed of the car, Eleanor could tell they were out on the open road. Good. No sudden stops likely on the highway.

"King?" Griffin asked, and Kingsley tossed Griffin a condom. He opened his pants and rolled it on. He was big definitely, but nothing she couldn't take and everything she wanted to take. When he was ready, Griffin crooked his finger at her, and Eleanor, eager to obey, straddled his legs facing him. She expected him to enter her immediately but instead he kissed her again almost tenderly.

"I've wanted to do this since the day I met you," he whispered.

"No whispering," Kingsley said, and Griffin rolled his eyes.

"I wanted it, too," she said, making sure only Griffin could hear her. The hum of the engine and the tires and the face-to-face position awarded them a modicum of privacy. To show Griffin how much she adored him, how much she'd wanted him, she took his erection firmly in her hand and brought it to the entrance of her body. Griffin gripped her by the hips and lowered her down onto him. She stretched open as she settled onto him, sighing as he penetrated her fully.

"It's only you and me now." Griffin mouthed the words and she nodded. As she moved on him slowly, relishing the fullness of him inside her, he unbuttoned her shirt and pulled it off her. It might have landed on the floor. She had a feeling, however, that when Griffin threw it, it had landed in Kingsley's lap. Or on his face. Her bra came off next, just as slowly, just as sensuously. Griffin lifted and kneaded her breasts in his hands as her head fell back in pleasure.

"I was meant to know you," Griffin whispered to her. "I don't know why but I was."

"Maybe we'll find out why someday," she said.

He kissed her on the mouth again and said against her lips, "Maybe this is why."

Griffin slid his hands from her breasts to her shoulders, from her shoulders to her arms, from her arms to her wrists. He held her arms behind her, forcing her to arch her back.

"Ride me," he said, and she was happy to oblige. With tight movements of her hips, she drove her hips against Griffin while he kissed and licked her nipples. She smiled in victory when her vagina contracted on him and he gasped from the shock of pleasure. But still he held her wrists in his viselike grip even as she pushed them both closer to coming.

Her body burned with the heat of his body and hers. Her arms ached from being held so tightly. And when she thought she couldn't take it one more minute, Griffin tossed her onto her back and slammed into her with rough and brutal thrusts that left her gasping. Blood surged through her thighs as she spread them wider for him. Her heart thudded in her chest. She contracted her stomach and tilted her hips until he was as deep inside her as any man could go. Finally she shuddered underneath him, as a fierce and forceful climax shook her to the core. Distantly, she was aware of Griffin's orgasm that he was pushing into her with his last and roughest thrusts.

It was over, done, and yet Griffin remained inside her.

"Not yet," he said when she wriggled underneath him in discomfort. He had her pinioned to the seat, impaled against it, and she couldn't move until he did. His eyes met hers and for a second she thought she saw something more than friendship in them, more than passion. But he blinked and it was gone. Griffin pulled out of her and carefully removed the condom.

Kingsley looked at Søren. Søren looked at Kingsley.

Kingsley held up an eight.

Søren held up a seven.

"Fuck," Griffin said. "I was hoping for at least one nine."

"You didn't stick your landing," Kingsley said. "Work on your dismount."

"Can you do better?" Griffin asked, sounding skeptical as he wiped himself off with a tissue and zipped his pants back up. It wouldn't be easy to fuck her more thoroughly and enjoyably than Griffin had fucked her.

"Of course I can," Kingsley said. He whistled, beckoning her to him. Eleanor crawled off Griffin's lap and over to Kingsley's. She waited, kneeling on the floorboard between Kingsley's knees. He reached down and tapped her under the chin, a signal that required no other words.

She unzipped his trousers and brought her mouth down onto his erection.

"See?" Kingsley said. "Practice makes perfect."

While she massaged and licked him with her tongue, he ran

his fingers through her hair. He lifted the black mass of it, and she felt the flick of a cane on her back and flinched, a carefully controlled flinch. She knew the rules of such a game. She went down on Kingsley while Søren inflicted pain on her in some way, and at no point was she allowed to pass the pain to Kingsley. In other words...no biting.

Søren flicked her with the cane again—the thin plastic cane that licked her skin like a tongue of fire.

Eleanor forced herself to concentrate on Kingsley's pleasure and ignored her own pain. It was the perfect torture. A few grunts of discomfort was all she allowed herself. And yet the cane came down again and again, a dozen or more times. Finally the caning stopped. Kingsley gripped her by the hair and forced her to look up at him.

"Good girl," he said in French. *Bien fille*. She smiled and he cupped her chin, raising her off the floor. He wrapped his arms around her back and unzipped her skirt. Seconds later she was completely naked but for her white strappy high heels. Kingsley inclined his head at the seat. "Arms and knees," he said, giving her a gentle order. Søren had moved to the other seat and now they had the back bench to themselves. Good, because they needed the room, especially when she moved into position and Kingsley entered her from behind.

With a few shallow strokes he readied her for full penetration. She did love the way Kingsley fucked her. He liked taking his time, making her squirm and beg for release. Even now he moved slowly inside her. Long slow thrusts that filled her and filled her and filled her. He slid his hand under her hips and pressed two fingers into her clitoris. Gently he rubbed the swollen knot until she hovered on the edge of another climax.

"Please," she gasped.

"Come," he said, granting her permission. She came with a hoarse cry but Kingsley didn't. He kept pumping into her long after her orgasm had come and gone.

"Show-off," she heard Griffin say, and she smiled into the cradle of her arms. Kingsley pulled out and dragged her down to her knees again. Once more she took him in her mouth, laving him with her tongue and lips until he came in her mouth, his fingers digging into her shoulders from the intensity of it.

Spent and exhausted, she sank to the floor, her head resting on Kingsley's inner thigh. His fingers curled in her hair and caressed the back of her neck.

Griffin held up a nine.

Søren held up an eight.

"You're worse than the Russian judge," Kingsley said, glaring at Søren.

"It wasn't your best work," Søren said unapologetically.

Kingsley shook his head. "Armchair critics."

Eleanor looked up and met Søren's eyes. They were bright and gleaming, full of secret mirth. He whistled at her, summoning her to his side like a master calling his dog. Griffin vacated the seat next to Søren, and she crawled to her owner, her master, her lover, her heart.

"Your turn, sir?" she asked.

"All turns are my turn." He slipped a finger between her collar and her throat and pulled her to him.

He kissed her and bit her bottom lip until she tasted a drop of blood. The kiss deepened and before she knew it, Søren had her on her back. He kissed her breasts, her nipples, her stomach and thighs and finally brought this attention to her clitoris. She was sore inside from being fucked twice already but it took only a few minutes of Søren's expert ministrations before she was panting and eager to be penetrated again. Søren ignored her pleas and continued to edge her closer to climax before pulling back again, edging her close again and once more pulling back.

"A master," Kingsley said to Griffin. "Sadism by pleasure is as vicious as sadism by pain."

"I'm learning this," Griffin said.

"Don't learn from him," Eleanor said between heavy breaths. "I have all the sadists I need already."

Søren replied by swatting her hard on the outer thigh, hard enough she knew she'd have a bright red handprint there for the next hour at least.

She flinched and Søren chose that moment to rise up over her, push her wrists deep into the seat by her head and enter her with one hard deep thrust. Eagerly she wrapped her legs around his lower back and locked her ankles together. She was so wet for him by now she could feel it dripping out of her and onto the leather.

Her wrists ached under his viciously strong hands. She hoped she would have bruises from them later. Only the other submissives she knew would understand why she wanted bruises, wanted welts, wanted something on her body to remind her of what had been done to her. But she and Søren couldn't live together, couldn't spend their days together. They had only a few nights a week, all stolen, and the bruises made a road map to her memory of everything he'd done to her. She'd be reliving this night for weeks...

Griffin and Kingsley were still in the car, of course. But they might as well have been a thousand miles away for all she cared about them. Søren was inside her and she was underneath him and they were the only two people in the world.

"Happy birthday, Little One," Søren said in her ear between kisses. But she said nothing in reply. She couldn't speak, lost as she was in his thrusts, in his kisses, in the moment of being used over and over and over again. "It's only beginning. You're ours all night..."

All night. Forever. She didn't care as long as he kept fucking her like this, as if it was the only thing keeping them alive. She couldn't stop her hips from meeting his, couldn't stop taking him deeper and deeper into her. When her orgasm came it was so hard she went silent, her body locked up and she opened her eyes.

Fuck.

The orgasm from her dream was so strong it had woken her up. Her vaginal muscles were contracting so hard against nothing her eyes watered. She slid her hand into her underwear and rubbed her pulsing clitoris, trying to make the orgasm go on and on.

She collapsed against the sweat-drenched sheets and kicked the blankets off the bed. Her body still buzzed and trembled from the force of her climax. Craziness...she hadn't orgasmed in her sleep since she was a teenager. But ever since coming to her mother's convent, it happened once a week at least. It had been a dream, but a dream so vivid it was as if she were there, reliving every moment of her last birthday when Søren had surprised her with that incredible night in Kingsley's Rolls-Royce. She could still feel Søren inside her. She could still smell Griffin's soap. She could still taste Kingsley in her mouth.

Elle sat up, found her duffel bag and unzipped it. From the bottom of it she pulled out her collar. She held it in her hands and looked it at. She'd been wearing it the night she lost her virginity to Søren. She'd worn it every night she spent with him and not once since she'd left him. It was the symbol of his ownership of her and despite that, she'd kept it. If she could get rid of it, toss it away, throw it out, then she could be free, completely free.

But she wasn't free. The dreams proved that. And she couldn't get rid of her collar. Not yet. She put it back in her bag and resolved to forget about it. At least this time she didn't kiss it before putting it away.

The 5:00 a.m. bell rang. She grabbed the blankets off the floor, made her bed and pulled on the thick white terry cloth bathrobe she'd been given her second day here. Even in a house of all women, modesty was to be maintained at all times. No running to the bathroom at night wearing only underwear and a T-shirt. She had to be covered up, neck to toe, every day, at all times.

In the bathroom at the end of the hall, Elle took a quick shower, pulled her hair back in a tight knot and dressed in the black tights, long black skirt and white blouse that had become her uniform here at the abbey. No one would have mistaken her for a nun, but no one from her old life would have recognized her now in such conservative clothing.

Alone in the kitchen, Elle had her usual breakfast of coffee, eggs, fruit and toast. Only on Sunday mornings did the menu change to something more exotic than the breakfast basics. While the sisters were at Lauds, Elle headed to the laundry room where she would spend the next five hours until lunchtime.

Her life at the abbey had been difficult at first. She argued with the more irascible nuns, she'd been unceremoniously tossed out of the kitchen for ruining one too many dishes with her bad cooking and she'd been kicked out of the library for rearranging all the books. Who on earth had decided to put the books in order by title? No one who'd ever worked in a real library or a bookstore would arrange books in such an ass-backward way. She'd worked in a bookstore for years and had even fucked a librarian. She knew how books worked. But the sisters had their own idea of order and didn't appreciate any attempts at improvement.

That left her alone in the laundry room all day. She washed sheets. She dried sheets. She folded sheets. The next day she did it again. She washed habits. She ironed habits. She folded habits. The next day she did it again. Hardly slave labor, but it certainly didn't excite her. Then again, no one came to a convent for excitement. She'd come to the convent for the opposite of excitement, and the opposite of excitement was exactly what she'd found here. She had safety. She had peace and quiet. And she hadn't seen Søren and Kingsley in months.

Elle refilled her coffee mug, put her dishes in the sink and left the kitchen. Once in the laundry room she tried to work up the energy to do something. All she wanted was to go back to bed and sleep until the second coming. Of course, in her theology the second coming had nothing to do with Jesus's return and everything to do with having another orgasm.

She hopped onto the tile counter by the sink and looked out the window while she drank her coffee. She could see the road from the window, see the front lawn of the abbey and could see the wrought-iron fence that surrounded the convent's acreage—one hundred twenty in total, give or take a few square feet. All of it from the sides of the abbey to the edge of the farthest field was fenced in in one way or another. The side and back gardens were fenced in by iron. The fields of farmland and well-manicured forest were fenced in with white wood. And the entire abbey was fenced in by the rules. Rule number one—never leave the grounds without permission. Elle didn't have permission to leave, so here she stayed.

Since she couldn't leave and didn't want to, she stared out at the road and watched the occasional car pass on its way to or from town. She saw one now, a blue Audi, but instead of passing by like every other car she'd seen since coming here, it turned into the long abbey driveway. Slowly it crept toward the convent before coming to a gentle stop.

As if on cue, a dozen sisters in their black-and-white habits streamed from the front doors toward the car. Elle had never seen the sisters leave the abbey. They did, of course. Sometimes they had doctors' appointments or dentists' appointments or Mother Prioress would visit with someone important in the city who wanted to buy their land or sell them more. But Elle had only heard about sisters leaving, never seen it happen.

The car doors opened and a man got out of the driver's side, a woman out of the passenger's. They looked about midforties, married, not terribly interesting. But then the woman opened the back door of the Audi and out stepped a young woman. She had reddish-brown hair sun-streaked with pale gold highlights that reminded Elle of feathers, like the tips of a dove's wings. Her hair fell in waves down her back. She had flowers in her hair—white flowers. And the long dress she wore was simple and white. The man pulled a small suitcase from the trunk. The woman took the girl's hand in hers, but only for a moment.

Now the sisters surrounded the trio and quickly pried the young woman from her parents. Yes, of course, they had to be her parents and this girl was entering the order. It didn't seem right, though. The girl barely looked twenty-one. And what a beauty…a tiny thing who couldn't have weighed more than a hundred pounds.

"Don't do it, sweetheart," Elle whispered. "Get back in the car and drive…"

As if the girl could hear her, she glanced up at the window and squinted. Elle froze. Did the girl see her? Probably. What did it matter? The girl raised her hand and waved at her. Elle didn't know what to do so she waved back. Mother Prioress turned and glanced up at the window, but Elle had already ducked away from it out of sight. She panted in nervousness and didn't know why. Nothing but a girl, a beautiful young girl who'd waved at her. Nothing to panic about.

Still, Elle walked to the other window in the room and peered out.

The sisters had formed two even lines like an honor guard, and the girl was between them walking toward the front door of the convent. Elle knew what would happen next. There would be a ceremony in the main chapel and the girl would be dressed in her habit and veiled. She'd choose a new name— Sister Mary Something—and profess her temporary vows. And by lunch, she'd be a Sister of St. Monica.

Her old life would be over. Even her name would be gone.

Halfway through the line toward the door, the girl stopped, turned around and ran back to the car. She embraced her mother and her father. Poor thing. She must be scared to death, heartbroken, sobbing...

Or was she?

The girl, using her mother as a shield of sorts, glanced up to the window again and stared straight at Elle. And then—and Elle was entirely certain she didn't imagine it—the girl winked at her.

Elle laughed and shook her head. Then she composed her face. If Mother Prioress had told her one time, she'd told her a thousand times—behave.

She wrenched herself away from the window and promptly resolved to forget she'd seen that beautiful girl and her mysterious wink. After all, she was about to become a nun and nuns had to abide by vows. Vows of obedience and vows of chastity.

Then again, when had a little thing like a vow of chastity ever stopped Elle before?

11

Haiti

THE WOMAN ROSE OFF THE GROUND AND DUSTED THE sand off her knees, brushed the tears off her face.

"Thank you for your help," she said. "Have a lovely day."

With that cool dismissal, she reached down and picked up a canvas tote bag by its handles, turned around and walked away from him. Kingsley didn't like that. At all.

"What's your name?" he asked, jogging to catch up with her.

"Why do you ask?"

"No reason."

"If you don't have a reason for wanting to know my name, I don't have any reason for telling you."

Kingsley winced. She had him there.

"Sorry. I don't have reasons for much of what I do. If you asked me why I'm even in Haiti, I couldn't tell you why."

"Then I won't ask," she said. She started walking off again.

"May I carry your bag for you?" he asked, adjusting his strides to keep up with hers. She had magnificently long legs and walked briskly. "It looks heavy."

"It is heavy. And no, you may not carry it for me."

"Would you like me to leave you alone?" he asked, not wanting to admit defeat but willing to admit it if necessary.

She stopped and looked at him. A long studied look. He was grateful he had sunglasses on over his eyes; her gaze was so piercing, so searching, that he almost took a step back away from her.

"No," she said at last. "You don't have to leave me alone."

"Then I'll walk with you, if you'll allow it."

"I will," she said, and started off walking again. Kingsley walked at her side and readjusted his strategy.

"I'm Kingsley," he said.

"Are you?"

"I am. That's my name."

"Just Kingsley?"

"I have a last name. Two of them actually. Do you have a name? First? Last? Middle?"

"Yes."

"Good. If you didn't have a name I would have given you one. I have extras."

That got a smile from her. A small one but he'd take what he could get.

"Juliette," she said. "My name is Juliette."

"Beautiful name. Do you have a last name?"

"I do."

When she didn't volunteer it, he gave up that line of conversation. He needed a new strategy.

"Your French is perfect, by the way." A compliment usually worked in these situations, Kingsley had found.

"Yours isn't," she said. "You must live in America."

"I do. Haven't been back to France in years. You can tell?"

"I can tell."

"Keep speaking your perfect French to me and perhaps my French will improve."

"I have nothing to say." She went silent again.

She had nothing to say? Well, fuck. Kingsley could have respected that statement, and they could have walked on in silence. But he didn't like silence, especially not from this woman with her voice and her perfect French. So instead of respecting the silence, he broke it. Dramatically.

"I fucked an eighteen-year-old girl this morning," Kingsley said. "And last night, although I was too drunk to remember much of it."

"Are you still drunk?" She sounded utterly disgusted with him, but at least she was speaking, so disgust was better than nothing.

"Look, I'm not proud of myself. I didn't mean to fuck her. It was an accident."

"Accident?" she repeated. She had a low voice and everything she said sounded like a secret. "Isn't that the excuse men use when they do something stupid and don't want to take full responsibility for it? That sort of accident?"

"She didn't tell me her age."

"Did you ask?"

"No…" he admitted.

"How old are you?" she asked.

"Thirty-nine."

"Old enough to know better."

"I should. I do. I won't ever do it again," he said, hoping to wheedle a smile out of her.

"I don't care," she said. "What you do doesn't matter to me."

"I want it to," he said.

"Why?"

"I want you to like me," he admitted. "Do you?"

"Not yet. Why do you want me to like you?"

"Because you are the most beautiful woman I've ever seen." She stopped and turned to face him.

"That's a stupid reason to want someone to like you." She shook her head and walked off again.

Kingsley stared after her a few seconds before catching up with her.

"I know," he admitted. "But I'm male and feeling eighteen today for some reason."

"Did that eighteen-year-old girl infect you with her immaturity?"

"I have only myself to blame for this."

"You're honest. I can appreciate that at least," she said, taking long purposeful strides. A woman who didn't mince or waste time. He liked that about her.

"You like honesty? I can tell you more horrible things about myself if you like. I have a list."

"I think I have enough to work with here already." Juliette reached a point where the path forked and she took the fork to the right.

"I've made a bad first impression."

"I've seen worse."

"Can you tell me what I can do to make a better impression?" he asked. "Gifts? Quests? Orders? I can take orders."

"Priestly orders?"

He glared at her.

"Not those kinds of orders. Order me to do something for you, and I'll do it to prove my worth."

Juliette faced him again. She gave a heavy sigh as if he'd found her very last nerve and had stomped on it.

"Take your clothes off," she said.

"Here?" They were standing on a path near a village and two hundred tourists on a beach.

"Here."

"If I'm arrested for public indecency, will you get me out of jail?"

"No."

"You're serious, aren't you?"

"If you were serious about me, you'd be naked already."

Was he serious about her? She was unbearably beautiful, yes. And she'd stoned an obnoxious spoiled white American child. And she seemingly loathed him, which made her all the more intriguing. And if she walked away from him now he'd be wondering about her for the rest of her life.

Kingsley pulled his shirt over his head, kicked his shoes off and dropped his beach-battered khakis to the ground.

To be as naked as humanly possible, he also pushed his sunglasses up to his head so she could see his uncovered eyes.

Juliette didn't look him up and down. She stared straight into his eyes and ignored every other part of his body, including his semi-erect penis.

"Are you lost?" she asked.

"Completely."

"I can't help you find yourself. I can't help you with anything."

"I don't want your help," he said. "I only want your body."

Juliette apparently liked that answer. She put her canvas tote bag on the ground. Kingsley glanced down and saw it was full of nothing but rocks. Why would a woman carry a bag of rocks with her?

He would have asked but before he could say a word, she'd stepped forward, put a hand in his hair at the nape of his neck and kissed him.

He kissed her back, greedy for anything and everything he could get from this exquisite mysterious woman. He didn't ask questions, didn't ask why she kissed him. He let her kiss him and he kissed her back because there was nothing in the world he'd rather be doing at the moment.

Her lips left his and she took a step back. Kingsley slowly opened his eyes.

"'Let him kiss me with the kisses of his mouth; for his love is better than wine...'" Juliette said softly, almost under her breath, but Kingsley heard.

"Song of Solomon," Kingsley said. Juliette looked at him.

"Put your clothes back on," she said, and he obeyed quickly

before anyone noticed the naked man standing on the beach. "You know the Bible?"

"A little," he said. "I went to Catholic school. I know the Song of Solomon when I hear it. It was my favorite."

"Mine, too," she said, her voice far away as if it had got caught in a wind. "'I am black but lovely, O daughters of Jerusalem.'"

"'Like the tents of Kedar, like the curtains of Solomon,'" Kingsley continued the verse. "I like the verse, but it needs improvement."

"You think you can improve on the Bible?"

"I can. It says 'I am black *but* lovely.' The woman I see is 'black *and* lovely.'"

"You're trying to seduce me."

"Is it working?"

"Yes."

"Good. I'm glad I could improve upon my dismal first impression."

"Come back to this place tomorrow at nine. I'll give you a chance to make a better impression."

"Why? Did you see something you liked when I took my clothes off?"

"Yes."

"What?"

"Desperation," she said.

"You like desperation?"

Juliette didn't smile when she answered. She merely picked up her bag of rocks and turned on her heel.

"I like that we have something in common."

12

Upstate New York

ELLE REMOVED A LOAD OF SHEETS FROM THE DRYER as soon as the cycle ended. As quickly as she could, she folded them before a single wrinkle could set in. Ten sheets in three minutes. If folding laundry had been a sport, Elle would be on a box of Wheaties by now.

How had it come to this? Elle wondered, as she stacked the sheets in a neat pile on the counter. Once upon a time she'd been the most well-known submissive in Kingsley's grand and infamous court of Manhattan kinksters. If she wasn't tied to Søren's bed, she was on Kingsley's arm somewhere—at a club, at a party, at his home where he hosted the rich and the infamous. On a regular basis she'd enjoyed erotic beatings, threesomes with Søren and Kingsley and enough notoriety to get her into any club in town.

And now here she was, spending her days doing laundry for a convent. And the most excitement she had was timing herself every day to see if she could beat her previous record. She reminded herself the lack of excitement was exactly why she'd come here. No men allowed. No men meant no Kingsley and no Søren and no temptation to misbehave. Of course she couldn't avoid misbehaving entirely. With so many rules it was impossible to not break one or two. But her sins were venial—she stayed up after everyone was supposed to go to bed, went to the library after lights-out, stole the occasional extra dessert from the fridge when no one was looking. She masturbated too, which was considered a sin here. Elle didn't consider it a sin. She considered it an act of self-preservation.

The buzzer on the washer sounded and Elle removed the wet sheets and threw them in the dryer. She'd washed the sheets, she'd dry the sheets, she'd fold the sheets. And in a week, she'd do it again. She'd wash habits, dry habits, hang up the habits on their fancy wooden hangers. And in a week, she'd do it again. Fifty women under one roof made laundry an endless eternal chore.

"Sisyphus, Sisyphus." Elle sighed after starting the dryer. "I feel your pain."

"Who's Sisyphus?"

Elle looked toward the door and saw a nun standing there, one she hadn't seen before. But no, she had seen her before.

"It's you," Elle said.

"Is it?" The nun looked down at herself. "You're right. It is me."

"Sorry. You're the girl I saw entering the order last week. Right?"

"Yes, and you're the ghost."

"I'm the what?"

"I saw you standing in the window. They said the only people in the abbey were nuns and you obviously weren't a nun so I assumed you were a ghost. And you work in the laundry room with all these white sheets, which are very ghostly. So... are you a ghost?"

"No, I'm not a ghost," Elle said slowly, as if talking to someone very young or slightly off her rocker, and this girl seemed to be both.

"Which is exactly what a ghost would say, isn't it?"

The young nun looked at Elle expectantly. She batted her eyelashes and Elle noticed the girl's baby blue eyes.

"I don't know," Elle said with a sigh. "Maybe I am a ghost."

"Thought so," she said.

"Can I help you with something?" Elle asked, ready to end this conversation as soon as possible so she could get back to work, back to being a ghost.

"You can tell me more about Sisyphus. Is he also a ghost?"

"Sisyphus, the mythological figure. The guy who had to roll a stone up a hill for eternity. Laundry is the ultimate Sisyphean task—clean, dirty, wash, rinse, dry, repeat ad infinitum."

"You know what would help?" the young nun said in her light and airy tone. "Nudism."

Elle stared at her.

"You are a weird nun," Elle said.

"I know. Sorry."

"Don't be sorry. You'll fit right in with all the other weird nuns here."

"You think we're all weird?"

"If you met a homeless person on the street who claimed to be the bride of Jesus Christ, what would you say to her?"

"I'd ask her if her husband was a good kisser."

Elle did something she hadn't done in so long she couldn't remember the last time she'd done it.

She laughed.

"Wow," the nun said. "Good laugh. Do it again."

"I can't laugh on command."

"I'll have to keep saying crazy stuff then and hope for the best. I'm Kyrie, by the way. What's your name?"

"It's Elle. And you're not Kyrie. You're Sister Mary Whatever."

"Sister Mary George."

"George?"

"He slayed a dragon. How cool is that?"

"Can I call you Sister George?" Elle asked.

"Call me Kyrie."

"I'm not supposed to," Elle said.

"I won't tell."

"Okay then, Kyrie. What can I do for you?"

"Sister Agnes told me to come see you. I have a boo-boo."

"A boo-boo?" Elle repeated. "Are we talking about a small injury or a tiny bear?"

"Neither." Kyrie held up her arm. "I spilled candle wax on my habit. Can you get it out?"

Elle examined the stain. It was about the size of a half-dollar and right in the middle of her sleeve.

"Hold still," she ordered Kyrie, and pulled a knife out of the utility drawer.

"It's only a stain. I don't think you have to kill me for it," Kyrie said.

"I have no choice. Stain on the habit is punishable by death. Now don't move."

Kyrie closed her eyes and braced herself dramatically. Elle shook her head, sighed and scraped the candle wax off her sleeve.

"Is it over?" Kyrie asked, popping one eye open. "Am I dead? Is this Heaven?"

"This is Purgatory."

"I'm in Purgatory? Well, crap." Kyrie sighed. "Mom told me this would happen if I didn't stop touching myself."

Elle stared at her.

"Go on," Kyrie said. "You know you want to laugh. And I know I want to hear you laugh."

"I'm not going to laugh. I'm going to iron your sleeve. Come here."

"Iron my sleeve? But I'm wearing my sleeve."

"Don't panic. I've done this before." Elle heated up the iron and pulled out a few sheets of white blotting paper. She pointed to the ironing board and Kyrie rested her arm on it.

"This doesn't seem safe," Kyrie said. "Maybe I should take the habit off."

"There's enough fabric in your sleeve to make a mini-dress. I won't get near your skin, I promise."

Elle placed the blotting paper on the red stain the candle wax had left behind. She pressed the tip of her iron over the stain, replaced the blotting paper and did it again. While she ironed she studied Kyrie out of the corner of her eye. Her novice's white habit covered every inch of her but her face and her hands. But she was still undeniably beautiful with her wide eyes and long lashes, her delicate lips and suntanned skin. Elle forced herself to focus on her task.

"*Voilà,*" Elle said, lifting the iron. "Though your sleeves are like scarlet, they shall be white as snow."

Kyrie held up her sleeve, now devoid of any sign of a stain.

"Rad. How did you do that?"

"The blotting paper sucks up the dye," Elle said.

"Do they teach you tricks like this in laundry school?"

"I didn't go to laundry school."

"Where did you learn how to get candle wax stains off fabric?" Kyrie asked, touching the now-pristine sleeve.

"Little skill I picked up a few years ago," she said. "I've had more than my fair share of candle wax accidents."

"Did you work at a church? I'm guessing candle wax accidents are an occupational hazard there."

"No." Elle shook her head. "I suppose you could say my candle wax stains were a *recreational* hazard."

"What sort of recreation uses candles?"

"Nothing," Elle said. "I was joking. You're done. Boo-boo is healed."

"You're trying to get rid of me," Kyrie said.

"Don't take it personally. I'm not allowed to distract you sisters from your prayer and your work."

"You aren't bothering me by talking to me," Kyrie said with a smile. "I promise. I don't need to be anywhere for a while. We can talk. I'd like to talk."

Elle looked up at the ceiling and sighed.

"Someone told you about me, didn't they?" she asked.

Kyrie blushed—guilty as charged. "Well…sort of."

"Sort of," Elle repeated. "May I ask what they told you about me?"

"Oh…" Kyrie shrugged. In her voluminous pure white habit, Kyrie's shrug looked like a bird adjusting its wings. "This and that."

"What specifically, might I ask?"

"If you must know, no one was gossiping. I asked someone about you. You know, since I thought you were a ghost. I didn't think anyone but sisters were allowed in the abbey. They said an exception was made for you because of extraordinary circumstances nonrelated to noncorporealness."

"Extraordinary circumstances. That's one way to put it," Elle said.

"Have you ever thought about how weird the word 'extraordinary' is? It means not ordinary but if something is extra ordinary wouldn't you assume it was very ordinary? Super ordinary?"

"*Extra* is a Latin prefix meaning 'outside.' If something is extra—it means it's outside. Extra ordinary means outside the ordinary."

"Wow." Kyrie's blue eyes widened. "You are really smart."

"Genius IQ, and I'm working in a laundry at a convent."

"How extra ordinary of you."

"Are you done talking to me yet?" Elle asked, hoping the answer was yes.

"Oh no. We've just gotten started here. I want to know what your extraordinary circumstances are."

"You really don't," Elle said as she started the washer. She pulled a wrinkled tablecloth from a basket and lined it up on her ironing board.

"Why don't I?"

Elle looked up from her ironing.

"You're a nun."

"I am?" Kyrie repeated. She looked down at herself as if noticing the habit for the first time. "Oh, you're right. I am. You were saying?"

"You're trying to make me laugh again."

"You have a really awesome laugh, Elle."

"It's not going to work. I checked my sense of humor at the door when I came here," Elle said, picking up her iron again.

"Do I at least get points for trying to make you laugh?" Kyrie asked, looking wide-eyed and hopeful.

"Two."

"Two what?"

"I'm giving you two points for trying to make me laugh."

"How many points do I need to win?"

"What game are we playing?" Elle asked, turning the steam up on her iron. She had a wrinkle that would not give.

"The 'Let's Be Friends' game."

"I don't need any friends."

"We all need friends," Kyrie said. "We'd go crazy without friends."

"You're already crazy," Elle reminded her. "And so am I."

"Is it true you're hiding from your abusive boyfriend?" Kyrie asked, and Elle stood up straight and stared Kyrie down. Daniel might have had The Ouch, but long ago Elle had perfected her own scary stare she used on the other submissives in Kingsley's circle. The second one of them crossed a line, stepped out of bounds, or even worse, in Elle's opinion, whined, she gave that Sub a stare so intense it had inspired tears. She gave Kyrie that same stare now.

"Are you a virgin?" Elle asked.

"What?" Kyrie blinked at her in confusion.

"If we're having a personal conversation, it's going to be two-sided. Are you a virgin?"

"Yes," Kyrie said.

"I thought so."

"What does that mean?" Kyrie demanded.

"It means that you are innocent. You have never let yourself be sexually vulnerable to someone. Since you are a virgin you cannot begin to imagine what my life was like before I came here. We will be speaking entirely different languages. I could tell you the truth about who I am and what brought me here and none of it will make any sense to you."

"How do you know that?"

"How do you think I knew how to get candle wax off your habit?" Elle asked.

"I don't know. You said it was, what? A recreational hazard. Recreation means play. You used to play with candle wax."

"I did. Any guesses how or why?"

"Not really. Candle wax doesn't seem all that fun."

"You don't run with the same crowd that I do then. Used to run with," she corrected.

"Sounds like an interesting crowd. The candle wax gang."

"We were. I guess." Elle sighed and folded her now-perfectly flat tablecloth.

"Do you miss it? Your old life?" Kyrie walked around her ironing board and pulled herself up onto the counter. Her feet, shod in black old lady shoes, kicked against the doors. Without the habit, Kyrie would look like a bored teenage girl sitting on a kitchen counter.

"Yes and no," Elle said. "I miss parts of it."

"What do you miss?" Kyrie asked.

Elle looked her straight in the eyes.

"Sex."

She hoped that would finally shut Kyrie up.

"Is it as much fun as it sounds?" Kyrie asked.

"Oh my God, I can't get rid of you, can I?" Elle asked, ready to break a window and run for it if necessary.

"You can't." Kyrie grinned ear to ear. "I haven't had this much fun since I came here. You are really grumpy, and I like it. Say something grumpy to me again."

"You must be a masochist."

"A what?"

"A masochist. Someone who takes pleasure from pain and humiliation."

"Well...I did join a convent."

"Good point," Elle conceded. "Look, you seem very nice."

"I am very nice. I am the nicest person I know."

"You're a real Polly-fucking-Anna, aren't you?"

"I am. Also, Polly Fucking Anna would make a great name for a lesbian porno."

Elle glared at her.

"Oh, scary face," Kyrie said.

"Stop," Elle said. "Please, just stop what you're doing here."

"What am I doing?" Kyrie asked, still smiling.

"You are clearly a girl on a mission to make friends with the poor abused little laundress who ran away from her big bad boyfriend. I don't know if your priest told you to do it or Mother Prioress or my own mother even, but I don't care. I don't need a buddy. I don't need a friend. I don't need your pity. I don't need anything you have to give me. I'm fine."

Kyrie's smile faded and it was as if the sun had set five hours early.

"My oldest sister's husband beat her to death," Kyrie said. "Two years ago. They had a three-year-old little girl who watched the whole thing happen."

Elle felt the bottom of her stomach drop out of her like a trap door had opened under her and everything but her body fell through.

"Kyrie…I'm sorry."

"Someone told me you'd run away from your boyfriend who used to beat you," Kyrie said. "If that's true then I wanted to say I'm happy you got away from him before he killed you. I really miss my sister."

Elle reached down and pulled a fistful of white linen napkins from the basket.

"I'm very sorry about your sister. If it makes you feel any better at all, my situation is nothing like hers was. I'm not here because I had an abusive boyfriend. I left him for other reasons. It's…it's complicated."

"So, he never hit you?"

"I told you…it's complicated."

"So he did hit you."

"Complicated."

"He was married? When women are with married guys and they don't want to admit he's married, they say it's complicated. I saw that on TV."

"My life is not a TV show," Elle said. "My life is—"

"Complicated. Got it."

"I'm not trying to be mean or grumpy or bitchy," Elle said. "I don't want to talk about why I'm here, and I shouldn't have to."

"Okay, you're right. I get it."

"You don't, but that's okay. Trust me. I'm doing you a favor. You seem like you really enjoy being a nun. I don't want to say or do anything to make you have second thoughts about the Catholic Church."

"Oh, I have lots of second thoughts about the Catholic Church. Third and fourth thoughts even. My sister's priest told her to stay with her husband because divorce is a sin. He suggested counseling. If she left him, she'd probably still be alive.

Why do we ask marriage advice from men not allowed to get married? That's my second thought about the Catholic Church."

"A good second thought."

"Third thought," Kyrie said, holding up three fingers. "Why can't women be priests? Doesn't it say there is no man nor woman in Christ Jesus?"

"Yes. The book of Galatians 3:28," Elle said.

"If that's true, then there's no reason women can't be priests."

"There is a reason. The Catholic Church hates women."

"*Hate* is a strong word, Elle."

"Did you know that if a Catholic priest is caught molesting a child, he's put into therapy and moved to another parish. Meanwhile, if a woman has an abortion she's—"

"Excommunicated."

"Not just excommunicated. *Latea sententiae*—automatically excommunicated," Elle said. "The act itself causes the excommunication. Your brother-in-law who beat your sister to death wouldn't even get excommunicated for what he did to her. There's a nice fourth and fifth thought about the Catholic Church for you."

"I know you said something really profound and worth thinking about, but all I heard was you speaking Latin there for a second and it was really awesome."

"Oh my God, you're certifiable."

"I'm sorry. Sort of. But you're right, lots of thoughts," Kyrie agreed. She folded her arms over her stomach.

"And here you are, one of them. A nun. Despite all your second, third and fourth thoughts, you still joined the ranks."

"You know, American nuns drive the pope crazy. We're all liberal and revolutionary, and we hold property in common and that makes everyone think we're communists. Which most of us are. At least socialists. God forbid everybody gets enough food and water and nobody gets to be a billionaire until everyone gets dinner every single day, right?"

"Pissing off the pope is a good reason to be a nun. Maybe the only good reason."

"There are other good reasons."

"There are?" Elle asked. "What are they?"

"Free fancy outfits," Kyrie said. "Three square meals a day. A girl who knows Latin to do your laundry for you."

"I only know a tiny bit of Latin. And don't get used to the laundry servicing," Elle said. "Once I leave here, one of you lovely ladies will take over laundry duty again. Maybe even you."

"Leave? Why would you leave?" Kyrie sounded horrified by the very idea.

"I can't stay here forever."

"You could if you joined."

"I'm not joining a religious order. Especially not this one."

"Why not?"

"No men allowed."

"You like men?"

"Love men. They're my favorite people when they're behaving."

"I like women," Kyrie said.

"Then you've come to the right place. Women galore. Lucky you." Elle ironed a crease into the napkin, folded it and ironed it again.

"When are you planning on leaving here?" Kyrie asked.

"I don't know. As soon as I can figure out what do to with my life."

"Any ideas?"

"Not yet. I don't have a lot of job skills. Working in a laundry for the rest of my life doesn't hold much appeal."

"I don't blame you. Did you go to college?"

"NYU."

"Did you graduate?"

"I did. English degree. See what I mean about no job skills?"

Kyrie laughed. "You can't do anything else?"

"I give good blow jobs. I'll leave the convent and become a prostitute."

"I bet I'd suck at blowing. It seems hard."

Elle looked up and glared at Kyrie.

"Did you make a dick joke?" Elle asked.

"I did!" Kyrie applauded herself. "I'm not sure if I've ever done that before. How many points do I get?"

"One point."

"Only one? Hmm…that means I have three points. How many points would it take for you to tell me why you're here?"

Elle sighed heavily. "I don't know. Lots of them."

"How about twenty-five? That's how you win a match in volleyball. I played volleyball. I'm crazy good at volleyball."

"Why am I not surprised you played volleyball?"

Kyrie looked her in the eyes. "That's a lesbian joke, isn't it?"

"It might be."

"I liked it. I give you two points."

"How many points to get you to leave?" Elle asked.

"You," Kyrie said, pointing at her. "You are a curmudgeon."

"One point for use of *curmudgeon*."

"Awesome. Now I have four points. Twenty-five of them and I get your story. Okay?"

"Fine. If you get to twenty-five points, I'll tell you why I'm here. You'll probably regret asking."

"I'm sure I will. Looking forward to regretting it."

"You can go away and leave me alone now," Elle said. "I really do have work to do, and you are seriously distracting me."

"I'm leaving. But I'm going to bug you until I get all twenty-five points."

"You're going to have to do better than a lame dick joke. I'm a tough grader, and I was telling better dick jokes than you when I was in middle school. Step up your game, okay?"

"Yes, ma'am," Kyrie said, giving her a little salute and hopping down off the counter. "I'll see you later tonight. You finish your work. I'll figure out what you can do with your life."

"Oh, you're going to figure that out for me?"

"I am."

"Good. One less thing for me to worry about," Elle said, picking up another napkin, a napkin that would be used at dinner tonight, soiled on some elderly nun's mouth, and returned tonight to be rewashed, redried, reironed and reused. Until the end of time.

"I'll catch you later," Kyrie said, heading for the door. "Happy ironing, Elle."

"Hey, Kyrie?" Elle called out. Kyrie stopped and turned around.

"What?"

"I meant it. Mother Prioress really doesn't want me bothering you all. If she finds out we're talking too much, she might not let me stay, and I don't have anywhere else to go."

"I wouldn't tell anybody we talked," Kyrie said. "Your secrets you won't tell me are safe with me. Mainly because you won't tell them to me."

"Thank you. Mother Prioress doesn't really want me here. She's doing my mom a favor."

"If it makes you feel better," Kyrie said from the doorway, "I want you here."

The words, so simple and kind, hit Elle like a high ocean wave and pulled her under like a riptide. They carried her down deep under the surface and it took a few seconds before she hit open air again.

"Elle? What's wrong?"

"Nothing," she said. "It's just…what you said—I said the exact same thing to my priest ten years ago."

"You said 'I want you here' to your priest? Why?"

"Why?" Elle said, smiling. "Because I was fifteen and he

was nice to me, and I would have done or said anything to make him happy."

"Oh," Kyrie said, nodding. "That's funny."

"Why is that funny?" Elle asked, meeting Kyrie's eyes. They were the strangest color of blue—like a spring morning so bright it hurt to look at it.

"That's the same reason I said it."

13

Haiti

KINGSLEY WAS OUT OF HIS ELEMENT. BACK IN MAN-
hattan if he met a woman he wanted to pursue, he'd find out
everything he could about her and use that information to his
advantage. If they were in Manhattan he'd know who Juliette
was, her last name, where she came from, who she ate with,
worked with and slept with. But he wasn't in Manhattan. He
was in Haiti, and he had no idea who this woman was or what
she wanted with him.

And he certainly had no idea what to expect tonight. He
wasn't even certain Juliette would show up. Maybe it was a
test, like making him strip naked on the beach. Asking him to
take his clothes off hadn't been much of a test. He'd take his
clothes off anywhere, anytime and for nearly any reason. Especially when asked nicely. It was getting him to put his clothes
back on afterward that was the real challenge.

Speaking of clothes…Kingsley looked himself up and down.
He'd debated about what to wear for his second meeting with
Juliette and decided to dress in a slightly cleaner version of
his usual Haitian uniform of sun-bleached khakis and white
button-down shirt. It was the beach, after all. He hadn't packed
any of his suits and ties and boots. The freedom of going in-

cognito was intoxicating. Right now, as far as Juliette knew, he was nothing more than a French-American refugee, who'd come to Haiti for an inexpensive vacation. Something about Juliette, the way she talked, the way she looked at him, made him think his money and power wouldn't impress her. What would impress her, he didn't know. But he would find out what it was, and he would do it even if it meant getting naked in public again.

Especially if it meant getting naked in public again.

The sun had barely set by the time he made it back to the fork in the path where Juliette had said to meet her. He waited for a few minutes, and then a few minutes more. He told himself he wouldn't wait another minute. And then another minute would pass and still he'd be there. Finally at nine-thirty he gave up and walked away. One minute later he un-gave up and walked back.

And there she was, wearing a scarlet red dress and holding a set of keys in her hand. He knew he should say something, anything. Perhaps "you're late" would be a good start to the conversation. But he had no words. The dress she wore had a deep V-neck that stopped at the center of her chest. She had full and firm breasts, which the dress did nothing to disguise and everything to display. The wind blew a cool evening breeze on them and caught her skirt in its fingers. He saw a flash of her strong thighs, both shapely and muscular. And he saw something else too, something that made him smile.

He was in the presence of a dangerous woman.

"Flight delay," was all she said by way of apology for her tardiness.

"Flight? You flew somewhere? Today?" he asked.

"No."

He waited for more of an answer and didn't receive one.

"Are you coming with me?" she asked, sounding both im-

patient and indifferent, a difficult combination she managed
to pull off beautifully.

"Where are we going?"

"A house."

"Is it your house?"

"No."

"Has anyone ever told you that you talk too much?" Kingsley asked.

"Never."

"Didn't think so."

Juliette said nothing to his joke. He'd got her to crack a smile
the morning they'd met. If he could make her laugh once tonight he'd call it a victory.

"So...yes or no?" Juliette finally asked. "Are you coming
with me?"

"After you, milady," Kingsley said with a smile. She set out
down the path, which wound around a patch of palm trees and
ended at a small gravel parking lot. There in the parking lot
sat a red Porsche.

He paused and stared at it a moment.

"I confess I didn't figure you as a sports-car aficionado."

"I'm not," she said. "It's not mine."

"Please tell me you aren't a car thief."

"I'm not a car thief," she said, sounding affronted. "I have
permission to drive it. But if you like it, feel free to steal it for
yourself. I don't care a thing about it."

"You're interesting," he said as she got behind the wheel.
Without waiting for an invitation that didn't seem forthcom-
ing, he got into the passenger seat. That was when he noticed
she had no shoes on. She drove barefoot. He liked that and he
didn't know why.

"I'm not interesting," she said. "You're bored."

She started the car and drove out of the parking lot.

"So this house we're going to..." he began.

"Oui?"

"Can you tell me where it is?"

"A few miles from here."

"You aren't planning on killing me at this undisclosed location, are you?"

She gave him a sidelong glance and her eyebrow went back up again.

"Are you scared of me?"

"You have a spear point knife on your thigh."

"How do you know that?" she asked, sounding intrigued. Intrigued was better than irritated. He'd take what he could get.

"First of all, I've been staring at your legs. Second, I'm trained to look for hidden weapons on people. Old habits die hard."

She flipped her dress to the side of her leg, exposing her right thigh where the blade rested in a leather and Velcro harness. She pulled off the Velcro strap, removed the knife and handed it to him.

"I have the knife to use in case the car breaks down at night, and I have to walk alone. I would never hurt anyone unless they tried to hurt me first."

"That's a noble philosophy of life," he said, rolling up his sleeve and strapping the knife onto his forearm. He didn't make a practice of carrying weapons with him these days, but if Juliette felt she needed a knife, he'd much prefer he be the one to use it if necessary.

Juliette shrugged. "It's not a philosophy. It's a religion. I'm Catholic."

"Pull the car over."

Juliette only looked at him. Then she laughed. Finally. And what a laugh. Musical, light, turning deeper at the end and coming straight from her belly. It hit him in the gut like a spear point knife.

"You don't like Catholics?" she asked.

"I have a long complicated history with a Catholic priest of my acquaintance."

"Is he a bad priest?"

"Very bad. He never preaches about sin, only God's love and forgiveness. He doesn't judge sinners and he works tirelessly at his parish on behalf of the poor and oppressed."

"Sounds like a good priest to me. Is he a bad person?"

"He would die for the people he loved. I think he would even die for me."

"And you hate him?"

"Completely and utterly."

"Why?"

"Because he hurt his lover and made her leave him."

"And?"

"She was my lover, too. Then again, so was he once. More than once."

If Juliette's eyebrow arched any higher, it would leave her face and hover above her head.

"I think I was wrong about you, Kingsley," Juliette said as she turned the car onto a winding road. "I think I like you."

"You didn't like me before?"

"No."

"Then why did you let me in your car?"

"I wanted you to fuck me," she said.

"Flattering. I think."

"You can take it as a compliment," she said, making it clear with her tone she hadn't intended it as such.

"You don't need to like someone to fuck them?"

"No. Do you?"

"No, but I thought I was special."

"I hate to tell you this," she said with an apologetic smile, "but I don't think you're as special as you think you are."

"That only hurts because it's true. You really like me? A little?"

"*Un peu*. Enough that I want to talk to you instead of letting you fuck me," she said.

"Oh," he said, and weighed his words. "But we are still going to fuck, right?"

Juliette smiled again. And in her flawless elegant French she purred two beautiful words.

"*Bien sûr.*"

Of course.

She went silent after she made another turn. The road was long and treacherous and wound up the side of a high, heavily forested hill. He could only imagine how Elle would tackle a similar driving challenge. They'd either have made it to their destination in half the time or died a fiery death rolling over a cliff in the attempt. He'd convinced Elle to let his driver take her everywhere she wanted to go. She thought he was being kind and generous. Little did he know he was simply trying to keep her alive. She was alive, wasn't she? Twenty-six years old, smarter than any other woman he'd ever met. Street-smart, too. She'd be fine without him, fine without Søren. Wouldn't she?

"What's wrong?" Juliette asked.

"Nothing."

"You're quiet."

"You were driving."

"I've spent thirty minutes in your company, and I already know quiet isn't your standard mode of operation," she said.

"Are you saying I talk too much?" Kingsley asked.

"Yes."

"Then you shouldn't complain when I'm quiet."

"It made me nervous." She gave him a smile and he was glad to see she was kidding. Hopefully anyway.

"I was thinking about someone."

"Your priest?"

"And his lover."

"You have unusual friends," Juliette said.

He smiled back at her. "Not nearly enough of them. Would you like to be my friend?"

"Do you sleep with your friends?"

Kingsley turned his head and grinned at her. "I'm very friendly. And terrible at monogamy."

She didn't seem to mind that answer. A good sign. So far he'd made her laugh and hadn't scared her off yet by confessing to A) being trained to kill people, B) being bisexual and C) fucking anyone and everyone who would let him.

Beautiful and brave. His type of woman.

Of course, he'd had that thought before. A brave woman would be his perfect woman. Last year he'd fallen madly in love with a girl he'd met at one of his clubs. She'd been a fire breather and she'd come home with him after five minutes of conversation. Unlike with Juliette, he'd known everything about Charlie before he'd gone to bed with her—her full name, her age, her background, her income, her family, everything. Everything except the one thing a file couldn't tell him. He hadn't known her dreams for the future. Turns out children weren't a part of her dreams as they were a part of his. She'd raised her gay younger brother after her mother died and her father kicked them out. Kingsley thought that was a sign she had a strong maternal instinct. But no. She'd already given up college to raise one child. She had no interest in raising another. Kingsley asked her if she'd ever have his children someday. Her "no" had broken his heart.

Juliette was altogether a different woman than Charlie. Juliette was mysterious, dangerous. He was pursuing her for no other reason than she intrigued him. This wasn't about love, wasn't about settling down and having children. A woman who threw rocks at little boys was not the future mother of his children. But she was the woman he was going to fuck tonight and that made her far more important to him than some dream girl he'd likely never find.

When at last they arrived at their destination, Kingsley couldn't see a house, only trees and a gate. She typed a number into a keypad, waited for the wrought iron gates to yawn open and drove through them at a glacial pace. On either side of the car, great trees loomed and cast long shadows. Far ahead he saw white light, and when they reached the end of the driveway, a house like a mountain loomed before them. Gleaming white. Four stories. Endless lines of balconies. Juliette parked the car in front of the stairs that led to the front door.

"Do you live here?" Kingsley asked as he got out of the car.

"Yes," she said.

"But it's not your house."

"No."

"Do you work here?"

"I wouldn't call it work," she said as she lifted the skirt of her dress and walked up the steps. She walked lightly, gracefully and without fear or hesitation. She said she didn't own the house, but she walked into it as if she did. He followed her with less confidence. He couldn't remember the last time he'd felt so nervous around a woman. Why was that? He was out of his element, definitely. He had no idea where he was other than in the mountains outside Petionville. And he was with a woman who wore a dagger on her thigh as casually as most women carried a purse. She was in control of this situation, not him.

Once inside the house, Juliette switched on a single light in the entryway.

"This is the house," was all she said. Apparently there would be no tour.

Kingsley glanced around. Even in the low light he could see the interior looked like a Caribbean palace. White furniture and polished wood floors.

"It's magnificent."

"It's a house. That's all."

"You aren't impressed?"

"I've lived here all my life."

"Your parents own this place?" he asked as she walked up a curving wooden staircase to the third floor.

"No."

"But you grew up here."

"Yes."

"And you speak French and not Creole?"

"I know Creole. I speak French."

"You're not going to tell me anything about your life, are you?" he asked as he followed her down another hallway decorated with white and pale green floral wallpaper.

"It doesn't matter." She gave an elegant shrug, and he fought the urge to bite the back of that arrogant shrugging shoulder. The red straps that crisscrossed on her otherwise bare back were begging to be ripped off her body. Flawless skin. He ached to leave it covered in welts and bites. She might not like that, though. Still...to be inside her would be worth anything he had to give up to get there. Even kink.

"Doesn't matter?" He almost laughed. "At this point, I think I'd rather know you than fuck you. And for me to say that... well...consider it my highest compliment."

"You would rather know me than fuck me?"

"I would."

She turned her back to the door and leaned against it. She crossed her arms over her chest and faced him.

"My name is Juliette Toussaint. I'm twenty-six years old. I was born in this house because my mother was the housekeeper here. My family has always worked for the family that lives in this house. For generations. We lived in the servants' quarters here. The owner's children had French tutors. I was allowed to learn with them instead of going to school. If I was here at the house, I could help my mother with her work. When I was fourteen years old, my mother got very ill. The owner of this house is paying for her medical treatments. I work for him now.

It's not a difficult job, which is why I don't call it work. Now you know everything there is to know about me."

"I highly doubt that."

"Do you want my autobiography or do you want to have me?"

"I want both."

"Both isn't one of your options," she said. "Look, we're wasting time."

"I don't have to be anywhere anytime soon."

"I do," Juliette said. She sighed heavily and glanced away. "Kingsley…"

He shivered. It was the first time she'd said his name.

"I can only give you tonight," she said. "One night. So please stop wasting time."

"What do you mean you can only give me tonight?"

"I have a life," she said. "With someone. Tomorrow I'll go back to it."

"Are you married?" he asked, realizing he should have asked that question before he'd got into the car with her. But it was too late now. No matter what she said, he would stay until she kicked him out of her life.

"No. It's different."

"How so?"

"You wouldn't understand."

"Try me," he said. "I'm very understanding."

"I'm…" She met his eyes again. "I'm owned."

Owned. Of course she was owned. A woman like Juliette was a prize, a crown, a work of art, a priceless jewel that would inspire the urge to own her in any man who looked at her. She should be owned, cherished and guarded. If he owned her, he would guard her with his life.

Kingsley nodded. "That I understand."

"You do?" She sounded skeptical.

"I do. I understand what it means to be owned."

"Good. He's gone tonight. He'll be back tomorrow."

"Do you make a habit of seeing other men behind his back?"

She shook her head. "No."

"Am I the first?"

"Second."

"Second man you've cheated on him with?"

"No," she said, her voice so quiet he could barely hear her. "Second man I've ever been with."

"Ever?"

"Ever," she said.

Kingsley inhaled deeply. He never dreamed a woman so beautiful would have had only one lover in her entire life.

"Why me?" he asked.

She met his eyes and lifted her hand. Gently, slowly, she trailed her fingers through his hair and brought a lock of it to her lips. She kissed the tip of his hair before she released it. The act was so intimate, so unexpected and so possessive it hurt like a spear point knife in his stomach.

"I like your hair," she said, looking at his face as if she was memorizing every detail of it. "That's all."

Kingsley was so hard for her already it hurt. He physically ached to be inside this woman.

"Now will you fuck me?" she asked.

"A few more questions. They'll be quick."

"What else do you need to know?" Juliette asked, sounding impatient.

"Well…for starters, how do you like to be fucked?"

He crossed his arms over his chest to match her posture and waited.

She met his eyes and they were so dark and so wide right then he imagined he could see himself in them.

"I like it rough."

"Rough?" Kingsley repeated. "On a scale of one to ten…"

"What's one?"

"You fall asleep while I'm on top of you."

"Ten?"

"Hospitalization."

Juliette seemed to ponder that a moment.

"Nine," she answered.

"Nine. Nine is very rough."

"If nine is too much for you, take the car and drive yourself home. I don't like having my time wasted."

She flicked the keys at him and he caught them easily. But after he caught them, he dropped them on the ground.

"Trust me," he said, taking a step forward and clapping a hand on her throat. He put his mouth to her ear and whispered, "I won't waste your time."

Now. Finally.

Kingsley was back in his element.

14

KINGSLEY'S HAND WAS ON JULIETTE'S THROAT AND HIS mouth was at her ear.

"You'll do everything I tell you to do," he said, an order, not a question. "Yes?" *Oui?*

"Yes" Juliette said, breathlessly.

"I won't cut you or burn you or choke you. But once we're in that room, everything else is possible. Every act, every hole," he said. "You understand?"

Juliette swallowed hard. He felt her throat moving under his hand.

"I'll use condoms," he said.

"Thank you."

"You have any requests of me?" he asked.

"Yes. Open the door already," she said. Kingsley smiled. If he wasn't careful, he was going to fall in love with this woman.

As requested, he opened the door.

He'd expected a bedroom and it was a bedroom. But not a man's bedroom or a woman's even. Not a guest room or a hotel room.

It was a child's room.

He looked down into Juliette's face.

"It's the one room he's never had me in," she whispered.

The look on her face—almost embarrassed—touched his heart. She hadn't meant to say that out loud, that she wanted him in a room without memories of another man.

Only a single lamp burned on a small round white table but even in the low light it was unmistakably the bedroom of a young girl. The bedroom of the daughter of Juliette's lover, no doubt, still decorated in the fashion of a child even though she'd long ago grown up and moved out. The bed was small, no more than a full size. The sheets were an innocent shade of white and the rug on the floor a pale pink and blue. Mosquito netting hung down over the bed and a window onto the garden let in a cool rush of ocean air. The night was all around them and even in these strange surroundings, Kingsley burned to be inside her. He hadn't fucked in the bedroom of a teenager since he'd been a teenager. But it didn't matter. As hard as he was right now, any horizontal surface would do.

Kingsley kicked the door shut behind him and locked the door. With one arm he swept Juliette to him, meeting her face-to-face, eye-to-eye. She put her hands against his chest, not to push him away but to steady herself. An unnecessary precaution. He had no plans on letting her go until morning.

Juliette looked into his eyes. He saw no fear in them, only desire. She lifted her hand to his face and then swept her fingers through his hair. When she reached the end of a lock she brought it to her lips. No woman had ever kissed his hair before like that, as if it was an act of worship more than affection.

"Will you kiss me?" she asked. Not a humble request, merely a question.

"When you've earned it."

She nodded. "Let me earn it then."

Far rougher than necessary, Kingsley grasped the fabric of her dress and pulled it down and off her body. Her spine stiffened as he stripped her, but she made no protest. When she was naked but for her woven hemp sandals, he took a step away from her.

"My turn," he said. He stared at her body, grazing it with his eyes from ankle to neck. She kept her chin high, her eyes forward, and she didn't try to cover herself in any way. She was beautiful, with a body that could only be described in superlatives—exquisite, striking. Lean, long muscular legs, full hips, a slim waist, large high breasts and shapely shoulders. His dream woman. In spite of her nakedness or perhaps because of it, she looked regal, almost imperious, and definitely defiant. She dared him with her eyes to find fault in what he saw.

There was no fault to be found.

He reached for her and gripped her hard by the back of the neck. She'd asked him to be rough and it was good that she had. Scalding hot desire had burned all the gentleness out of him tonight. He swept the white diaphanous mosquito netting aside and pushed her onto her back at the center of the bed. Kneeling over her, he shoved her legs wide and pried her inner lips apart with brutal fingers. He stared at the opening to her body, red and wet already. His chest heaved, his heart contracted. Juliette lay there with her thighs wide and her eyes half shut. They watched him, her eyes did, from under the veil of her lush eyelashes. Without warning he shoved two fingers into her, as deep as he could go. Juliette's back arched hard off the bed, her vagina clenched his fingers.

Without mercy, he pulled back and shoved in again, even deeper. Her body opened to him more and he pushed in a third finger. Her wetness coated his hand and she let out a groan in the back of her throat.

Another minute would be a minute too much for him. Kingsley pulled his hand out, yanked his shirt off and opened his pants. He grabbed her by the hips and pulled her toward him. Once the condom was on, he wasted no time entering her body. He thrust in deep and she took every inch. It must have hurt. He could tell from the tension in her body that taking so much into her hurt. But he could also tell—from the moan that escaped her lips and the way she raised her hips to take even more of him—that she liked that it hurt.

"You like pain?" he whispered as he thrust again, right into the core of her.

"Yes…please…" she breathed. *Oui…s'il vous plaît.*

"So do I."

"I know," she said. "I know you do."

How she knew, he didn't know. He didn't care either, now that he was inside her. He placed his hands next to her shoulders and rode her with long, slow, hard thrusts.

"I want to fuck every part of you," he said as the heat of her surrounded his cock, enveloped it.

"You can."

"Does he fuck you like this? Does he make it hurt?"

"Yes," she whispered.

"You like it?"

"Yes…"

"Does it feel this good?"

"Nothing feels this good," she said, and he heard a note of regret in her voice. Regret? But why? He was too far gone in lust to ask.

He grasped her breasts in both hands and squeezed them. Her fingers caught into the white fabric under her and inside her a muscle pushed back against him. It was too much. He almost came from that alone. With a grunt of frustration, he pulled out of Juliette's body and brought his mouth down onto her, licking and kissing her wet seam. The lips parted for him and he pushed his tongue up and into her. She writhed under his mouth, twisted and groaned. He knew he was hurting her. He also knew she wanted him to hurt her. Her clitoris swelled against his tongue even as he bruised her hips with his hands as he pinned her hard to the bed.

He yanked her to him and shoved his cock back inside her, impaling her hard and deep. She rewarded him with a cry of pleasure tinged with pain. When she slammed her hands against his chest he grabbed them, pinned them behind her back and pushed into her with a punishing thrust.

"You want this," he said, fucking her with abandon now. Every muscle in his hips had coiled into the tightest knot of need and pressure.

"No," she said, even as she pushed back against him to take him deeper.

"Liar." He pushed her onto her back once again and forced her legs even wider. It wasn't enough. Not matter what he did he couldn't fuck her hard enough, get into her deep enough. He forced her legs around him, rose up over her and mounted her again. It was so rare that he could let himself go entirely with a woman, let himself fuck her as roughly as he wanted to. But whatever he gave her, she took. She came with a cry as he filled her and came again not long after. He dug his hand into her hair at the nape of her neck and pulled, bending her body, forcing it into greater submission to his.

They were a tangle of limbs on the bed, limbs and flesh and bodies entwined so fully, joined so deeply, that it was as if they were sealed together. The heat had melted and merged them. They weren't even human now, but sex in its rawest, purest form. Juliette had gone silent underneath him even as she worked herself against him with hungry thrusts of her hips. When she came again with a shudder and inner contractions so hard they hurt him, he rammed his own orgasm into her.

At last they were still. His body. Her body. Neither of them moved for any reason but to breathe. He was still inside her, reluctant to leave her even though he needed to. He needed to pull out, pull away, remember who he was and why he was here. He needed space, time, rational thinking, something.

Or he could just fuck her again.

He lifted himself off her, stood up and threw the condom away. Juliette remained on the bed, flat on her back, staring at him. Her legs were still splayed wide. An open invitation.

"Did I hurt you?" he asked when he rejoined her on the bed. The mosquito netting surrounded them like a cloud. It was all too easy to believe they were alone in the world.

"Yes."

"How much?"

She slipped a hand between her legs and when she held it up to him, he saw a blood smear on her fingertips. He'd fucked her so hard he'd made her bleed. There were two ways to respond to such a situation. One was to apologize. That was the vanilla way. He didn't respond the vanilla way. He responded the Kingsley way.

"Good thing you have two other holes," he said.

"I'm yours," she said with a tired smile. "Make me yours in every way."

"But only tonight?"

She nodded and whispered, "Only tonight."

"What if tonight isn't enough?"

"It has to be," she said.

"Then start praying," Kingsley said.

"Praying for what?"

"That this night never ends."

Juliette came to her knees in front of him. She touched his naked chest with her hands, kissed the scar over his heart, looked up at him.

"That is my only prayer," she whispered.

Kingsley took her face in his hands and forced her mouth to his. He kissed her with a hunger he'd forgotten he could feel for anyone who wasn't Søren or Elle. He'd thought with them he'd reached the end of his passion, that he'd bottomed out in them and given all he had. But with Juliette he found a new reserve of desire, a deeper hunger, a longing to have something with her he had with no one else. He pushed his tongue past her lips and into her warm mouth. She tasted of salt and ocean water and the more he drank of her the more he needed to drink. He would never be quenched of his thirst for her.

"Juliette…" he murmured against her lips. "My Juliette, my jewel." She shivered in his arms.

"Your name is Kingsley?" she asked. "It's your real name?"

"It is."

"Are you a real king?"

"Yes," he answered. He was. He had a kingdom. He had dominions. He had a court who served him. Yes. He was a real king.

"Then let me serve you, *mon roi.*"

She kissed her way down the front of his body, taking her time as she kissed every inch of him except the inches that most craved her kisses. As she neared his cock she blew softly on his penis. The cool air from her mouth washed over him. Then she breathed hot air and set his blood boiling again. With her tongue and lips she teased his lower stomach, his hips, his inner thighs. When he reached the point of desperation, she wrapped a hand around his length. He'd come only minutes ago, but he was already hard again. She'd got in his blood, made it burn, made it boil. He was lost in his lust for her.

"Tell me if you don't like this," Juliette said.

"Like what?"

She didn't answer with words. Her mouth was too occupied to speak. She'd cupped the head of his penis and pulled the foreskin to the tip, making a sort of halo with it. Then she licked around the center with her hot wet tongue. Kingsley died. The visual coupled with the sensation—that glorious carnal salacious voluptuous sensation—nearly did him in. He saw stars and he saw the heavens and he might have seen God but only if God looked like Juliette. Every part of him throbbed.

"I've never seen a more beautiful man," she said, looking

up at him as she cradled his testicles gently in the palm of her hand. "You're so beautiful I wish I'd never seen you."

He would have answered her, but she brought her mouth down onto him again and his words were gone. She went deep, taking him all the way into her throat. Her full lips on his cock sent him straight to the edge and left him there, tense, taut, his body one pulsing nerve of need. Juliette worshipped him with her mouth, showering him with hot wet kisses, licks, hard strokes of her hand that made him gasp wide-eyed with the shock of pleasure. She lavished every inch of him endlessly with her tongue. She stretched out over him and rested her hands on his chest as she buried her face into his hips, sucking him all the way into her mouth. He'd never been so fully taken before for so long, so deep, so much. Too much. He grasped her wrists in his hands and came so hard his shoulders rolled off the bed, his stomach bowed. Somewhere he heard a cry, almost a shout, and knew it had to have come from him.

She swallowed his semen, even licking the last drops off the tip. When he winced, she stopped.

"Don't stop," he said. "Take it all."

"It hurts?" she asked, dipping her lips to lick him again.

"Yes."

She asked no more questions. She obeyed him as if she'd been born to obey him. And he wanted to believe she had. Was this what Søren had felt the day he met Elle? That he'd found the one woman created for him? Designed for him? If his desire for her had burned anything like Kingsley's for Juliette, it wasn't a surprise the priest had waited four years to fuck her. It was a miracle.

"*Arrête*," he said. Stop. Juliette stopped.

Kingsley closed his eyes and merely rested. Juliette slid up his body and lay next to him on the bed.

"I want to beat you," he said.

"We can't. He'll see the marks."

"But you want that?"

"I do," Juliette said. "I want everything from you."

"One night isn't enough."

"How many nights would be enough?"

Kingsley opened his eyes and gazed at her face, met her eyes.

"All your nights."

"You're drunk on sex." She started to roll up. "On pleasure. You found a new girl to fuck, and you've convinced yourself she's different from all the other girls you've fucked. You don't mean what you say."

"I'm not a teenage boy in love for the first time. I've been with hundreds of women."

"Congratulations. I'm sure your parents are very proud."

"My parents are dead."

"Is it because they heard what a whore you are?" she asked.

He grabbed her by the back of the neck and dragged her back down to the bed.

"Behave," he said, sliding on top of her. "And keep a civil tongue with me."

She glared up at him.

"You want to pretend you don't feel the same," Kingsley said. "You want to pretend this was just sex so it won't hurt as much when you never see me again."

"Tell me more about what I feel. Tell me more what I think. Tell me what it is I want, since you think I don't know."

"This," he said, and grabbed her hair, pulling it hard enough to force her back into a bend. He dropped his mouth to her breast and sucked deeply on her nipple.

"He gives this to me. He gives everything to me."

"If that were true, I wouldn't be here," he whispered against her skin. "Or here."

He pushed four fingers deep into her wetness.

"I'd never been with anyone but him," she panted as he

opened her body with his fingers. He felt her inner muscles pushing against him, fluttering with pleasure, pulsing with need.

"Do you love him?"

"Yes."

"Are you lying?"

"Maybe."

"Do you want me to fall in love with you?" Kingsley asked.

"He loves me," she said. "Love is the last thing I need from you."

"Tell me what I can give you that he can't." Kingsley pushed in deeper until she enveloped his hand.

"It doesn't matter. You won't give it to me."

"How do you know until you tell me what it is?"

"I know. I promise you, I know already," she said, and Kingsley heard despair in her voice. "Fuck me. That's all that matters."

He did as he was told. He pushed her onto her stomach and dragged a pillow under her hips. She tensed at first when he pushed his tongue into her tightest hole but relaxed after a minute and opened up for him. He rolled on a condom and entered her again. The tightness was ecstasy around him. He lasted only a few thrusts before he came.

But he didn't pull out. He wasn't ready to pull out. He would never be ready to leave her body. Kingsley lay on top of her, his naked chest to her naked back, his cock still buried in her, and their breaths intermingling.

"Anything," he whispered. "I'll do anything you ask of me."

"No, you won't."

"Ask it."

He slid out of her and turned her onto her back.

"Tell me what it is I can give you that he can't."

"You won't give it to me."

"Tell me," he ordered again. "Whatever it is, I'll do it. Any price, any prize, anything you want—I will find a way to give it to you."

He cupped her face, caressed her hair.

She looked up at him with tired, hooded eyes.

"Death," she said.

Kingsley sat up and looked down at her in utter horror.

"You're right," Kingsley said. "That is the one thing I can't give you."

She only smiled.

"I told you so."

15

Upstate New York

AFTER ALL THE SISTERS WENT TO BED AT THE UNGODLY hour of eight o'clock, Elle crept down the stairs to the library. Every night she made this little pilgrimage. She'd go stir-crazy if she had to lie in her tiny bed in her tiny cell and stare at the ceiling while she waited for sleep. Only in the library did she feel a little like her old self. She threw wood in the fireplace, switched on a lamp or two and sat and read anything she could find that wasn't the Bible.

Surrounded by books, Elle could pretend she was at her old job at Wordsworth's where she'd worked part-time during college and full-time until she was twenty-five. She'd hated to quit her job, but things were so busy at Kingsley's that working by day and helping him manage a stable of submissives, Dominatrixes and various Fetishists who worked on and off his clock became too much for her. She didn't need her minuscule paycheck anyway. Kingsley let her live in luxury at his town house for free. He'd even given her a credit card that he'd ordered her to use for everything she wanted or needed. But she was no kept woman, no pampered princess. She trained the submissives for Kingsley, kept his house in order and did anything he asked her to do, in and out of the bedroom. And not a week passed that she didn't go to bed with Kingsley and Søren and give her body up to them both, all night long. Oh yes, she earned her keep.

The physical memories of all those nights threatened to flood her senses. Elle pushed them out of her mind as she pulled a book off the shelf—a decaying copy of *Bulfinch's Mythology*. Elle carefully turned the dry and yellowed pages as she hunted for an entry. She and Kyrie had talked mythology a few days ago—Sisyphus specifically. She knew in the legend Sisyphus had been given his meaningless task as a punishment, but for the life of her she couldn't remember what he'd done wrong. It hadn't been the act of giving the secret of fire to humanity. That had been Prometheus, not Sisyphus. And the gods had punished Prometheus by chaining him to a rock and having an eagle peck out his liver for all eternity.

Which was worse? Pushing the rock up the hill or being attacked by a bird? If she had to choose, she probably would pick the eagle. At least she wouldn't be alone then. Even if the bird was hurting her, at least there would be another living creature there. All Sisyphus had was the rock.

"Can I share your fire?"

Elle looked up from her book. Kyrie stood in the doorway in her long white bathrobe. Her white veil covered her hair but Elle could see wisps of blond and brown at her temples.

"You're not supposed to be talking," Elle whispered. "Great Silence, remember?"

"Mother Prioress said the sisters aren't supposed to talk to each other during the Great Silence." Kyrie stepped into the library uninvited. Elle noticed she wore nothing on her feet. Bare feet. Bare ankles. When was the last time she'd seen anyone's bare feet but her own? "You aren't a sister."

"Someone else who looks for the loopholes in the rules," Elle said, holding the large dusty hardback book to her chest. "A girl after my own heart."

"I am an expert in Loophole Theology," Kyrie said, dragging a chair over to Elle's and sitting down. She pulled her legs up to her chest and wrapped her arms around her knees. She looked unbearably young right now and tiny. Elle was only five-three but she had curves. In shoes, Kyrie might have been five-three and she had stick-thin ankles. If she had curves, her bathrobe did a good job hiding them. "Test me. Give me a rule or a commandment or something, and I'll find a loophole."

"Um...how about the big one? 'Thou shall not kill.' Where's the loophole there?"

"Spiders."

"Spiders?"

"Spiders are the work of the devil. If God didn't want us to kill spiders, he wouldn't have allowed Satan himself to invent them and unleash them on the world. Spiders. Give me another one."

"What about the priestly vow of celibacy?" Elle asked, giving Kyrie her best and therefore fakest innocent look.

"Celibacy means no getting married. So let priests have sex, but they can't get married."

"Yes, but the Bible also says no sex outside of marriage. So if they get married, they're breaking the celibacy vow. If they have sex when they aren't married, they're breaking the command against fornication."

"That is a tough one," Kyrie said, nodding her head. "Wait. I got it."

"What?"

"Hand jobs."

"That is your answer to the issue of priestly celibacy? Hand jobs?"

Kyrie raised her hands and wiggled her fingers.

"A hand job isn't sex. Right?"

"Not exactly, no."

"I mean, you could give a priest a foot rub, right? That wouldn't be sex, right?"

"Right," Elle said, remembering all the intimate massages she'd given Søren at his command.

"And a hand job is like a foot rub but not on the foot. It's a massage."

"A really intimate massage," Elle reminded her.

"But still, not sexual intercourse."

"Definitely not intercourse." Elle couldn't argue with her.

"There. Loophole Theology saves the day. I have solved the crisis in the priesthood. Priests can't get married. They can't have sex. But they can get handies to their heart's content."

"Great. I'll go give a priest a hand job," Elle said, opening her book up once more. "Again."

"Do I get points? I want my points," Kyrie said. "I'm stuck at four."

"You can have two points for spiders. Two points for hand jobs."

"Yes. Eight points. Getting closer."

"There are extra points if you actually give a priest a hand job."

"Ew. No, thank you," Kyrie said with a dramatic shudder. "I'm picturing Father Antonio."

"What? You don't find liver spots sexy?"

Kyrie smiled. "Men."

"That's right. You're a girl's girl."

"Does that bother you?" Kyrie asked.

"What? That you're a lesbian?"

"That."

Elle stared blankly at Kyrie. Then she laughed. She laughed and she laughed and she laughed.

Then she laughed a little bit more.

"Elle?"

"Sorry...."

She laughed again.

"Elle, you're laughing like a maniac."

Elle playfully wiped a tear from her eye.

"I'm done laughing," she said. Then she laughed again.

"Elle, seriously. Are you having a seizure? Is this demonic possession? Holy laughter?"

"No, none of those." Elle finally took a deep breath and stopped laughing. "The irony of someone, anyone, thinking I'd be bothered by a girl who likes girls."

"So I'm guessing you…"

"I'm bi," Elle said. She was also the most famous submissive in the Manhattan Underground, but she decided not to tell Kyrie that part. Yet. "Which is either the best of both worlds or the worst of both worlds."

"I'm an optimist," Kyrie said. "We'll go with best of both worlds."

"I could use some optimism."

"I could use some points. I'm still working on my twenty-five points. I think I should get more than four points for hand jobs and spiders."

"You get one bonus point for using them in a sentence together."

"So I only need sixteen more points until you tell me what you're doing here?" Kyrie asked, grinning eagerly.

"Sixteen more points until you regret asking."

"I can't wait." Kyrie stretched her legs out and let her bare feet hover in front of the fireplace.

"I can."

"Is it bad?" Kyrie lowered her legs and looked at Elle. "Really bad?"

"It's…you know."

"Complicated." Kyrie nodded. "Right, you said that earlier this week."

"It's still complicated. Things haven't ceased being complicated in the last three days."

"Maybe you only think they're complicated because you're inside the situation? And maybe if you were outside of it like I am, it wouldn't be so complicated. You know, like a person trapped in a maze. You can only see what's in front of you. But if you were above the maze looking down at it, you'd know exactly where you are, what's happening and where to go."

"It's a nice thought," Elle said, resting her hands in the cradle of the open book. "But I promise, there's no way out of this maze. No matter how you look at it."

"I just…" Kyrie smiled at Elle. "I want to help."

"You can't. But don't feel bad. No one can."

"Not even God?"

Elle laughed again.

"God got us into this mess," Elle said with a tired smile. "He seems in no hurry to get us back out again."

"Who's us?" Kyrie asked.

"Stop." Elle raised her hand in a warning. "You're getting nothing else out of me tonight. I didn't come down here to spill my guts. And I'm certainly not in the mood to give anyone my confession."

"Why did you come here? Tonight, I mean. Is this your usual nine-o'clock hangout?" Kyrie asked.

"I used to work at a bookstore. I like being around books."

"Me, too. You know my sister was a writer."

"The one who—"

"Who was murdered?" Kyrie asked. "Yeah, her."

"What was her name? I'd rather call her by her name than 'your sister who was murdered,'" Elle said.

Kyrie gave her a strange look. And then a smile.

"You're the first person who's asked me her name after I mentioned her."

"She only spent one day of her life dying. Who was she the rest of the time?"

"Bethany. Although her pen name was Marian Sherwood."

"Robin Hood fan?"

"It was her favorite story, favorite movie, favorite everything."

"What did she write?"

"Romance novels. The kind set in the past when everyone dressed better? What are those? The men with the great boots?"

"Regencies?"

"Those. They were good, too. I loved reading her books. She even dedicated one to me."

"Do you have any with you?" Elle asked, desperate to read anything other than a book of Catholic theology or church history.

"I wasn't allowed to bring them with me," Kyrie said. "But they're up here." She pointed at her head.

"I'm really sorry about what happened to her."

"It was on the news, you know. National news. Young mother and bestselling writer murdered by her husband. Well, it was on the news for one day and then something else more important happened. Some celebrity got divorced or something."

"Nothing's more important than losing someone you love."

"I thought so." Kyrie sighed heavily. "It's crazy that a romance writer would get killed by her husband. You'd never imagine a woman who wrote about true love for a living would be in such a bad marriage."

"The face you show the world isn't always your real face," Elle said. "You can look at someone and think you know everything about them...but you don't. We all have masks on. Or veils." She looked pointedly at Kyrie. "I know someone who lives a double life. Actually...almost everyone I knew back home did." Kingsley, Søren...all of them.

"So what are you reading?" Kyrie asked, clearly ready to stop talking about her sister. "Anything good?"

"*Bulfinch's Mythology.* I'm trying to figure out what Sisyphus did to deserve his rock and rolling for all eternity punishment."

"Nothing," Kyrie said, taking the book off Elle's lap. "Nothing anyone could do merits eternal suffering."

"You sure about that? What about rape?"

"Nope."

"Murder?"

"No."

"Child molestation?"

"Not even that. I mean, think about it. Eternity, Elle. Forever and ever without end. Infinite time. No crime causes infinite suffering. At some point the victim dies, goes to Heaven and lives in bliss. If the victim's suffering isn't eternal, how can the punishment for a crime be eternal?"

"Hell is in the Bible."

"So are talking donkeys. You see a talking donkey anywhere?" Kyrie asked.

"I know a few talking asses."

Kyrie glared at her. "Hell is where we put people we don't want to think about. Like my ex-brother-in-law who killed Bethany. I mean, he…" Kyrie paused and closed her fingers into a fist. "He slammed her head against the wall until she died, Elle. But you know what? Bethany's in Heaven. She's with God, and she's happy and rejoicing for all eternity. And he, Jake…Jake was abused by his father so badly when he was a kid that at age thirty-five he still wets the bed when he hears loud noises at night because he thinks it's his dad coming to his bedroom again."

"That's horrible." Elle winced. "I know a man who was sexually abused by his own sister when he was eleven. But he never used that as an excuse to harm other people. We all have free will."

"I'm not saying Jake shouldn't be punished. But it's like the maze we were talking about," Kyrie said. "A person's heart is a maze. When you're in the maze, you can't see your way to the center of it. Only if you're above the maze can you look down and really see what's happening. I think that's how God looks at us. That way he can see the entire maze at once, can see where the twists and turns are, and where the center is. Jake was a victim, too. Do I love him? No. Do I hate him? Yes. But I want to forgive him. God says to forgive him. And if God expects fallible human me to forgive him, why shouldn't I expect perfect, infallible God to forgive him?"

"You want to put a sign on the front doors of Hell that says Going Out of Business."

"Good," Kyrie said. "Hell is a fun concept. Hell is where you damn the guy who cuts you off in traffic or the girl who breaks your heart or the lady at the customer service counter at Sears who refuses to give you a refund on your underwear even though they fell apart after only one washing and of course you don't have the tags still on it because who would wear their underwear with the tags on it?"

"Not that you speak from experience or anything," Elle said.

"Once. I wore those panties once and they disintegrated in the washer."

"Hand wash in the sink, cold water, soak overnight, hang to dry."

"Where were you when I needed you last summer?"

"Here," Elle said. "Pushing a rock up the hill, letting it roll down and then pushing it back up again. I'm still here."

"I'm glad you're still here. Even if means you're pushing a rock up a hill every day. Even if it means…"

"Means what?"

"Even if it means me getting in trouble for talking to you during the Grand Silence."

Elle had a feeling Kyrie wanted to say something else, meant to say something else. But she'd somehow lost her courage.

"You won't tell anyone, will you?"

"Tell anyone what?"

"That I don't believe Hell exists. It's kind of a heresy."

"I am a walking heresy," Elle said. "And no, I won't tell."

Kyrie looked at Elle but didn't smile. She didn't frown, either. She simply looked at her as if trying to memorize Elle's face. Elle let her.

"Anyway, I should go to bed," Kyrie said, standing up. "You're reading and I'm supposed to be sleeping. Instead of, you know, touching myself or something so I'll end up in Purgatory."

"You don't believe in Hell, but you believe in Purgatory?"

"I do. That's weird, right? I kind of like the thought that there's a process you have to go through to get into Heaven. I mean, I had to fill out paperwork just to return a pair of disintegrated panties. Heaven has to have some sort of returns policy, right?"

"Red tape. No escaping it."

"I should take a book back with me to bed. Something to help me keep my hands off myself. Any suggestions?"

"What do you like to read?" Elle asked, the standard bookseller question when any customer asked for a recommendation.

"I'm guessing there aren't any romance novels in here?" Kyrie glanced up at the shelves.

"Nope. Trust me, I looked," Elle said. "If you want anything fun to read, you'll have to write it yourself."

"Bethany was the writer in the family. I'm a reader. Any romances in there?" Kyrie nodded at her book of mythology.

"Sort of. There's Leda and the Swan. More bestiality than romance, though. Psyche and Cupid's pretty good. Daphne and Apollo. They're my favorite. The original love-hate relationship."

"Who were they?"

"Daphne was a forest nymph and beautiful beyond imagining. Apollo was the god of music, reason and healing. He came upon Cupid one day playing with his bow and arrows—"

"Masturbating?"

"No, I think these were literal bows and arrows."

"Continue the story please. I'll adjust my mental images," Kyrie said.

"Apollo teased little Cupid about his prowess with his bow."

"Are we sure they're not talking about penises?"

"Might be in the subtext," Elle said. "Apollo teased Cupid about his little bow and arrow or maybe his penis. I don't know. So Cupid, pissed off at Apollo for his arrogance, picks up two arrows. One is tipped in lead. One is tipped in gold. He shoots the arrow tipped in lead into the heart of Daphne the beautiful forest nymph. The arrow tipped in gold he shoots into the heart of Apollo. At once Apollo is seized by desperate love for Daphne. And she is seized by hatred of Apollo. He chases after her through the forest while she runs from him as fast as she can. But Apollo gains on her so she prays to her father the river god to turn her into something so Apollo can't have her. Her father turns her into a laurel tree. From there and ever after, the laurel became the symbol of Apollo."

"Wait. This girl turns into a tree rather than let Apollo have her?" Kyrie asked. "That's crazy."

"I know. But what do you expect from a patriarchal society that prized virginity so highly? Better a woman be a tree or a stone or some kind of mindless but pure object than be sullied by sex."

"Terrible ending," Kyrie said. "Very disappointing."

"I didn't write it. If I wrote it, there would be much more sex in the story."

"Then write it."

"What?"

"Write it," Kyrie said. "Fix the ending."

"You want me to rewrite the story of Daphne and Apollo?" Elle looked at Kyrie as if she was crazy. After all the talk about spiders, hand jobs, mazes, Hell and penises, Elle was starting to think Kyrie was.

"You said if I want something fun to read, I'd have to write it myself. I can't write so you write it for me."

"I'm not going to write you a book."

"My sister wrote a book for me."

"You're using your dead sister to guilt trip me into writing a book for you."

"She would have wanted it this way. Come on, Elle. Don't you want something fun to read, too?"

"I'd give my left arm for a single copy of *The Story of O* right now. In French or English. Preferably fully illustrated."

"You write me the story, and I'll do something nice for you," Kyrie said.

"What?"

"Anything. You name it."

Elle narrowed her eyes at Kyrie.

"*Anything* is a dangerous word where I come from," Elle said.

Kyrie didn't look the least intimidated.

"I trust you. Is it a deal?"

"Not a deal. Definitely not a deal. I haven't written anything since college. And you really shouldn't trust me. For a lot of reasons."

"Too late. I already do."

Elle rolled her eyes.

"Fine," she said at last. "But only if I get a perfect idea for the story. Otherwise I'm not going to waste my time trying to fix a three-thousand-year-old myth that's doing fine without me."

"It's got a terrible ending. It needs you."

"If, and only if, I get a perfect idea. Then I'll write it. And if

I write, then you can do something nice for me. Maybe sneak me extra dessert or something."

"I can do that."

Kyrie stood in the darkened doorway of the library. This girl…this crazy girl…what on earth was she doing letting this crazy girl into her life? Not just a girl. A nun. An intelligent, weird, wonderful, breathtakingly beautiful nun…

"Have a good night," Kyrie said. "I'll say a prayer God hits you with a good idea."

"Gotta be perfect. Not good. Perfect. Otherwise I'm not writing it."

"God can handle perfect. That's His strong suit."

Kyrie gave her one last smile, turned around and on her naked feet disappeared into the darkness.

Elle exhaled. In that exhale she realized she'd been tense for the past half hour. Tense? Why? Kyrie, of course. She liked her. Liked her much too much. And the last thing Elle needed was a friend in this place. Especially a very pretty friend under a very serious vow of chastity. She'd come here to get away from people, get away from the world, get away from love and sex and men and complications.

Kyrie had the potential to be a serious complication.

For the first time in years, Elle had begun to feel completely safe someplace. She was safe in the abbey, far away from her old life where every day carried with it the risk that Søren would get caught, she would get hurt, or Kingsley would get killed. Here at the convent she had nothing to fear. She had a roof over her head, three meals a day, a small warm bed and a library full of books—boring books. And even worse, she'd read them all by now.

But still…this was what she needed now. Safety. Peace. Quiet. Complications were the last thing she needed. She'd had enough of those for a lifetime. She'd back away from Kyrie. Far far away from her. She'd get away from Kyrie if she had to turn herself into a tree to do it. And tonight would mark the first and the last of their late-night fireplace conversations. No more of those. Never. No. Not a chance.

Elle returned the copy of *Bulfinch's Mythology* to the shelf. She went to bed and slept and when she woke up she was still thinking about Kyrie. About Kyrie and her sister the writer, who'd died, and Kyrie's demand that Elle write her a romance novel.

Sweet girl. Very pretty. Totally delusional.

Outside the window in the light of dawn, she saw a blur in the distance. Elle pulled on a sweater and squinted into the new morning. It was a woman out jogging in winter running clothes. Jogging. That was all. The abbey had neighbors, normal people who lived out in the country. Sometimes Elle saw them driving or walking. Nothing special about a woman jogging in the morning.

Or was there?

In the back of Elle's mind she saw something.

Not something…someone. A girl.

And the girl was running for her life. Elle closed her eyes, let the picture come into focus. It was a teenage girl who was running. Long stick-thin legs, arms pumping, feet pounding the fresh green earth under her feet and trees racing past her with every step. She ran because someone chased her. A man. A beautiful man who was beauty and music and reason personified.

"Don't run…" Elle whispered to the girl. "He's the only one you shouldn't run away from."

Elle's eyes opened, but the vision remained.

"Fuck…" Elle sat down on her bed with a groan.

Kyrie's prayer had been answered.

Elle had the most perfect idea.

16

Haiti

BY DAWN THE NEXT MORNING, KINGSLEY HAD RE-
turned to his beach hut. He'd only slept an hour or so the night
before. He hadn't wanted to waste a single moment he had with
Juliette sleeping. When she wouldn't talk to him, he'd fucked
her again. And again. He'd spent most of the night inside one
part of her body or another. They'd had so much sex he could
hardly move this morning. And he didn't want to move, didn't
want to think. But when he closed his eyes all he could hear
was Juliette's voice speaking her perfect French.

"Mort," she'd said when he asked her what he could give her.
Death.

She wanted to die. And she wanted him to kill her. But he'd
kill himself first before he killed her.

Madness. She'd refused to say anything more to him about
last night. She'd only kissed him until he forgot everything.
But this morning, he remembered.

Rolling out of his bed hurt but he did it anyway. He found
his cell phone and dialed home. Calliope answered on the
third ring.

"Yes, Mr. King?"

"Report?"

"It's too quiet here," she said. "The dogs are napping. The house is closed up like you asked. Are you coming home soon?"

"Not yet. Look, I need you to find out some information for me."

"Absolutely," she said, and he could hear the smile in her voice. His assistants were always chosen for their interest in and ability to find out things they shouldn't know and get themselves in trouble. Calliope, although painfully young, was no exception.

"I have an address," he said. "A house outside Petionville. I need you to see who owns it." He gave her the address. "Also, look up a name for me. Juliette Toussaint."

"Is she pretty?"

"Stunning. I've never seen her equal."

"Good. Are you bringing her back with you?"

"I will or I'll die trying."

Calliope laughed. "You sound much more like your old self," she said, and he could hear her typing in the background. "I've missed you. Everybody really misses you."

"That's not true."

"Okay, your ex-girlfriends don't miss you, but everyone else does. People think you're up to something since you've been gone so long. They're talking about you and Elle both being gone."

"What's everyone saying?" he asked, curious despite himself.

"Um…well, one rumor I heard is that you and Elle fell in love. You stole her from her priest and eloped with her. You two are supposedly on an around-the-world honeymoon."

"She would commit ritual suicide in Times Square before she married me. Anything else?"

"Some people think you're on a talent scouting mission, and you're out to find new Subs and Doms for the club."

"Not true, but much more likely than the first rumor."

"I heard someone say you'd run out of money and that's why you sold the Cuffs and Le Cirque."

"I have so much money I couldn't spend it all in ten lifetimes. Especially now that I sold the clubs."

"You might not want to know this...but there's this new Dom around who's talking shit about you."

"Who?" Kingsley demanded.

"He works for a new kink club. His name is Brad Wolfe."

"I refuse to believe that's his real name."

"He was at a party me and Tessa were at. Wolfe said you probably got in trouble with the law and you're on the run from the cops."

"If you see him again, tell him I'm on vacation. With his mother."

"I'll send him that message today. With pleasure. Are you ever coming back?"

"I'll come back as soon as I can. I have unfinished business here, however."

"Well, you have the most beautiful woman in the world to deal with, right?"

"Absolument."

"We need a new white queen around here now that Elle's gone."

"Juliette's black."

"Okay, a new black queen then," Calliope said. "I don't care what color she is. But it's really boring around here without you and Elle. It's like..."

"What?"

"It's like the lights went out when she left." Calliope paused. "Literally. I've never seen the town house this dark. No one ever stops by anymore. It feels like the whole Underground's gone dark."

"I know," Kingsley said. That's exactly what it was. And now she was gone and everything had gone dark.

"Elle was supposed to teach me how to sub. She said I was a natural."

"I'll find you a teacher when I get back."

"I don't want another teacher. I liked her."

"Has anyone heard anything from her? Has she contacted anyone at all? Griffin? Tessa? Irina?" Kingsley asked, already knowing the answer. He knew Calliope would have called the second she had news.

"No. Sorry, King. No word from her or your priest. Do you want me to send someone to check on him?"

"Leave him be. He'll be fine."

"Are you sure about that?"

Kingsley considered lying. Reconsidered it.

"No. If she doesn't come back to him, I doubt he'll ever be fine again."

"King, it's been eight months. I don't think she's coming back."

"That's her choice then." He kept his voice flat, but inside his guts churned with the idea he might never see Elle again. That maybe no one would ever see her again. "Did you find anything for me?"

"Yeah, here it is. That address? It belongs to Gérard Guill-roy."

"Why do I know that name?"

"Did you have to see him about your passport?"

"Why would I have to see him about my passport?"

"Because he's the French ambassador to Haiti."

Kingsley's blood went cold.

"The man who owns that house…the address I gave you, he's the French ambassador to Haiti?"

"He is. Has been for over fifteen years. Forty-eight years old. Two children in their late twenties. One grandson. Rich wife lives in Paris. They're still married but apparently separated. She stays in France. He spends most of his time in Haiti. What about him?"

"He's forty-eight you say?"

"But incredibly handsome. Silver fox."

"What?"

"I mean he has gray hair. But he's really handsome. French George Clooney."

"And rich?"

"Super rich. He's got Oprah money. Should I send you all this stuff I have on him?"

"No. And pretend we never had this conversation."

"I pretend that with all our conversations."

"What about Juliette? Did you find anything on her?"

"Nothing but the basics. Age and birth date. Born in a Petionville hospital. Parents aren't married. Father's and mother's names are listed. That's it."

"There has to be more."

"This is Haiti, not Manhattan," Calliope reminded him. "Not every country has computerized records on everything."

"They should. It would make my life easier."

"Yours and mine both, boss. But if you want to know more about this girl, why don't you ask her yourself?"

"I've asked. I can't get anything out of her."

"Why not? Did you piss her off?"

"I fucked her for eight straight hours last night."

"Eight hours? Tell me again why we're not sleeping together." Calliope sighed.

"Because you're eighteen, and I don't sleep with my assistants."

"You're no fun."

"I'm old enough to be your father, and you should remember that."

"Juliette is thirteen years younger than you are."

"Do as I say, not as I do."

"I don't know why I put up with you," Calliope said. "Except you're gorgeous and you pay me really well to put up with you."

"I'll give you a raise if you can find out anything about Juliette. Anything at all. Parents. Siblings. Hospital records. I'll see what I can do on this end."

"Got it. I'll call if I find anything," Calliope said. He could hear one of his dogs barking in the background.

"Who is that? Brutus?" he asked.

"Max. They miss you."

"I miss them, too," Kingsley said. "Talk soon."

"Hey, King?" Calliope asked before he could hang up.

"Oui?"

"She's never coming back, is she?"

"I don't know. But I wouldn't get my hopes up if I were you."

"Fuck."

Kingsley laughed.

"Sorry, boss," Calliope said.

"Don't be sorry, *chérie.* I feel the same. If…" He stopped and took a breath. "Cal, if she calls for any reason, give her a message for me."

"What's the message?"

"Tell her I'm sorry."

"You're sorry? For what?"

"She'll know."

"Okay," Calliope said, her voice soft. "I'll give her the message. Do you have any idea when you're coming back?"

"I'll come back when I can convince Juliette to come back with me. I'm not leaving this island without her."

"Then stop wasting time talking to me. Go get her, boss."

Kingsley smiled. "Yes, ma'am."

He hung up the phone and threw on clean clothes. For months now he'd been living the life of a beach bum. Doing nothing, going nowhere except from one beach to another.

Weeks had passed when he hadn't even bothered putting on shoes.

But he had never desired any woman the way he'd desired Juliette. And he hadn't been exaggerating. He would not leave Haiti without her. Enough killing time. Enough hiding. Enough grieving.

It was time to go back to work.

He made a call to his accountant and had money wired into a Haitian bank account.

Then Kingsley got dressed and went shopping.

First he rented a car using the fake ID he'd brought with him in his duffel. They didn't care about who he was at the rental place anyway, as long as the money was real. He picked out a black Jaguar. Something sleek and shiny, but not ostentatious.

Second he purchased five suits in beach-appropriate colors. He felt more like himself already.

Third purchase, a gun and ammunition. By sleeping with Juliette he'd inadvertently found himself swimming in the deep end of the ocean. He needed to be prepared.

In two days, he had transformed his beach hut into a home worthy of a woman like Juliette. Complete with a much larger bed.

Without waiting for an invitation Kingsley knew wouldn't come, he drove the long winding road up to Guillroy's home, where Juliette had taken him. In the light of the late-afternoon sun, the road appeared far less treacherous than it had when Juliette had driven him there two nights earlier.

He'd paid close attention to everything she'd done, every turn she'd made. He even knew the security code she'd punched into the gate. He didn't punch it in, however. He parked the car far back from the gate to the house and walked through the trees on the side of the road until he found the edge of the property. It was easy enough to scale the wall and jump down onto the lawn. He stayed away from the driveway, from the one security camera he'd noted, and took the most circuitous, most hidden route possible to get to the house.

He couldn't get caught. He knew that. If he got caught breaking into Guillroy's house, he could be arrested and deported.

But he had to see her again. She'd said they could only have one night together but he refused to believe she'd meant it. He needed all her nights, not just that one. And he needed to give her all of his.

Kingsley made it to the house at last and carefully walked its perimeter, looking everywhere for Juliette. The house was open on every level—open doors, open windows. Anything to keep the air flowing and the heat at bay. Finally he saw her. She emerged from a set of open double doors at the back of the house and stood on the balcony looking out onto the garden. The sight of her alone swept the breath from his body. She wore a white dress, strapless with an ankle-length skirt that moved with the breeze. Every kiss of wind bared her long beautiful legs to her knees. He grew hard simply looking at her. He'd been joking with Calliope when he'd said he would have this woman or die trying. Now he made the vow to himself. Whatever it took, she would be his.

He started to step out from the shadows of the trees, but then a man appeared behind her. He was tall, gray-haired, handsome as Calliope had said. He dipped his head and kissed Juliette on the side of her neck.

It was nothing but a kiss, a gentle kiss between lovers. But the sight of Juliette's passive resigned acceptance of the kiss sent possessive rage welling up within Kingsley. It took everything within him, all his sanity, all his willpower to not pull his gun right then and shoot Gérard between the eyes.

Gérard took her by the arm and together they walked along the balcony and disappeared through another door.

Without knowing why he did it, Kingsley walked up the

steps. He took off his shoes and as silently as he could, followed them.

The door they'd passed through led to some kind of sitting room. He went through the room and out into the hall. Carefully as he could, he looked in every room he walked past. One room was well decorated with a woman's taste—French novels on the shelves, a Bible by the bed and the scent of jasmine perfume in the air.

Juliette's room.

Kingsley entered it, shut the door behind him. He opened the closet door and found her clothes hanging there. A few of the island print dresses still had tags on them. They were from the finest fashion houses, the most luxe designers. One dress cost more than one of Kingsley's hand-tailored suits. He saw the canvas bag she'd carried on the floor of her closet. It still had the rocks in it. Why did she have a bag of heavy rocks? It made no sense. He closed the closet door and gazed around her bedroom. The bed was queen-size and the sheets were white, soft, and the bed looked inviting and luxurious. This was a room designed for seduction, for sex. It even had a slatted headboard and he noticed dings in the wood and faded areas. Someone had been cuffed and/or tied to this headboard on many occasions. His own bedposts bore the same marks. The candles on the bedside table no doubt served a dual purpose—ambience and sadism. He opened a drawer and found further evidence of this—lubricant, handcuffs, a small flogger. But he saw something else, too. A book. Kingsley fully expected it to be a book about sex, but it wasn't. It was a biography of Virginia Woolf translated into French. He flipped through it and found where someone had left in a bookmark. It was on the page that detailed Woolf's suicide.

Woolf filled the pockets of her coat with stones, waded into the river, and drowned herself.

Kingsley closed his eyes and felt the life go out of him. Juliette was planning to kill herself. That's what the rocks in the bag were for, why she'd had rocks at the ready when the boys attacked the birds.

Sickened by his discovery he shut the book and shoved it back into the drawer.

He withdrew quickly from the room and walked down the hallway again. He had to see her if only to see that she was alive and well. Or at least alive. If she had a plan to kill herself, she certainly wasn't well.

Kingsley found a room with a door that led to an interior garden. At the far end of that room was another door, a glass door standing open.

Quietly...so quietly he didn't let himself breathe, Kingsley came to the glass door. He angled himself so that he could see out, but no one could see him inside.

They stood in the center of the garden, Gérard and Juliette. And now the kiss they shared was one of ardor, at least on Gérard's part. Juliette stood before him, receiving the kiss and returning it, but without any of the passion Kingsley knew she had within her.

Gérard's mouth moved from hers to her neck. He pulled her dress down and bared her breasts to him. He cupped the back of her neck, forced her to arch her back, and then kissed her breasts like a man possessed. Juliette put her hands on his shoulders to steady herself and she received his attentions without protest. Not only did she not protest, she seemed to enjoy it, him, all of it.

With a show of strength that Kingsley found in poor taste, Gérard lifted Juliette and carried her five steps to the chaise longue that sat under an umbrella by a clear blue swimming pool. He stripped naked in seconds and pushed the skirt of Juliette's dress to her stomach. She had nothing on underneath and when he mounted her and entered her, she gave him no resistance at all. She simply opened her legs, received him into her and let him have his way with her body.

Gérard sucked hard on her nipples and she lay beneath him, running her hands through his short silver hair, whispering words that must have been encouragements, though Kingsley couldn't hear them. He thrust hard into her body and she lifted her hips to take him. He gripped her shoulders as he bore into her with his most powerful thrusts. She should have just lain there. She should have hated it. She should have borne it in stoic silence, made a martyr of herself, or a corpse. Instead, as his hips pumped into hers and his hands grasped her breasts, pinched her nipples and rubbed her clitoris, she pumped back, moving with him, an equal partner in pleasure.

After a few minutes Gérard pulled out, motioned with his hand, and Juliette turned over onto her hands and knees. He entered her from behind now, gripping her hips, pulling her back hard against him as he pushed forward and into her.

Kingsley took the tiniest step forward and Juliette's eyes flashed open. Had she heard him? He knew Gérard had not. He was too lost in his own pleasure to even notice her utter indifference to him. But Juliette, she stared into the shadows where Kingsley stood.

"Go." She mouthed the word at him. "Go."

It was the last thing he wanted to do. But Gérard gave a hoarse cry as he finished inside her and rested his body on top of hers.

Gérard pulled out of her body and she rolled onto her back. She smiled up at her lover and mouthed, *"Merci."*

He had two choices as he counted them. He could kill Gérard right now for no other reason than he'd touched the woman Kingsley already considered his own property.

Or he could do what she'd ordered him to do.

She'd told him to go.

Kingsley left.

17

JOHN APOLLO CHASED DAPHNE ALL THE WAY INTO THE *woods behind the school. Daphne feinted left, but he didn't fall for it. She took a sharp turn right, and he followed close behind. He was fast but she was faster. But he was male and had better stamina. After two miles on rough terrain she couldn't go another step. She collapsed against a tree and swallowed air until she coughed.*

"Don't touch me," she said when he came to stand in front of her.

"I won't." He was panting just as hard as she was. She'd never seen perfect John Apollo looking so wrecked. His dark hair fell over his forehead in a wet mass, his jeans splashed with mud and muck, his shirt stained with sweat. "I just need to talk to you. Please talk to me."

"You killed my brother." Her hatred for this man in front of her was like a poison arrow in her heart. She felt the point digging in deeper with every breath.

"I know," he said between heavy breaths. "I know I did."

Those were the last words she expected from him.

"I killed your brother, yes," he said, and it sounded as though he were exorcizing a demon with his confession. "And I don't regret it."

"How can you say that? He was—"

"He was bashing another student's face into the wall, Daphne.

You're sixteen years old now. Grow up and face the truth that your brother was a time bomb. And he went off."

"You didn't have to kill him."

"Do you think that's what I wanted? I was trying to restrain him, not kill him."

"It doesn't matter what you were doing. He's dead."

"He's dead and another boy isn't. My conscience is clear."

"Well, good for you," Daphne said, anger boiling as hot as her blood. "My brother's still dead but you sleep like a baby at night."

"I don't. I don't sleep at all at night. I can't sleep."

"Because you killed my brother?"

"Because I'm in love with you."

Daphne only stared at him. He bent over and coughed.

"You're in love with me?"

"Of course I'm in love with you. Do you think I'd run after you for three goddamn miles in the woods in loafers if I wasn't?"

Daphne ran her hands through her hair.

She laughed.

She laughed and then John laughed. The laugh rolled through her like a wave washing all the anger out of her heart. It poured out sobs that crested and ebbed. Before she knew it, John had her in his arms.

"He tried to choke me once," Daphne whispered in his ear. "I thought my own brother would kill me. But he loved me. He did love me."

"He loved you," John whispered, stroking her hair. "I'm sure he didn't want to be how he was. He was lucky he had you to love him back."

"I don't love you back." Daphne met his eyes. "I can't."

"I know." John nodded. "It's fine. I don't expect you to. Just let me love you, and let me help you and that'll be enough."

"It's not enough."

"What else is there then?" he asked, wiping her face with the end of his sleeve.

She raised her face to his and kissed him. He pulled back and looked at her. She saw in his eyes it was the last thing he expected her to do.

His eyes changed from shock to something else. The change scared her, but she didn't look away. And when he kissed her, she wasn't shocked at all.

She opened her mouth and his tongue slipped inside. He grabbed the strap of her tank top and yanked it down her arm. A rough hand reached into her bra and cupped her breast, pinching the nipple and squeezing it. She'd never been touched like this before, and the pleasure of it left her gasping. He rolled her nipples between his fingers and she moaned into his mouth. His hips pushed into hers, and she felt something big and brutally hard against her, and it made her ache with a new kind of wanting. John lowered his head to her chest, pulled her bra down to bare her breasts and sucked on her nipple.

Nobody had taught her how to be kissed like this. She'd taken sex ed, but it hadn't prepared her for being pushed up against a tree in the woods with a twenty-four-year-old cop sucking and fondling her breasts. She thought about asking him to stop, but right then he chose to slip his hand into her running shorts and touch her clitoris. All words, all rationality even, left her, and all she could get out of her lips was one desperate, "Please…"

Please stop? Please don't stop? She didn't know what she begged for, only that she had to beg for it.

John grasped her shorts and pulled them down and off her. He ripped her shirt up and off her and her bra joined the rest of her clothes on the ground. She needed skin, needed contact. With terrified fingers, she unbuttoned John's shirt and got it halfway down his arms before he lifted her off her feet and brought her down onto him.

She cried out, a sound that echoed through the quiet forest around them.

Instinctively Daphne wrapped her legs around his waist and her arms around his shoulders. The bark on the tree cut into her naked back but she couldn't feel it, couldn't feel anything but him inside her.

"Shh…" John whispered in her ear. "It's all right. I'll make it all right."

"I've never—"

"I know," he said. His fingers dug into her hips. Why did this pain feel so good? So necessary? Like only this pain could banish the pain from her brother's death? This was the pain she'd been waiting for. "Let me hold you. I'll stop when you tell me to."

She buried her head into the crook of his neck and nodded. She didn't want him to stop but she didn't know what to do, how to proceed. John knew, though. He pulled her hips toward him as he pushed against her. When he did it again, it felt as if something gave way inside her and she opened up for him. Her body wanted him in it. Her head fell back and her hips moved on his, working against him and with him until he lifted her up again and brought her down once more, harder this time, impaling her on his cock all the way to the center of her stomach. His mouth was on her mouth again, his tongue in her mouth. The kiss was wild, hungry, violent, as were the thrusts that he slammed into her. She couldn't get enough of this part of him inside her. She'd never get enough of it.

The heat of their joined bodies rose to a fever pitch. She moved her mouth from his so she could breathe. He'd pounded her so hard against the tree behind her she felt as if she would become one with it as she became one with John. Her hands grasped his broad muscular shoulders and her nipples tightened painfully against his burning chest. He'd said he would stop if she told him to but she knew they were both too far gone to stop now. Ecstasy writhed and trembled along every nerve inside her hips. Her vagina poured wetness over him, a mix of blood and desire. Her muscles contracted into a knot and with a cry she couldn't contain, she exploded around his still-thrusting length. As she spasmed and flinched, he slammed into her with rough jerks of his pelvis, at last coming inside her with a burning rush.

Finally it stopped. Her heart rattled against her rib cage like a prisoner banging on the bars. But John lowered her feet to the ground. He pulled out slowly and she winced in fresh agony.

"Daphne..." he breathed as he kissed her stomach, caressed her nipples with his tongue, kissed her neck and mouth. Even as his semen dripped down her thighs, he couldn't stop touching her.

"Stop, please..." At last she got the words out. As promised, he stopped. He stepped away from her and nervously straightened his clothes. Before he buttoned his shirt again, she saw she'd left deep red scratches on his shoulders.

In pain like she'd never felt before, she got onto her hands and knees and gathered her clothes.

"Daphne, I—"

She raised her hand.

"Don't talk to me," she said. "You killed River and fucking me doesn't change anything."

She pulled her shorts on and winced as the fabric met the ravaged flesh. Her arms shook when she hooked her bra and pulled on her running tank again.

"Tell me what I can do to help," he said. He was begging, pleading, offering her anything. She saw it in his eyes—he would do anything she asked.

"Take me to your house," she said. "And what you just did to me—"

"What? Tell me."

She looked up at him.

"Do it again."

"What do you think?" Elle asked, bracing herself for Kyrie's judgment. She sorted through a pile of towels she needed to fold. If she looked busy maybe Kyrie wouldn't notice how nervous she was, letting someone else read the story she'd been writing.

"You made Apollo into a cop?" Kyrie asked, flipping through the sixty handwritten pages Elle had created over the past week.

"Yeah, and Daphne and her brother lived in a group home— no parents. Seemed like a good idea at the time," Elle said. "Trying to make the story more contemporary. Daphne's a runner. That's the only thing I could think of that would be like a wood nymph—a girl who runs cross-country."

"He's also a music teacher?"

"Well, Apollo was the god of music," Elle said, "and I needed a reason for him to be at the group home. He volunteers there with the kids in the home, teaches them music. He's an off-duty cop, so when her brother goes off and starts beating another kid to death, he intervenes and Daphne's brother dies in the process."

"Where did the arrows go?"

"I thought it would be more interesting if Daphne had a really good reason for hating Apollo rather than just getting hit by an arrow from a pissy little cherub with an inferiority complex. So I gave her a twin brother who was emotionally unstable and then had Mr. Apollo accidentally kill him while restraining him. Daphne blames him and *voila*! Hate."

"That's kind of dark," Kyrie said, flipping through the pages again.

Elle smiled. "I like dark."

"Cop–teenage girl affair. Interesting," Kyrie said, putting the pages back down.

"Just interesting?" Elle had been hoping for more of a reaction.

"Very interesting. And hot."

"Kyrie."

"What?"

"You're a nun. You're not allowed to find anything hot."

"If I put my hand on a stove, I'm allowed to find it hot. This story is the fictional equivalent of putting your hand on a hot stove."

"I'll take that as a compliment. Don't tell me if it isn't, okay?"

Kyrie's eyes went wide and she whistled to herself. Kyrie could whistle? Cute.

"This is wow," Kyrie said.

"Wow? I can live with wow." Elle tried to hold back her smile.

"Really wow. I love it. I have never loved a story as much as I love this story. I want to read it again. And I want to read more of it. I want it to be one thousand and ninety-five pages long so I can read one page a day for three straight years. Wait. Leap year. Better make it one thousand and ninety-six pages long."

"I think you're exaggerating."

"I'm not exaggerating," Kyrie said. "I love this story. You have to keep working on it. Please?"

"Sure, why not?" Elle said. "Nothing else to do around here. Except laundry."

"You could come to Mass."

"I could. I won't. But I could."

"Your mom is a nun. You're obviously Catholic. Why do I never see you at Mass?"

"I've gone to Mass enough for a lifetime."

"Are we getting into an area you don't want to talk about again?"

"Very much so," Elle said. "I'd rather talk about why you're still a virgin at twenty-one."

"Is it that surprising?"

"No girls even?"

"Elle," Kyrie said as she hopped off the counter, "I've never even been kissed."

"You have got to be kidding me." Elle stared blankly at her, the towel in her hand forgotten.

"I'm not counting the kisses you get in elementary school from boys who grab you from behind."

"No, those definitely don't count. Nothing before puberty counts."

"Well, what can I say? I come from a very Catholic family. I have three brothers and two sisters and the most conservative parents ever. And the day I realized I liked girls and only girls was the same day I realized I wanted to be a nun."

"How old were you?" Elle asked.

"Thirteen."

"You knew you wanted to be a nun when you were thirteen?"

"Sister Mary Patrick came to my high school and gave a little talk on joining religious orders. I fell in love with her and the idea of being a nun all at once. I think…"

Kyrie leaned back against the counter and crossed her arms. If Sister Mary Patrick had looked anything like Kyrie did now, like an angel all in white, no wonder Kyrie had fallen for her. "I think they became the same thing to me. The idea of love and the idea of joining a convent. They were one and the same, two strands of the same cord. If I wanted one I had to have the other."

"How's it working out for you so far?"

"So far…" Kyrie smiled. "So far the past month has been the happiest month of my life."

"Honeymoon phase," Elle said. "It'll pass."

"You think so?"

"I've been here long enough to see three novices go from 'This is Heaven on earth' to 'Get me the fuck out of here' already."

"But they didn't leave?"

"One did. Two are still here. She's better now. At least she stopped having panic attacks during Vespers. Sister Aquinas calls it progress."

"Your mom seems to love it here."

"She does. But Mom's wanted to be a nun since she was—I don't know. Forever, she says."

"What took her so long to join?"

"Me," Elle said with a shrug. She placed her folded towels into the basket and started on a new stack.

"She got pregnant with you?"

"When she was seventeen. Then she got divorced and of course you can't join a religious order if you're divorced and you have a kid. But then my father was killed and that meant she was technically a widow. She went back to college, got her degree and joined here a couple of years ago."

"Good for her."

"Yeah, I guess it is. I didn't see that at the time. I'm starting to see it now."

"You can see a change in her?"

"In Mom? Definitely. She used to be really angry," Elle said. "Angry at herself, but she took it out on me a lot. Not physically. She wasn't abusive or anything. Just…sad. Really sad and I made her even sadder." The memories of a hundred mother-daughter fights flashed through her mind in an instant. "She wasn't who she thought she should be. And now she finally is."

"It's a terrible thing to not be who God called you to be. I think that's the cause for most of the suffering in all the world," Kyrie said. "People trying to be who they aren't supposed to be or not getting to be who they should be."

"Maybe. But what do you do when you don't know what you're supposed to be?"

"Ask me. I'll tell you."

"Great. What am I supposed to be?"

Kyrie held up the pages again.

"This."

"That? A girl having sex with a cop?" Elle asked, arching her eyebrow. "I don't think I've ever fucked a cop. Or a music teacher."

"A writer," Kyrie said. "You should write books. Professionally. For money. Like my sister did."

"Write books," Elle said.

"Professionally," Kyrie repeated. "For money. There. I told

you I would figure out what you should do with your life. You can even do it here. You don't have to leave to do it."

"I'd probably have to go somewhere with a computer," Elle said. "You know, for typing. I doubt publishers have accepted handwritten manuscripts since 1890."

"Mother Prioress has a computer in her office."

"That's good. I'll ask her if I can borrow it to type up my novel about the rookie cop deflowering a high school girl against a tree after killing her brother."

"Well…you might not want to word it quite like that." Kyrie laughed. "Maybe call it a dissertation."

Elle winced at the word *dissertation*.

"What?" Kyrie asked.

"Force of habit. Sorry. Anyway, it's a fun idea, writing books. I've been writing short stories since I got here. Very depressing ones."

"Toss them," Kyrie said. "No money in short stories. Write novels."

"I'll think about it."

"You say that in a tone that makes me think you won't think about it."

"I'll think about it, I promise."

"You'll finish the book, right?" Kyrie asked. "I want to know what happens next."

"I don't know what happens next."

"You're smart. You'll figure it out. You should write more tree sex, though. That was fun."

"It's not as fun in real life. The bark on your back is really itchy."

"You've had tree sex?" Kyrie asked, her eyes wide.

"Not with a tree. Against a tree."

"Oh my." Kyrie grinned and leaned over Elle's ironing board. "Tell me all."

"I had sex once and it was against a tree. The end."

"Okay, maybe you shouldn't be a writer." Kyrie stood up straight again and sighed.

"I'm not going to tell the dirty details of my sex life to a virginal nun who's never been kissed."

"Elle, I will tell you the truth and you should believe it because it is the truth."

"What?"

Kyrie reached out and took Elle's hand in hers. It had been so long since someone had held her hand that Elle had forgotten how good it felt, the simple act of fingers touching fingers, of palms pressed to palms.

"The truth is…there is no one on earth who needs to hear the details of your sex life more than a virginal nun who has never been kissed."

Elle stared at Kyrie. She thought they'd been joking, only joking. And while Kyrie's words were joking, the way she said them was serious.

It wouldn't hurt anything, would it? A kiss? A kiss was such a small thing, small as a hiccup, small as a firefly. And maybe if she kissed Kyrie, it would scare the girl enough to send her running away. Then Elle could have her peace and quiet back. Worth the risk anyway.

It was only a kiss.

"Ellie? Ellie, are you here?"

Kyrie dropped Elle's hand as if it had caught fire.

They both turned to the door. Elle's mother rushed into the laundry room. Her pale skin was whiter than usual, almost as white as her habit.

"I'm here. What's up?" Elle glanced at Kyrie who was discreetly sliding Elle's pages underneath a pile of towels.

"Have either of you seen Sister Mary Angelica?"

"Which one is she?" Elle asked.

"The old one," Kyrie said. "Really old, right?"

"Yes, she's ninety-two. And she has dementia. She's wandered off again, and no one can find her."

"I've been in here for three hours," Elle said.

"When is the last time you saw her?" her mother asked Kyrie.

"Breakfast," Kyrie said. "Not since then."

"Everyone is looking for her," her mother said. "Can you help?"

"Yeah, sure." Elle dropped her towel back into the basket. Kyrie followed her out of the door. In the hallway they were met by Sister Aquinas.

"She's locked herself in the supply pantry in the infirmary," Sister Aquinas said. Her words were rushed, her faced flushed.

"Can't you unlock it?" Elle asked.

"No. It used to be an office so it's got an old lock on the inside. We haven't had the key in years."

"Did you call a locksmith?" her mother asked.

"Yes, but he's on a call and can't be here for another hour. There are needles in there, scalpels. We're going to have to take the door off the hinges," Sister Aquinas said. "Or call the fire department to come."

"Is it a normal lock?" Elle asked. "A key lock? Nothing fancy?"

"Nothing fancy," Sister Aquinas said.

"Hold on," Elle said. "I'll meet you in the infirmary."

She raced off down the hall to her cell.

"Elle?" Kyrie stood in the doorway of her room.

"I got this," Elle said. She pulled open her purse and dug to the bottom of it. From it she pulled out a leather case.

"Got what?" Kyrie asked. But Elle didn't answer. She ran off down the hall again and down the stairs. She could hear Kyrie behind her racing to catch up.

"What room?" Elle asked once she was in the infirmary. But she already saw it. Three sisters were kneeling by the door, their ears against it.

"She's crying her eyes out," one of them said. "She might be hurt."

"Get up," Elle said. The nuns hesitated a moment but then moved out of her way. She knelt on the floor in front of the lock and examined it. Sister Aquinas hadn't been kidding. The metal works were old and tarnished. This wouldn't be easy. She opened her case, pulled out a lock-pick tool and inserted it into the keyhole. It took some doing to get the ancient tumblers to move. By the time she'd pushed the first one up, sweat had beaded on Elle's forehead.

"Elle, can we help?"

Kyrie sounded as scared as Sister Mary Angelica but Elle only shook her head and pushed up the second tumbler. She wiped her sweaty palm on her jeans and a minute later, had the lock picked. Elle got up and wrenched the door open. Her mother and Sister Aquinas raced inside the pantry and brought out the weeping elderly nun.

Elle's mother took her gently by the arm and put her in a chair. She called for water and a towel and every nun in the room rushed to help Sister Mary John calm Sister Mary Angelica down.

Every nun in the room except for Kyrie.

"How do you know how to pick locks?" she asked Elle.

"Long story," Elle said, and put her lock-pick tool back into the case. She got off her knees and left the infirmary. She walked to the nearest bathroom. Kyrie followed.

"I'm serious. I want to know how you did that."

"Just a hobby," Elle said. "I was curious about how to pick locks. I figured out how to do it."

"Are you a cat burglar?"

Elle laughed. "I haven't stolen anything since I was fifteen years old. Well, one car, but I gave it back."

"You stole a car?"

"No, I was kidding. I borrowed it. It was a friend's."

"Who? The complicated guy?"

"No. A different guy. Doesn't matter. I'm not friends with him anymore." She turned on the water and washed the dirt and oil from the lock off her hands.

"Who taught you how to pick locks?"

"Kyrie, I'm not going to talk to you about any of this, okay?"

"Why not?"

"I told you. I don't want to talk about my life. I want to keep my head down, do my work and figure things out. I don't want to get into trouble because a little virgin nun has a crush on me and won't leave me the hell alone."

The smile and the delight washed out of Kyrie's eyes like color fading from too many washings.

"I don't have—"

"Yes, you do. You follow me everywhere, you ask me a million personal questions, you are obsessed with finding out why I'm here even though I've told you a dozen times I don't want to talk about it. You're not the first girl who's had a crush on me. I know what it looks like. And I'm not interested, okay? Go be a nun. Go back to the infirmary and help them with Sister Mary Angelica. Stop thinking about me."

Kyrie clasped her hands in front of her. They disappeared under her bell sleeves.

"I can't, Elle," Kyrie said. "I try to stop thinking about you and there you are, back in my mind again. I ask you about your life because I told myself that the reason I'm thinking about you is because you're a mystery to me. And if I solve the mystery then you won't be so interesting to me anymore, and I won't think about you anymore. But it's not working. You won't tell my anything about yourself and here I am, still thinking about you, morning, noon and night." Kyrie paused, and when she spoke again her voice had become a whisper. "Especially at night."

"That's not my problem," Elle said, grabbing a paper towel to dry off her hands.

"I know it's not. But maybe if you tried to help me…maybe if you told me something about you…how you know how to pick locks or why you came here or why your complications are so complicated. I mean, I know complicated. I'm a nun with a crush on another woman who's standing two feet in front of me. That's complicated."

"He's a priest."

"What?"

"You really want to know why my situation is so complicated? There. I told you. My lover who I ran away from is a Catholic priest. He was into hardcore kink, sadism and bondage, and I taught myself how to pick locks so I could get out of anything he put me in if I wanted to. There you go. Your questions are answered."

Kyrie stared at her. Her eyes were wide with shock. She said not a word, made not a sound. It was the longest Kyrie had ever been silent in her presence. The shock in her blue eyes turned to horror and then something worse.

Disgust.

Kyrie turned and walked out of the bathroom without another word.

And as she'd wanted, Elle was finally alone.

18

ELEANOR TURNED THE PAGE IN HER BOOK, PUSHED A second pillow under her head and read. She was so engrossed in the story she barely heard the door to her bedroom open. But she wasn't so engrossed in the story that she didn't feel the bed move when someone sat on it.

Still, she kept reading, not looking away from the words in front of her.

"The Count of Monte Cristo," Kingsley said, as he reached out and plucked the book from her hands. "Excellent choice. A story of bitter vengeance with a perfect ending."

"I'm enjoying it," she said. "*Was* enjoying it, until someone rudely interrupted." She took the book back from him with a flourish and settled into her pillows. It was nearly midnight so she wore only one of Kingsley's shirts—a white one with pearl buttons down the front. She crossed one leg over the other and attempted to resume her reading. Then she felt Kingsley's hands on her legs. He uncrossed them for her.

"Kingsley…"

"Are you feeling better, *chérie?*"

She looked over the top of her book at him.

"Much."

"Bon. Très bon," Kingsley said as he bent and kissed her thigh. She kept reading.

Kingsley opened the third button on his shirt she'd stolen to sleep in. He pushed the fabric aside and kissed her left nipple. She felt a delicious pull in her stomach.

"Kingsley, are you here to seduce me?" she asked. "While I'm trying to read?"

He rolled his tongue around her nipple before answering, *"Oui."*

"Oh," she said, closing the book with a loud snap. "What the fuck am I doing reading this then?"

She tossed the book across the room. Kingsley laughed and sat up.

"You should be nicer to Dumas," he said. "The greatest French novelist."

"I'd rather be nice to you, *monsieur.* The greatest French lover."

Kingsley straddled her knees and kissed her on the lips. It was a slow, soft sensual kiss, merely a prelude to whatever decadent plans he had for her that night. As much as she missed Søren when he was gone, at least he always left her with the world's best babysitter.

Kingsley slipped his hand under her shirt and rested it on her stomach. Like the well-trained submissive she was, she opened her legs for him and gave him access to every part of her he could possibly want.

He parted the folds of her vulva with his fingertips and gently massaged the outside of her vagina. When she grew wet from his touch, he pushed one finger into her.

"You're the only woman I come inside," he said, kneading her favorite spot right under her pubic bone. "Did you know that?"

She flushed a little at his words. Kingsley was adamant about using condoms. There wasn't a room in the house that didn't hold a crystal bowl of them. But with her he never used one. Her and only her.

"I know, *monsieur*."

"Do you know why?" he asked, pushing in a second finger.

"No."

"He comes inside you," Kingsley said. "And that makes this hole very special to me."

She laughed and raised her hips.

"Come inside me all you want. He gave me to you. Until he gets back, I'm all yours."

They kissed again, kissed for a long time as he fucked her with his fingers. He spread them apart inside her, opening her up for him. Soon she was dripping wet and panting.

"I was thinking of trying something special with you," Kingsley said. "Since you are so special to him and to me."

"Anything you want," she said. "You know I'll do whatever you tell me to do."

Kingsley kissed her earlobe, her neck under her ear.

"Come to my bedroom. I'll tell you there. But…"

She raised an eyebrow at him.

"But what?"

"What we do, it will have to stay a secret," he whispered.

"A secret? From who?"

"From him."

She stiffened a moment.

"Why do we have to keep it a secret from Søren?" she asked. "He doesn't care what kink we do."

"He'll care about this," Kingsley said with a smile that for one split second looked almost nervous.

"What is it?"

Kingsley pulled his fingers out of her.

"Come find out. If you dare," he said, and the old roguish smile was back.

He left her alone in her bedroom as he walked back to his.

Eleanor wanted to follow him, but she hesitated. What could Kingsley have planned for them tonight that was so kinky he didn't want her to tell Søren about it? She and Kingsley had done every sort of kink she could think of, even the harder stuff like rape-play, breath-play, blood-play. Søren was usually there for it, but not always. All that mattered to Søren was that she was a good girl, submitted to Kingsley when told to and told Søren all the erotic details of whatever happened afterward.

Something they couldn't tell Søren? A mix of desire and curiosity led her down the hall to Kingsley's bedroom. When she opened the door she found he'd lit half a dozen candles. They burned on each side of his big red bed. And the dogs that always slept in his room at the foot of his bed were nowhere to be seen.

"Lock the door," he said, a rare command. No one would dare interrupt the master of the house in his bedroom without knocking first.

She locked the door behind her.

"King, I'm a little freaked out here," she admitted as she walked to him. He stood by the bed and had already started undressing. He was barefoot and had removed his jacket. He could have been the Count of Monte Cristo with his fitted black trousers, his white shirt and black-and-red embroidered vest. His hair was looking particularly Byronic tonight. His ex-girlfriend Charlie had cut it short, but he'd started growing it back out and now it curled its way to his earlobes.

"If it makes you feel better, so am I."

"That doesn't make me feel better at all. None of this does."

She nodded at the candles, shivered at the quiet, the quiet that radiated from Kingsley outward. He was different tonight. Nothing like the Kingsley she was used to, the Kingsley who could silence her with a stare, put her onto her knees with a nod. Some days she couldn't get within five feet of him without him grabbing her, throwing her over his lap and spanking her until she collapsed into screams and laughter. Nothing was right about this. Kingsley nervous? Humbled? She shouldn't be making eye contact with him now. She should already be on her knees, at his feet, obeying, serving, submitting.

He took a small quick breath and laid a hand on the side of her neck. His thumb massaged the ticklish spot under her ear.

"I know you know what I am," he said.

Eleanor swallowed.

"I know," she said.

"You can say it. I want to hear you say it."

"You're a switch," she said.

"And?"

"And a masochist."

"Did he tell you how much of a masochist?"

"He told me everything he did to you. And he told me you liked it."

"I didn't like it," he said. "I loved it. And more than that, Eleanor. I needed it."

"I understand. I need it too sometimes."

"Sometimes?" he asked. She heard the note of curiosity in his voice. "Not always. Only sometimes?"

"I always like it," she said. "Always love it. But I'm saying I know what it means to need it some nights."

"Are there nights you need something else?"

"What do you mean?"

"Are there nights you'd rather give pain than receive it?"

And then she knew what Kingsley wanted her to do. Her heart stopped. Her blood went cold. This was every kind of bad idea Kingsley had ever had.

"King…no," she said. If she hadn't had Kingsley's hands on her, she would have turned around and walked right out that second. "This absolutely cannot happen."

"Please," Kingsley said. "He won't have to know."

"Kingsley…" Unexpectedly tears sprang into her eyes. She was scared. Not scared. Terrified.

"I want you to hurt me, Eleanor. I need you to hurt me. Please?"

He lifted both hands to her face and brushed the tears away with his thumbs. He didn't seem the least surprised to see them on her face. In fact, he seemed to recognize them.

"I can't..." She pressed her face against his chest and he wrapped her in his arms.

"You can." He whispered the words into her hair. "We both know you have this desire in you. *Oui?*"

She paused only a moment before nodding her head against his chest.

"Oui," she said. She pulled back and looked up at him. "Are you sure you want me to do this?"

"Yes."

"You want me to hurt you?"

"Hurt me and use me. Anything you want from me, ask it."

"Anything? No limits?"

"The only limit is collars. I hate them."

"I know, I know. Collars are for dogs. Where are the dogs anyway?"

"I put them downstairs."

"Why?"

"The dogs, they love you, but they're trained to protect me," he said. "If they witnessed someone hurting me, they wouldn't react well."

"You were so sure I'd say yes that you locked the dogs downstairs?"

Kingsley smiled. Kingsley nodded. Kingsley was an arrogant son of a bitch and she loved him for it.

"Yes," she said. "I mean, yes, I'll try. I don't know if I'll be any good at it. But I'll try. But I'm only doing this because you told me to do it. You're still topping. You ordered me to hurt you. Right?"

"If that's what you need to believe..."

"I do."

"You might be surprised how much you like it."

"I've never done this before." She felt nervous as a virgin. No, far more nervous. She hadn't been nervous at all the night she'd given her virginity to Søren. This seemed like a far more terrifying threshold to cross. And yet...

"You have done it. I watch you with the other Submissives and they do everything you tell them to do. You scare the shit out of them every day."

"If they weren't such whiny little pussies, I wouldn't have to."

"See?" He cupped her face with both hands. "There it is. Pure dominance. It's in you. I saw it in you the night we met. You aren't afraid to make decisions. You aren't afraid to give orders. You aren't afraid to be hated."

"Neither is Søren."

"*Oui*. And there is no one more dominant than he. But maybe you..."

"Maybe me, what?"

"Maybe you could give him a run for his money, no?"

Eleanor took a long shuddering breath.

"Well, it's worth a shot anyway," she said.

Kingsley laughed then, a low sensual laugh that made her toes curl and her skin shiver. She did want him. She felt desire for him as acute as pain. It had been over two weeks since she'd had sex. She wouldn't last a night more without it. Without him.

"Any other limits?" she asked.

He shook his head.

"Hurt me," he said. "You know where everything is in the room. Whatever he does to you, you can do it to me."

"If Søren finds out I topped you..." Eleanor said. "Without him here? Without his permission?"

"What he doesn't know won't hurt us." He raised one finger to his lips.

She would have been less scared had she agreed to kill someone for Kingsley. But still, she raised her finger to her lips, as well.

Now, here they were, alone in Kingsley's bedroom. And she was going to hurt him. And she'd never done anything like this before in her life. Where did she start?

She took a step back and looked Kingsley up and down. He needed something. Not a collar but something, something to make everything different between them.

"How do you feel about blindfolds?" she asked.

"I don't mind them, but I'd rather see you."

"You see me all the time," she reminded him.

He gave her a long look, heated and heavy with meaning. "But not like this."

She took a quick breath. "No." She couldn't argue with him there. "Not like this."

Stepping back in front of him she started to unbutton his vest. She'd undressed him before at his command, but never of her own volition. He stood there, still and submissive, letting her pull the vest down and off his arms. She thought about folding it, thought about hanging it up. This was part of one of Kingsley's sexiest Regency-style suits, after all. And likely one of his most expensive. Instead, she paused, looked at it and then dropped it on the floor.

"You're more like him than you can possibly know," Kingsley said.

To which Eleanor replied, "Don't speak until spoken to."

Kingsley bowed his head in apology. She felt something new surging through her veins, something sweet and spiked and utterly intoxicating.

Power.

Kingsley remained still as she unbuttoned his shirt and pulled it out of his trousers. He had such a beautiful body—all lean muscle and old scars—that she couldn't stop herself from kissing his naked shoulder as she pushed his shirt down his arms.

First a kiss on the naked shoulder, then on the naked bicep, then the naked forearm and the naked wrist.

The naked wrist.

She left him standing there while she went down on her hands and knees by the bed. She pulled out a suitcase and opened it up. Inside was bondage equipment—ropes, adjustable spreader bars, cuffs and collars.

And gauntlets.

She took out two black leather gauntlets and laid them on the bed. She'd seen male submissives at The 8th Circle wearing various sorts of leather. Bicep cuffs, chest harnesses, but her favorite were the gauntlets. They looked so medieval, like something a knight would wear under his armor. And after a battle he'd strip down to nothing but the dirt and sweat and the leather braces on his wrists.

Eleanor lifted Kingsley's arm and held it against her chest. She wrapped the brace around his forearm and laced it. Her hands shook as she did it and she knew Kingsley could see it. But he didn't tease her for once.

"You like leather?" he asked. His voice was soft and the gentleness of his tone made her even more nervous.

"Yeah, I do. On men especially."

"Why did you never tell me?"

She glanced up at him.

"You never asked."

Kingsley narrowed his eyes at her. "I should have asked. What other secrets are you keeping in here?"

He touched her temple and let his fingers trail down until they rested on her chest under her shirt and over her heart.

"Lots of secrets," she whispered.

"Tell me all your secrets. Tell me everything you want."

"You," she said. "Like this."

"Like what?"

"Submissive to me."

"You've fantasized about this?" he asked. "About me submitting to you?"

Finally she had the wrist brace on his left arm. Lacing the brace onto his right arm went much more smoothly. She could do this. She could.

It scared her to answer the question. The question wasn't a question but a box, and if they opened the lid to this box, God only knew what would come out.

"Please tell me, Elle," he said so quietly she could barely hear him even in the potent pregnant silence of the room.

"Yes."

And with that yes, she yanked the laces on the gauntlet and tied a neat quick bow.

When she had the braces on his arms, she looked him up and down.

"Almost perfect," she said, appraising her handiwork. She unbuttoned his trousers, pushed them down and told him to step out of them.

"Perfect," she said with a smile. "Absolutely perfect."

Eleanor had only ever been on the receiving end of a beating. She had no idea how to throw a flogger, wield a single-tail. And she certainly wasn't going to try to figure it out tonight. But there were other ways to hurt someone, ways she did know.

"Lie on your back," she ordered, and Kingsley did as he was told.

Wild. For years she'd been doing everything Kingsley and Søren told her to do.

Go here. Do this. Spread for him. Suck me here.

Stand there and take it and take it and take it…

Time to give as good as she got.

Kingsley was lying naked on the bed, naked but for the elaborate leather arm braces laced from his wrist halfway up his forearms.

Eleanor looked down at Kingsley. He kept his eyes lowered.

She snapped her fingers in front of his face, one of Søren's least endearing ways of getting her attention. It worked. Kingsley met her eyes.

"Are you sure?" she asked. "Completely 100 percent sure about this?"

"Elle, listen to me." He met her eyes and looked deep and hard into them. "Yes."

She nodded and took one more long breath. What to do... what to do... She'd been hurting herself since she was a teenager. She knew how to give pain, right? She'd been the first person to hurt her own body.

Then she had an idea.

She opened the drawer in his nightstand and pulled out a scalpel from a leather case. Then she picked up the lit candle.

"Blood-play or wax-play?" he asked. Both seemed amenable to him.

"Neither," she said.

She crawled onto the bed and straddled Kingsley's hips. She pushed herself against his erection but didn't let him inside her. His cock pulsed against her wet seam. She wanted him in her, yes, but she wanted to make him wait even more.

"I did this to myself when I was a kid. Except I used a curling iron. My curling iron's all the way in the other room, so we'll have to improvise a little."

She brought the blade of the scalpel into the flame of the candle and watched while the fire heated the metal.

When it turned a glowing red, she lowered the scalpel and pressed the flat of the blade against Kingsley's stomach.

With a gasp of pure pain, he closed his eyes tight and arched underneath her, arched so hard his cock went inside her. She shuddered as their bodies joined. She settled in on top of him, moving her hips to take him as deep as she could.

"Vicious bitch," he hissed through his clenched teeth. She'd given him a first-degree burn.

"Did I hurt you?" she asked, worried she'd crossed a line already.

"God, yes. Do it again," he said between harsh breaths. "Please."

Eleanor laughed. "Well, since you asked so nicely."

Then she brought the blade into the flame again, heated it once more and brought it back to his stomach.

The red-hot metal left half-moon shaped burns on his stomach. Every time she touched him with the flat of the scalpel blade, he shuddered as if in agony, grunted in the back of his throat and pushed his hips into her.

After the fifth burn, and the sixth, sex and pain became the same thing to them. Their bodies were joined but only when she pressed the blade against his stomach, his hips, his chest, against the tender flesh of his inner bicep, did he thrust up and into her.

Her own wetness poured out of her and coated him, sealing them together.

"How are you feeling?" she asked, more curious than caring.

"It's excruciating," Kingsley said. "Thank you."

"You want more?"

"As much as you can give."

"Will you heal in time before Søren comes home?"

"He's back when? Six weeks?" Kingsley looked down at the burns on his chest, hips and arms. "Maybe."

"Well, in for a penny, in for a pounding," she said, firing up the blade again.

She burned him a seventh time. Then an eighth. She went all the way to sixteen and then stopped.

"Sixteen's a good number," she said, putting the candle down.

"What does it mean to you?" he asked.

"I was sixteen when I saw you the first time. On the stairs at that orgy you were throwing. Remember what you said to me?"

Kingsley grinned. "I said, 'No children allowed.'"

"And yet…here I am." She pushed her hips forward and clenched her muscles around his cock.

"Ah, but you're not a little girl anymore. Not a virgin anymore."

"I haven't been a virgin since I was twenty."

He raised his hand and swept it through her hair. He touched her cheek, her chin, her lips and tapped her lightly under her chin.

"Not that kind of virgin," he said softly. "Not after tonight."

She turned her head and kissed his palm.

"Hold still," she said.

Kingsley lowered his arms. After that he didn't move even to breathe.

With the tip of the scalpel she carved a small "ES" into the delicate skin of his lower stomach, near enough to his cock to make him nervous. She went deep enough to draw blood but not so deep the cuts wouldn't heal in a day or two. Kingsley could blame his burns on someone else if it came to that. Her initials on this most intimate part of Kingsley's body would damn them both if Søren saw them.

"Beautiful." Kingsley sighed. His pupils were so dilated his eyes appeared solid black.

"It's not quite finished yet," she said. She picked up the candle one more time and let a drop of wax fall onto the broken skin.

Kingsley's fingers dug into the sheets, his shoulders lifted up and with a hot spurt, he came inside her. His orgasm caught them both off guard. He grunted and gasped as his hips rose and fell beneath her. The pleasure of it was so intense she almost came from the force of his climax. She'd never been aroused this way before, never felt this mix of pleasure and power. It scared her how much she loved having Kingsley underneath her, hurting him as she did, pushing him to the edge until he lost control and came without any warning.

He lay back on the bed, panting and breathing.

"I think you liked that," she said. Eleanor bent over and kissed him hard and deep.

"*Like* is not the word, *chérie*," he whispered against her lips.

"We can't ever tell him we did this," she said.

Kingsley smiled. "Our little secret."

Laughing softly she started to move again on him, riding him hard, chasing her own orgasm. She dug her fingernails into his chest, hard…harder…they broke the skin and kept breaking. Kingsley was brutally hard again inside her and when she came again, he came, too.

And when he came again inside her, Elle woke up.

She lay on her stomach on her bed at the abbey. Her hips pushed down and into the bed and her vagina clenched emptiness. When her orgasm faded out, she groaned into her pillow, rolled onto her back and stared up at the ceiling.

Another dream. She was losing her goddamn mind here.

Elle crawled out of her bed and pulled on her black silk pajama pants and camisole, and a black sweater. She shoved her feet into shoes, and she left her room and her burning bed behind.

Even now, almost eight months after leaving Søren, she still feared the front door that led to the outside world. Instead, she went out the back door into the garden and found a path to follow. It was brisk out on this spring night, and the air cooled her skin.

At the center of the garden stood a statue of the Virgin Mary, solid white stone and life-size, her belly rounded with the unborn Christ inside her. A full moon gave her enough light to see Mary's face. She looked so peaceful, so calm and serene. Elle had trouble believing a fourteen-year-old girl who got pregnant by God would be that relaxed about the situation.

"Can I tell you a secret?" Kyrie asked from behind Elle.

"Are you following me?"

"Yes. But only because I couldn't sleep. That's my window." Kyrie pointed to the nearest window looking out onto the garden.

"It's okay. I don't mind the company. What's your secret?"

"When I was twelve, I had the biggest crush on the Virgin Mary. Is that weird?"

Elle turned and found Kyrie standing in her white bathrobe and white veil behind her.

"Not really. She's beautiful. At least in all the paintings and statues she is."

"I like that she submitted to God. I always thought that was sexy what she said to God when He told her she would get pregnant with His child—'Behold the handmaid of the Lord. Let it be done unto me according to Your word.'"

Let it be done unto me... Elle had said similar words so many times in her life to Søren. *I am yours, do what you want to do with me. Whatever you want with my body, you can do it...*

"When I was fourteen, I wanted her life," Kyrie said. "I like to think Mary was a lesbian. I mean, it's the perfect situation for a closeted lesbian."

Elle laughed. "It is?"

"Well, of course. She can't come out to her family so the best way to pretend to be straight is by getting married. But she gets pregnant with God's child through the Holy Spirit. And then she's a perpetual virgin. Never has to have sex with her husband and yet he protects her and provides for her."

"Sounds like you," Elle said.

"Me?"

"Can't come out to your Catholic family. Married to a man

you'll never have sex with. That's what they call you all, right? Brides of Christ?"

Kyrie held up her left hand. She wore a wedding band on her ring finger.

"That's us."

"A warning, don't tell anyone but me your theory about Mary being a lesbian," Elle said. "Lots of people don't handle erotic speculation about Mary and Jesus very well."

"I'm not saying she was. Just my theory," Kyrie said.

"Søren had a theory like that, too," Elle said.

"Søren? Is that his name?"

Elle nodded. She hadn't spoken his name aloud in months.

"One of his names," she said. "He's half-Danish."

"What was his theory?"

"When Søren was in seminary, he wrote a paper positing that Jesus had been married and was widowed. Only explanation for why this thirty-something Jewish man would be unmarried, and no one would remark on it. Married young. Wife probably died in childbirth or for a thousand other reasons people died back then. Søren's professor called him a heretic. He was proud of that label. Then again, he's a Jesuit."

"This is the first time you've ever smiled while talking about him."

"I think this is the first time I've really talked about him in months," Elle said. "Telling a nun you used to sleep with a priest doesn't go over well."

"Yeah, I'm sorry for the way I reacted," Kyrie said. "That was...not cool of me."

"You're a nun and a virgin. I'd be surprised if you weren't a little disgusted with me."

"Reflex," Kyrie said. "Priest seduces a girl in his church. Hard not to flinch."

"It sounds sordid when you put it that way. It wasn't like that."

"Yes, but how am I supposed to know what it was like if you won't tell me anything?"

Elle shrugged. "Good point."

"I guess you couldn't sleep, either." Kyrie came to stand beside her.

"I was sleeping. I had a dream. It woke me up."

"Nightmare."

"Opposite of a nightmare."

"What's the opposite of a nightmare?"

"The dream I had." Elle laughed to herself. She could still feel Kingsley inside her. "About once a week I'll dream something that actually happened to me. These vivid erotic dreams. I've never dreamed like this before. It's like I'm reliving the entire moment, second by second. I woke up having an orgasm."

"I've had some pretty crazy dreams since coming here, too. They warn you that being isolated like this, cut off from the outside world, will cause your mind and your soul to dredge things up and force you to deal with all your unfinished business from your old life."

"What do you dream about?" Elle asked her. "What's your unfinished business?"

Kyrie shrugged. "I dream about Bethany a lot, my family. Everyone sort of fell apart after she was killed. The trial, the publicity...it's like a shipwreck. You start off strong, everybody holding on to each other for dear life. And then you drift away on the tides of your grief and hope you wash ashore someday."

"Is this where you washed up?" Elle asked. Kyrie always seemed far more interested in learning about Elle's life before the convent than talking about what hers had been like. Elle didn't blame the girl. Everyone deserved a fresh start free of baggage. Unfortunately no one ever really got what they deserved.

"This is my dry land," Kyrie said. "Being here...I finally feel like I'm on steady ground again. You?"

"I'm still at sea," Elle admitted. "Especially on nights like this when I wake up from my dreams and don't know where I am for a few seconds. Lost at sea and I can't find my sea legs. Maybe they were right about being here. Maybe I do have unfinished business."

"What were you dreaming about?"

"Do you really want to know?" Elle asked. "Or are you asking to make conversation?"

"I want to know. I want to know everything about you. Maybe for the wrong reasons, but there's at least one right reason in there. I do want to help you. Will you let me?"

Silence settled over them, over the garden, over the moment. In that silence, Elle made a decision. She was lonely and scared, and she didn't know what to do with her life, didn't know what to do now that she'd left Søren. And no amount of running and hiding was making the way any clearer. She needed help.

And so she answered.

"I was dreaming about the night I got pregnant."

19

Haiti

PARFAIT...THERE WAS NO OTHER WORD FOR THAT NIGHT with Elle, the night she burned him sixteen times. Every waking moment the day after, Kingsley's brain had buzzed with the memories of the pain, the intensity of the agony and the incredible release she'd pulled from him again and again. He was drunk with happiness, nearly delirious with sexual satisfaction. It was all coming together. The clouds were clearing, the pattern appearing. For years he wondered what it meant, that Elle had become part of his life. He loved sharing her with Søren. Kingsley loved watching Søren fuck her, loved being watched by Søren as Kingsley fucked Elle. Those were his most potent erotic encounters when sin and sex and sadism merged into one and spent the night in his bed.

But for all that, it hadn't been enough. As much as Kingsley loved to give pain and to dominate others, he himself needed pain and domination, as well. And if Søren would not give Kingsley what he needed, then perhaps Elle would.

And finally she had.

And not only had she done it, she'd loved it. He'd seen that gleam in her eyes as she'd fired up the scalpel. He'd known exactly what it was that burned in those dark green depths.

Sadism.

Pure, delicious, unadulterated sadism.

It had been too long since he'd let someone hurt him the way he needed hurting and have the sex he needed having. The Dominatrixes in his employ—he couldn't have sex with them. They worked for him and they never had sex with any of their clients. Mistress Felicia had moved back to England five years ago. And Søren had clearly repented of the night six years ago he'd lost control and beaten and fucked Kingsley in his own house. Another night like that with Søren? It had become nothing but a fantasy.

But another night like that with Elle? He bore sixteen burn marks on his body and eight deep scratches on his chest to prove it had been real. And it would be real again as soon as he found what he was looking for.

Two days after the night Elle burned him, Kingsley left on his quest. It took three days of driving through New England, stopping at every antique store he'd ever heard of and a few he hadn't before he found what he'd been looking for. At last in a tiny antique shop that specialized in equestrian equipment, there it was. It had cost a small fortune as it was two hundred years old and had belonged to a rather notorious duchess who supposedly did more than ride her horses. Triumphant, he returned to his town house and waited until nightfall to find Elle again.

He found her in his music room sitting near the piano. She did that whenever her longing for Søren grew painful. The piano was his and to sit near it was to be close to him. He'd seen similar behavior before among the priests at his old school, St. Ignatius. Sometimes they'd simply sit by the Eucharist with their eyes closed. They believed Jesus was incarnate in the blessed communion wafers. To sit by the Eucharist was to sit near Him, the man they'd devoted their lives to in service, in love and in marriage. Did Elle believe Søren was incarnate in the piano? Music, after all, was Søren's communion.

"I'm not talking to you, King," Elle said as she threaded a thin metal pick into what looked like a bicycle lock.

"Pourquoi pas?" he asked, suppressing a smile. He loved her bad moods. They always boded well for a good evening.

"You know why not." She didn't look at him, merely focused her entire attention on gently twisting the pick in the lock. She'd been doing this a lot lately, playing with locks, prising them open, learning their secrets. Why? Who knew? Although Kingsley had a theory, one he didn't want confirmed.

"It was all in good fun," he said, taking a seat behind her on the striped sofa. She must not be too angry at him for she wore one of his shirts again, a black button-down with the sleeves rolled to her shoulders. Her legs were tantalizingly bare and smooth and he traced a line with his fingertips from her knees to her hips.

"Good fun?" The lock popped open. She shut it again and went to work unlocking it again. "You tied me facedown, spread-eagle to your bed and fucked my ass for half the night without letting me come. Then you disappear for three days. Do you have anything to say to that?"

"You're welcome?" Kingsley said.

Elle glared at him.

"Don't pout, *mon chaton*. I only tied you up and fucked your ass all night to reassert my dominance. You know how it works. And you weren't complaining at the time."

"I wasn't complaining at the time because I assumed at some point you would let me come. That did not happen. Then you disappear, leaving me sore and horny. So don't even try to butter me up with the French accent and the finger-fucking. It's not going to work. Shoo. I'm done talking to you."

"Mais—"

"No buts. And no butts, either. You're cut off."

"But...I brought you a present."

She raised her eyebrow.

"Present? What is it?"

"Come and see."

"I'm not falling for that line again, King."

"See and come?"

"Better."

She set her pick and lock aside. He took her hand and led her from the music room and up to his bedroom.

"You're smiling," Elle said, her voice awash with suspicion. "I get nervous when you smile."

"You shouldn't be nervous. I should be nervous."

"Why should you be nervous?" she asked as he opened the door to his bedroom, shut it and locked it behind him.

"Because I'm giving you this."

He nodded toward the bed and Elle looked down at it.

"What is it?" she asked.

"It's a riding crop," Kingsley said. "An antique bone and ebony riding crop. Hand-carved, carved bone handle, two hundred years old. Rare, valuable, vicious. And..."

"And?"

Kingsley picked it up off the bed and presented it to her.

"And yours."

Elle stared at the crop but didn't take it.

"For me?"

"Pour vous, mademoiselle."

"Why are you giving me a riding crop?"

"Why do you think?"

"Because you hate me, and you're secretly plotting to get Søren to kill me?"

"Non."

"Because you're suicidal and you're secretly plotting to get Søren to kill you?"

"Non."

"Because you're masochistic and you want me to beat the shit out of you again?"

"We have a winner. Take it. See how it feels."

He saw the subtlest tremor in Elle's hand as she reached out and grasped the crop by the bone and pearl handle. The wood of the crop was black, the handle white.

"This is the most incredible riding crop I've ever seen," she said. "Do I want to know how much it cost?"

"If you sold it you could buy a car," he said, speaking to her in terms she'd understand. "A small one."

"This is better than a car."

"I'm pleased you like it." He bowed to her. Hopefully, by the end of the night he'd be doing more than bowing. He wanted to kneel at her feet, bury his face in her pussy, service her until she screamed, and then let her thank him for his service by beating him until blood ran down his back.

She looked at it through narrowed eyes, bringing it to her face to study the carvings on the handle. She tested the weight and the balance of it. With a flourish she swished it. He heard the whipping sound it made as it sliced the air in two.

"Do you want to hurt me again?" Kingsley asked.

"Oh, Kingsley," she said, smiling up at him. "I want to hurt everybody."

"Start with me."

Elle looked up at him and once again she was transformed. Gone was the good little girl who sat at Søren's feet, napping in his lap while her priest wrote out his homily for that Sunday using her back as a desk. Gone was the good little girl who said "Yes, sir" and "If it pleases you, sir" and "I am yours, sir. Do with me what you will, sir."

It was a bad little girl who looked up at Kingsley and without smiling asked him one very important question.

"Why do you still have your clothes on?"

Kingsley couldn't help but smile at the memory.

"Was I supposed to take them off?" he asked her.

She took a step back and brought the leather tip of the crop under his chin.

"You weren't supposed to have them on to start with."

He would have laughed at the memory she'd conjured with those words but he was already too turned on to do anything but obey.

"My apologies," Kingsley said and quickly—but not too quickly—stripped out of his clothes.

Once he was naked she pointed the crop at the bed.

"Bend over. Hands on the bed. Feet apart."

"You're welcome to fuck me," Kingsley said as he did what she ordered. "I certainly deserve payback for sodomizing you all night."

"I might," she said, wrapping black leather cuffs around his ankles and buckling a foot-wide spreader bar to them to keep his legs open. "But I think I want to beat you first. No..."

"No?"

"No. I know I want to beat you first."

"Beat me then. And don't be afraid to hit hard. Most new Doms are too gentle, too careful. You can strike me as hard—"

Kingsley screamed.

No, not quite a scream. He was too well trained to scream. But it was the closest he would ever get to a scream.

She'd hit him so hard on the back of his thighs with her crop that Kingsley's arms gave out under him.

As he gasped and coughed and forced his arms to straighten again, he heard Elle's voice from behind him.

"You were saying?"

"Nothing," Kingsley said. "I was saying nothing."

"Good. Shut up. Stand there. And don't talk. Unless you want to say 'ouch.' That you can say."

Ouch was the least of the exclamations she dragged from him that night. She wrung every French curse and every English curse he knew out of him. The crop was as vicious as a bamboo cane and in no time she had him welted from shoulder to shoulder, neck to knees. The back of his body burned as if it had been stung by a thousand angry wasps instead of one very calm young woman who was having too much fun tearing his body to pieces.

She hit the same spot three times in a row at the bottom of his rib cage. One, two, three vicious strikes with the thin wooden crop, and he released a cry of utter agony.

"Jesus Christ," he gasped, his fingers digging into the bed. He saw red, all red. The red light of pain flashed in front of him and he'd never see any color other than red again. "Do they teach all Catholics how to hurt people like this? Or is it just you two monsters?"

"Søren's sadism is self-taught," she said. "And I learned from Søren."

"No one's ever hurt me as much as he has," Kingsley said.

"Good."

"Why is that good?" Kingsley asked.

"I love a challenge."

She hit him again. By the time she tired of beating him, his back was a solid red knot of burning welts. His cock was excruciatingly hard and throbbing with the need for release. If she even touched it, he would come. He breathed to calm himself. He was still angry he'd come so fast the first night she'd hurt him. He wanted to savor his arousal, let it build to the breaking point before coming anyway and anywhere she ordered him to. On her, in her, he didn't care as long as it pleased her.

It pleased her now to lay the riding crop on the bed and run her hands up and down his broken body.

"Your skin is hot to the touch," she said. "The welts are on fire."

"I'm on fire," he said, forcing the words out between rasping breaths.

"You're beautiful like this." Elle pressed her palm to his

lower back where she'd concentrated her most vicious attentions. "Did you know that? When you're submissive and suffering and so turned on your cock is dripping? It's beautiful."

"Merci," he said, flushing slightly. Praise like that was a balm to his soul.

"Remember that night I told you about Wyatt, my college boyfriend for like a week? Well, you and I were in the music room. You unbuttoned your vest and your shirt and put my hand against the scar on your chest. I had this fantasy right then about pushing you onto your back and riding your cock into the ground."

"I would have let you."

"I was a virgin."

"Only because he saw you first."

Elle kissed his back between his shoulders. She reached around his hips and grasped his cock with two hands.

"What do you think would have happened if you'd seen me first?" she asked, stroking him so that he groaned.

"I've wondered that myself," he confessed. "I know one thing—if I had seen you first, you wouldn't have been a virgin at twenty. You would have been lucky to make it to sixteen."

"Lucky is not the word I would choose," Elle said, stroking him harder now. "Would you have shared me with Søren the way he shares me with you?"

"I would have shared you, but not in the same way."

"How then?"

"I would have let him beat you and fuck you. And then let him watch while you beat me and fucked me."

"You want him to watch me hurt you?"

"Oh, *oui.*"

"So he can see what he's missing?"

"No." Kingsley shook his head. "So he can see who you really are."

"And who am I?" she asked, massaging his cock so that his eyes rolled back with the dizzying ecstasy of it.

And Kingsley grinned. She might be beating him and he might be submitting to her right now but that didn't mean he'd given up all his power.

"That's for me to know, and for you to beat out of me."

And she did.

Kingsley opened his eyes and stared out upon the ocean before him. It had been a week since he'd seen Juliette coupling with her lover in their garden. A week since she told him to go. A week since he'd chosen to stay for no reason he could think of except he wasn't ready to go back yet. He'd tried to push thoughts of Juliette out of his mind, but thoughts of Elle had come and taken their place. Every evening he walked alone on the beach at sunset, a slow ramble from his hut to the edge of the bay and back again.

Kingsley took a deep breath. The vastness of the ocean spoke to the submissive in him. He was nothing compared to the endless waters. Their power and might humbled him as nothing else could. Vaguely he wondered if this was how Søren felt when he contemplated God. Small. Humble. Unimportant and yet loved despite all that. No. Surely Søren never felt small or humble. Not even God could humble that man.

Søren...for months now Kingsley had kept thoughts of Søren at bay. They'd intruded, of course. There was no escaping them entirely. But now Kingsley invited the thoughts in, let them swim to the shore and walk along the beach beside him.

"I miss you, *mon ami*," Kingsley said to the silent shadow that strolled beside him. "But I am still so angry at you."

The shadow didn't speak. Kingsley kept walking.

"With Elle...it wasn't like you and me. Or you and her. I had to work to love her. It didn't come easy. You chose her over me and it hurt, and it will always hurt. But I learned to love her despite all that, and that should tell you how close we are that I could overcome how much I wanted to hate her. You were right about her, about what she could be to us. But I was right, too. I was right about what she is and what she needs. I was right, and you didn't listen to me."

Kingsley paused and faced the waters. The wind blew through him and he inhaled the clean salt air. The sound of the surf drowned his every word, his every breath. He could hear nothing but the ocean.

"And now she's gone. And it's your fault. And it's my fault."

The shadow at his side bowed its head. Kingsley pulled a length of carved bone from his pocket. A broken piece of what had once been an antique riding crop.

"What happened between me and Elle...it was between me and Elle. Not you," Kingsley said, readying himself to toss the bone fragment into the ocean. "You had no part of it. And that's why you were angry, no? That's why you did what you did and made her run away from you, away from us?" He lifted his arm to throw it as far into the water as he could. "Because there is a part of her that has nothing to do with you and you were..."

And then Kingsley understood. He lowered his arm.

"And you were scared."

From behind him he heard Juliette's voice.

"Who was scared?"

20

Upstate New York

"PREGNANT?" KYRIE REPEATED. "YOU WERE PREGNANT?"

"I was," she said.

"And you…"

"Had an abortion."

"I see." Kyrie's voice was calm. Elle gave her credit for that.

"I'm not making this easy for you, am I?" Elle asked. "Just when you think it couldn't get any worse…"

"It's okay," Kyrie said. "I'm still here. Is that why you don't go to Mass?"

"I'm excommunicated."

"You can still go. You're just not supposed to take communion."

"Consider me quietly protesting that aspect of Catholicism."

Kyrie said nothing and Elle pitied her. The poor girl, a virgin, a nun, and here she was fighting off sexual, possibly even romantic feelings for a woman who'd fucked a priest and had an abortion.

"This is why I didn't want to tell you about me, about why I'm here," Elle said. "It's a lot for one person to carry."

"Too much for one person to carry," Kyrie said. "That's why I want you to tell me."

"Regret asking yet?"

"Not yet."

"You might if I keep talking."

"Keep talking," Kyrie said. "I want to know it all."

"Not here. Not tonight. It's cold out."

"Tonight," Kyrie said. "Before you change your mind. We can go to my room if you want somewhere warmer."

"No. We should go to mine. They put me up on the third floor away from everybody else."

"What? Do they think pregnancy is contagious?"

"I think Mother Prioress thinks sin is contagious, and I'm a carrier."

"We're all carriers. Original sin, remember?"

Elle laughed. "If you saw the crowd I used to run with... let's just say we put the *original* in original sin."

"Who were they? Your crowd?" Kyrie asked as they walked back to the abbey.

"I don't know what you'd call us. There's this man—Kingsley Edge. He has a town house on Riverside Drive in Manhattan. That's where all the rich people live, if you didn't know."

"I didn't know. So he's rich?"

"Filthy." Elle smiled. So many memories flooded her mind—good and bad. "He owns and operates a big S and M club. There's a group of us who practically live at that place."

"S and M? Like hitting people and stuff?"

"Pain and bondage and sex parties. Kink. Kingsley's our king, of course. He wouldn't have it any other way. But he has a court all around him. I was part of the court. Life is pretty luxurious inside Kingsley's inner circle."

They stopped talking when they reached the back door. They entered the abbey in silence and tiptoed up three flights of stairs. Elle's cell was near the end of the hall. The abbey had once boasted nearly one hundred sisters. Now their numbers were halved and dozens of cells on the third floor sat empty.

Elle opened her cell door for Kyrie but didn't turn on the light.

"Sister Luke walks the halls at night," Elle explained in a low whisper. "If she sees the light, she might listen at the door."

Kyrie sat on the bed. Elle pulled up her desk chair and sat close but not too close to her.

"I don't want you to get into trouble," Elle said.

"You, either. They wouldn't kick me out. They might kick you out, though."

"That's the last thing I need," Elle said. "I have no idea where I'd go if they kicked me out."

"Why can't you go back to your friends?"

"I could," Elle said as she took her shoes off and shoved her cold toes under the blanket on the bed. "I could go back tonight if I wanted. I was living at Kingsley's house."

"You lived with someone? That sounds serious."

"Not really. I had a room there. My own room. My own bathroom. I wasn't living *with* Kingsley. I was living *at* Kingsley's. Subtle difference."

"So you two are friends?"

"More than friends."

"But what about your priest?"

"Søren's a Jesuit but he's also a parish priest. He lives alone in his rectory, but it's not safe for me to be there all the time. I'd go over after dark and hide my car. I'd almost always leave before morning. I had to live somewhere, and I couldn't afford my own place. I moved in with King. King and Søren are best friends. And brothers-in-law. But that is a long story. And trust me, you don't want to get into that long story."

"If you say so. So what happened? You got pregnant and your priest, Søren, made you have an abortion?"

"No. It was nothing like that. Søren was out of the country for ten weeks, in Rome finishing his dissertation on Canon Law. I wasn't pregnant when he left. I know that because I was having my period. And then I got sick. Fever, stomach and back pain."

"What was wrong?"

"A kidney infection. Two weeks of antibiotics. My regular doctor couldn't get me in so I went to Søren's. When she asked me if I was sexually active I lied and said no. I didn't want her asking me any more about my sex life. So she didn't tell me that antibiotics can mess with your birth control. As soon as I felt better, Kingsley and I had sex."

"Wait. You cheated on your priest with Kingsley?"

"It wasn't cheating. Søren and Kingsley…" Elle stopped and took a breath. If Kyrie hadn't looked so confused and so beautiful, she would have laughed. "This is really hard to explain. No. Wait. It's very easy to explain. I was sleeping with both of them. There. I explained it."

"But how is that not cheating if you're having sex with two different men?"

"We're in an open relationship. Sort of. I'm…I was Søren's submissive, and he—"

"What's a submissive?"

"It's like being someone's property. But not exactly."

"But how can you be someone's property? Isn't that illegal?"

Elle raised her hand.

"This isn't working."

"What do you mean?"

"I can't sit here and try to explain my life to you with you saying 'but' every five seconds after I've said something weird like, 'My priest is a sadist, but that's one of his most endearing qualities.' And you'll say?"

"What's a sadist?"

Elle laughed. "We're going to be here all year if we keep this up. You and I, we speak different languages."

"Please try, Elle. I want to know."

"Why?"

"Because…" Kyrie took a ragged breath. "I've wanted to be a nun for so long that I don't remember what it feels like to want anything else. And then you…I met you and now I know what it's like to want something else. But I don't know you. You don't tell me anything so I don't even know what it is I want, and it's driving me crazy. Please, Elle…who are you?"

"Who am I?" Elle repeated. "I wish I knew who I was. I wish I knew how to tell you."

"Can you show me?" Kyrie asked.

Kyrie looked at her in silence and then pulled the veil off her head. She ran her fingers through her long blond hair and let it fall down her back where it belonged.

Elle reached out and touched a lock of Kyrie's hair. It was soft, so soft, like a baby's hair. But Kyrie was no child. In the moonlight streaming through the window and with her hair down, Kyrie looked like a nymph, beautiful and ethereal. She didn't seem real. More like a shadow or a shade from a dream. Elle had been dreaming her memories for months. Was she now living in her own dreams?

"If you can't tell me," Kyrie asked again, "can you show me?"

Elle laughed. Could she show her? One easy way to do it.

"Give me your hand," Elle said. Kyrie obeyed without question. "I'm going to bite your wrist. Is that okay?"

"Will you do it hard?"

"Yes. But I won't break the skin. Do I have your permission to bite you?"

"Sure, I guess. Yes."

"Good." Elle raised Kyrie's wrist to her lips and sank her teeth deep into the soft flesh at the wrist bone. Kyrie flinched but didn't cry out.

Then Elle kissed her in the same spot. A warm, soft, sensual kiss on the bite mark and the inside of her wrist.

"Elle…" Kyrie breathed. Elle released her hand and Kyrie pulled it back against her chest, cradling it in her other hand.

"Did you like that?" Elle asked.

"I liked the kiss after you bit me. And the bite, too."

"What would you say if I said I would do it again, but only if you let me bite you again?"

"I'd say...bite me."

"What if I said I'd make you feel amazing but only after I hurt you? Would you let me hurt you?"

"Yes."

"What do you think would happen if every time I hurt you I also made you feel good afterward?"

"I don't know. I guess I'd want you to hurt me so I could feel good."

"You'd associate pain with pleasure?"

"I would."

"You'd want the pain because it meant you'd have pleasure, too?"

"Probably."

"Would the pleasure mean more to you because you earned it?"

"I think so."

"If I told you it turned me on to hurt you and then pleasure you in that order, what would you think?"

"I would think you should do that to me then. Hurt me and then pleasure me."

Elle smiled. "That's kink. It's also kink when your deepest sexual fantasy is to be treated like a sex slave or punished by a teacher or tied up like a prisoner or spanked like a child."

"People do that?"

"I do that," Elle said.

Kyrie held out her hand again to Elle. "Will you do it me?"

"Kyrie—"

"Please?"

Almost nine months...Elle hadn't been intimate with anyone in that long. No wonder she dreamed of sex almost every night and woke up coming. And Kyrie…she wanted her. This young virginal…

"You're a nun." Elle took Kyrie's hand but only to hold it. "If we do this—"

"I'm just a starter nun."

"It's called a novice, not a starter nun."

"You know what I mean. I don't take final vows for two years," Kyrie said. "I want to know what I'm giving up."

Elle closed her eyes and shook her head.

Somewhere out there, far in the distance, she heard a sound she thought she would never hear.

"Can you hear that?" Elle asked.

"No, what is it?"

"God laughing at me."

Elle opened her eyes.

Then she stood up.

She pushed her chair under the doorknob.

Kyrie was already on the bed, her hair down and unbound. She was a vision of loveliness and innocence. And Elle wanted her. Wanted her as she'd never wanted a woman before in her life. But she wasn't a woman. Not yet. She was a girl, chaste and pure, and she'd never even been kissed. The hunger to be the first lips on Kyrie's lips was physical in its urgency. Elle wanted hers to be the first hands on Kyrie's body. But even more than that, she wanted to feel again what she felt those nights with Kingsley, the nights he'd let her hurt him, dominate him, use him. She needed to feel that power again.

She needed to own this girl, body and soul. In two years, Kyrie would take her final vows. In two years, her beautiful long hair would be shorn to the scalp. In two years the door on Kyrie's life would lock and it would never be opened again. Kyrie would never be opened again.

Innocence had its virtues, but ignorance had none. To let this beautiful girl walk away from the world without ever having tasted the pleasure it offered was more than a crime. It was a sin. A shame. And Elle wouldn't allow it.

"Are you praying?" Elle asked, seeing Kyrie's head bowed. The starlight made itself a halo in her hair.

"Yes. The prayer of St. Augustine." Kyrie looked up at Elle and met her eyes in the dark. "Lord, make me chaste...."

Elle finished the prayer for her.

"But not yet."

21

Haiti

"WHO WAS SCARED?"

Kingsley closed his eyes. Juliette's voice carried over the air and the waves and the water on the sand. It carried over the beach like the signal of a lighthouse to a ship lost at sea.

"No one." He shoved the length of carved bone into his pocket. He turned and found her standing ten feet behind him. She wore a yellow dress, bright as the sun. "I was talking to myself."

"It didn't sound like it. Were you praying?" She walked on bare feet across the sand to him.

"Something like that."

"To God?"

"To a man," he said. "A man who thinks he's God sometimes. But he can't be God, can he? Not if he's scared."

"I don't know," she said with a graceful tilt of her head, a graceful lift of her shoulders. "I think God gets scared."

"You do? Seems unlike Him. All-knowing. All-powerful. What is there for Him to fear?"

"Us," she said. "His people. He loves us and we're..." She turned her gaze onto the water. "Small. Weak."

"Fragile," Kingsley said.

"We're fragile, yes. And He's new to us, as new as we are to Him. He doesn't know His own strength. He doesn't understand yet how weak we are." She paused and looked at her feet in the sand. "I've seen mother birds crush their own eggs by accident. The mothers aren't evil. They aren't trying to hurt their babies. But still, the eggshells, they're too fragile."

Kingsley felt something in his chest, something like an eggshell. He felt it in the place where his heart should be.

"Imagine," Juliette whispered. "Imagine how terrifying it is to know you could crush your own creation simply by loving it."

"I can imagine."

"I suppose that's the price we pay," she said, looking toward the horizon.

"Pay for what?"

"For loving and being loved by something so powerful."

Kingsley nodded. God was so vast, and they so small—was it any wonder so many of His children got crushed? And yet, living in a world without God's power would be like living in a world without oceans.

"How did you find me here?" Kingsley asked.

"I'm good at finding people. I found where your hut was and when you weren't there, I followed your footsteps. Do you walk here often?"

"Every evening."

"Can I ask you something?" Juliette took a small step closer to him.

"Ask."

"Why are you here? In Haiti, I mean?"

"Something bad happened," Kingsley said, trying to speak as vaguely as possible. What happened between him and Elle was between him and Elle and no one else. Not even Søren. Especially not Søren. "I didn't handle it as well as I should have, and someone important to me was harmed in the process. If I'd stayed, I would have made it worse for her. And it was bad already."

"*Elle est partie,*" Juliette said. Kingsley looked at her in shock.

"How do you know her name?"

"Her name? You talk in your sleep. I heard you say 'She is gone.'"

In French "She is gone" was "*Elle est partie.*" He'd been speaking of Elle in his sleep. She is gone. Elle is gone. Same thing.

"Her name is Elle," Kingsley said. "Eleanor."

"I see. Were you in love with her, with Elle?"

"No. It was different with us. Love but not in love. Friends but not friends. I can't explain us."

"Love but not in love. Family?"

Kingsley smiled. "We were lovers."

"I know married couples not in love with each other. But they are family."

"Family," Kingsley said, thinking of her and him and Søren and what they were to each other. Would they ever be that close again? "Perhaps she was family. There are two people in the world who know all of my secrets. And she was one of them." Kingsley's throat tightened painfully. "I failed her when she needed me the most. But she's gone and I can't even tell her how sorry I am."

"Can I tell you how sorry I am?" Juliette asked.

"For what?"

"I shouldn't have slept with you if one night was all I could give you. I shouldn't have brought you into the mess that is my life."

"We barely know each other. You don't owe me any apology or explanation."

"I do. Spending the night with you…it was selfish of me."

"You aren't selfish very often, are you?"

She raised her hands in a question. A question, or maybe a surrender.

"I don't have the luxury of being selfish."

"Why not?" Kingsley asked.

"Because I'm owned."

"I know many men and women who are owned. They are quite capable of being selfish. Some of them have made an art of it."

"I'm not owned the way they are."

"How are you owned then? What other way is there?" he asked.

"The people you know, they are owned by choice? Because they want to be owned?"

"Yes, very much so."

"I'm not."

Kingsley turned and faced her finally. "What do you mean? Slavery was abolished in Haiti two hundred years ago."

"Don't be naive," Juliette said with a smile. Kingsley was certain that was the first time anyone had ever accused him of being naive. "As long as there are men with money and power and women without it, there will be slavery in this world."

"But you're here with me right now. On this beach. You can walk away from him. I could take you back to Manhattan with me tonight."

She shook her head. "No, you can't."

"No one can own another person. There are laws against it."

"This isn't about laws."

"How can he own you like this?"

"He owns me because I owe him. A debt. A huge debt I can never repay."

"And you pay it to him with your body?"

Juliette nodded. "It's the only currency he accepts."

"What do you owe him?" Kingsley asked.

Juliette took a step forward and let her toes touch the water. The tide ebbed around her ankles and slid back into the sea.

"My family has always worked for his family and his family has been here since before the Revolution. My great-grandparents, my grandparents, my mother...our families are intimately intertwined. *Maman* was a housekeeper for Gérard's father. And more."

"They were lovers."

"Of course. I say of course, but you haven't seen my mother. In her youth, she was beautiful."

"I can imagine," Kingsley said, admiring Juliette.

"Gérard was appointed ambassador to Haiti when he was only thirty-three or thirty-four. But it's an old family, the Guill-roys. Old name, great power. That story."

Kingsley knew that story well.

"Gérard has an understanding with his wife. They own companies together, properties. Better to stay married and live apart than divide the assets."

"Very practical," Kingsley said. "Very French."

"It is," Juliette said with the smallest of smiles.

"What happened?"

"Growing up in his house? Nothing." She crossed her arms, shrugged her shoulders. "He was kind but distant with me. He had his own children to occupy him. Twin girls four years older than I am."

"Something must have changed along the way."

"Maman changed," Juliette said. "All her life she was a little unstable. Emotional. She overreacted to things. But she was smart and strong. She took good care of me even if she did scare me sometimes with the things she said. But when I was thirteen..."

She paused. The pause scared Kingsley enough that he said, "You don't have to tell me."

"I want to tell you. I want you to know. When I was thirteen, Maman changed. She..." Juliette took a ragged breath. "She went quiet. She was withdrawn, and then in a flash, angry. She grew paranoid and scared. She heard things, voices. And she started hurting herself. I walked into the kitchen one day and found her bleeding from both arms."

"Suicide attempt?"

"No, she said she saw snakes under her skin and had to cut them free."

Juliette shuddered and crossed her arms over her chest. Kingsley wanted to hold her and comfort her. He didn't deserve to hear this story, so personal and painful.

"The doctor said schizophrenia. And Maman must never be left alone. She couldn't work anymore, of course. I tried to watch her on my own, I did. But it was too much for me."

"You were only a child."

"I was but I wasn't," she said. "I was smart, too. I had the same education as Gérard's girls, who were four years ahead of me, and I did better in our lessons than they did. I was smart and I knew...I knew how the world worked."

"What did you do?"

"When summer came and his daughters went back to Cannes to be with their mother, I went to Gérard and asked him to put my mother in a hospital. A good one where she could get the care she needed. The doctor had mentioned a place in Switzerland where people like my mother got very good care."

"What did he say?"

"He said such a place was expensive. And that although he was very sorry, my mother no longer worked for him. I told him I would take her place. I told him I would do the work she did for him if he would pay for the hospital. I told him I would do anything he wanted. In bed and out of it."

"I assume he took you up on your offer."

"I was fourteen by then, tall, a woman already in many ways. We were alone in the house. He brought me to his bedroom, and he took my virginity. That was over twelve years ago."

Kingsley stomach turned. "You were fourteen."

"I was scared, but the truth is, I enjoyed it. Eventually," she said. "He's a good lover. Handsome. Passionate."

"French."

"Of course," she said with a smile. Then the smile faded. "I thought I was in love with him. For a long time I thought that. We did everything in bed two people could do. But I never forgot, not once, that my mother was at his mercy."

"What would happen to her if you left him?"

"What are mental hospitals in New York like?" she asked.

"Hell," Kingsley said. "Even the good ones are like Hell, they say."

"Imagine what one in Haiti is like."

"I don't want to. Truly, I have seen enough horrors to last a lifetime."

"I believe you," Juliette said. "So now you know. Gérard takes care of Maman. I take care of him. If I stop taking care of him, he stops taking care of her. And when I say he owns me, I mean it."

"Is this why you want to die? Is that why you're planning to kill yourself?"

She looked askance at him.

"I saw the rocks in your bag," he said by way of explanation. "I saw the book in your nightstand. Planning to follow in Virginia Woolf's footsteps?"

Juliette's lips formed a hard line. It took a few moments before she seemed ready to speak again.

"When I was eighteen, Gérard gave me a ring. Diamonds and sapphires. Worth a fortune. I have a cousin—he's gone to Miami now, but when he lived here he worked outside the law. I had him sell the ring, and I told Gérard it was stolen at knifepoint. He kissed me, said he was sorry and called the insurance company. He had a check for the full cost of the ring and then some in a week and I…" She held up her right hand to display a diamond and sapphire glinting on her ring finger.

"Life insurance policy?"

Juliette nodded. "I took the money from the ring and bought insurance. My mother's the beneficiary on my policy. If I die and it's ruled an accident, then there would be enough money to take care of my mother for at least ten years. People drown in the ocean all the time here and their bodies wash up on the beach."

"There has to be another way," Kingsley said.

"There isn't. If there were another way I would have found it by now." She took his hand and he wished she hadn't. Her long slender fingers felt as if they belonged in his grasp. And the time would come when he would have to let her go again.

"I'm not certain I can go through with it. I am Catholic, after all."

"This is a new feeling I'm experiencing now. I've never been grateful for someone's Catholicism before."

Juliette laughed softly and squeezed his hand.

"In the car on the way to the house, you took off your knife and gave it to me. Were you hoping I'd use it to kill you?" he asked.

"All I wanted from you was a night with a man of my choosing. A night with a man I wanted and who I owed nothing to. A night with a man who didn't own me." She paused for a long time before speaking again. "Before I died."

Juliette stepped out of the reach of the tide. Side by side they walked back toward Kingsley's hut.

"You should know," she said, squeezing his hand, "he doesn't abuse me. The pain he's caused me has been the kind you and I both enjoy. And he's faithful to me. He and his wife haven't been intimate in years. He has no other lover, only me."

"He owns you," Kingsley said. "He's rich. Beyond rich. It would be pocket change for him to pay for your mother's medical treatment."

"I made the offer. He accepted it."

"He should have helped your mother without making you pay for it with your body. You grew up with his own daughters, for God's sake. You should have been like a daughter to him."

"I never said he was a saint. I only said he doesn't abuse me. I live in luxury. Anything I want he gives me."

"Except your freedom."

"Except my freedom."

She squeezed his hand.

"I shouldn't complain," she continued. "It's like a marriage of convenience. How many women out there have made the same bargain with a wealthy man that I have?"

"But it's not marriage. If you were married, the law would be on your side. You could divorce him, take half his money and pay for your mother's treatments yourself instead of putting rocks in your pockets and walking into the ocean."

"I should have asked him to marry me then. Oh wait, he's already married. There goes that idea."

Her flippant tone only made Kingsley angrier.

"Even an indentured servant knows when his service will end. How long will your mother need to be in the hospital?"

"They say she's treatment resistant. And self-harming. There is no cure for what she has. Only constant monitoring and good care."

"So you will be his…"

"Until the day she dies," Juliette said. "Or until I do."

"Do you ever see her?"

"Oh yes, twice a year I'm allowed to visit her for a week. She's happy where she is, and safe."

"Does she know what you do for her?"

Juliette shook her head. "She thinks Gérard's father is still in love with her, that the family pays for her care because of what they were. I haven't disabused her of the knowledge. It comforts her."

"You are a good daughter. But you do too much for her. I

don't know of any mother in the world who would ask her only child to make the sacrifice you have."

"Sacrifice? You've seen the house I live in, the clothes I wear, the car he lets me drive."

"His house. His clothes. His car. Your life."

"Yes," she said. "They are. But I try not to think about it that way. My mother lives in a dreamworld. I try to live in my own."

"Dreaming and lying to yourself are very different things."

"I know. I have always known," she said in her flawless, elegant French. *Je sais. Je l'ai toujours su.*

"What would you do with your freedom if you had it?" Kingsley asked. "If your mother were cured tomorrow, what would you do?"

"Go away from here," she said. "Travel for a while. Then I would go to school."

"School? For what?"

"Business," she said. "I'm good with money. I handle all of his."

Kingsley laughed and the sound carried across the ocean and back.

"What?" she asked.

"I never would have expected that from you."

"Why not?"

"I don't know. I shouldn't be so surprised. I have an eighteen-year-old assistant who is a computer hacker."

Juliette laughed. "You have an eighteen year-old girl working for you? Do I want to know what it is you do?"

"I wouldn't ask if I were you. Only because it would take so long to explain."

"Is she just an assistant? Or more?"

"Only an assistant. She flirts with me, but I remind her she's young enough to be my daughter. I hope she's doing her homework while I'm here. Usually you have to make her get off the computer to eat. She's always up to something. But I can't scold too much. So am I."

"You sound like a proud father."

Kingsley winced. Father of an eighteen-year-old girl? Possible, yes, but God, he couldn't imagine having a child who was already a teenager.

"She's a sweet girl. That's all," Kingsley said. And then he asked a terrifying question. "Do you want children?"

"I've thought about it. Under other circumstances I would."

"Could you have them with him?"

She shook her head. "He won't allow it."

"Why not?"

"His daughters don't know about me. And considering I grew up in his home…it would be a scandal. Even for the French it would be a scandal. I'm nothing but the housekeeper to anyone but us. He wants to keep it that way."

"You've asked, haven't you? Asked if you could have children?"

Juliette visibly swallowed. "I've asked, yes."

"And what did you do when he said you weren't allowed to have children?" Kingsley asked.

She raised her hands again. They were still empty.

"I gathered a bag of stones."

Kingsley closed his eyes and exhaled. He felt his heart crack like an eggshell.

"Bastard," he breathed.

"C'est la vie," she said.

Kingsley stopped walking. They were near his beach hut now.

"I could help you," Kingsley said. "I have money, too."

"And what would I do? Be your lover?"

"Of course."

"Be your property?"

"Not like you are now. You'd have freedom."

"Trading his bed for your bed, his money for your money… that's not freedom. That's merely transferring the deed of ownership."

"It wouldn't have to be like that."

"What if I left you?" she asked. "What if I cheated on you? What if I betrayed you? Would you still take care of my mother even after I'd moved on from you?"

Kingsley didn't have a good answer to that.

"What's that English phrase?" Juliette asked. "Better the devil you know?"

"I won't leave Haiti without you," he said, meaning the words more now than he had when he first said them.

"Then I hope you love it here. Because you will be here for a very long time."

"I suppose I will then."

She stood in front of him, raised her hand to his face.

"Don't be angry. Don't be hurt," she said. "And don't be afraid to leave me here. I'm fine. I won't kill myself, I promise."

"You swear?"

"I do. It was a foolish idea. In truth, I'm blessed in many ways. I have food, shelter. He spoils me. My life isn't perfect, but name me one person who does have a perfect life. Can you?"

He tried to think of a name. Nothing came to him. He stayed silent.

"I thought so," Juliette said with a tight smile. "No one."

"Do you love him?" He'd asked before and she'd lied.

"I can't leave the house without his permission. He always grants it, but also, I always have to ask."

Kingsley couldn't imagine how much that must gall her, this beautiful intelligent capable woman to have to ask permission like a child to leave her lover's property.

"But…" she continued. "He didn't have to help my mother at all, and he did. And he doesn't threaten me, or her. He and I, we work well together, play well together. Despite everything."

"Then why did you find me tonight?"

"Because his work has called him back to Paris for a week," Juliette said, taking a step closer to him, close enough he could smell the scent of jasmine on her skin. "And I want to spend every moment until he gets back with you."

"You'll go back to him when he returns?"

"I will. I have to."

"Spending more time with me will only make it harder for you, harder for both of us. You know that."

"I know that," she said.

"Answer this…why should we spend another night together if it's only going to end with you going back to him?"

She gave him a reason he couldn't and wouldn't refuse.

"Because I'll let you beat me."

22

"DO YOU HAVE A HYMEN?" ELLE ASKED, AND EVEN IN the dark she could see Kyrie blush. "Some virgins do, some don't."

"I think I do. Why?"

"I want to know what I'm working with." Elle sat on the bed in front of Kyrie.

"What are you going to do to me?" Kyrie asked.

"I don't know yet," Elle said, and she didn't. She'd never done anything like this before. Never topped a woman. Never taken anyone's virginity.

She brushed her hand through Kyrie's hair again. The waves in the sun-streaked mass looked like feathers in the darkness.

"You remind me of a dove," Elle said. "All white and light and nervous."

Kyrie smiled and pulled her knees to her chest.

"You'd be nervous too if you were me."

"Yes," Elle agreed. "You should be nervous."

"Is it going to hurt?"

Elle nodded.

"Will I like it?"

"If I do it right you will."

"Are you going to do it right?"

"I am," Elle said, making the words a solemn vow. "But don't think about what's going to happen. Think about this instead."

"What?"

Elle kissed her.

In the beginning, the kiss was nothing but light. A light brush of lips on lips. Elle let her mouth linger on Kyrie's, waiting, patiently waiting. Elle would do the work, but Kyrie would set the pace. They had all night and tomorrow night. They had all week, all month, all year. As sweet as the kiss was, as beautiful as the girl she kissed, Elle was in no hurry for it to end. Only in a hurry for it to begin.

Kyrie tilted her chin up and parted her lips. Elle deepened the kiss. With the tip of her tongue she touched Kyrie's teeth, lightly and without pressure. But Kyrie took the hint and opened her mouth even more to Elle.

She tasted sweet, like warm honey, and Elle cupped the back of her head to hold her mouth right where she wanted it— against her own. Kyrie whimpered at the force but didn't pull away. The kissed deepened further, grew heated as Kyrie fell into the rhythm of lips on lips and tongue to tongue.

Elle moved her hand from Kyrie's head to her shoulder, from her shoulder to her neck. She felt Kyrie's pulse throbbing in the vein under her ear. She was scared, aroused, everything Elle wanted her to be.

From her neck, Elle dropped her hand to Kyrie's waist. She found the tie of Kyrie's white robe and unknotted it.

"Elle?" Kyrie made her name a question, a panicked question.

"It's all right," Elle said, resting her palm on Kyrie's burning face. "You'll get used to this."

"Get used to what?"

"Get used to me undressing you. I'll go slowly tonight. But when we're alone together in my room, your body belongs to me. I'll touch it when I want to touch it, undress it when

I want to undress it and use it however I want to use it. You understand that?"

Kyrie nodded.

"How does that make you feel?" Elle asked.

"Better," she said. "Scared, but better. I don't know what I'm doing. I want…I want you to do it all."

"I will. I promise. And I'm taking care of you."

"You'll take care of me?"

"Yes," Elle whispered. "That's what I want to do. You do what I tell you to do. And I'll take care of you."

"Thank you," Kyrie said. And Elle had to stop herself from laughing. Thank her? Kyrie was letting Elle kiss her and touch her and dominate her and Kyrie was thanking her? Submissives were so cute sometimes.

Elle kissed Kyrie again, a slow sensual kiss. A kiss to distract the girl while Elle finished unknotting the tie of her robe. Once it was untied, Elle parted the robe and rested her hand on Kyrie's stomach. She felt the muscles fluttering like bird's wings with every nervous breath.

Beneath the robe Kyrie wore an old-fashioned gown of white cotton, tied with a drawstring at the neck. On the other sisters, the gown looked like a relic from another era. On Kyrie, it looked unbearably erotic. One little bow to untie and the gown would fall open like a flower.

"Are you okay?" Elle asked, between kisses.

"I think so."

"Scared?"

"Terrified."

"Good. I like that you're scared," Elle said.

"Why?"

The question caught her off guard. She didn't have an answer for it.

"I don't know. I just do. Maybe…" She kissed Kyrie's neck under her ear and over the pounding vein. "Maybe I want you to be afraid of me. That way your trust means more than if you weren't afraid."

"I do trust you," Kyrie said.

"I know. You'll be brave for me, and do everything I tell you to do even if it scares you?"

Kyrie took a breath, looked away. "Whatever you want, Elle. Do whatever you want. I'm yours."

Let it be done unto me…

"Good. I'm going to take your robe off you. Just the robe. For now."

Kyrie took a breath as if bracing herself. Elle bit back a smile. With her mouth on Kyrie's neck, Elle pushed the robe down her back and off her arms.

"Tell me if you get cold," Elle asked.

"I'm okay," she said. "I'm anything but cold right now."

Elle pulled back and wrapped a leg around either side of Kyrie's waist. They were face-to-face now, Kyrie sitting in the circle of her legs and arms.

"Do you like kissing?" Elle asked, kissing her again on the mouth, the cheek, the ear.

"I love it." Kyrie's head fell back, giving Elle better access to her neck and throat. Without any warning Elle nipped Kyrie's neck with a quick snap of her teeth. Kyrie flinched but didn't protest. A good sign. "I was just thinking kissing felt so good I wished I'd done it a long time ago. But then maybe I wouldn't have come here, and I wouldn't have met you. And you're my first kiss, Elle. I'm so glad you're my first kiss."

Their lips met again in renewed passion. All gentleness had fled from the kiss. Elle took Kyrie's face in her hands and kissed the girl until she moaned. While their lips were otherwise occupied, Elle raised her hands to Kyrie's neck and found the bow of her nightgown. She untied it and yanked lightly on the silky string.

Kyrie inhaled sharply and froze.

"Trust me," Elle said in a warning tone. "Don't forget to trust me."

"I trust you," she said again. "It's just…"

"I know. I was a virgin once, too. I promise, I know."

"I don't want to stop."

"We're not going to stop until I'm done with you. Remember that?"

Kyrie smiled and laughed softly.

"I remember."

"Do you need to stop for a minute or two?"

"Maybe…maybe just a minute. What are you… I mean—"

"I'm going to push your nightgown down to your hips, and then I'm going to touch and kiss your breasts. That's what I'm going to do. Just that. For starters."

"For starters."

"Kyrie, you won't be a virgin when you wake up tomorrow. Are you sure you're ready for that sort of morning?"

She didn't answer at first, not with words. But then she sat up straighter and brought her own hands to the tie of her nightgown. She loosened the fabric and, with a tiny shake of her shoulders, let the gown fall down her arms, baring her body to her waist.

Elle stopped breathing for two or three tense seconds. Kyrie had beautiful breasts, small and high and with the pinkest, most pert nipples. There was nothing voluptuous about the girl. She had a thin petite frame, almost boyish, but the breasts were flawless. Elle cupped one in her hand. Kyrie breathed in at the contact but didn't say a word, didn't protest. Not even when Elle massaged her areola with her thumb, making a slow circle until her nipple tightened and grew hard.

She raised her other hand and pinched both of Kyrie's nipples. She didn't pinch hard, not enough to hurt her, but hard enough a little gasp escaped Kyrie's parted lips.

"How does this feel?" Elle asked as she rolled Kyrie's nipples in her fingers, massaged and teased them.

"Amazing," Kyrie said. "I didn't know it could feel this good when someone else touched me."

"I want to make you feel things you've never felt before. Pain and pleasure."

"How will you hurt me?"

Elle brushed the pad of her thumbs over Kyrie's nipples. That was something that never failed to make Elle aroused. Søren would do it until she was cursing the day he was born for getting her so aroused and then making her wait for penetration.

But Søren was her past now. Kyrie was her present. And like a present, Elle wanted to open her.

"I want to open your vagina up. It'll probably hurt if you've never had anything bigger than a tampon or a finger in you before."

"I haven't."

"I'm glad. I want to be the one who opens you up."

"I want it, too. I want to feel you inside me, Elle. Please?"

"Soon. Lie back for me now."

Carefully, Kyrie rolled down and rested her head on Elle's pillow. Her hair surrounded her shoulders like a veil. What a waste of God's beauty to cover this girl's hair with anything. But Elle was glad then that Kyrie covered her hair with a veil. Now she and she alone got to see Kyrie like this—unveiled in every way.

Elle bent over Kyrie's chest and kissed her right nipple.

"Oh, God."

Elle smiled.

'That's how I feel about it, too. Now don't talk," Elle ordered. "Enjoy it."

Like a good girl, Kyrie said nothing. Elle focused all her attention now on Kyrie's breasts and nipples. She licked them, both breasts. Easy to do with breasts so petite and perfect. And then she took the right nipple into her mouth and sucked it and she used her fingers to pull and tug on her left nipple. Beneath her mouth, Kyrie's breasts heaved with her ragged breathing.

"I can feel it…" Kyrie said in a low strained voice. "In my stomach."

"Where else?" Elle asked, sucking her left nipple now.

"In my hips and back."

"Where else?"

"Inside me," Kyrie said.

"Are you getting wet? Can you tell?" She'd ordered Kyrie not to talk, but now she had to know everything she was feeling.

"I am. I'm sure of it. God, it feels so good."

Elle took her time with Kyrie's breasts. No rush. No hurry. She wasn't a man rushing through the process, counting every second until he'd got his girl ready enough he could stick his cock in her with a clear conscience. No, Elle was a woman too and knew everything Kyrie was feeling and wanted to feel, everything she needed to feel. If Kyrie wanted her nipples kissed for half an hour, an hour, Elle would do it. She would do it with pleasure and with patience.

"Elle…" Kyrie breathed as Elle drew her nipple deeper into her mouth. "I want…"

"Tell me."

"I don't know. I just…I want."

Elle rose over Kyrie and kissed her again on the lips. A sheen of sweat covered Kyrie's forehead and Elle pushed a lock of damp hair off her face.

"Me, too," Elle whispered. "I want it, too."

"Do you really like doing this? I know you're not—"

"I'm a not a lesbian, no. I love having sex with men. But I also love having sex with you. And that's what we're doing now."

"We are, aren't we?"

"We are. I hope it's as good for you as it is for me."

"Better," Kyrie said. "You're doing all the work."

Elle shook her head. "This isn't work. You aren't work."

"Will you touch me inside now?"

"Soon. I told you I'm enjoying myself. Don't rush me, my dove."

"Dove?"

"When I first saw you, your hair and your skin reminded me of a dove. I don't know why."

"I like it. It sounds like 'my love.'"

"It does, doesn't it?" With one more smile, Elle dropped her mouth back to Kyrie's breasts. She kissed them again, kneaded and molded them in her hands and with her mouth until Kyrie panted.

Elle sat up finally and moved between Kyrie's knees. She lifted the hem of the gown up to Kyrie's waist and pushed her thighs open. Kyrie said nothing. Her body had gone limp. She was weak with desire. Exactly the way Elle wanted her.

"I'll try not to hurt you too much," Elle said, forcing her eyes to Kyrie's face.

"You couldn't hurt me now if you tried."

"Don't say stuff like that. Knowing me, I'll try."

With both hands, Elle stroked the lips of Kyrie's vulva. She had the softest pubic hair, like a young girl's. Elle pushed the folds open and looked down at the small pink hole of her vagina. Carefully she slipped a finger into her and pushed up against the soft hollow right inside her body.

"You are soaking wet," Elle said.

"Is that good?"

"Unbelievably good. Let's make it better, though."

"How?"

Elle bent down and licked Kyrie's clitoris with the tip of her tongue. One lick and a second one. One the third one she lightly sucked it between her lips. Kyrie went stiff and still from the shock of pleasure.

"Relax," she ordered the girl. "Trust me. Even if this makes you nervous at first, after a couple times it will become your new favorite thing."

"Okay. Trying to relax. But…"

"But what?"

"Doesn't it taste weird?"

"If you want me to tell you it tastes like candy and straw-berries, you're going to be disappointed. If I wanted candy and strawberries, I'd go grocery shopping. Since my head's between your thighs, I think it's safe to say I'm in the mood for some-thing else to eat. Now shut up. My mouth has better things to do than answer silly questions. Like this, for example."

Elle licked Kyrie from her clitoris to the base of her vagina and back up again. Kyrie groaned in the back of her throat and Elle did it again. While she kissed and licked Kyrie, she pushed her finger into that soft spot as deep as she could.

Kyrie flinched.

"Good flinch or bad flinch?" Elle asked.

"Good flinch."

"I wish I'd packed a vibrator. I hadn't planned on deflower-ing a nun while I was here."

"Better than doing laundry, right?" Kyrie asked. She was flushed and shivering. She'd never looked more vulnerable or more beautiful.

With every minute that passed, Kyrie grew wetter and her breaths faster and more desperate. She was on the verge of or-gasming any second now. Under her mouth, Kyrie's hips rocked up and down. Her fingers grasped at the sheets, at the pillow around her head.

"Are you close?" Elle whispered.

"Yes. Please don't stop."

"I'm not stopping. Not now or ever. But when you come, I'm going to put my hand inside you."

"All of it?"

"Most of it."

"That's going to hurt, isn't it?"

"I have small hands. It won't hurt any more than a penis would, which means it will probably hurt. Try not to scream."

"What if I scream?"

"You will not scream. That's an order."

Kyrie gave a scared little laugh, and Elle went back to work on her, sucking her, licking her, fucking her…first with one finger, then two. Two fingers…then three. Kyrie was so wet it was dripping onto the sheets underneath her and forming a small puddle. Good thing Elle did the laundry. That could be incriminating.

Elle focused her attention solely on Kyrie's clitoris. It pulsed against her tongue while Kyrie's tight wet passage slowly opened itself to her fingers.

Then Kyrie went silent, completely silent. She was there, on the edge, on the verge. She'd hit her climax and hit it hard.

"Elle—" Kyrie gasped the warning and Elle slammed her left hand over Kyrie's mouth and pushed her right hand into Kyrie.

All around her hand Kyrie's body throbbed and pulsed as the muscle contracted wildly, clamping down onto Elle's intruding presence. Kyrie's legs opened even wider and her hips rose half a foot off the bed and lifted them again and again. Against Elle's palm, she cried out with either pleasure or pain. Who could tell in that moment?

Kyrie pushed her heels into the bed and pulled back. As quickly as she could without hurting her even more, Elle slid her hand out of her. With a whimper, Kyrie collapsed back onto the sheets in a sweaty, panting, tired mess of blond waves and tears.

"It's okay," Elle said, sliding up to lie beside her. "You're okay. It's over."

Kyrie closed her eyes and nodded.

"You did so good." Elle took a corner of the sheet and wiped the blood and fluid off her hand. Then she gently stroked

Kyrie's burning forehead. She looked so lovely right now, spent and tired with her lips swollen and her nipples taut and her stomach quivering. Elle couldn't stop herself from kissing her on the mouth one more time.

"How good?" Kyrie asked.

"Gold medal. You didn't even scream."

"Surely that's worth a few points, isn't it?" Kyrie asked. "One or two...or ten?"

"You want me to give you points for losing your virginity?"

"No, I want you to give me points for having my first kiss *and* losing my virginity all in one night. And extra points for not screaming."

Elle laughed. "You have a one-track mind."

"I should get points for that, too."

"Okay. Three points for the first kiss. Five points for not being a virgin anymore. And a bonus two points for not screaming when I broke your hymen with my hand."

"Nine plus three plus five plus two is...nineteen. I'm only six points away from getting the truth out of you. So close. Let's have sex again so I can win more points."

"You already know most of it."

"But not all, right?"

"No," Elle admitted. Not all.

"So is that a yes for more sex?"

"You need to recover. You're bleeding a little."

"I know," Kyrie said, sighing. She closed her eyes and the smile on her face faded.

"Are you okay?" Elle asked, pulling Kyrie's nightgown back up to cover her breasts. She'd be cold any second now as her temperature plummeted. "You don't have to answer until you're ready. And when you're ready there's no right answer. If you're not okay, you can tell me that, too. I've had 'not okay' sex, too. We can talk about it."

Kyrie still didn't speak. Not a word.

"Kyrie?" Elle prompted. "Are you okay?"

Kyrie rolled onto her side and stretched an arm over Elle's chest and threw her leg over Elle's leg. Elle gathered Kyrie's small shivering self close to her and kissed her on the forehead. She felt a wave of happiness flow through her and a surge of possessiveness. Hers. All hers.

"Elle," she began, "what you just did to me?"

"What?" Elle asked, bracing herself.

"Do it again."

"That's my girl."

23

Haiti

THE SUN HAD SET BY THE TIME THEY MADE IT BACK TO his beach hut. The moon was on the water. The stars had woken up and come out to watch them. And the instant they were inside his beach hut, Kingsley grabbed Juliette by the arm and pulled her hard against him.

She went limp in his arms, resting her weight against him in an act of total surrender.

He kissed her deeply and she wound her arms around his neck. Her height brought her body into perfect alignment with his. She had substance to her, warm flesh and lean muscle, rounded hips and full breasts. He felt her strength even in her surrender and he adored her for giving it up for him, if only for the night.

"You want me to beat you?" he asked her, sliding his hand down her hair and pressing his palm against the small of her back.

"Please," she said. *S'il vous plaît.* "I've dreamed of you doing that to me."

"Has he beaten you?" Kingsley asked when he pulled back from the drugging kiss.

"Yes."

"Was it his doing? Or yours?"

"Mine," she said. "I asked him to hurt me."

"Why? Did you have those fantasies?"

"Sometimes." Juliette sighed heavily. "But the truth? By the time I was twenty, I had been his lover for six years. I was tired of him, bored. My love for him was fading. It was hard to pretend, especially since his interest in me had only grown in that time. I'm the center of his life now and he…" Her voice trailed off. "I used to love him and hate him in equal measure. Now…now the scales have tipped."

"So you asked him to hurt you."

"I did. A few years ago. I needed something, anything to make me look forward to going back to his bed every night."

"Did it?"

She nodded. "It did. It does. I didn't want him anymore, but I wanted *it*, wanted what he gave me at night—pain and fear and power. I wanted that even if I didn't want him."

"Did he like it as much as you did?"

"He didn't want to hurt me at first. I had to beg him to do it."

"Why didn't he want it if you did?"

Juliette shrugged. "He's white. I'm black. He's French. I'm Haitian."

"And that's what pricked his conscience? Skin color and French colonialism? Not that you were fourteen and bargaining for your mother's life when he took you the first time?"

"Don't judge him," Juliette said, pointing a finger at the center of his chest. "You didn't see me when I was fourteen. I would have fucked me, too. And so would you."

"I have a conscience," Kingsley said.

"Is that what you call yours?" she said with a wicked grin.

"You do want me to beat the hell out of you, don't you?"

"Bien sûr," she said with a wide smile.

"Is there anything you don't like, don't want?" he asked. "Any limits?"

"He'll be back in a week. I need to be healed by then. That's all. He and I, we've done everything."

"Does he rape you?"

"When I want him to. He hates it but it's my favorite. If I make him angry, he'll do it, and then he hates us both afterward. I like making him hate himself." She smiled, and Kingsley caught a glimpse of the darkness in her, the mirror image of the darkness in him.

"Do you wear a collar with him?"

"No. He gives me jewelry and expensive clothes. That's how he shows he owns me. I'd rather have the collar. At least that would be something private."

"I've never collared anyone. Collars are for dogs."

"You collar a dog so if it gets lost it can be returned home to its rightful owner again. The collar isn't for the dog. It's for the owner."

Kingsley looked at her and found himself unable to speak for a moment. Finally he managed to get a few words out.

"I want to own you," Kingsley said.

Juliette only laughed and shook her head. "Stand in line."

Kingsley pulled her to him and kissed her.

Juliette had dreamed of him hurting her, she'd said. And Kingsley had fantasized about hurting Juliette since their first night together. Giving and receiving pain was the most intimate act two people could share with each other. More intimate even than sex, which required so little courage. It was a biological itch and that was all. But pain was life and trust and everything he needed from Juliette, everything he needed to give her.

But he hadn't planned for this night, merely fantasized about it. And he had nothing with him—no floggers, no canes, no whips, no chains. That hadn't stopped Søren when they were boys back in high school. But that was Søren and Søren could beat Kingsley breathless using nothing but…

Of course.

Kingsley unbuckled his belt and pulled it out of the loops of his khaki trousers. He'd lost weight while living on the beach, weight he hadn't needed to lose. A month ago he'd dug a belt out of his bag, the one he'd packed in the leather duffel he'd kept in that locker, the bag that contained anything he would need to run for his life if the time came. And the bag that contained the last and only objects that mattered to him. The belt was in that bag.

Juliette took a nervous step back toward the bed.

"Do you know what this is?" Kingsley asked.

"Your belt," she said.

"It is mine, and it isn't." He held it up. The black leather was scuffed and faded, but otherwise it was in pristine condition. It was high quality and had no doubt been expensive when purchased over twenty-five years ago.

"This belt," he continued, "belonged to the first person who ever beat me. He was a boy at my high school, and I loved him. I loved him so much I gave him my body in every way possible. And this was the belt he used when he beat me. His belt. I've kept it all this time."

"It's special to you," Juliette said, eyeing the black leather.

"He is special to me. Was special…"

"Is," she said. "If he wasn't still important to you, you wouldn't be telling me about him."

Kingsley nodded. "He is special to me. Then and now and always. So special I've never beaten anyone with this belt. I kept it hidden away like treasure. Hidden away with all my memories of him and what he did to me."

"You loved him?"

"I did. And I do. Although I wish I didn't sometimes. It's been a knife in me for twenty-three years."

Juliette nodded. "I know that kind of love. A love like a knife," Juliette said. "But the knife is what carves us into who we are. Don't repent of the knife."

"The knife brought me here," he said. "I repent of nothing. Not even making love to you again when I know you'll leave me."

"Not by choice," she said. "I promise, not by choice."

"If you could choose—"

"Don't ask me to choose when I can't. Just…"

"What?"

"Just hurt me tonight until I forget who I belong to. Hurt me until I forget who I am."

Kingsley cupped the back of her neck, kissed her throat. Into her ear he whispered, "I'll make you forget."

He untied the back of her dress and pulled it down and off her body. Would he ever get enough of her body? It seemed impossible. The well of his desire was bottomless and he dived into it headfirst.

He kissed her again, held her breasts in his hands, gripped her hips and pulled her hard against his erection. Then, without warning her, he turned her back to him and shoved her against the rough wooden wall.

She held still, said nothing. Waited with her eyes closed and her head bowed.

He struck her hard between the shoulder blades and harder still a few inches lower. She didn't cry out even when welts appeared on her skin, and he aimed for them. The only sound she made were a few quiet gasps that pleased him more than any scream he'd ever wrung from the lips of a weaker woman. A whip or a flogger made the work easy for him. With a belt he had to throw hard, strike hard, concentrate his energy and his strength. It was as much work for him to hurt her as it was for her to take it. After two or maybe three dozen vicious strikes up and down the entire back of her body, he stopped with as little warning as he'd started.

Juliette remained standing with her eyes closed, panting. He was hard already, eager to have her. Too eager. Dangerously eager. If he took her right now he'd no doubt hurt her with his ardor.

Then again, she'd admitted she liked rough sex. If rough sex was what she wanted, he was more than capable of giving it to her tonight.

Kingsley dropped the belt on the floor and stepped behind Juliette. He pressed his naked chest against the scores of raw welts on her burning back. Then, finally, she cried out in real pain. Sweat and heat against battered flesh…sensual salt rubbed into sublime wounds.

"I'm going to fuck you now," Kingsley whispered in her ear as he opened his pants and let his cock rub against her naked bottom. He let her feel it, let her feel the length and the width and the hardness against her like a threat. Behind her with his back still pressed to her, he rolled on a condom. "And you have one job to do while I'm fucking you."

"What is my order?"

"Try to stop me."

Kingsley grabbed the back of her neck with his left hand. With his right arm he wrapped it around her waist and dragged her toward the bed. Juliette dug in her heels and pushed back against him. She was strong but he was stronger. His fingers dug into her soft skin. No matter how she twisted and turned in his arms, she couldn't get away. He threw her onto the bed and she landed on her back. Before he could get on top of her she had hands up and she pushed hard against his chest.

Blood surged in his veins as he caught her wrists in an iron grasp and forced them down onto either side of her head. She gave a cry of rage and he'd never heard a sound so electrifying. She tried to kick at him but he'd already got a knee between her thighs and was forcing them open. He pressed his full weight onto her, onto her wrists and her thighs. With a burst of sudden strength she jerked under him, nearly succeeding in throwing him off her. But he tightened his grip to the point of pain and beyond.

At last her will to fight back was broken. She went slack underneath him, surrendering. He pulled her wrists together and trapped them in one hand above her head. With his free hand he claimed her body, squeezing her breasts, pinching her nipples, thrusting his fingers inside her wet body until she groaned with unwanted ecstasy. He caught a nipple between his lips and pulled it deep into his mouth. The struggle had made him wild with desire. He shoved his cock inside her and Juliette arched underneath him so hard her back bowed. All around his thrusting length, her vagina pulsed wildly with her orgasm. He kept thrusting, harder and harder, slamming into her with all his might. Sex became fucking became rutting became something else he didn't know because he was too lost in the unbearable pounding pleasure of it.

This woman...this incredible woman...Kingsley couldn't get enough of her, using her, ramming into her until every thrust hurt him as much as it hurt her. And yet the pain was as sweet as white wine and it drugged him like no intoxicant he'd ever taken. And he forgot...everything. Inside her body he forgot his anger at Søren, his anger at himself, the women he'd lost—Marie-Laure, Sam, Charlie, Elle... He forgot everything and everyone but Juliette, whoever she was. He didn't care. She was his. Right now, this moment, she was his. His property, his body, his lover, his treasure.

He'd come to Haiti to drink, to sleep, to forget everything that had happened. By accident he'd stumbled into a dragon's treasure room and found a jewel, rare and priceless. He held a fortune in his hands. Endless wealth. If only he could claim and keep it, he'd be the richest man in the world. How could he walk away from such a treasure? No man could. It would be like walking away from a pile of diamonds, a chest of gold. He'd no more leave Juliette in Haiti than he'd leave an emerald on the ground, a pearl on the beach.

"My Jules..." he whispered into her ear when he came inside her, his semen pouring out of him in aching bursts. "My jewel."

A second climax overtook her and she writhed and shivered underneath him.

"Listen to me," he said between kisses. She was still trapped by his arms and his knees. But the struggle was over and their bodies were still joined. "You belong in my kingdom. You always have. But you were lost to us, and now I've found you again. Your king has found you and I will bring you home where you belong."

"Mon roi," she said in her exhaustion as she went limp against the sweating sheets. My king. "I want to tell you something."

"Don't say it."

He felt her laugh more than heard it. "You don't know what it is," she said.

"I know."

"You know I'm in love with you?" she asked.

"Oui. But don't say it."

"Why not?"

"Because I can't have you. I can't keep you. You aren't mine."

"Then I don't love you," she said, tracing the old and faded scar on his chest with her fingertips. "I don't love you with all my heart and with every inch of my body. I don't love you now and always."

"I will never love you, either," Kingsley said, closing his eyes.

"I don't know about your priest, but my priest says it's a sin to lie," Juliette said, looking down on him. He rested his hand against the side of her face. "The Devil is a murderer and the Father of Lies. When we lie we are like the Devil, killing the truth."

"God will absolve us," Kingsley said. "He knows our lying isn't murder."

"What is it then?"

"Self-defense."

24

THEY KISSED FOR A LONG TIME, ELLE AND KYRIE. NOTH-
ing but kisses, gentle and sleepy. Elle had forgotten how plea-
surable, how sensual, the simple act of kissing could be. She
wasn't designed for chastity. She needed a body in her bed other
than her own. She needed to touch and be touched. And she
needed this girl, this beautiful fragile little girl in her arms as
she needed air and water and food.

"Do you want me to touch you?" Kyrie asked between kisses.
"I mean, like you touched me?"

Elle shook her head. She couldn't stomach the thought of
being touched intimately yet by anyone other than herself. "No,
you don't have to. I already had an orgasm tonight."

"Were you masturbating?" Kyrie asked, a fair question.

"Dreaming," Elle said. "I woke up from the dream having
an orgasm."

"You said you were dreaming about the night you got pregnant. You know exactly when it happened?"

"I do," she said without hesitation. "I remember the day
Søren left for Rome. I remember the day I went to the doctor
because of my kidney infection. I was on antibiotics for two
weeks. When I felt better, Kingsley and I had sex. The next

night we only had anal. Can't get pregnant from anal. The next morning he left for a few days. I remember…" She paused, closed her eyes… She could feel Kingsley inside her again, see him underneath her. And she missed it. Him. She missed him.

"I'm sorry. We don't have to talk about it if you don't want to."

"We can talk about it. But you're the nun, and I'm the unrepentant slut. It'll probably bother you a lot more to hear about it than it'll bother me to talk about it."

"I'm not…" Kyrie paused. "Let's just say I haven't made up my mind about abortion the way the Catholic Church has. I can't imagine it's ever an easy choice. But I can imagine that sometimes it's the only choice you'd have."

"It was the right choice," Elle said. "But no, I wouldn't call it easy."

"Why did you do it?"

"When I was seventeen, God and I had a long talk. I told him that I would never ask Søren to leave the priesthood if God would let Søren and I be together. Something happened that night and whatever childish dreams I'd had of marrying him and having his children burned to ashes. I have new dreams now. Children aren't part of my dreams. Is that selfish?"

"Children aren't part of my dreams, either. How can I judge you without judging myself?"

"Even if I did want children, I don't think my life is…was the sort of life you should bring a child into." She rubbed her forehead and laughed. "You know what Friday night is at Kingsley's house?"

"I don't know? Game night?"

"Orgy night," she said. "He throws these wild parties on Friday nights and all the rich beautiful people of Manhattan show up and get off. You walk around and there are naked women everywhere with men fucking them over and on top of every piece of furniture in the place. Except the piano. The piano was off-limits."

"Why not the piano? Is Kingsley some big music lover?"

"The piano was Kingsley's gift to Søren." Kingsley had bought the piano even before he and Søren had reunited. A gift? More like an altar.

"What about Kingsley?"

Elle sighed heavily and closed her eyes.

"Kingsley...that's the only knot I can't quite untie. Kingsley wants children. He always has. I took that chance from him."

"He'll have other chances."

"I tell myself that. I hope I'm right."

"It's not your job to provide a baby for every man who wants one," Kyrie said. "If God wanted women to be baby makers, He wouldn't have called so many of us to religious orders."

"Kingsley's special," Elle said. "And he would never have wanted me to have a child against my will. I know that. But I also know that he wished I'd wanted it. That's what still hurts, knowing he's still hurting."

"So when did you realize you were pregnant?"

"It was a few days before Søren was due to come back from Rome. He was defending his dissertation at the Jesuit university there. PhD number two."

"Two PhDs? That's crazy. He must be really smart."

"He's the most intelligent man I've ever known. And such a nerd," Elle said, smiling. "But he's a Jesuit. PhDs are like catnip to Jesuits. They pop a boner around academic degrees like a teenage boy with his first *Playboy*."

"Oh God, my great-uncle's a Jesuit."

"Sorry," Elle said, wincing. "How many PhDs does he have?"

"Three. Which is probably the same number of boners he's had since becoming a Jesuit."

Elle laughed.

"Not the sexy, vow-breaking kind of Jesuit then?"

"Dry as dust and about as sexy," Kyrie said.

"Søren is sexy," Elle said. "You've never seen a more beautiful man in your life. Blond hair. Darker than yours but still very blond. Handsome. Strong nose and jaw. Gray eyes like the color of a cloudy morning. And he's tall—six foot four. Tall and strong. I used to sit on his back while he did push-ups in the morning. Five hundred of them without me. Or one hundred of them with me."

"Wow, that is seriously strong."

"Once we spent the night at Kingsley's and Kingsley took over push-up duty. He stood barefoot on Søren's back. Søren only made it to fifty Kingsley push-ups, but that's still pretty good. Kingsley's six feet tall, weighs about one-ninety, I think."

"Oh my God. I weigh ninety-five pounds. He's exactly two of me."

Elle gave a wistful sigh. "I was living in this erotic Paradise. If Søren was busy there was always Kingsley. If Kingsley and Søren were free at the same time, it was both of them in the same bed. All night long."

"It sounds perfect. Apart from the men. Change them to beautiful women, and it's my secret Heaven."

"It was as close to perfect as you can get in this life, I guess."

Kyrie rolled onto her side and sat up halfway. She rested her weight on her right hand and looked down at Elle. Her nightgown fell off her shoulder and Elle had to fight off a wave of desire for her.

"So why…why if everything was so sexy and perfect, why did you say you've had 'not okay' sex?"

"What?"

"You know." Kyrie shrugged. "After you and I were done having sex…" She blushed as she spoke. "After we were done, you said it was fine if I wasn't okay. You said you'd had 'not okay' sex before. That doesn't sound like Paradise to me."

"Why do you care so much?"

Kyrie flashed hurt eyes at her.

"Because it's you, and I care about you. Do you think I would be in bed with you if I didn't care about you?"

"I'm sorry. I didn't mean it that way."

"Elle, you loved him, right? Your priest?"

"Yes." She couldn't deny it so she didn't bother denying it.

"You loved him, but you still left him. That scares me."

"Why would it scare you that I left *him*?"

"Because if you can leave someone you're that much in love with, how much easier would it be to leave me?"

"Kyrie..." Elle pulled Kyrie close to her and wrapped her arms tight around the girl's thin shoulders. "Listen to me. There is no way in Hell you will ever make me as angry at you as I am at Søren. And I'm not going to leave you like I left him. I can't stay here forever but remember, you're the one in the convent, the one who's taken a vow of chastity."

"Temporary vows," Kyrie said.

"But you've got final vows coming up."

"In two years."

"Okay, in two years, you'll take final vows and go back to the abbey in California, right?"

"I know. I'm sorry. This is all new to me."

"It's new to me, too," Elle said. "I've never been in a relationship with another woman before. We'll have to figure it out together. But I'm not going to run away from you, so put that thought out of your pretty little head."

Elle tapped her on the forehead between the eyes. Kyrie's eyes crossed and Elle laughed.

Kyrie stretched out again along Elle's side and laid an arm across her stomach.

Elle took a deep breath.

"I did love Søren," she said again. "And I do love him. Still. Do you know how hard it is to leave someone you're in love with? To walk away from them? Or worse," she said, remembering the near-crippling pain she'd been in that night, "to crawl away?"

"I can't imagine. I don't want to imagine…"

"I think about it all the time. Why I left Søren. Why I haven't gone back yet. I need to think about it otherwise maybe I'd forget why I left him and then…"

"You'd go back?"

Elle nodded.

"And I don't want to go back. Even if I did, I shouldn't go back. So I think about bad times, the bad things about being with him. It's a short list but…"

"What's on the list?"

"Not getting to spend as much time with him as I want to. Not getting to go out in public as a couple. We've never spent Thanksgiving together, you know? He spends it with his sister Claire at her place with her family. She knows about me but bringing me along would be asking for trouble. All it takes is one person making one phone call, and we're front-page news, Søren and I. But it's not just stuff like that."

Elle felt Kyrie's eyes on her but didn't meet her gaze. She raised a hand to her forehead and rubbed between her eyes.

"I've never told anyone about this," Elle finally said.

"Told anyone what?"

"The list of things I tell myself to keep me from going back to him… Something happened once—only once—but once was enough. If it had happened twice, I think I would have left him a long time ago."

"What did he do to you?" Kyrie asked, the same question Daniel had asked her. This time Elle would answer.

"It's not easy being the sexual property of a sadist," she said with a tired smile. "It's sexy. It's fun. It's intense like you can't imagine. Fear makes it potent. Doing something dangerous makes it potent. But there's always a risk that you can go too far and someone can get hurt."

"You got hurt?"

Elle nodded.

"In kink, we have a thing called a 'safe word.' It's nothing special, just a word that means 'Stop, I mean it.' If you're doing heavy role-play stuff and you want to be able to say 'Oh no, not that. Don't put your big cock in me, sir, and force me against my will to have an orgasm. Anything but that,'" Elle said, putting the back of her hand on her forehead and pretending to play a pearl-clutching virgin. "You know, stuff like that. You need a word that means 'stop' that isn't stop. Mine is Jabberwocky."

"Good word. Sounds nothing like stop."

"Easy to remember, too," Elle said, glancing away from Kyrie's searching gaze. "Unless you get so freaked out you forget it in the moment."

"Is that what happened? You forgot your safe word?"

"We'd only been lovers a couple weeks," Elle said. "I was a virgin until Søren, a virgin until I was twenty years old. But after our first night together, I felt like we'd done everything there was to do. But we hadn't actually. We hadn't even scratched the surface of everything…"

"Did he put his entire hand inside your vagina?"

"Not that night."

"Then I still win."

"You win," Elle said, touching Kyrie's face, tucking a lock of hair behind her ear. She kissed her again but Kyrie wasn't to be deterred or distracted from her question by so obvious a ploy as a kiss.

"What happened?" Kyrie asked, and Elle knew she had to answer.

"It was after our third night together, a Thursday night. I remember that because Søren didn't have anything to do until noon on Fridays so we could actually stay in bed together longer, spend the whole night and the morning after together. And it was a rough night. Rough in the good way. Lots of kink. Lots of sex. Afterward we were curled up together in bed. I was laying on his chest. Laying? Lying? I can never remember which. And we were talking."

Elle closed her eyes. And when she opened them she lay on Søren's chest, her head against his heart.

"How are you feeling, Little One?" he asked as he stroked her back with his fingertips. He'd left her covered in welts from his cane and even his gentle touches burned. But she didn't stop him from touching her. She would never stop him from touching her.

"Sore. Happy. You?"

"Happy," he said.

Søren happy was her favorite sort of happy. She knew everything there was to know about his past, his pain, everything he'd suffered growing up. To know that right now in this moment he was happy, that the darkness was outside the room tonight and not in it, that made her happier than her own happiness ever could.

"I want to make you happy," she said, kissing the center of his chest.

"You please me very much."

"Is there anything I can do to please you more?" she asked, hoping the answer was yes. Whatever it was, she would do it, allow it, enjoy it. Anything for him.

He sighed heavily and she grinned as she rose and fell on the wave of that big breath.

"There's something I'd like us to do together. When you're ready."

"What is it? And I promise, I'm ready."

"You don't know what it is yet," he said, rolling onto his side. She lay on hers and faced him. "So how do you know you're ready?"

"It's like the numbers game we play when you make me pick a number between one and ten and you don't tell me what I'm picking. One kiss? Ten kisses? One strike of the cane? Ten strikes of the cane? I pick a number and you do whatever it is you want to do."

"This is different." He reached out and ran his fingers through her unbound hair. He caressed her face, traced her bottom lip with his thumb.

"Is it something you want to do?" she asked.

"Very much. It's been a fantasy of mine since I saw you."

She smiled at him. Her eyes were bright with the untold secret. She even bit her bottom lip, an act that he punished by kissing her and biting her bottom lip for her.

"I'm yours," she said into the kiss. "Do anything you want to me, my sir. My body is yours…"

"Yes, it is," he said, stretching out on top of her and deepening the kiss. "You're all mine. Now and always…"

Whatever it was, she wanted him to do it to her right then, right there. She'd waited years to be with him and now that they were lovers, she wanted him all the time. She couldn't get enough of his body inside hers, couldn't get enough of the pain he gave her. Nothing made her feel more beautiful than to kneel naked at his feet and let him mark her with welts and bruises. And to know he'd fantasized about doing something to her since the day they met excited her beyond reason.

"Please…" she whispered as he pulled her back against his chest and settled into bed once more.

"Not tonight. But soon."

"Never soon enough," she said as he ran his finger around the edge of her white leather collar. She would fall asleep in it tonight and by morning he would have taken it off her and put it away. And she drifted off to sleep in the safety of his arms.

★ ★ ★

"What was it?" Kyrie asked. "What was his fantasy?"

Elle took a deep breath and smiled as Kyrie rose and fell on the wave of that breath. Now she was the Dominant and she had her a little Sub all her own. And she had no idea what to do with her.

"I found out the next morning," Elle said. "I woke up in his bed and my collar was off my neck. I could hear water running down the hall so I went to take a shower with him."

She wanted mornings with Søren almost as much as nights. Nights were a secret time, dark and erotic. A time for sin and whispers, passion and pain. But mornings…mornings were an everyday time. Light and bright. Drinking coffee together. Reading the newspaper. Discussing the day ahead and plotting how to make it through the hours until the next night they could be together came again. As much as she loved the sins and the secrets, Elle also longed for the light, for the simple pleasures of fighting over the sink while brushing their teeth and making the bed—he took the right side, she took the left— and, of course, taking a quick shower together.

She stepped into the shower and in an instant she was in his arms. His mouth was on her mouth, on her neck, on her breasts. The hot water poured over them both. She reached up and slicked his hair back, marveling at how much darker the blond turned when wet.

"Did I say you could get out of bed?" he asked, biting her hard on the neck. She shuddered at the sting of his teeth on her tender skin. He pulled her hair hard enough to elicit a gasp. He bit her lips again between kisses, dug his fingers into the soft flesh of the small of her back.

"No, sir," she said, smiling in her defiance. She felt the tip of his erection pressing against her belly.

"Did I say you could steal my water?" he asked, pinching her nipples to the point of pain.

"No, sir." She pushed her hips against him, eager already to have him inside her. They'd never made love in the shower before, and she treasured all of their first times. First kiss, first touch, first time he beat her in his bedroom, first time he beat her in the living room and then took her on the floor by the fireplace…she wanted all their firsts and all their seconds and all their thirds and she couldn't get them fast enough. "But what are you going to do about it?" she taunted. "No floggers in the shower. No whips, no toys. How are you going to punish me in here?"

And then he smiled. The smile scared her.

"Like this," he said and pushed her face-first against the tile wall. "This is how."

There was, in her memory, a split second of pause. And in that split second she'd had three distinct thoughts.

I know what he's going to do to me.

I don't want him to do it.

How do I stop it?

Before she could remember the answer to number three, he was inside her with one vicious thrust. She screamed into her arm as he penetrated her anally. It felt like a burning blade sliced her body in half from neck to knees. His mouth was at her ear and she heard his breath catch in ecstasy. Her pain was his pleasure, he'd told her. So surely now he experienced the greatest pleasure of his life as she had never known pain like this. It was without beginning and without end and for all she knew in her blind panic she would feel like this forever. He came inside her.

And then it was over.

He pulled out of her and kissed the back of her neck. She stood stock-still as he stepped out of the shower. Slowly she sank down onto the floor of the bathtub. Her arm bled from a small cut. Wide-eyed and without recognizing her own body, she wondered how the cut had got there, whose arm that was and why it was bleeding. Oh, it was her arm. Of course it was. And the cut came from her teeth. She'd been bracing herself against the wall and had bitten her own arm. Silly her.

"Eleanor? Are you staying in there all day?" Søren pulled back open the shower door and looked down at her sitting with her knees to her chest, her arm bleeding, the water beating off her like a storm she didn't notice was happening.

She looked up at him.

"I forgot my safe word."

Elle turned and looked at Kyrie, who was staring at her wide-eyed with horror.

"That's it," Elle said.

"What is?" Kyrie whispered the words.

"The way you're looking at me now is exactly the way he looked at me when I told him I forgot my safe word. I had never seen that look on his face before. I didn't think you could shock Søren. No, it wasn't shock. It was horror."

"I can believe it," Kyrie breathed. "What did he do when he realized what happened?"

"He turned off the water and opened a towel. He held it open and waited. I got up and stepped into the towel. What a pair we must have made right then. He was already dressed—collar and everything. And here was this naked girl, soaking wet, wearing nothing but a white towel. He picked me up and carried me to his bedroom. He didn't say anything, not a word. He dried me off and checked to make sure I wasn't torn or bleeding. I wasn't except for my arm. So he cleaned the cut on my arm and put a Band-Aid on it. I think...I think I laughed then—when he put the Band-Aid on. I asked him why he didn't have Snoopy Band-Aids. Those were my favorite as a kid. I'd get so excited when I scraped my knees or elbows as a kid because then I had

an excuse to cover myself in Snoopy Band-Aids. Anyway…"
She paused and took a much-needed breath. "He dressed me
in my underwear and one of his white T-shirts. And then he
held me in his arms, in a chair. He held me and I held him.
And we didn't talk about what happened. And we didn't need
to talk about it. It never happened again."

"Never?"

"Don't get me wrong, he hurt me. A lot. But never like that
again. And he always had my explicit consent before doing anything new. But even when you've given your consent, sometimes you still don't know what you're in for."

"Sounds like joining a religious order. Before I got here…I
had no idea what I was getting myself into."

"Søren said the young seminarians he knew were all so
bright-eyed and happy—thrilled even—to take their vows of
celibacy, to give up family life for God and the church. He said
you could watch that light visibly fading year after year. Ten
years into their priesthood, twenty years, and they were running
on fumes, drinking heavily, cheating every chance they got, or
worse. They didn't know what they'd signed up for. Same with
being a submissive. You go into it wide-eyed and then reality
comes along and kicks you in the ass—sometimes literally."

"Were you angry at him?" Kyrie asked. A good question, she
had to admit. Elle wished she had a good answer. She wished
she'd been angry at him. That would have been healthier than
blaming herself. But she'd given him permission, and he'd taken
her at her word. Who was to blame? Maybe nobody.

"Back then I was only mad at myself for forgetting my safe
word. And I was ashamed. Which was a foreign feeling for
me that day. I felt so stupid. I had one job as his submissive—
say my safe word if and when I wanted the scene to stop. That
would have stopped it. One word, and I couldn't even do that
right. It took me a few weeks to get over that feeling. Søren,
he was more careful with me after. And when we had anal sex

the second time about a month later, it was amazing. Like the best sex we'd ever had. I think he was trying to make up for what happened in the shower. That morning in the shower, I think maybe…"

"What?" Kyrie asked.

Elle smiled and remembered the story Kingsley had told her about his first time with Søren on the forest floor. *He fucked the life out of me, Elle. Every other time we used lube but that night, there was only blood. My blood. And I hope God is as understanding as you two like to tell me He is, because if I get to Heaven and God wants to wipe my memory of the night and take away the blood and the pain, I'll turn on my heel and walk straight into Hell just to keep the memory.*

"Søren had one other lover before me, a hard-core masochist. I think Søren forgot who he was with for a second. If so, he never forgot again. And I never forgot, either. But that didn't stop me from whispering my safe word to myself over and over again for the next two weeks until it was the only word I knew. At night before bed, when I woke up the next morning, before lunch, after lunch and into my coffee. It's a miracle I didn't introduce myself to people that way by mistake. 'Hi, I'm Jabberwocky, nice to meet you.'"

"Why did you pick that word?"

"I loved Lewis Carroll's books as a kid. So did Søren. It was something we had in common, and if you compare his childhood to mine, you'd see how crazy it was we had anything in common at all. I loved the books because I thought they were funny. But he… When Søren was five years old, his father sent him to England to live with relatives and go to boarding school. He said he loved *Alice's Adventures in Wonderland* and *Through the Looking Glass* because he wanted to believe there was another world out there he could get to by stepping through a mirror or falling down a rabbit hole. But he didn't want a Wonderland with Mad Hatters and March Hares. He wanted to see his mother again, and he didn't know how to find her. He'd walk past a mirror and catch a glimpse of his own blond hair and he would…he'd think for a second it was her waiting just around the corner of the world inside the mirror."

Elle closed her eyes and let herself love the lonely little boy Søren had been once upon a time.

"So Jabberwocky was my safe word because it meant something to both of us," Elle said, clearing the knot from her throat with a cough.

"Did you ever use it?"

"Once more," Elle said. "The night I left Søren once and for all. But that's a longer story than this one and you need to get back to your room. It's almost 3:00 a.m. You have to get up soon."

"I don't want to go. I want to stay with you all night."

"I know," Elle said, kissing Kyrie on top of her head. "I know that feeling. But if you want another night with me, we can't get caught."

With obvious reluctance, Kyrie rolled up. Elle saw her wince.

"How are you?" she asked Kyrie. "Are you sore?"

"Sore," she said, nodding. "And happy. Are you happy?"

"I feel better than I've felt in a long time."

"I'm going to be thinking about you…what we did, all day tomorrow."

"Me, too," Elle said, tying a knot in the cord of Kyrie's white robe. "All tomorrow and the day after and the day after…"

"We can do it again, right?"

"Yes, definitely. But we'll wait a couple days until you're healed. Take warm baths. That's an order."

Kyrie grinned. "Yes, ma'am."

"Kiss me good-night. That's another order."

Kyrie bent down and kissed Elle on the mouth. It should have been a quick kiss but it lasted far too long and yet ended all too soon.

"Good night, my dove," Elle said, brushing Kyrie's hair over her shoulder. "Sleep well."

She started for the door but stopped and turned back.

"You used your safe word the night you left him?" Kyrie asked.

"I did."

"Was what he did to you that night…was it worse than what he did to you in the shower?"

Was it worse? The night she'd left him Søren hadn't laid a hand on her. He hadn't hit her, hadn't touched her and didn't fuck her in any way.

Elle glanced away, let herself remember what had happened, forced herself to forget.

"Much worse."

25

Haiti

"ARE YOU OUT OF YOUR HAITIAN MIND?" KINGSLEY DEmanded, to which Juliette had a cruel retort.

"Are you out of your French courage?"

"I'm half-American."

"I thought Americans were supposed to be brave, always running off to play war."

"You're getting courage confused with stupidity." He leaned forward and looked down. "I shouldn't have done that."

"It's not that far down. You'll be fine."

"You have gone mad in the heat," Kingsley continued. "Sunstroke? Heatstroke? That would explain this."

"Pussy," Juliette said.

"Meow."

"You know you want to…" Juliette gave him a cat-eyed smile.

"I know nothing of the sort. I have no desire whatsoever to do this. You are living in a dreamworld, a dreamworld where gravity does not exist. I live in the real world. I have been shot four times. I have looked death in the face, shook his hand and said we have to stop meeting this way. So if you think I'm going to do this, you are as foolish as you are beautiful."

Juliette leaned over the edge of the cliff. Kingsley followed her eyes fifty feet down to the blue-and-white water below.

"I must be," she said. "Because I'm going to jump. And you're going to follow me down."

"Is this a cry for help?" Kingsley asked, forcing his gaze back up to the sky. The view down to the water had made his head swim with dizziness.

"Diving's fun," she said. "And it's not as hard as it seems. You have to close your eyes…listen to the waves. You hear that? That crash when they come in? That's when you jump. By the time you hit the water, the wave will be on its way out away from the rocks."

"You've done this before?"

"I have."

"Many times?" he asked.

"So many times."

"And you've never been killed?"

"I'd hardly be standing here talking to you if I had been," she said, still smiling. They'd spent the past few days in his bed at the beach hut. They'd hardly come up for air or water or food. They'd survived on sex, thrived on it, feasted on each other and been sated. But this morning Juliette had woken him at noon, dragged him from bed, told him she had a surprise for him.

It was a terrible surprise.

"Mon roi," she said, wrapping her arms around his neck. She wore nothing but a red bikini and a skirt around her hips festooned with white-and-red flowers. And he had on nothing but his khaki pants rolled up to his calves. "There is something I want to show you and I can't show it to you unless we go down to the water. And there's only one way down to the water."

"Then how do we get back up again?"

"Maybe we don't," she said. "Maybe we stay down there forever."

"Because we've crashed against the rocks and died?"

"Because it's Paradise. And who would ever leave Paradise?"

"Adam and Eve left Paradise."

"Adam and Eve were expelled from Paradise. They weren't allowed to stay. And ever since God sent Adam and Eve from Paradise, we've been trying to get back there."

"And you know the way?"

"I know a shortcut."

"Is death your shortcut?"

"Trust me," she whispered, looking at him with her bright and gleaming eyes. "I've done this dive a thousand times. You wait for the wave to hit, you jump, and in seconds...there you are, in the water, safe."

"What if I jump at the wrong time?"

"Then the water throws you against the rocks, your spine shatters, your skull explodes like a dropped egg, and you die."

He saw the mirth shining in her eyes. She was trying to scare him. Oh, she would get it later for this. If he survived this insane leap.

"I'm going back to the hut. Paradise is not worth the risk."

"Paradise is the only thing worth the risk."

She pulled away from him and untied her skirt.

"What are you doing?"

She looked back over her shoulder at him. "Everyone thinks Paradise is up...high up in the sky and far away. But it's not. It's down there. And I'm going. With or without you."

"You can't go without me."

"We all go alone. But you're welcome to meet me there."

Then she winked and turned away. He fell silent and watched her close her eyes. She was listening, listening to the water. With her eyes still closed she took a step and another. And then she was running and with the ends of her red wrap in her fingers she launched herself off the cliff. Kingsley raced to the edge and watched her swan dive down to the water, the wrap in her fingers still floating and flying behind her like red-and-white wings. She hit the water with the smallest of splashes and he held his breath. Between the inhale and the exhale he lived and died a thousand deaths.

When she surfaced again and waved up at him, he breathed out finally.

"Why can't I ever fall in love with a normal woman?" he sighed to himself. "Just once…"

He looked up at the sky hoping for an answer.

"Too much to ask? One normal woman?" He held up one finger. "Or man. I'm not picky. You know me. Someone without a horrible childhood and no kinks that will get me killed."

He leaned over the edge of the cliff and yelled down at Juliette.

"Cliff diving is one of my hard limits!"

She must not have heard him because all she did was wave.

He closed his eyes, took a breath. He thought he heard something somewhere, something like laughter. But surely it was only the waves on the water below.

God didn't answer so he took the silence for a no. So when the water hit the rocks Kingsley jumped feet first. It seemed he hovered in midair a moment. The way down passed in a second and lasted an eternity. In the final second before he hit the water, he thought of all that he'd done and all that he wanted in his life. Everything he'd wanted to do he'd done but for two final things on his to-do list. He wanted to save Juliette, and he wanted to have children. And if he survived this foolish leap to his imminent death he would do both.

He hit the water with so much force he went blind and deaf. He couldn't see the way to the surface, couldn't hear the sound of the surf. Up and down became meaningless. Life waited in one direction. Death in the other. But which?

He felt a hand on his hair, a tug on his arm. He went where he was pulled and surfaced with a gasp of breath. The rocks were fifty yards away. Juliette was right there. Smiling. Laughing. Alive. Both of them. Alive and beautiful.

"It's this way," she called out over the rolling waves. She kicked off and he followed her. She might have been guiding him to Hell—he didn't care. Where she went he would follow. If she was there, it was Paradise no matter the destination.

After a few minutes of fighting the choppy surf, they entered calmer darker waters. Kingsley spied Juliette's destination—a large basalt rock formation a hundred yards out. She swam toward it with graceful powerful strokes of her arms and kicks of her long legs. Kingsley went underwater and kicked his way to her. They reached the rocks at the same time and carefully climbed up the tallest of the boulders.

"What is this place?" Kingsley asked as he sat to her right and raised a hand to his forehead to shield his eyes from the sun.

"Playground," she said.

"Playground?"

"Watch."

Silently she peered out over the dancing waves. Kingsley followed her gaze. It was beautiful here with the sound of the surf filling the air and the call of the seabirds and the sun skipping over the waves.

"There," she said, pointing. "Do you see?"

Kingsley looked and laughed. Two dolphins breached the surface of the water and shot steam into the air. Ten yards away, three more dolphins came up for air. They glided along the surface with incredible power—their sleek bodies pure muscle and energy.

"You never see that in Manhattan, do you?" Juliette asked.

"No," Kingsley breathed. "If there are dolphins in the Hudson River, I've never seen them."

For a long time they didn't speak, only watched the dolphins play. Was it play, though? They surfaced to breathe, swam fast to hunt, frolicked to learn how to fight. It was life to them—life and death. Not a game at all. And Kingsley wondered if something was out there, something greater than himself, greater than Juliette, perched in the distance and watching him and watching her, sitting together on this rock, making love in his bed, watching the pain he gave her, the worship she gave him, and smiling at what looked like play, what looked like a game. But it wasn't a game to him and Juliette. It was their lives.

"You could stay," Juliette said at last. "Here in Haiti."

"I could stay," he repeated. "And why would I do that?"

"For them." She pointed at the pod of dolphins that had moved in closer to the rocks. One of the larger ones swam right in front of them, his dorsal fin pockmarked with old battle scars. Kingsley could sympathize.

"For the dolphins? A good reason. Anything else?"

"Maybe for the food?"

"There is a very good Haitian restaurant in Manhattan."

Juliette laughed. "Then maybe stay for me?"

"You belong to someone else," he said. "And it sounds like he wouldn't be interested in sharing."

"He wouldn't have to know. I could come to you at night after he's asleep. I could try."

She wasn't looking at him now, only at the water and the waves and the ever-shifting sunlight.

"How long could you do that before he found out?" Kingsley asked turning to look at her. Water ran down her face. Ocean water from her hair? Tears? Both? "And what would happen when he caught us?"

"I don't know," she said, "but it wouldn't be good."

"Let me help you," Kingsley said. "Please."

"You can't buy me," she said, blinking hard. "I've already been bought. I'm not for sale."

Her words hurt more than any weapon used against him ever had. They hurt not because they were false, but because they were true. He did want to buy her. He wanted to own her. And she wanted nothing but her freedom, the one thing he couldn't give her.

"There has to be a way. Let me help you."

"Just kiss me," she said. "That's how you can help me."

Kingsley kissed her. She tasted like the ocean and the ocean tasted like tears. He cupped the back of her neck and held her steady, held her against his mouth as he kissed her harder and deeper.

"I've never…" she began and stopped.

"Never what?" Kingsley asked.

"I've never brought him here. I've never brought anyone here. This is my secret place."

"Then why did you bring me here?"

"Because you are my other secret place now." She rested her hand on his bare chest over his heart.

Kingsley took her by the wrist and lifted her arm to his lips. He kissed her hand, turned it and kissed inside her palm.

"I can't let you go," he said. "Not even when he comes back."

"You can," she said, kissing his lips, his cheek, his jaw to his ear. "You can and you will. And you'll go home to your world, and I'll stay in mine. And we'll be fine, you and I. I'll be fine. Eventually. Someday."

"I won't. Don't pretend you will, either," Kingsley said. Juliette didn't argue. He knew she felt as he did, that what they were to each other they could only be to each other.

He kissed her again, more passionately now. There was no way to make love to her out here without tearing her back to shreds on the rough rocks. And they had nothing with them, not a single condom. But he had to touch her. They were far from the shore, no other people in sight. He untied her suit top and pulled it off her. Her naked breasts were magnificent in the sunlight with water sliding down her skin. He dipped his head and licked a water droplet from her breast before taking a nipple in his mouth and sucking deep. He cupped her other breast in his hand, massaged it. She arched her back as he kissed and licked her nipples.

When her breaths grew ragged and harsh, he untied the bow on her right hip and slipped his hand between her legs. She opened her thighs for him, leaned back on her hands and tilted her hips for him in an invitation.

Kingsley pressed his fingertip lightly against her clitoris. He brushed it gently again and again and Juliette panted between her parted lips. Her eyes were closed and her long thick lashes lay on her cheeks. He kneaded the swollen knot harder now, making circles with his finger. It pulsed against him as her hips moved in time with his touch. He entered her with one finger and found her wet inside, wet and hot. He pushed a second finger inside her. He didn't rush the moment, didn't force her climax. All he needed was to touch her as deeply and intimately as possible.

Inside her he pressed his fingertips into the soft indentation under her pubic bone. Juliette's inner muscles clenched him and she gasped again. Her fingers curled tight on the rocks. As wet as she was, it was easy to push a third finger into her. He pushed against the walls of her vagina, slipping his fingers into the inner folds, opening her up, exploring, learning every inch of her. He found a pulse point inside her and pressed his fingertip into it. Against his hand he felt the wild pounding beat of her heart.

He turned his hand again and penetrated her with his thumb and index finger. Juliette gripped his thigh and squeezed to the point of pain.

"There," she said, the words coming out in sharp rasps. "Like that."

He fucked her with his fingers now and her thighs fell open. His hands were covered with her wetness. He'd never felt such raw sexual chemistry with a woman before, such incredible aching hunger. He would die before his desire for her ran out. For days she'd played his sexual property, submitting to his every order, his every need. And it was a cruel trick the gods were playing on him, for whenever he entered her, penetrated her, it was Juliette who dug her way deeper inside of him.

She was close to coming now. He could feel her muscles tightening on his hand, gripping him hard, pulsing and contracting. She cried out in her release, but Kingsley didn't stop. He pushed on, still touching her past the point of pleasure until she winced and flinched in pain.

"It hurts," she said but didn't tell him to stop. He didn't stop. He rubbed her still-throbbing clitoris until she cried out again with a second orgasm. He didn't let her catch her breath, didn't let her rest. He knew her body by now, knew what it was capable of. Inside her she bore an inexhaustible supply of ecstasy and he knew how to find it and release it. He gave her pleasure until it turned to pain, gave her pain until it turned once more to pleasure.

"You're punishing me," she said, her voice weak and tired. Still he worked his hand inside her, and still she stayed open for him, letting him use her as he willed.

"I am," he said. "Every time he touches you for the rest of your life you'll think of me. I will burn myself into your mind like a fucking brand and it will never heal."

She cried out with her fourth orgasm. Her body shook and her vagina spasmed with the tremors of her climax. He let her rest at last and reluctantly he pulled his hand from her. While she watched, he licked her wetness off his fingers. She opened his trousers and took his length in her hand. He hadn't ordered her to do anything but he didn't stop her from taking him in her mouth, sucking him hard. The rocks underneath him hurt his hands and his back. The pain spiked his pleasure. Not since Søren had he felt this particular brutal combination of desire, of agony, of ecstasy and fear. When they were lovers, Kingsley had feared Søren and what could happen between them.

Kingsley's life had been in Søren's hands because Kingsley had put it there. With Juliette, Kingsley feared something far more terrifying—he feared what might not happen. He might lose Juliette, he might lose this game. But now he only lost himself in the impossible bliss of this moment with the sun warm on his body and the waves cold against his feet and Juliette's mouth wet and hot around him. And when he came, he came with blinding force oblivious now to the rocks scoring his back. He felt only the movement of Juliette's tongue as it coaxed his cock deeper and her throat as she swallowed every drop of him.

When it was done and over and they had nothing else to give or take from each other, Juliette rested her head on Kingsley's chest and he wrapped an arm around her naked back.

He had to have her. He had to. He couldn't imagine a world where she belonged to any man but him. So he would have her. Whatever it took. He would have her. No matter what he had to do. He would have her. Even if it killed him.

He would have her.

Even if he had to kill for her.

26

ELLE COULDN'T STOP SMILING. AT FIRST SHE TRIED TO stop when she realized someone might notice her behaving oddly. After all, she probably hadn't smiled five times in the past six months. But when alone she gave up the battle against her own happiness. Why not smile? She'd had one of the most amazing nights of her life without Søren, without Kingsley, without a man anywhere near her. All day long and all night, all the next night long and all the day after, she thought of Kyrie. Kyrie's face with its elfin beauty and her small body that fit so nicely against Elle's, and her scent like ocean water and the beach and the warmth of the California sun...

Flashes of memory from their night together intruded into all of Elle's thoughts. The sheets she washed and folded reminded her of the sheets she'd taken Kyrie's virginity on. And the sunlight breaking through the spring cloud cover reminded her of Kyrie's smile. And for two nights Elle had lain alone in her bed praying Kyrie would come to her again. But the girl was too good at following orders already. Elle had told her to wait a few days, and wait Kyrie did. So Elle waited, too. Impatiently, wistfully and in a near-constant state of arousal. Images from their night together hit Elle's brain like an electric current. Her knees went weak—literally—and she'd have to stop every few minutes and brace herself on the counter, catch her breath, refocus her thoughts. She hadn't walked around in this sort of lust-filled daze since she was a teenager waiting for Søren to have her. She needed Kyrie, needed her now, in her bed. And Elle needed to top her, dominate her, use her. For years, Elle had ignored her dominance fantasies but now she gave free rein to them, all of them. There was no one to stop her now from doing whatever she wanted to do to Kyrie. No priest, no king. And not even God would get in the way of Elle doing to Kyrie everything she dreamed of doing.

And these were her dreams.

Next time she and Kyrie were in bed together, she would tie that girl spread-eagle to the cot and give her so many orgasms they'd need a calculator to total them all up.

Gagging might be a good idea. That many orgasms could get loud, after all.

Oh...maybe a blindfold? Kyrie would be able to focus on what she felt if Elle took her sense of sight away.

Would Kyrie like pain? She could start with a spanking and together they could work their way up to harder stuff.

Wait. Had Elle ever spanked anyone in her life? Swatting Kingsley on the ass when he wore a pair of particularly tight and well-tailored trousers didn't count.

This was a convent. Candles everywhere. Maybe Kyrie would like candle-wax play. Who didn't like candle-wax play?

So many ideas, fantasies, dreams...all Elle needed was another night with Kyrie. And another. And another. Then a whole week with Kyrie. A whole year. They needed their own bedroom, their own house, where they could do everything they wanted.

House?

"Oh my God, one night with a girl and I'm already packing the U-Haul," she said out loud.

No to the house idea. They'd start with a hotel room and see where things went from there.

Elle gave up her work and stared out the window of the laundry room. The trees swayed in a spring breeze. The sun dappled the leaves that shone with morning dew. The sky was a brilliant blue. This was her world and it was good. And she, she was happy. Elle was happy for the first time in a long time. She was happy without Søren. It was possible. It could happen. It had happened. She could leave him and move on with her life. Hope was Heaven, and she had Heaven in her heart.

Once upon a time she thought the world would end if she ever had to live without him.

And here she was, without him. And here was the world, spinning on its axis as usual.

She had survived the end of the world and found at the end a new beginning. And if she'd survived the end of the world, surely she could survive anything now.

"Eleanor Louise Schreiber, what the hell do you think you're doing?"

Elle started and dropped the sheet she'd been halfheartedly folding and spun around.

Her mother stood in the doorway of the laundry room glaring at her with fire in her eyes.

"Mom? You scared the shit out of me."

Her mother shut the door behind her. That wasn't good. Mother Prioress discouraged private conversations at the convent. Whatever her mother had to say, Elle knew she wouldn't like it.

"I will ask you again," her mother said as she stood in front of Elle. "What do you think you're doing?"

"Laundry?"

"Don't be a smart-ass."

"I don't know what you're talking about. I'm doing laundry. Like I do every day."

"You know exactly what I'm talking about."

"No, I swear—"

"Answer me this then. Do you want to get kicked out of here? Do you?"

"Of course not." Elle stammered as she answered, scared and confused.

"This is an abbey. We have rules here. Vows. And while you're here you have to respect that."

Oh shit. Kyrie.

"Mom, I didn't mean to—"

"Oh no, you never mean to do anything you do. I bet you didn't mean to sleep with your own priest, either. And you didn't mean to keep sleeping with him for six years."

"We're having this fight again? I was twenty years old when I lost my virginity to him. How old were you when you had sex the first time?"

"I've repented. And clearly you haven't."

"I'm a sexual being, Mother. I know you don't want to accept that your daughter has sexual thoughts and feelings, but I do."

"I know you do. We all do. But we don't go around writing about them, do we?"

"What?"

"Did you think I wouldn't catch you?"

"What exactly did you catch me doing?" Elle asked, more confused now than ever.

Her mother reached into the pocket of her robe and pulled out a sheaf of bent and folded papers.

"You left this here in the laundry room the other day. And it's a damn good thing I'm the one who found it. Mother Prioress would have you out on your ass in five seconds if someone had brought this smut to her."

Elle saw it now. Her story. Her Daphne and Apollo story. She laughed.

"You think this is funny?" her mother demanded.

"You found my book," Elle said. "That's why you're mad."

"What did you think I was talking about?"

"Nothing," she said hastily. "I didn't know you'd found it."

"I did find it, and I read it. You can't have pornography in a convent. Have you lost your mind?"

"Mom, it's not pornography. It's a romance novel. They sell them in grocery stores. Last time I was in a grocery store I didn't find any porn. I looked."

"This is what you think romance is? No wonder you fell in love with that man."

"Yeah, no wonder." Elle tried to compose her face into a mask of sincere contrition. Or at least a passable fake. "I'm sorry. Seriously. There's nothing good to read in this place. It's all theology and politics, and I got bored. It's a novel based on a mythology story."

"It has explicit sex in it."

"People do have sex sometimes. So I hear. Every now and then. When they're not in a convent."

"You don't have to write about it."

"I don't have to. But I want to."

"Are you trying to get thrown out of here?"

"Well, no."

"Then if I were you, I'd burn this trash. Burn it today. Get rid of it before anyone else finds it and reads it. And stop wasting your talent on this garbage. Use it to write something good. When God gives you a gift, you use it to glorify Him, not to glorify sin. Or worse, to glorify yourself."

"Some people don't think sex is a sin, Mom."

"And some people think the world is flat and that there's nothing wrong with letting a priest beat you and abuse you. Those people are wrong." Her mother threw the pages down onto the counter. She pointed her finger at them. "Now get rid of that before someone else finds it. I find it again, and I'll throw you out of here myself."

Elle swallowed. "Okay," she said. "Sorry."

"Good. Thank you."

Her mother shook her head in disgust one last time. She walked to the door of the laundry room. Elle could have wept from relief. She'd been so sure her mother knew about her and Kyrie…but this. A dirty story? That was nothing.

But…

"Mom?"

Her mother paused by the door and turned around.

"What, Eleanor?" she asked in clipped tones.

"Do you really think I'm talented?" Elle's voice sounded small even to her.

Her mother didn't answer at first. She looked at Elle, who squirmed under the intensity of the gaze.

"I read every page," her mother finally said.

"You did?"

"I didn't need to read every page to know what it was I was reading. I'll admit, I kept reading long after I told myself I should stop reading."

"I guess that's a good sign," Elle said, smiling. She hated how much she wanted and needed her mother's praise. "I've had fun writing it. I think…maybe…I think it's pretty good."

Her mother fell silent once more. Her lips pursed tight and her eyes revealed nothing. Elle tried to see her mother as her mother, not the nun she'd become. If she took off the habit and put on her old white bathrobe and grew her long black hair out again, a little makeup…she'd be Mom once more.

"Do you remember a day in school…you must have been six, I think. First grade. And they took all the children out of your class one by one and gave you tests out in the hallway?" her mother asked.

"I think so. Yeah," Elle said, nodding. "There were flash cards and different colored blocks and we had to do puzzles for these people."

"You know what that was for, right?"

"No."

"They were administering IQ tests to all the first graders."

"So that's what that was. Anything to get out of class for a few minutes. They gave us cookies and orange juice."

"I never told you this, but the school called me a week later and said you'd scored higher than any other student in your grade. Your IQ was—"

"One hundred and sixty-seven," Elle said.

"Genius."

"I wouldn't test that high now," Elle said, shrugging. "Kids tend to test high."

"Did they tell you your score?"

"He did," Elle said. He meaning Søren.

Her mother's body stiffened. "He did? Why?"

"He was in charge of my probation, remember? And I had to keep my grades up. One day I was struggling really hard with my pre-calculus. I was in tears because I couldn't figure it out. He caught me crying into my math book. So he made me some hot chocolate and sat next to me on that bench that's across from his office door. And he told me he'd seen my school records and that my IQ was something very special. I told him I didn't feel very smart right then. He said IQ wasn't a measurement of what you know but how fast your brain works. If the brain was an athlete, then math wasn't my event. But someday I would find my event and when I did, nothing would stop me from doing whatever I wanted to do with my life. Then he helped me with my homework until I had it halfway figured out."

For a long time her mother only looked at her. Elle picked up the pages off the counter.

"Maybe this is my event," Elle said, clutching the pages to her chest.

"I should have told you how smart you are," her mother said. "I shouldn't have let that be something he got to tell you."

"So why didn't you?"

"I don't know. You were so confident, so arrogant growing up…I assumed you already knew you were the smartest girl around. You certainly acted like you knew everything."

Elle laughed a little. "I was an arrogant little shit."

"Was?"

"Okay, I am. Still am."

"You know, I'd have to send you to your room sometimes instead of fighting with you because I was scared you'd be able to talk your way out of whatever trouble you'd gotten into. You certainly ran circles around me with your logic sometimes."

"Still don't know what the point of making a bed is if I'm only going to sleep in it that night and mess it up again."

"Same reason we get up every morning and try to make our world better even though we know someone is going to mess it up. That's why."

Elle laughed and nodded. "That's actually a good point. You're pretty smart, too, Mom."

"Thank you. Glad you finally noticed that."

"Only took me, oh, almost twenty-seven years." Elle would be twenty-seven soon. Too soon. Time was passing quickly and she still didn't know what to do when and if she left the abbey.

"You'll behave, won't you? You'll get rid of that story?"

"Sure. Of course. It never existed."

"I sleep easier knowing you're here and not out there. I don't want them to make you leave."

"Are you sure?" Elle asked. "I mean, really? This is your world. Being a nun was your dream. I know it's probably distracting having me here."

"Out there," she said, nodding toward the windows, toward the big wide world outside the walls of the convent. "Out there, I can't see you, and I don't know what's happening to you. I don't know if you're safe or if you're scared, if someone is hurting you or helping you. Here, I can keep an eye on you. I know you're safe. I know you can't stay here forever. But while you're here…yes, I'm glad, Ellie."

"Thanks, Momma. Thanks for taking me in despite…you know."

"You left him and that life you were in. All is forgiven. And yes, I think you're very talented. But write a real book, please."

Elle took a step forward but her mother was already gone. She sat down on a chair and laid the handwritten pages of her book on her lap.

She'd spent all morning folding laundry, but now she unfolded. She unfolded every single sheet of paper that her mother had crushed and crimped. With a sweep of her hands she flattened the pages and put them back into order.

She had no intention of destroying her story. She'd cut her own hand off before she burned any book, especially one she'd written. No, she would do something else entirely. She'd finish writing the book. And she would get it published. And she would make money off it. And then her mother would see that her book was a real book. People did have sex, after all. Why shouldn't she write about it?

It needed a title, her book did. That would make it real. A thing must have a name. She couldn't go on calling it "the story" or "the book." And once it had a title then she could figure out what to do next. Although she'd read books all her life, she had no idea how to get one published. But she'd figure that out later. Finishing the book was step one.

Elle flipped through a few pages and stopped to read a random section.

"Why didn't you tell me you were a virgin?" John asked as he soaped his hands and ran them over her inner thighs and the raw skin of her torn hymen. He'd taken her home like she'd asked him to but instead of putting her in his bed and making love to her again, like he had in the woods, he'd run a bath, set her in it and washed the dirt and blood off of her.

"Does it matter?" she asked, wincing as the hot water scraped the most sensitive places inside her. "Would it have stopped you?"

Daphne looked at him and saw him now as if for the first time. Before she'd lost her virginity, he'd been a monster to her. Mr. Apollo—six feet four inches tall, powerful, able to kill her brother without breaking a sweat. But now she saw he was a man, a human man, not a monster, not a god. A scared man who had made a terrible mistake and had made loving her his penance.

"Yes," John said. "It would have stopped me."

"That's why I didn't tell you I was a virgin."

Elle stood up and opened the junk drawer where all the random things she pulled out of the nuns' habit pockets ended up. The drawer was filled with thimbles and keys, half-used packages of tissues, small tubes of hand lotion, small prayer books and worn-out rosary beads. Elle pulled out a pen from the jumble and removed the cap. At the top of the first page of her story she wrote the title. At least it would act as the title until she thought of something better.

THE VIRGIN
By Eleanor Schreiber

A moment later she crossed out her own name and changed it.

By Elle Schreiber

27

Haiti

GÉRARD RETURNED AND JULIETTE RETURNED TO HIM.
Kingsley did nothing but lie on the beach for one entire week
after she left him.

He wasn't grieving.

He wasn't mourning.

He was planning.

It would be easy. He knew his way around the house. He
could stage a break-in at night, shoot Gérard and get Juliette
off the island before they even found the body.

Or he could fuck Juliette. He'd spent a whole week fucking Juliette and he'd got very good at it. And he could do it
under Gérard's roof and time it so that he saw them together.
It could drive Gérard into a rage. Kingsley had been trained to
kill a man with one well-aimed punch to the Adam's apple—
asphyxiation would ensue—or a sudden hook to the jaw could
break the neck if sufficient force was applied. If Gérard attacked
him, then anything Kingsley did after that would be considered self-defense. Juliette wouldn't have to know it had been
Kingsley's plan all along.

Then she would be free.

Violent fantasies consumed Kingsley. Once plotting to kill

had been all in a day's work. His ability to plot an assassination remained as keen as it was in his days doing his quiet cleanup work for the French government in Russia and Eastern Europe. His skills were just as sharp. If only he could get his conscience out of the way so he could go through with it.

The men he'd killed in the past had all warranted his intervention in their continued existence. He'd killed killers. Gérard wasn't a killer, though. His crime was taking advantage of a scared fourteen-year-old girl trying to save her mother, using her love for her mother to hold her hostage, and to deny her children, the one solace she'd begged for. It was a crime. A crime that needed punishing.

And he would. He could. For Juliette he could.

On the night of the seventh day of his plotting, Kingsley went for a long swim in the ocean to clear his mind and focus his attention. He would go to Gérard's and watch, only watch. When did Gérard wake up? When did he go to bed? What was his routine? What rooms did he frequent? Did he drink heavily? When did he like to fuck? Morning? Noon? Night? All of them? He wouldn't let Juliette know he was there. No one would know. And once Kingsley knew everything he needed to know, he would do what he had to do, anything he had to do as long as Juliette was his by the time he was done doing it.

Kingsley dressed in dark clothes and sandals. He'd need to be barefoot in Gérard's house. Silence was the difference between life and death. Life for Juliette. Death for Gérard. He drove to the house and parked far away, hiding the car well out of sight of any passersby. He didn't bring any weapons with him. He didn't need them. Gérard was a politician. He'd never even served in the military. He might be tall and strong and handsome, but tall and strong and handsome would be no match for a trained killer on a mission.

Once near Gérard's home, Kingsley walked its perimeter. He stayed hidden behind the trees and ornamental gardens that surrounded the estate like a green wall. Gérard no doubt saw himself as untouchable on this island. Here he was—rich, powerful, from a white French family that had been here for three hundred years. They'd come before the Revolution and stayed long after many French colonists died or returned to the old country. He had diplomatic immunity, a house like a castle and enough money to buy his way out of any problem.

He wouldn't buy his way out of this one.

Kingsley entered the house through a sliding glass door using his elbow to open and close it. He stood in the dark room, a small office or library, and let his eyes adjust to the interior light. At the door he listened and heard voices in the house. More than two. Gérard had company.

When the sound of the voices dimmed, Kingsley eased the door open and stepped into the hallway. He stayed close to the wall and took note of every door, every window. If he were caught by anyone other than Gérard, he'd have to escape quickly.

He turned a corner, walked up a short flight of stairs. A door at the end of a hallway was ajar and light streamed through it. Kingsley crept to the door and peered inside. He saw Juliette. She was alone, and appeared to be packing or unpacking someone's suitcase. In the lamplight she glowed with quiet beauty. She wore a white dress with a long white scarf in her hair trailing over her shoulder. She looked serene as she bent over the open suitcase and sorted through the contents. When finished she walked to a large wooden birdcage hanging in the open window and whistled at the little yellow bird inside who danced on its little legs for her and fluttered about the cage.

He shouldn't let her see him. She shouldn't know yet he was there. He needed to watch, to wait, to assess the situation before acting. But he couldn't look away from her.

When she moved her head, the light caught her face, and he saw tears on her cheeks. Juliette turned her back and Kingsley stepped into the room and shut the door behind him. His plan was discarded in an instant. All that mattered was her.

Kingsley clapped a hand over her mouth from behind and held her tight against him. Her body tensed, ready to fight or flee.

"It's me," he whispered in her ear. At once she relaxed into his arms. "Good girl."

He let her go and she turned to face him. Before she could say a word, his mouth was on hers, and he had her backed against the wall.

"He's home," she said against his lips, but it was the only protest she made.

"Good. If I fuck you hard enough do you think he'll hear?"

He didn't let her answer. He thrust his tongue into her mouth and kissed her so brutally she whimpered. She wanted him as much as he wanted her. Her hips pushed into his, and she reached between their bodies to open his pants. He had the condom on as quickly as possible and her panties off and on the floor in seconds. He lifted her off the floor and brought her down onto him, impaling her with one thrust.

Once Kingsley was inside her, time stopped. The rush and the urgency ceased. He was in her and that was all that mattered and would ever matter.

He kissed her gently now. Their tongues mingled, their breath… He held her thighs, stroking them, gripping them. She had one foot on the floor and one leg wrapped around his back. She smelled like a tropical garden, like Eden, like Paradise before the Fall. His tongue traced the line of her neck, slid over her collarbone, her shoulder. He pushed the straps of her dress down and bared her breasts.

The heat inside her was incredible. She burned him from the inside out. They pressed their bodies into each other. She had her hands flat against the wall to steady herself as she tilted her hips up. Kingsley pressed his thumb against her clitoris and she shuddered silently. The day's heat hadn't worn off yet and sweat covered them both. He tasted the salt on her skin as he dropped his head and took a nipple in his mouth, sucking deeply.

Juliette raised her arms, twined them around his shoulders, holding him to her breast.

"Mon roi," she whispered, a sob her in voice, and Kingsley went weak. He kissed his way up to her mouth again, kissed the tears off her face. She buried her face into his neck and he held her there, held her close and let her cry.

He couldn't stop and she didn't want him to. He thrust into her, and she took it. She took it until he came hard enough the world went black, and he had to blink to clear his vision.

Juliette looked at him and he raised his hands to her face and wiped away her tears. More came to take their place.

"I can take these away," Kingsley said.

"How?"

"I have a plan."

"To do what?" she demanded. Juliette pulled away from him and straightened her dress.

"I can kill him."

Juliette laughed, laughed right in his face.

"You're out of your mind," she said.

"I'm not joking."

"I'm pretending you are."

"You'll be free."

"Free? Killing a man isn't freedom. Death isn't freedom. Running away isn't freedom. I could walk out of this house tonight of my own volition if I wanted to."

"Then why don't you?"

"I choose to stay. I told you why. He takes care of my mother."

"Who takes care of you?"

"I don't need taking care of."

"Yes, you do."

She opened her mouth to say something else, but a cry echoed from the next room. Kingsley recognized the cry at once. It was the cry of a baby, shrill and piercing.

"Who is that?" Kingsley demanded.

"His grandson," Juliette said, obviously annoyed. But not with the baby. With him. She strode purposefully from the room and Kingsley followed her into the guest room next door, where someone had set up a nursery. She reached over the side of a crib and lifted the crying baby boy from his bed. She put a cloth diaper over her shoulder and bounced him a few times until he quieted.

She carried him past Kingsley, ignoring him studiously, and walked down the hall. Kingsley switched off the light behind her and stayed in the shadows of the doorway. At the end of the hall Gérard met her. He patted the baby on his head and kissed him. He listened as Gérard complimented his grandson for his impressive lung capacity. He took the boy from Juliette's arms and held him to his chest, rubbing the boy's back and sooth-ing the last of his tears.

"Let's go find your maman," Gérard said to his grandson. "She'll talk some sense into you."

"I should go to bed," Juliette said to Gérard.

"Go, but stay awake," Gérard said. "I'll be there soon."

"Your daughter is here," Juliette said. "You shouldn't come to me tonight. She might hear."

"She's going out soon to meet friends. He'll sleep. You don't." He kissed her on the cheek and walked off, bouncing his grand-son in his arms and laughing.

And in that moment Kingsley felt something hit him like an ocean wave, knock the breath out of him, kick the legs out from under him and send his heart to his knees in the sand.

Envy. Envy the likes of which he had never before felt in his life. Envy of this man and the life he had. Children, grand-children, Juliette in his home, in his bed, in his heart. And if

Kingsley had been offered the chance to take Gérard's place, and all he had to do was go back in time and fuck fourteen-year-old Juliette, he would have done it. He would have done it in a second. He would have done it in a heartbeat, in an instant, and he wouldn't have regretted one second of it. And that meant he couldn't pass judgment on Gérard and certainly couldn't sentence him to death.

They were the same.

Juliette came back to Kingsley.

"You have to leave," she said.

"I'll go."

"Leave for good. Leave me. We're only making it worse."

Kingsley leaned back against the door frame.

"I want to have children," he said to her.

Juliette glanced away from him as if she couldn't bear to meet his eyes. "So do I."

"I got someone pregnant, and she didn't want it."

"That's why you're here in Haiti? You're grieving?"

"Yes," he said.

Juliette leaned against him, clasping the back of his neck with her hand and resting her head on his shoulder.

"I want to rescue you," he said. "Please let me."

"You're not a real king," Juliette said, looking up at him. "And I'm not a princess in a tower. He's not a dragon. We're real people and a sword's not going to solve this problem."

"I know." The two hardest words he'd said yet to her.

"I can't save you. You have to save yourself," Juliette said. "Go."

She let him go, took a step back and met his eyes.

"I'm sorry," she whispered. *Je suis desolée.* She touched his face and walked off, walked away, following the path Gérard had taken.

And Kingsley was sorry, too.

He left the house and walked back to his car, drove to his

hut and stood alone on the beach watching the moon glide across the ocean.

Save yourself, Juliette had ordered. He loved her enough to take that order from her.

Haiti and Manhattan were on the same time. He returned to his hut, and dialed a number.

"Hey, boss," Calliope said when she answered the phone. She sounded sleepy. He'd probably woken her up. "What's up?"

"I need you to do something for me," he said.

"Sure. What is it?"

"Book a flight for me."

"Sure. Where are you going?"

"Home."

"France?"

"No. Home. I'm coming home, Cal."

"Seriously?" The joy in her voice was small comfort, but he'd take any comfort he could get. "When?"

"As soon as you can get my flight."

He heard clicking in the background, her fingers flying over a keyboard.

"Then guess what?" she asked.

"What?"

"I'll see you tomorrow night, boss."

She booked his flight and gave him his confirmation. Then before she got off the phone he gave her three more orders.

He packed his bags and left nothing behind that would let Juliette know who he was or where he'd gone.

Then he did the one thing he'd sworn he would never do.

He left Haiti without Juliette.

28

ELLE RAN THROUGH THE WOODS CHASING AFTER Kyrie. The girl had played volleyball in high school and she ran like an athlete—fearlessly and tirelessly. She sprinted like a gazelle with her long-legged gait, jumping gracefully. Elle pursued her deeper into the trees, following the sound of her laughter, the rustle of leaves.

At the far end of the abbey's grounds stood a small marble oratory hidden among a cluster of trees. Elle hadn't stepped foot in it yet, but Kyrie said it was her favorite place to pray. They weren't planning on praying much tonight.

When she reached the oratory, Elle stopped and looked around. It was night and the moon loomed large above the trees. The spring night was crisp but Elle wasn't cold even though her breath hung like a cloud in the air whenever she exhaled. After running she had to wipe sweat off her forehead. She had on jeans and a T-shirt but no shoes. They'd both run like hoydens through the woods, heedless of twigs and stones and the cold ground. Angels must be watching tonight. Neither one of them had tripped in their flight from the abbey to the chapel.

But where had Kyrie gone?

"Kyrie?" Elle whispered. Her voice coiled around the trees and sprang back to her own ears.

"Boo!" Kyrie said from behind her. Elle spun around and caught Kyrie by the forearm before she could run off again.

"You're terrible at hiding," Elle said, pulling her close.

"I am *not* terrible at hiding. I'm wonderful at being found." Kyrie kissed Elle on the mouth and laughed.

"Why are you running from me?" Elle asked.

"Because I want you to catch me."

"I caught you. What do I get?"

"I have a present," Kyrie said.

"For me?"

"For you."

"Is it wrapped up in a white bow?" Elle tugged on the ribbon on Kyrie's white nightgown. It tied under her breasts and when loosened would allow the gown to fall off her. She wore no socks, no shoes, no veil. Her blond hair hung loose and wild around her shoulders. In the moonlight she glowed like a candle, and Elle followed the light to its source, kissing her on the mouth as she held her in place. Kyrie would not get away from her again.

"Come inside," Kyrie said against Elle's lips.

"I plan to."

Elle pushed Kyrie against a tree and kissed her even harder. She yanked on the bow of Kyrie's nightgown and pulled it down her shoulders. In the cool air, Kyrie's nipples had peaked hard and Elle bent her head and ran her tongue over them until Kyrie moaned. She loved making Kyrie moan, making her gasp, making her come. Pleasuring this girl had become the raison d'être of Elle's entire existence.

Kyrie laughed for seemingly no reason. She danced away from Elle, clutching her nightgown to her neck.

"Come and get me," Kyrie taunted, running to the small chapel. She crooked her finger at Elle before disappearing through the wooden door.

Elle didn't follow at first. She looked around, eyeing the trees, the twigs on the ground. At last she found what she needed, a long thin twig with smooth slick bark and a lot of give to it. Elle bent it and released the tip. It bent easily and sprang back in an instant. Perfect.

After she peeled the leaves off the cane and stripped it of extraneous twigs, Elle entered the oratory and found Kyrie at the front by the prayer altar spreading blankets on the floor.

Elle grabbed her by the wrist and dragged her in for another kiss.

"I brought these here earlier today and hid them," Kyrie said with a bright smile when she saw Elle.

"Premeditated sexual assignations," Elle said. "You'll have so much tell Father Antonio next time you confess."

"He'll be so excited," Kyrie said. "Hope I don't give him a heart attack."

"Priests hear everything. Takes a lot to shock them, I promise."

"Still…it'll be fun to try." Kyrie sat on the blanket right in the middle.

"So where's my present?" Elle asked. The only light in the oratory came from the moon through the windows. Elle took two candles out of her duffel bag and lit them. She wanted light but not too much. She didn't want anyone from the abbey waking up in the night and seeing light emanating from the chapel windows.

"I'll give you your present later," Kyrie said. "I don't want to distract you from, well, me."

"A nuclear bomb blast couldn't distract me from you right now."

Once they had light, Elle sat on the blanket in front of Kyrie and unzipped her duffel bag.

"Did you bring me a present, too?" Kyrie asked.

"Nothing for you," Elle said. "This is for me."

"What is?"

Elle pulled out a comb and a hair band.

"What are you doing to me?" Kyrie asked as Elle moved to her side and gathered a lock of hair in her fingers.

"Anything I want to do to you," Elle said. "As usual."

"Good. I like everything you do to me. Even if it means pulling my hair."

"Not pulling it, braiding it. You're my fairy princess tonight so you need princess hair."

With nimble fingers that had twenty-seven years of experience taming her own wild tresses, Elle plaited Kyrie's hair into a thin French braid at the side of her head. She moved to the opposite side and gave Kyrie a matching braid. While Elle worked, Kyrie closed her eyes.

"That feels good," Kyrie said of Elle's hands in her hair. "I miss having my hair touched."

"You'll miss it even more when you don't have any hair at all."

Kyrie didn't say anything to that. Elle wondered how much their one night together had changed Kyrie's thoughts about taking her final vows. Did she still plan to become a nun? Would she stay? Go? Had she thought about it? Elle didn't ask her. She didn't want to know.

When she finished the two braids, Elle gathered them in the back of Kyrie's head and used the band to tie them together. Now her two braids formed a crown, like a Daphne wreath.

"Perfect," she said, pleased with her work.

"Is it?" Kyrie asked, smiling shyly.

"You're so beautiful. I can't believe you're mine."

"I am yours," Kyrie said, and leaned in for a kiss, a kiss Elle was only too happy to give her. As they kissed, Elle pulled Kyrie's nightgown down to her stomach. She pushed Kyrie onto her back, not breaking the kiss once. She licked and kissed a path from Kyrie's lips to her quivering flat stomach and lower as Elle dragged the gown all the way off her and tossed it aside.

"Are you warm enough?" Elle asked as she surveyed Kyrie's naked body, her small pert breasts and long lithe limbs.

"I am," Kyrie said, a nervous hitch in her breath.

"I want to hurt you tonight. Can I?"

"You can do anything you want to me."

"Do you want to be hurt?"

"I want to do anything you want to do," Kyrie said, and Elle could have laughed at her eagerness. Those could have been Elle's own words to Søren seven years ago on their first night together. *Anything…anything at all…* His pleasure and happiness had meant so much more to her than her own.

Elle kissed Kyrie on the forehead.

"I want you to touch yourself," Elle said. "Like you do when you're alone."

"You're going to watch?"

"I am. And while you're doing that, I'll hurt you. And I'll keep hurting you until you come. And once you come, I'll stop hurting you."

Kyrie swallowed and took a ragged breath. She spread her legs and slipped her right hand down her stomach.

"Nervous?"

"No one's ever watched me do this before," Kyrie said. "You?"

"I have lost count of how many times I've done this for an audience," Elle said as she ran her hand up and down Kyrie's soft inner thigh.

"It's a little embarrassing," Kyrie admitted.

"That's why Søren would make me do it for him."

"Is that why you're making me do it? To embarrass me?"

"No," Elle said. "I think it's sexy. There's nothing embarrassing about a girl touching her own body."

She gave Kyrie one more kiss on the lips, then a kiss on each of her nipples. She watched for a moment as Kyrie's middle and index fingers found her clitoris and stroked it.

Elle picked up her makeshift cane and flicked Kyrie on the smooth skin above her knee. Kyrie flinched.

"Hurts, doesn't it?" Elle asked, smiling.

"I can't believe a little thing like that can cause so much pain."

"Canes are vicious bitches," Elle said.

"I was talking about you."

Elle laughed. "I'm a vicious little bitch, too."

Kyrie closed her eyes and Elle silently counted to ten. Every ten seconds she would strike Kyrie somewhere on her thighs. She worked her way up the leg and back down again. Kyrie continued stroking herself, kneading her own clitoris until she panted.

As Elle hurt her, she felt herself falling into a place of deep tranquility and calm. Everything outside the chapel ceased to exist. And all that mattered in the world was the world in front of her, this beautiful naked girl who'd given Elle her body.

Along with the tranquility, Elle felt something else. Power. Another human being had given up control of her body to Elle, had put her life into Elle's hands. Elle cherished that trust. It honored her and aroused her. Was this what Søren felt with her? Did he miss feeling it now that she was gone?

Eight...nine...ten.

Elle hit Kyrie again. She could see angry red welts on Kyrie's pale flesh. Elle smiled at them, loving the sight of them, knowing she'd given them to Kyrie and they wouldn't fade for at least a day or more.

Kyrie's breathing grew more labored. Her breasts rose and fell rapidly. She let out a soft cry, music to Elle's ears. Her pain and her pleasure sounded the same to Elle's ears—like music.

Her narrow hips rose an inch off the blanket and pulsed upward. Elle waited and watched. At the moment Kyrie inhaled hard, Elle struck her repeatedly while her orgasm washed over her. She collapsed back on the blanket with a sigh and a laugh.

"That's my good little girl," Elle said, stretching out at Kyrie's side and stroking her face.

"That was really strong," Kyrie said.

"Pain will do that," Elle said. "I don't know how or why, but it's like putting nitrous oxide in a car engine. It's a performance booster. Zero to sixty in five seconds flat."

Kyrie laughed again and wrapped an arm around Elle's neck.

"You're explaining orgasms using car metaphors. You are the weirdest woman in the world," Kyrie said. "No wonder I'm so crazy about you."

"I might be crazy about you, too." Elle slid her hand down Kyrie's chest and stomach. "Especially this part of you." She pushed two fingers into Kyrie and found her slick with her own wetness.

"That part of me is inordinately fond of you, as well."

Kyrie opened her legs wide, and Elle massaged her inner muscles with two and then three fingers. She didn't try to bring her to another climax again. She only wanted to touch, to explore, to feel. But it didn't take long before Kyrie panted again and dug her fingers into Elle's thigh. Elle lowered her head and sucked hard on Kyrie's nipple. Soon she felt Kyrie's vagina tighten and convulse around her hand with her second orgasm.

Elle pulled her fingers out and wiped the wetness off on the blanket.

"How was that?" she asked Kyrie, who slowly blinked her way back to awareness.

"I love orgasms. I say a prayer of thanks to God for them every day."

"You say a prayer of thanks for orgasms?" Elle asked.

"Of course. I mean, they're a gift from God, right? A woman doesn't need to have an orgasm to get pregnant, right?"

"Right."

"So if they have nothing to do with reproduction, then why do women have them?" Kyrie asked. She raised her hand and pointed a finger up at the ceiling, at the sky, where God lived. "Orgasms are God's way of saying He's sorry about periods and cramps."

"Apology accepted," Elle said.

Kyrie said, "Amen."

Still laughing, Elle sat up and looked around the chapel. "This might be the weirdest prayer meeting ever held in here. Lord, we thank You for orgasms…"

"I don't know. This place has been around for over a hundred years," Kyrie said. "I'm sure we're not the first people to use it for less than entirely angelic reasons."

"You think other nuns have come out here for their liaisons?"

"Maybe," Kyrie said. "And locals, maybe."

"Can outsiders get in here?" Elle asked.

"Definitely. There's a door. A secret door."

"Where does it go?"

Kyrie sat up now and pulled her gown back on. "I'll show you."

She stood up and Elle followed her to what she'd thought was a storage room behind the prayer altar. But the door didn't lead to a room. It led outside to a path in the woods. A long tall wooden fence stretched as far as the eye could see all the way from the chapel to the abbey in one direction and from the chapel to the edge of the convent's acreage in the other.

Elle didn't cross the threshold to the outside world. But she stared at it almost hungrily.

"The door locks from the inside," Kyrie said. "Nobody from out there can come in unless someone in here unlocks the door for them. But maybe that's happened. Maybe someone from inside the abbey had someone outside the abbey they wanted to see."

"Why do they have a door back here? We're not allowed to leave the abbey without permission."

"It was for the workers who built the oratory. They cordoned off this area while they built it. They didn't want big burly construction workers tromping through the abbey so they had them come in through the back door of the chapel. They never sealed off the door, though."

"Lock it," Elle said.

"But—"

"Do it."

Kyrie shut the door immediately and locked it up.

"What's wrong?" She looked at Elle in confusion.

"I don't want anyone coming in here," Elle said, her heart racing for no reason she could or would name.

"Who would come in?"

"Nobody."

"Then why—"

"We should get back to the abbey," Elle said, taking a step away from the door.

"Elle, what's wrong?"

"Nothing."

"You're a bad liar," Kyrie said, taking Elle's hand. "You don't really think he'd break in here, do you?"

"No," Elle said. "But I might break out."

Kyrie looked up at her sharply, hurt in her eyes.

"You want to leave?" Kyrie asked.

"No. Yes."

"Which is it?"

Elle shook her head. "I don't know."

"Yes, you do."

When Elle looked Kyrie in the eyes, she saw fear there. Her gut instinct was to take it away. This girl was hers to protect and to cherish. Dominants were supposed to take care of their submissives. Being a Dominant was harder than she'd anticipated.

"Elle, please. You're kind of freaking me out."

"I want to leave," Elle said, choosing honesty. "But I don't want to leave you."

"I see." Kyrie let go of Elle's hand and returned to the blanket on the floor. She pulled her legs in tight to her chest.

It wasn't until she'd seen the open door that she'd realized how much she wanted to walk through it. Not walk—run. She wanted to run through and keep running until she'd put a thousand miles between her and this convent.

"Are you leaving?" Kyrie asked, looking up at Elle.

"No. I can't leave. I don't know where I'd go, what I'd do."

"I do," Kyrie said.

"What?"

"I said I know what you can do. I told you I'd figure out what you could do with your life. So I figured it out."

Elle laughed coldly. "You figured out what I can do with my life?"

Kyrie stood up and walked to the back room where she'd hidden blankets.

"I told you I had a present for you." Kyrie came back out holding an envelope. She gave it to Elle. "So here."

The envelope had already been opened. It was addressed to Kyrie, not her. One single sheet of paper was inside. Elle unfolded it and held it near the candle.

Dear Kyrie, the letter began.

It was wonderful to hear from you. I think of Bethany every single day. Her books are on my shelves and her memory lives in my heart.

"Who is this?" Elle asked, looking up from the letter.

"My sister's literary agent," Kyrie said. "Keep reading."

I'll admit I was surprised to receive fifty handwritten
pages of an erotic novel from a convent in New York,
but Bethany did tell me her baby sister was the odd duck
in the family. We have submission guidelines here, but I
certainly couldn't tell any sister of Bethany's no. I'm glad
I didn't say no. Your friend Elle is an extremely talented
writer. I couldn't put the pages you sent me down and was
most unhappy when I reached the end and found there
was no more to read.

"You sent my book to your sister's agent?"

Kyrie grinned in the dark. "I made photocopies of the first
fifty pages and sent it to her. But keep reading."

The letter now shook in her hands.

Please tell me when your friend has finished her novel.
And ask her to send it to me as soon as she can. If the rest
of the book is as strong as the pages you sent, we can absolutely sell this. I have a list of editors already who would
be interested. My contact information is below. When
your friend is finished with the book, tell her to email me
the completed manuscript and call me as soon as she can.

Elle read the letter again. Then again. She had trouble believing it was real.

"You're shitting me," Elle said. "When did you do this?"

"You gave me the book to read so I read it all," Kyrie said.
"I snuck into the offices and used the copy machine to copy
the pages. I sent them to my sister's agent. She and Bethany
were close. I knew she'd do me a favor and read it for Bethany's sake. But she's tough and honest. If she says she can sell it,
she means it."

"Oh fuck. I have to finish the book."

"How long will that take you?"

"I don't know. A month. Six weeks. It takes a long time to write it out by hand."

"You can do it. I know you can finish it."

"I can."

"Are you losing your mind?"

"I kind of am." Elle's brain reeled. She had a thousand thoughts all at once. She knew how to finish the book. She'd had the ending in mind for weeks. But everything she'd written was a mess, all handwritten notebook pages. She needed to type the entire book up now. Not on a typewriter. She needed a computer. And a telephone. She had access to neither of them here. It might be 2004 out there in the real world, but the entire convent was stuck in 1904. Mother Prioress had a computer but there was no way Elle could use it to type her novel.

"My kingdom for a laptop," Elle said.

"What are you going to do, Elle?" Kyrie asked.

"If I pursue this…"

"I know," Kyrie said. If Elle pursued this, she couldn't do it from the abbey. She would have to leave.

"You could have gotten into a lot of trouble doing this," Elle said. "Breaking into Mother Prioress's office—"

"She doesn't keep it locked. I snuck in."

"You snuck in to make photocopies of an erotic story written by the woman you're sleeping with."

"We weren't sleeping together at the time," Kyrie reminded her.

"Why did you do this for me?"

"I'd do anything for you. You know that."

"Would you leave with me?" Elle asked.

"Leave the abbey with you?"

"I won't go unless you go with me," Elle said, meaning it.

"Where would we go?"

"I don't know."

"What would we do for money?"

"I don't know." Elle was quickly running out of the cash she'd had with her.

"Where would we stay?"

"I don't know. But I can't walk through that door without you."

"Okay then," Kyrie said.

"Okay what?"

"Okay. If you can't leave without me, then I'll go with you."

"You're serious," Elle said, not quite believing her.

"I am. Now how many points do I get for getting my sister's agent interested in your book?"

Elle shook her head. "I don't know. Infinity points." She pressed the letter to her chest.

"Then I win," Kyrie said. "You have to tell me why you left him."

The joy went out of the room.

"Why do you want to know?" Elle asked as she folded the letter up and slipped it back in the envelope. She would keep this letter all her life.

"Because it's the one thing you won't tell me. And if I'm leaving here with you, I want to know the truth about why you're here. I want to know the truth about you. All of it. If I can walk out of this place—this place that's my home now—then the least you can do is tell me the truth about you and him."

"It's not important."

"If it wasn't important you would have told me already."

"Fine. It is important but it doesn't matter to us."

"It matters to me. It matters that you're keeping something life-altering from me. If I'm leaving my life because of you, you have to tell me why you left your life because of him. If we're going to be together, we can't keep secrets from each other."

Elle took a long heavy breath and looked away from Kyrie. At the front of the oratory near the ceiling was an octagon-shaped clear window. The moon shone through the window.

A moon like a Cheshire cat's smile. Wonderland was out there, outside the door.

But there were Jabberwockys out in Wonderland. Kyrie was right. If she was to leave the safety of the abbey behind, she needed to know what was out there.

"Fine. You want to know why I left him. This is why."

She picked up her little makeshift cane and broke it into three pieces. She dropped the three pieces in front of Kyrie on the blanket.

"He broke something?" Kyrie asked.

"Yes," Elle said, staring at the broken twigs of nothing on the ground.

"He broke a cane?"

"No," Elle said. "He broke me."

29

SØREN WAS COMING HOME AND ELLE WANTED TO BE there when he arrived. Someone from Kingsley's entourage would pick him up at the airport in the Rolls, as usual, and drive him to the rectory in Wakefield. Kingsley himself might go and meet him. She'd asked him not to. She wanted to be the one to tell Søren what had happened while he was gone. But she never knew with Kingsley whose side he would take. Sometimes hers. Sometimes Søren's.

More often than not Kingsley took Kingsley's side.

She borrowed Kingsley's BMW and drove it to Søren's. A few times she had to stop, pull over and throw up on the side of the road. Lucky for the road it had started to rain.

When she arrived at last, she was light-headed with dehydration and exhaustion. The overnight bag she had over her shoulder felt like a lead weight she could scarcely carry. She dragged herself up the single set of stairs in Søren's rectory, smiling with a tiredness that bordered on delirium. Her first night with Søren he'd carried her up these stairs. She'd kill for someone to carry her now.

Elle went to the bedroom first and unlocked the box that contained her collar. She didn't put it on. She just wanted it.

For five minutes she lay on his bed before rushing to the bathroom to throw up again. Afterward she stretched out on the floor. It felt oddly comforting, lying there with the cool clean tile pressing against her burning skin. She breathed through her nose, which helped alleviate some of her nausea. The cramps came and went and she ignored them when she could, accepted them when she couldn't. And when at last she was cool enough and comfortable enough to almost fall asleep, she heard footsteps on the stairs.

She struggled into a sitting position when Søren called out her name.

"I'm here," she called back. "In the bathroom. You can come in."

Her heart was pounding now. She hadn't seen him in ten weeks and so much had happened. She started to stand but a wave of light-headedness hit her so she stayed on the floor. Søren opened the door and whatever pleasure had been in his eyes a split second earlier evaporated with one look at her.

"I'm sick," she said. "Not contagious."

She didn't know why she'd added that part at the end about not being contagious. If she'd had leprosy, Søren still would have done what he'd done just then. He shrugged out of his coat and tossed it onto the floor behind him, came down to his knees and pulled her into his arms.

It hurt. Moving hurt. Breathing hurt. Being loved and held by him hurt.

"What's wrong, Little One?" he asked in her ear. He smoothed her hair back, tucked it behind her ear, kissed her forehead. All the actions of a loving father.

"You don't want to know."

"Tell me anyway. It's an order."

"Yes, sir," she said, trying to smile for him, but she didn't have any smiles left in her. Not even for him. "It wasn't yours. You should know that first."

"What wasn't mine?"

And it seemed as soon as he asked the question he knew the answer. Before she could speak again, explain herself, his eyes closed and he let out a breath.

"Kingsley's." It wasn't a question.

"Kingsley's," she said. "I went to the doctor yesterday. They gave me pills."

"You went to the doctor." His voice was devoid of emotion. "Who did you go with?"

"Kingsley's driver took me," she said.

"Did Kingsley go with you?"

"You know how much he hates doctors."

Søren didn't say anything.

"It'll take a few days for it to all work out," she continued. "The nausea's normal, the doctor said. And the cramping. I'm bleeding pretty heavy, but that's normal, too. And…"

And she stopped talking. She'd lost her train of thought and it didn't matter anyway. Søren's back rested against the bathroom door, and she lay across his lap, in his arms, tired and helpless as a child.

"I'm sorry," she said at last, and then the tears came. "I'm so sorry."

Her body shook with her tears, which set off spasms of pain in her back and stomach. But she couldn't stop crying, not now that she was in Søren's arms. He tried to console her, to comfort her, but it was useless. Everything hurt, inside and out. Over the sound of her own racking sobs, she heard his voice speaking to her in soft murmurs.

"I love you, Little One. Now and always. And nothing you can do will take my love away from you. I will never leave you. You're mine now and always…"

And still she cried. She cried until sheer exhaustion silenced her sobbing.

She could have fallen asleep right there in his arms on the

floor of his bathroom. She should have fallen asleep. She needed sleep. It had been twenty-four hours or more since she'd slept.

"We'll be married," Søren said.

Elle came instantly awake.

"What?"

"I said we will be married. You and I."

"Married? Are you serious?"

"Of course I am."

Married? Her and Søren? Husband and wife? It was tempting, she had to admit, if only to herself. They had never talked about getting married before, but as soon as he said the word she had a vision of it. Søren in a tuxedo. She would be in a dress—off-white, not pure white. And Kingsley would stand next to Søren, his best man. Søren's confessor, Father Ballard, would perform the ceremony. Søren's mother would come, of course. And his sisters, maybe even Elizabeth. They'd honeymoon in Denmark. They might move in with Kingsley when they got back to New York. Knowing his sister Claire and how much she wanted Søren to leave the priesthood, she'd buy them a house of their own as a wedding gift. They could go out in public together whenever they wanted. That would be nice. They could have kids, too. Did Søren even want children? He'd never said anything to her about it. Obviously she didn't want kids. If she did she wouldn't be sitting here on the bathroom floor in the worst pain of her life. They'd have to do something for money, of course. Søren could work at the United Nations as a translator. She would...what? What did she want to do?

Not get married. That's what she wanted to do. She hadn't even figured out who Eleanor Schreiber was yet. How the fuck was she supposed to be Eleanor Stearns?

"No," Eleanor said. "I'm not marrying you."

"It's not up for discussion."

"Of course it's up for discussion. Why in hell do you think getting married is going to solve anything?"

"I can't leave you alone anymore. I leave you alone too much. If I had been here, this wouldn't have happened."

"If you had been here, it might have been yours."

"And you wouldn't have gone through this alone. I'll call the bishop now."

He stood up off the floor. Elle reached out and grabbed his leg at the ankle.

"Søren, no."

He looked down at her as if he couldn't understand what it was that had grabbed his leg.

"Eleanor, let go. I have to make a phone call."

"Don't call him. Calm down. Getting married isn't going to make this go away."

"I'm perfectly calm. This will give me peace of mind, which is more than I have now. I thought I could trust you with Kingsley. That was my mistake. It won't happen again."

He started off down the hall and Elle fought her exhaustion and pain to get to her feet. But she did stand and she stood up straight. She followed Søren down the hall to his bedroom. He'd already picked up the phone. She slapped her hand down on the receiver to hang up the call.

"I'm not marrying you," Elle said. "So don't even bother calling anyone."

"I've made my decision."

"It's not your decision to make. Marriage takes two people. I said no."

"You're exhausted, you're ill and you've been through something traumatic. You're not thinking clearly right now."

"I'm not the one out of my damn mind right now. I am not going to marry you. No. Not now. Not ever. You are a Catholic priest. You can't get married."

"I'll leave the priesthood."

"You will do no such thing," she said, standing as straight as she could despite the pain in her stomach and back. "God and I made a deal a long time ago. If He'd let us be together, I would never take you from the Church. I plan on keeping that promise."

"And I'll keep mine. I promised I would do anything to protect you. I will."

"I don't need protection. I don't need to get married."

"What you want is immaterial in this matter. Go to bed. I will handle this."

"Immaterial? Have you forgotten I am a twenty-six-year-old adult woman and not a child? You do not get to decide what I do."

"Of course I do. I own you."

"You own me. That's fine when we're in bed. That's fine when I've got my collar on. It's not fine when you're telling me I have to marry someone I don't want to marry."

"You promised you would obey me forever. Did you not make me that promise?"

"When I was fifteen. Do you think I'm still fifteen?"

"You're certainly acting like it."

"I promised God I would never take you from the Church. That's a deal He and I made when I was seventeen."

"I think I know what God wants for my life more than you do," he said.

"And I know what God wants for my life better than you do."

"I highly doubt that."

"Oh, you arrogant prick," she said. "You might be a priest but that doesn't mean you know more about me and God than I do. I have my own faith. It's mine and not yours." And here she broke into furious tears that she just as furiously wiped from her face. "And you can't take it away from me. I won't let you."

Søren ignored her and picked up the phone again. Once more Eleanor slammed her hand down to cut off the call.

"Eleanor, I will handcuff you to the bed if I have to," he said.

"Don't you dare lay a hand on me when you're like this," she said, pointing at the center of his chest. "You are out of control."

"I have never been more in control. You are the one being irrational and emotional."

"I had an abortion, which means not only did I break Kingsley's heart, I'm also excommunicated. I'm allowed to be emotional right now. But there is nothing irrational about me not wanting to marry you. That might be the most rational decision I've ever made. You are a Catholic priest who loves being a priest. You are called to the priesthood. If you've told me once, you have told me a thousand times how happy being a priest makes you. You will be miserable if you leave the church. I know you. Being married to me will not make you happier than being a priest does. It's your calling. Marrying me is not your calling."

"My happiness is also immaterial to this discussion."

"Not to me, it isn't. I will not let you resent me for the rest of our lives together, because I let you do something in a fit of madness that can't be undone. I will leave you before I let you throw your happiness away on some misguided attempt to make an honest woman out of me. Søren—that ship has sailed."

He met her eyes and looked down into her face. He was a wall, a granite wall, concrete and steel-reinforced.

"I have made my decision," he said as coldly as he'd ever said anything to her.

Eleanor bent down and unzipped her duffel bag. From it she pulled out the riding crop Kingsley had given her. She took it by the handle, and when Søren reached for the phone again she slapped it hard against the table.

"I topped Kingsley while you were gone," she said in answer to the look of confusion he gave her.

"You did what?"

"I topped Kingsley while you were gone," she repeated.

"Several times. I hurt him. I beat him, cut him, burned him and fucked him up the ass with a strap-on. And I loved it."

"You loved it."

"I loved it. I loved every second of it. I was scared at first. But once I started, I couldn't stop. The more I hurt him, the more I wanted to hurt him. He bought me this riding crop as a gift, and I used it on him."

"I see."

"I'm a Switch," she said. "Maybe not even a Switch. Maybe I'm a Dominant and it took me this long to figure it out. But I'm not a sub. If I know anything, I know that."

"Then what, pray tell, have we been doing together for the past six years?"

"I love submitting to you. Most of the time. Tonight, I hate it. I loved dominating Kingsley. I want to do it again. I want to do it with other people. I want to have a submissive of my own—maybe Kingsley if he'll let me—and I want to hurt him as much as I can, as often as I can and as hard as I can."

She'd said the words to hurt Søren but as she spoke them, she knew them to be the truth.

They stared at each other in silence. Finally Søren spoke.

"No," he said.

"No, what?'

"You don't have my permission to top Kingsley again."

"Your permission? I don't remember asking your permission to top Kingsley."

"You didn't ask. If you had I would have said no. I'm saying it now. No."

"Why not? You don't want him anymore. Why can't I have him?"

"Do not presume to tell me how I feel about Kingsley, Eleanor."

"Fine, then I'll tell you how I feel about Kingsley. I want to top him as often as I can. I'm not a submissive. I'm a switch."

Then he took from her hand the antique wooden riding crop with the carved bone handle and broke it into three pieces.

"Also," he said as he threw one broken piece across the room, flinging it like a newsboy tossing the morning paper. "Entirely." He threw the second piece. "Immaterial."

The wooden fragments of the riding crop hit the wall with a heinous crack and clattered to the floor.

A sound came out of Elle's mouth. A sort of animal whimper like the sound she'd once heard a dog make after being hit by a car.

On leaden feet she walked over to the pile of now-worthless wood and dropped to her knees. One by one she picked up the pieces.

"You bastard," she said, looking up at him with tears in her eyes. "That was a gift from Kingsley to me."

"You're no longer allowed to have any contact with Kingsley. Not until I say you may."

"He gave this to me. It was mine. Not yours."

"Everything that is yours is mine," Søren said. "I own you. Your body is mine. Your heart is mine. Your future is mine. Your decisions are mine. Your life is mine. You are mine."

She didn't think she could do it. She didn't think she had the strength to stand up one more time. But somewhere she found the strength and she came to her feet a final time.

"I am mine."

"What did you say to me?" Søren asked, narrowing his eyes at her.

"I am mine," she said again, gathering the broken pieces of her riding crop to her chest. She turned her back to him and started to walk away.

"Where are you going?" Søren called out.

Eleanor didn't answer. She kept walking. She walked down the hallway and down the stairs. She found her coat and her purse and walked to the back door.

"Eleanor, where do you think you're going?" Søren asked, his tone chiding. *You're not leaving,* his tone said. *You and I both know you aren't actually leaving.* "Eleanor, come back here this instant."

At the door she stopped and turned around. She looked at Søren and spoke one final word.

"Jabberwocky."

30

ELLE LOOKED AT KYRIE WHO HAD TEARS ON HER FACE.

"Then I left," Elle said. Three little words to sum up the hardest thing she'd ever done in her life. "After I safed-out, I got into the car, and I drove away. I shouldn't have been driving, not then. And not with all the pain I was in. But I did it. I left him."

Kyrie didn't speak. Elle reached out and brushed the tears off Kyrie's face with her hand. Elle's throat was tight, painfully constricted. But she had no tears, none. She'd cried them all out on the floor of the bathroom when she told Søren what had happened. She had no tears left for herself or him.

"Why are you crying?" Elle asked, smiling at Kyrie. "I'm the one who left him."

"He broke your riding crop," Kyrie said, gazing down on the three pieces of the broken twig on the blanket.

Elle reached out and grazed them with her fingertips.

"It would have hurt less had he broken my own body into three pieces," Elle said. With each snap of the wood as he broke the crop, Elle had felt something snapping inside her. As he'd thrown the pieces across his bedroom, she'd felt as if he was throwing her against the wall, throwing her away.

"You did the right thing, leaving him," Kyrie said.

"I know. But knowing it doesn't make it any easier. You'd think it would." Elle took a long ragged breath. "I used to think I wanted to marry Søren. I mean, I did want to marry him. When I was sixteen and that was the only thing I knew you were supposed to do with someone you'd fallen in love with—get married, have babies. I got older and my dreams changed. He was always in them, though. And in my dreams, he was always a priest. Because he is a priest. That's not what he is. That's who he is. And a good priest, too. I couldn't let him give up who he is for me."

"He wanted you to give up who you are for him."

"Yes," Elle said. "Yes, he did." She gathered the pieces of wood on the floor in her hand. "That's why I'm here. He can't get to me here. If I stayed, he would have called the bishop, told him he was leaving the priesthood and made me marry him. If he can't get to me, he can't make me marry him, and he doesn't have any reason to leave the priesthood."

"You walked away from him so he could lead the life he was supposed to live."

"Even when I hate him I still love him," Elle said.

"I couldn't have done that," Kyrie said. "I couldn't leave someone I was in love with. I don't think I'm strong enough to do that."

"I didn't leave him because I'm strong," Elle said. "I left him because I had no other choice. I couldn't let him throw away the most important part of himself for me."

"He might have done it anyway," Kyrie said. "Left the priesthood, I mean. You haven't spoken to him since you left, right?"

"I haven't," she admitted. She hadn't given that possibility much thought, that Søren had left the Jesuits, left the priesthood while she was here hiding at the convent. "I hope not. If he has, then me leaving him was for nothing."

"Not nothing," Kyrie said, and Elle gave her a look of deepest apology.

"No, not for nothing. I met you here. I wrote a book here."

"'All things work together for the good for those who love God and are called according to his purposes,'" Kyrie said. "That's my favorite Bible verse."

"You think I was meant to come here?"

"If you're here, then there's a good chance you were. Maybe you were supposed to meet me so you'd write that book and have an agent who wants to read it."

"Maybe I'm here because you're not supposed to be a nun and this was the only way for you to find out."

Kyrie smiled. "Maybe so."

"So when do we leave?" Elle asked. "You and me?"

"When you finish the book. As soon as it's done, we'll go."

"That'll give me time to figure out where we can go," Elle said. "Surely I know someone who could put us up for a few weeks while we decide what to do. Maybe I can get my old job at the bookstore back. My boss there loves me."

"I can get a job too," Kyrie said. "I have a college degree."

"In what?"

"Biblical studies."

"A BA in BS. That'll pay the bills."

"Oh, shut up, English major."

"Did you tell me to shut up?"

"I did," Kyrie said, crossing her arms in playful defiance. "What are you going to do about it?"

"I'll find a way to shut us both up," Elle said, and grabbed Kyrie by the wrist. She dragged the girl to her and pushed her onto her back on the blanket. Elle lay on top of her and kissed her with the deepest passion. Kyrie moved beneath her, pushing her hips into Elle's, rubbing her back, panting for more. Elle pulled Kyrie's gown all the way off and tossed it aside.

Elle sat on her knees and took a length of rope out of her bag.

Not real rope. She couldn't find any at the abbey. But she did have old sheets at her disposal and she'd torn them into strips and braided them into her own makeshift rope. She wrapped the white sheet rope around Kyrie's two wrists and tied them to the ornately carved leg of the nearest chapel pew.

"*B* is for *Bondage*," Elle said as she tied off the knot. "And *D* is for *Dominance*. If you want another orgasm, don't you say a fucking word until I give you permission to speak again. Nod if you understand."

Kyrie nodded. Vigorously.

"And *S* is for *Sadism* and *M* is for *Masochism*," Elle said, pinching Kyrie's nipples until she recoiled in pain. "Thus ends your alphabet lesson for the day."

Elle shoved the girl's thighs apart with her knees, and pushed two fingers into her wet hole.

Kyrie's back arched and Elle smiled, drunk with the power she had over this girl's beautiful little body. She lowered her head between Kyrie's legs and lapped at her swollen clitoris. Kyrie grunted softly from the pleasure but didn't speak. Elle rolled her tongue over all Kyrie's most sensitive spots and soon the grunts becomes moans, and when Elle pushed her fingers inside Kyrie and stroked her softest places, the moan became one long groan of ecstasy.

When her climax came and passed, Kyrie lay spent on the blanket, taking short shallow breaths. Elle spent the next hour doing nothing but rubbing and touching every inch of Kyrie. As she massaged Kyrie's body, she claimed it for herself.

"My hands," Elle said, caressing Kyrie's palms and fingers, one by one. "Aren't they? You can speak."

"Your hands," Kyrie said, wiggling her fingers for Elle.

"My arms," Elle said, rubbing up and down the length of Kyrie's arms.

"Your arms."

"My back," Elle said, massaging Kyrie's back. She took special pleasure in the small of her back, the small waist and hips.

"Your back."

Elle claimed every inch, every orifice, every single finger and toe and eye and nose. And the lips. Of course the lips.

"My Kyrie," Elle said with one last kiss. "My dove."

"Your Kyrie," Kyrie whispered into Elle's mouth. "Your dove."

When Elle had finished taking ownership of every part of Kyrie's body, she helped her dress and rise to her feet. She'd made her come three times, and Kyrie was light-headed now, weak from pleasure as Elle was weak from happiness. She had something in her heart she hadn't had when she came here months earlier—hope. A real agent wanted her book. Kyrie wanted her. They had a plan to leave, to go back into the world. Elle could work and pursue a writing career. She could do that. She wanted to do that. She could see it all happening, the dominoes falling ahead of her, the tumblers clicking into place. They could have a life together, her and Kyrie. She could make this work somehow and she'd do it on her own, without Søren.

Hand in hand they walked through the trees back to the abbey. Silently they slipped inside and Elle escorted Kyrie all the way to the door of her cell. Somewhere in another hallway, footsteps echoed. Kyrie pulled her inside the tiny room and shut the door silently behind them.

Elle grabbed her and kissed her over and over again, the thrill of almost getting caught sending her heart racing and making her blood burn. She remembered this feeling, the exhilaration of reveling in the forbidden. Sometimes she'd wondered if she desired Søren so much in spite of the fact he was a priest, or because of it.

"Thank you for telling me the truth," Kyrie said in the smallest of voices. If they were caught…well, what did it matter? They were leaving anyway. "I needed to know."

"You earned it."

"Will you be okay?" Kyrie asked. "When you're back out there, out in the world?"

"What do you mean?"

"I mean, you won't go back to him, will you?"

"No," Elle said.

In the distance she heard a sound. Nothing more than a motorcycle in the distance, its engine purring and humming as it lingered at a stop sign. Søren's? Maybe. She walked toward the window to hear it better, walked toward it as if drawn to the sound by an invisible cord wrapped around her heart.

Kyrie reached out and took Elle's hand in hers, stopping her in her tracks.

"Come to bed," Kyrie said. "Please? Be with me again. One more time tonight."

Elle pushed her to the bed and laid her down onto her back. They would be tired tomorrow, but who cared?

And outside the gate she heard the motorcycle drive off.

She was safe. Whoever it was had gone.

She'd told Kyrie the truth. She wouldn't go back to him.

Not now.

Not ever.

Not yet.

31

CALLIOPE SENT THE ROLLS-ROYCE TO PICK KINGSLEY up at the airport. But when his driver took the turn to head back to Riverside Drive, Kingsley called to the front.

"Wakefield first," he said.

His driver, a young semi-unemployed actor named Roland, did as Kingsley said.

A bone-deep exhaustion suffused Kingsley's entire body. He felt like a soldier again, returned from battle, wounded and tired and numb. His driver had noted the unnecessary weight he'd lost and quoted Shakespeare at him. Kingsley had a lean and hungry look about him, according to Roland, and Kingsley found the Julius Caesar reference appropriate. Men with too much power were on his shit list today. Time to have a little talk with one of them.

"Should I leave you and come back?" Roland asked when he opened the door of the Rolls for Kingsley.

"Wait for me," Kingsley said to the boy. "This won't take long."

Today was Saturday and Søren always said Mass on Saturday evenings. It would be over by now, but knowing Søren's habits, he'd still be at the church or in the rectory. He couldn't have gone far.

Kingsley was pleased to see the church empty of the faithful when he entered it. He was hardly fit for human company at the moment. His last bath had been yesterday in the ocean and he'd neither shaved nor slept in two days. He had on yesterday's clothes—dark pants, a black T-shirt. He'd left his black jacket in the Rolls and Juliette he'd left behind in Haiti.

He knew he would never see her again. The one woman he could have spent his life with, and she'd ordered him away from her and out of her life.

He'd lost it all. Again. He should be used to it by now, he thought, losing everything and everyone he loved. He'd certainly had enough practice to be an expert at it. If only one could get paid for losing the people you loved, Kingsley could turn pro.

Inside the sanctuary Kingsley saw a familiar blond head facing the front of the church. The head was slightly bowed. He was praying. Good. Kingsley hoped God was listening right now. Kingsley had a few things to say to Him, too.

Kingsley took one step forward on the hardwood floor, and it was enough to alert Søren to his presence. The blond head turned and the priest rose from his pew. It might have taken him a second longer than usual to recognize Kingsley. The Caribbean sun had turned his olive skin to bronze. His hair was longer now and needed taming, and he hadn't changed back into his usual uniform of expensive custom suits and boots and everything fine. Søren walked toward Kingsley with long purposeful, almost-eager strides.

Søren too appeared gaunt, as if he'd grieved in secret all this time.

His steps quickened as they neared Kingsley, and it took everything Kingsley had in him to not hasten the inevitable and go to him.

"Kingsley." Søren breathed his name more than spoke it. A sigh of relief, of surprise. And Kingsley was relieved to see him alive, relieved to see him standing, relieved to simply see him, this man he'd loved all this life.

Søren started to stay something else, but Kingsley stopped him with a quick vicious punch to the face.

Søren's head snapped to the left. Kingsley had to give the man credit. He took the punch well. He'd put other men on their backs by hitting them as hard as he'd hit Søren. For good measure and because he deserved it, Kingsley punched him in the chest. He aimed for under the rib cage and he was fairly certain he felt something crack.

"This isn't kink, by the way," Kingsley said. Søren clapped a hand onto Kingsley's shoulder to steady himself. He wasn't doubled over but close to it. "Consider it a lesson in empathy."

"I missed you, too, Kingsley," Søren said, his voice steady, but with a note of discomfort. He looked down and saw Søren's clenched hand. And slowly, ever so slowly, Søren relaxed his hand.

"Turning the other cheek?" Kingsley asked. "Maybe you did learn something in seminary, after all."

Søren stood up straight at last and raised a hand to his nose. A line of blood trickled from it. He touched it and looked at the blood as if surprised to see it there.

"To what do I owe the pleasure of this greeting?" Søren asked, his voice composed but hard as granite.

Kingsley reached into the pocket of his trousers and held out the handle of the riding crop he'd given Elle, the handle of the riding crop she'd left for Kingsley as a message, the handle of the riding crop Søren had broken.

He dropped it onto the floor of the church in front of Søren's feet. Kingsley looked Søren in the eyes.

"Don't ever break my toys again."

Kingsley turned to leave, but Søren stopped him with a question.

"Why weren't you with her?"

Kingsley froze. Slowly he turned back around.

"So much for turning the other cheek," Kingsley said. He smiled. "It's impressive, really. You don't even have to hit me to hit me. You are indeed the greatest sadist in the world. Congratulations. I hope you're proud."

"You shouldn't have let her go through it alone."

"No, I shouldn't have. I should have been there. But where the fuck were you?"

"I was in Rome, and I left her with you. I left her for you to take care of and instead I come home to find her bleeding in my bathroom and sick as I've ever seen her."

"Yes, and what did you do when she was bleeding and as sick as you've ever seen her? You did that." He pointed at the broken riding crop on the floor at Søren's feet. "And now she's gone. Maybe you should have stayed in Rome with the Pope. She'd still be here."

"If I'd been here, I wouldn't have let her go through it alone. If you'd called me—"

"I told her to call you. She refused. She said she didn't want to burden you with the decision. She had to make it herself so it would never be on your conscience. That was the most scared I've ever seen her, and even then, she was thinking of you."

Søren didn't speak but he didn't look away. He held Kingsley's gaze, unapologetic.

"It's funny," Kingsley said as he made a sudden realization. "For over ten years I've thought one thing about her. Yes, she's beautiful, beyond beautiful. Kinky. Smart. Every man's dream. But I always thought perhaps…she wasn't good enough for you. This little girl from Nowhere, Connecticut, with a nobody mother and a piece of shit father. How could she ever be worthy of you? Now I'm starting to think something different.

You hide behind your collar and get to play God while the rest of us do your bidding and suffer the consequences. You get the glory. She gets the bruises. Maybe it's you who's not worthy of her. Maybe it's you who's not worthy of me, either."

"Have you spent the last year planning this speech?"

"No," Kingsley said. "The last twenty years."

"Twenty years? I would have expected a longer speech then." For that Kingsley almost hit him again.

"I used to think you walked on water," Kingsley said, meeting Søren's eyes. "Now I know you're drowning like the rest of us."

"I am drowning," Søren said, and Kingsley paused in the doorway. There it was again—the sound of an eggshell cracking inside his heart. He ignored it.

Kingsley walked out of the sanctuary and out of the church before Søren could say another word or before Kingsley could say anything he might regret someday.

Roland was out of the car in an instant, opening the door for Kingsley.

"Where to now, sir?"

"Home," Kingsley said tiredly.

An hour later, Roland pulled the car in front of the town house and Kingsley got out on his own, his bag in his hand. He'd forgotten he had people to open doors for him, to carry his bags for him. He'd been gone too long. So long he'd thought he'd feel *something* when he arrived at his house. Relief? Happiness? Contentment? But he felt only resignation. He'd run away from home like a child who'd fought with his father. He'd gone out into the big wide world and the big wide world had sent him back home again. So much for the return of the prodigal. No fatted calf for him. No feast. No fanfare.

He opened the front door and sixteen feet raced at him in a flurry of love and fur. He dropped his bags and hit his knees as his four black Rottweilers whined and whimpered, almost mad with happiness to see him again. He let them paw at him, lick him, knock him flat on his back with their joy.

"I was going to throw you a welcome home party," said a voice from the top of the stairs. Kingsley looked up and saw a girl with bobbed brown hair skipping down the steps. "But the kids said they didn't want to share you."

Calliope was dressed in her usual uniform of a plaid skirt, kneesocks and an oversize cardigan. She was his devil in disguise—a wicked computer genius who looked like a schoolgirl, because she was one.

"They're very possessive," Kingsley said as he pulled himself off the floor. Calliope stood on the bottom step and Kingsley walked to her. "You look different."

"It's the haircut," she said, tossing her head left and right. "Like it?"

"It's *très* French. You look like Coco Chanel."

"I'll take that as a compliment."

"I said you looked French. There is no higher compliment." She laughed and crossed her arms over her chest.

"Am I allowed to hug my boss?" she asked. "Or would that be weird?"

"You aren't going to hit on me, are you?" he asked.

"No. I'll behave."

"Then yes, you can hug me."

Calliope leaned forward and wrapped her arms around him.

"You're too skinny," she said in his ear. "You need to eat. I'll get us takeout from La Grenouille. And then we can watch *The Matrix* again."

"I'll need wine for that," Kingsley said. "Lots of wine."

"Can I have some, too?" she asked, pulling back to smile ingratiatingly at him. *"S'il vous plaît, monsieur?"*

"You're underage."

"Yes, but you're French."

"I am, aren't I?" He paused and pretended to mull it over. He held up one finger. "Drink all you want then. But no driving."

"That's what we have Roland for, remember?" She embraced him again and for a moment Kingsley did feel what he wanted to feel upon arriving back at home after his journey—contentment, peace, happiness. But it was gone again in a flash.

"What about your Juliette?" Calliope asked. "When's she coming?"

"She's not," Kingsley said.

"But what about everything I—"

"She's not coming," he said again. He forced a smile, but Calliope didn't buy it.

"King, I'm so sorry." She hugged him again, long and hard, and he let her.

"It's fine," he said, patting her on the back, comforting her as she tried to comfort him. "Some things aren't meant to be."

"Do you love her?" she asked, a child's question. No adult would ask a question so honest.

"Yes," he said. "But I'll survive. That's what I do. It's what we all have to do whether we want to or not."

"You better survive. I don't want to have to get a real job."

"This is a real job," he said, pulling away from her. "You're the personal assistant to a business magnate."

"I've spent the last ten months having dungeons cleaned and hacking into the French governments personnel files."

"And?"

"And I love it." She grinned broadly at him. "So it's good you'll survive. And if she doesn't see how awesome you are after all you did, she doesn't deserve you."

"You're too kind. But I don't want to talk about it. I want to play with my dogs and eat all the *boeuf bourguignon* in the city."

"I'm on it," she said, clapping her hands. "Your wish is my command. Come on, kids. Dinnertime." She snapped her fingers and his four dogs—Brutus, Dominic, Sadie and Max—got to their feet and followed her like four huge black ducklings following their mother. He laughed at the sight of them. It was good to be home. He picked up his bag off the floor and tramped up the stairs. He'd take a long shower, shave, put on his favorite clothes, his favorite boots…then he'd feel like himself again. Or even better, he'd feel like someone else.

When he opened the door to his bedroom, he inhaled deeply. Calliope had done a good job. She'd kept the house in perfect order while he was gone. He could smell the wood polish on the bedposts, the leather polish on his boots in the closet. The air, however, carried the scent of abandonment. It was time he came home. He had the feeling his bed had missed him as much as he'd missed it.

He undressed and stood in the shower for a long time, willing the hot water to burn his misery out, willing the hot water to wash his heartbreak away. It didn't, of course, but he felt better when he was clean again. He was only half dressed when he heard his phone ringing—the private line that rang only into his bedroom. He checked the caller ID. It wasn't her. Would he be hoping it was her every time any phone rang?

"Edge," he said into the phone.

"You broke a rib," came the reply.

Kingsley laughed, his first real laugh in over a week.

"I thought you'd be happy about that."

"How's your face?"

"I have a bruise. Should be interesting explaining that to my church."

"Welcome to the company of we who must lie about our bruises. Your Little One was one of our founding members."

"I've never left bruises on her face."

"Then I suppose you deserve a medal," Kingsley said with more venom than he intended.

"I didn't call to start round two."

"No," Kingsley said. "I know. I'm done. *C'est fini.*"

"Good. Because if you try that again, I will hit back."

"I haven't taken a beating in months. Your threats aren't having the desired effect."

"They never did."

Kingsley paused and prepared his confession.

"I met someone in Haiti."

"Is that where you went?"

"For a while."

"Who is she? He?"

"Her name's Juliette. But it doesn't matter," Kingsley said. "It didn't work out with her. I might have taken my unhappiness about that out on you."

It's the closest Kingsley would get to saying he was sorry. Mainly because he wasn't.

"She must have gotten to you for you to assault a priest in his church."

"She was…is very special to me," Kingsley said, hating the past tense. "I'm not telling you this for any reason other than…"

"What?" Søren asked, the slightest note of compassion in his voice.

"If what you feel for Elle is like what I feel for Juliette…"

"If you feel anything close to what I'm feeling and have felt since she left…then you have my deepest sympathies. I wouldn't wish this on my worst enemy."

"I want to ask you how you are, but I don't want to know the answer," Kingsley said.

"You know my life. You know my past."

"I do," Kingsley said.

"Then you know what it means when I say this is the worst thing I've ever been through."

Kingsley winced. "For that I am sorry."

"It isn't your fault. I promise, if I could make it your fault, I would."

"Do you think she's coming back?" Kingsley asked him.

"Yes," Søren said.

"You're sure about that?"

"I know my Eleanor. I know my Little One. She will come back to me."

"And if she doesn't?"

Søren didn't answer that, and Kingsley was glad. He didn't want to know the answer to that question, either.

"She told you I asked her to hurt me?" Kingsley asked. "She told you she did hurt me?"

"She did."

"You didn't like that."

"No. I still don't."

"I told you what she was a long time ago. That girl is no submissive. She's a—"

"She's mine," Søren said. "Nothing else matters but that. She is mine. The end."

"She's yours, is she?" Kingsley pushed a wet swath of hair out of his face. "Too bad someone forgot to tell her that."

"Are you finished now?"

"Finished with what?"

"Finished trying to hurt me?"

"I think so," Kingsley said. "But I'm not ready to forgive you yet."

"Is that because you haven't forgiven yourself for letting her go through it all alone?"

"You smug bastard, I should have put you in the hospital."

"Where do you think I've been the last hour? Good thing I have a doctor in my congregation."

"How convenient." Kingsley sat on his bed and hung his head. He and Søren were silent for a long time, long enough for Kingsley to get angry again. "Ten years ago the three of us stood in the hall of your church and had our first little conversation. There'd been a wedding and she was cleaning up afterward. You went over and I followed you and found her there. And I asked you if I could have her. Do you remember what you said?"

"Remind me," Søren said, although Kingsley was utterly certain Søren remembered every word from that night.

"You said 'Wait your turn.'"

"So I did. And?"

"And you should know," Kingsley said, "if Elle ever comes back, it's my turn."

32

THE DAY HAD COME.

Time to go.

Those were Daphne's first thoughts when she woke up for the last time in John's bed. The clock on the bedside table read 5:17 a.m. She dressed in the darkness as the sun wasn't up yet and if it had been, the curtains were closed tight to whatever light was out there. She'd been living behind closed curtains since her first night with John. She went to his house at night in the dark and left before sunrise. In a book or a movie maybe she would have been a vampire who woke at sunset to her life and fell into a sleep like death at dawn. That had been her life, such as it was, for the past six months. From dawn to dusk, she lived in a daze, the hours empty of purpose and meaning. At sunset she came to life the moment she crossed his threshold.

This morning she would cross it again for the last time.

She pulled on yesterday's clothes that had ended up here and there on the floor. John had been playful last night and tossed her panties in one direction, her socks in another. Did he have an inkling of what she'd planned? Had it been a delaying tactic? No, of course not. She knew John. If he had any idea at all she was leaving him today, she would have woken up tied to the bed by her wrists and ankles, her car keys hidden and her money gone. And she'd been disappointed when she woke up and found her hands and her ankles free, her keys where she'd left them, her money all in her purse.

Once dressed, she stood by the bed and looked down at John asleep on his stomach, his hands to either side of his head. He had a beautiful body and she'd spent every night of the past six months underneath it. She ached to touch him but he always slept lightly, something he blamed on his military training. She couldn't speak either lest she wake him. So in the temple of her mind, she spoke one silent prayer to him.

"I can't do this anymore, John. I'm sorry. I got a letter that I've been accepted to UC. So I'm going there today. You don't know that. No one knows that. I wanted to tell you but I know you and you'd find a way to talk me into staying. You'd find a way to keep me here. It wouldn't be hard. You'd only have to say 'Stay' and I would stay. That's why I couldn't tell you. I couldn't give you the chance to talk me out of this, because you would. I don't know if this helps or makes it worse but you're the only man who's ever protected me. You need to stay a cop so you can protect other people. And someone would have found out about us eventually and you'd never be a cop again. I couldn't live with that, knowing I'd taken you from the life you love. So this is the only way. I promised you once I'd never run away from you again. There's two things you should know. I love you. But I lied."

Daphne turned around, picked up her car keys, walked out the back door and got into her car.

She started it, she backed out of the driveway and she drove.

She drove to the end of the street and stopped at the stoplight.

There was no one else on the road. She was alone, all alone.

The light turned green.

But Daphne didn't go.

She had to go.

The light turned red again.

Daphne waited. If she went back, she could slip into his bed and he'd never know she'd gone.

Or she could drive away and start a new life without him.

Stay? Go? Stay? Go?
The light turned green.

"So what happened?" Kyrie asked, flipping over onto her side to face Elle. "Does Daphne go back to him right then? Or does she drive away?"

"That's for you to decide," Elle said. "I left it open-ended. What do you think she did when the light turned green again?"

"I don't know," Kyrie said, smiling. "I kind of want her to go back to him. But then again, she's only seventeen. Can you really find your true love in high school?"

"I thought I did."

Kyrie met Elle's eyes and she braced herself for a question. But Kyrie didn't ask it and Elle thanked God she didn't have to answer it.

"What would you have done in her shoes?" Elle asked. "When the light turned green, would you go back or go forward?"

"I think…" Kyrie paused. "I don't know. Let me think about it."

"You think about it and get back to me." She loved that Kyrie wanted to think about it, wanted to mull it over. That's what Elle intended with the ending. It would be something different for every reader. The romantics at heart would say Daphne went back to him. The realists would say she left him.

"So it's done?" Kyrie asked, putting the pages of the book in order. "The whole thing is done? Beginning, middle and end?"

Elle nodded. "The end," she said. "Now I just have to find a computer, type it up, clean it up and email it to your sister's agent."

"So it's time?" Kyrie asked. Elle saw a flash of fear in her eyes. Elle didn't blame her.

"Yeah, time to go. Are you ready?"

"I'm…" It was as far as Kyrie got with her answer. A sob escaped her throat. Elle held her close and tight, rocking her as if Kyrie was a child in her arms.

"I know," Elle said. "I'm scared, too. But the longer we stay the harder it will be to leave. You do want to leave, don't you?"

"I want..." Kyrie began and stopped. She seemed to be debating her answer, weighing her words, searching for something to say, the right thing to say. Then she nodded and when she spoke again her voice was clear and steady. "Yes, I want to go."

Elle pulled her close and Kyrie cried quietly in her arms. They did everything quietly—laughed, talked, fucked. They hadn't been caught yet, but it was only a matter of time. And Elle was tired of being quiet all the time. She needed to raise her voice; she needed to laugh as loudly as she could. She needed to tie Kyrie to a real bed and make her come until she screamed.

"When are we going?" Kyrie asked, looking up at Elle.

"Tomorrow night," she said. "We'll wait for tomorrow night when everyone is asleep and just go. We can go out the back door of the oratory and walk to the road. We'll have to walk all the way to Guilford but when we're there, we can get a hotel room for the night and figure out where to go from there."

"I know it's really far away, but we could go to California," Kyrie said. "My brother would let us stay with him."

"Are you sure?" Elle asked.

"He left the Church after Bethany died. He didn't want me to be a nun."

"Does he know—"

Kyrie shook her head.

"Nobody does. You'll have to say you're my friend. Sorry."

Elle shrugged. "Being lying about my love life ever since I had one. I guess I can keep doing it."

"You can tell my brother and his wife you're leaving your boyfriend. They can guess why."

Elle laughed mirthlessly. She was getting tired of lying about herself.

"Leaving my boyfriend. Sounds so vanilla," Elle said. "I was the sexual property of a sadistic Dominant Catholic priest and now I'm 'leaving my boyfriend.'"

"You can't tell people the truth," Kyrie said. "They'll freak out, and they won't help us."

"You're sure your brother will?"

"Yeah," Kyrie said. "He's a good guy. Conservative. But he loves me. He and his wife have a pretty big house. I know we can stay there for a while, at least while we figure things out."

"Okay. We'll go to California. I've always wanted to swim in the Pacific Ocean."

Kyrie laughed. "You'll need a wetsuit. The water is freezing."

Elle sighed. "There goes that dream."

"I'm sorry."

"It's not your fault the ocean's cold out there." She held Kyrie's face in her hands and kissed her. "I have other dreams. Better dreams."

"Am I in them?"

"You're in all of them. We'll go to your brother's house, and I'll get a job. We'll make it work. Maybe your sister's agent can sell the book."

"I'm sure she can. The book is so good. I love it."

"I'll write another one. And another one."

"Good. I want to read them all."

"Maybe I'll write one with two girls next time. Athena and Aphrodite fall in love."

"Weren't they sisters?"

"They can't breed. Who cares?"

Kyrie laughed, and Elle kissed her again, happy to see a smile.

"That's better," Elle said. "We've got a long journey ahead of us. I need you to be strong for me, okay? Once I leave, they won't let me back in here. When we go, we have to go, and there's no coming back."

"I understand."

"I can't leave here without you."

"Yes, you could. You just don't want to." Kyrie smiled.

"Of course I don't want to leave without you. Not now or ever. But I have a reason to leave now, and it has nothing to do with him."

Kyrie held up the handwritten pages of Elle's book. "We'll do it for this."

"I didn't believe you when you said you'd figure out what I was supposed to do with my life."

"I told you I would."

"Now I believe you. You were right."

"Good. That's all I needed to hear." Kyrie reached for Elle again and they kissed. Elle pushed Kyrie onto her back and caressed her face, her hair, her neck and arms.

Elle took the lit candle off the bedside table. Kyrie raised her hand.

"Can we just sleep tonight?" Kyrie asked. "For a while, you and me. We've never slept together."

"Will you wake up in time?"

"Does it matter if I don't?" Kyrie looked up at Elle and smiled nervously. "We're leaving."

"Good point. I guess if we get caught now...what's the worst they can do? Kick us out?"

"Exactly."

"Okay. We can sleep." Elle blew the candle out and slid under the covers. She was small herself, but Kyrie was smaller. She pulled Kyrie against her, her back to Elle's chest. They lay together spooned tight until they fell asleep. When Elle woke up at dawn, Kyrie had already returned to her cell.

Elle took deep breaths to calm herself. They had a plan. Meet at night, leave through the oratory. Walk to the city. Buy bus tickets.

And then...who knew? And who cared? She'd have Kyrie

with her, someone to take care of, someone to be with so she
wouldn't have to do it all alone.

Nothing left to do now but pack.

The day had come.

Time to go.

33

New York City

TWO MONTHS SINCE LEAVING HAITI AND KINGSLEY was still alive, still functioning. He wasn't sure how he did it, but he did it. He survived losing Juliette. He didn't drink— not much. No more than usual. He didn't slip back into his old drug habits. He didn't engage in any wildly self-destructive behaviors. Of course, he did fuck as often as possible. When in doubt, Kingsley fucked. That had been his coping mechanism all his life, and it had always served him well.

Kingsley played smart and fucked only people he trusted. Women he'd known for years, who'd known him for years and had no interest in pursuing a relationship. He fucked Simone, one of the better pro-submissives of his acquaintance and Søren's go-to masochist when his Little One was unavailable. He wondered how much time Simone had spent on Søren's Saint Andrew's Cross lately. He didn't ask. Kingsley was certain he didn't want to know. There was also Tessa, who'd worked for him on and off for years. He went out a few nights with Griffin and seduced a beautiful twenty-seven-year-old gold-medal-winning diver named Hunter, whom Griffin trained with at his gym. Kingsley had hunted Hunter, and now Hunt, as he preferred to be called, had been Kingsley's most constant bedtime distraction for the past month.

For all his coping, he did have a weak moment and considered, for almost an entire minute, taking Calliope to bed. He discarded the idea quickly. She was eighteen and her adoration and affection for him made it easier to get through the day, to get back to work. He adored her and wanted only the best for her. And sleeping with her might compromise the high esteem she held him in, and he needed someone's love right now, even if it was from the eighteen-year-old girl who picked up his dry-cleaning.

It was for the best, really, that Juliette had made him go. Monogamy simply wasn't in Kingsley's blood. He loved fucking men too much. And other women. And pain, he loved that too, and Juliette only wanted to receive it, not give it. Cold comfort, but it was comfort. He needed all the comfort he could get.

"Mr. King?"

Calliope's soft voice interrupted his solitary reverie. Good. He needed to stay out of his mind as much as possible. He looked up from the book he hadn't been reading and smiled at her.

"Yes?"

"Are you done with me for the day?" she asked, standing in the doorway to his sitting room.

Kingsley checked his watch. It was a little after seven in the evening.

"I suppose. You have somewhere to go?"

She grinned. "I have a date."

Kingsley slammed his book shut and set it on the table next to him.

"A date? With whom?"

"No one you know."

"Why don't I know him?" Kingsley took his glasses off and tossed them on top of the book.

"Because I barely know him. It's a first date."

"You can't go on a date with someone you barely know. What if he's a criminal?"

Calliope pointed at him. "You're a criminal." She pointed at herself. "I am a criminal. We—" she pointed back and forth at both of them vigorously "—are criminals. Half of what I do for you is illegal. You caught me using a fake ID I made to get into your clubs and you hired me because it was such a good fake."

"We're not talking about me or you. We're talking about him."

"He seems nice. He's friends with Tessa."

"Nice? He's not vanilla, is he?"

Calliope screwed her face up in disgust. "Ugh. Don't even joke about that."

"What's his name? And birth date? And place of birth?"

"You are not allowed to make a file on him," she said, pointing her finger at him. "You are not allowed to do a background check."

"I'm your boss. I can do anything I want."

"No," she said again firmly.

"Does he know about me?" Kingsley asked. "Did you tell him I used to kill people for a living?"

"I hope you never have a daughter if this is how you act when your assistant has a date."

"Don't get pregnant."

"I don't believe in getting pregnant on a first date."

"Good. Do you need condoms?"

"I'm not having this conversation with you. I'm leaving. Right now. This instant."

"You come to my room when the date is over so I know you're safe. That's an order."

"Anything else, sire?"

"Take a gun."

"Oh my God." Calliope shook her head and sighed. Kingsley considered having her tailed.

"I don't want you getting hurt," he said.

She sighed and smiled at him. "I know. I'll be fine. It's sweet that you care."

She walked over to him and kissed him on both cheeks in the French manner as he'd trained her to do. He heard the doorbell and willfully ignored it. Calliope's date must be picking her up here. Maybe he should go say hello to her suitor…ask him a few questions.

But no. Calliope would kill him. Eighteen years old, he reminded himself. Almost nineteen. A legal adult. And intelligent. And responsible, apart from her association with him. And hardworking. She deserved a date without her boss giving her a hard time about it. Of course, if this boy harmed her in any way Kingsley would be forced to kill him. But that went without saying. He picked up his glasses and his book again—*Wide Sargasso Sea*, a book Elle had recommended to him long ago. A beautiful book but a poor choice for a man trying to forget the woman he loved who lived on a Caribbean island with a man who would never understand her.

"King?" came Calliope's voice again.

"If he stood you up, I'll shoot him," Kingsley said.

Calliope didn't laugh.

"What is it?" he asked.

"There's a woman here for you."

"Who?"

"She didn't tell me her name."

"What does she look like?"

"Stunning," Calliope said, sounding truly stunned. "I've never seen her equal."

Kingsley's eyes widened. He stood up and walked to the door. Calliope looked at him.

"I don't want you getting hurt, either," Calliope said with concern scrawled across her face.

Kingsley kissed her forehead. "Have fun on your date."

He walked past her and out into the hall. Down the hall to the entryway.

And there she was—Juliette. At first he could only stare at her in wonder. Juliette, in the flesh, standing in his foyer. She wore the loveliest turquoise dress and shoes and she shimmered like a jewel.

"That was a very pretty girl who answered the door," Juliette said.

"Cal. Calliope," he corrected. "My assistant."

Juliette nodded. "Calliope? Is that her real name?"

"She's a computer hacker. She says she has to have a mythological code name. Silly girl. She has a beautiful real name, but she won't let anyone call her that."

"What is it?" Juliette asked.

"Céleste."

"Yes," Juliette agreed. "Lovely name."

"Did you come here to talk about my assistant? We can if you like. She's going on a date tonight, and I'm not taking it well."

Juliette gave him a tight smile and laughed to herself.

"I came here because I can." She looked uncomfortable, nervous, out of her element. It took everything in his power to not grab her and drag her up to his bedroom. "Thanks to you."

"You said you wanted freedom. Freedom was the only thing you wanted. You wanted it more than you wanted me. So I gave it to you."

"I didn't expect you to pay for my mother's medical bills."

"I didn't expect you to find me. You wanted freedom. Now you have it."

He'd had Calliope set up a third-party medical trust fund account and had all of Juliette's mother's medical expenses paid through it. Everything was in Juliette's name and nothing was in his.

"You left without telling me where you lived, what your name was," Juliette said.

"You said you didn't want to be beholden to anyone. It was a gift. No strings attached." Kingsley had made sure of that. Calliope set up everything so that Juliette could never find him through the accounts. It was hers, free and clear. Leaving without telling her goodbye, without telling her how to find him had been the hardest thing he'd ever done.

"You didn't have to do that," she said.

"No, I didn't."

Kingsley didn't say anything else. He didn't trust himself to speak right now.

"I left him," she said at last.

"Did you?"

She nodded.

"I haven't really loved him in a long time. He's not an evil man. He's actually... I wish him well," she said. "I told him he should be with someone who does love him, but it would never be me."

"Was he angry?"

"Shocked. He wanted to know where the money came from."

"What did you tell him?"

"I said I found a buried treasure on the beach."

Kingsley swallowed hard. He would have laughed if he could have. Right now he could barely breathe, much less laugh.

"How did you find me?" Kingsley asked.

"Gérard had me help him with his work. I know how to find people. I knew your first name, your age, that you lived in Manhattan. Took a while, but here you are. Kingsley Edge—you weren't joking. You have your own kingdom. Must be nice."

"I'm afraid to ask you what you're doing here. But I'll do it anyway. Why did you come here?"

Juliette shrugged and crossed her arms over her chest.

"I went to visit my mother since I could. The first trip I've ever taken that he didn't pay for."

"How is she?"

"She's comfortable," Juliette said. "But her doctor said she's not improving."

"I'm sorry about that. Truly."

"She's happy and they treat her like a queen. That's all I care about."

"What did you do after visiting her?" Kingsley asked. Juliette glanced around the entryway. He hoped his home didn't disappoint.

"I traveled Europe. I liked Germany very much. And Italy. They were my favorites. After Paris, of course."

"Of course."

"I thought about you while I was traveling," Juliette said. "About what we had together and what you did for me. I thought about how I'd wanted freedom for years now and how you'd given it to me without asking anything in return. And I came to a conclusion…"

Kingsley had trouble speaking. His throat was tight and his hands were trembling. He shoved them into the pockets of his jacket.

"And what is the conclusion you came to?" he finally asked, keeping his voice as neutral as possible.

Juliette looked at him. Then she smiled.

"Freedom is overrated."

34

HER BAG WAS PACKED, AND INSIDE IT ELLE HAD ALL HER clothes, her handwritten copy of *The Virgin*, the copy of *Bulfinch's Mythology* that she'd stolen from the convent library and the two pieces of riding crop she hadn't been able to bring herself to throw away.

All day long she was an electric bundle of energy. She did everything she could to stay calm and stay focused, but she couldn't stop smiling, couldn't stop panicking. She was leaving. Finally. Getting out of here. She'd been trapped in a convent for months and months and was so ready to leave she could scarcely breathe the air inside anymore.

Elle had only one loose end to tie up. Her mother. She'd avoided thinking about her mom in the two months since she and Kyrie had decided to run away together. Her mother was certain that if Elle left here, she'd run right back into Søren's arms. Knowing her mother, she'd likely prefer that to Elle admitting she'd been sleeping with a woman for the past two months.

But still…Elle had to say goodbye somehow, some way. If she went and hugged her mother, that would be far too suspicious. And if she told her mother she was leaving, her mother would do everything in her power to get her to stay. She'd make a scene, start a fight. Kyrie was too fragile to handle leaving under those conditions.

And Elle too…this decision to leave felt fragile, as well. She was afraid to leave but more afraid not to. When would she see her mother again? They'd found a little peace together under this roof, behind these walls. But Elle couldn't stay just for her. Elle knew her destiny, unlike her mother's, didn't live behind these walls. As much as it hurt, she had to go. And since she had to go, she had to say goodbye. Elle decided on a letter. It was the only way.

Dear Mom,

By the time you get this letter I'll be gone. I can't stay here at the abbey anymore. I don't belong here and we all know it. But thank you for taking me in and giving me shelter. I promise I'm not going back to him. He's not the reason I'm leaving. You won't like hearing this, but there's a literary agent who is interested in my book. I used to dream about being a writer when I was a teenager. I hope you never found any of my journals that I was scribbling in constantly. They would have given you a heart attack. I'm only telling you this so you know writing was my first good dream I ever had for my life. The nicest thing he ever said to me was that I was a better writer than he was.

You might not believe me when I say this, but I love you, Mom. I'm sorry the choices I've made in the past have scared you and disappointed you. I would be lying if I said I had any regrets, but you should know, I don't feel good about hurting you. In my world, the pain is supposed to be consensual.

Please don't be angry with me, and don't be afraid. I'll be fine. You always told me growing up that God had a plan for me, a plan to give me a future and hope. If it makes you feel any better at all, for the first time in my life, I think I believe that.

Love,

Elle

She didn't add a postscript at the end. What more was there to say?

At 10:00 p.m., after everyone had gone to bed, Elle put on her jacket and her shoes and pulled her hair back into a ponytail. She walked out to the oratory and found Kyrie waiting there for her. She had on her habit, her full habit. She hadn't even changed clothes for bed. Elle had never touched her intimately while Kyrie had her habit on. She'd never touched Søren when he wore his vestments, either. They were sacred garments, and Elle felt awkward seeing Kyrie in them.

"I have clothes for you to change into," Elle said.

"Good. I'll put them on as soon as we get outside the gate."

Kyrie smiled big and bright, but something about her smile looked fake and fragile. Elle didn't blame her too much. They didn't have much of a plan or much money. They were scared, both of them. Elle's hand trembled and her breaths came faster than usual. Her voice sounded higher than usual, even to herself. Her mouth was dry and her muscles were tight.

She couldn't wait to get the fuck out of here.

"Well, I have everything," Elle said. "What about you?"

Kyrie had a suitcase. Elle reached for it but Kyrie held it to her chest. "I can get it," Kyrie said.

"Sure. Great. Ready?"

"You first," Kyrie said.

She reached out and took Elle's hand. Elle squeezed Kyrie's fingers and took a harsh, scared breath.

"Okay. I'll lead the way."

"Elle?"

"What?"

"Kiss me," Kyrie said. "Please?"

Elle laughed. "Absolutely."

She felt strange kissing Kyrie while she was wearing her habit and veil. But how could she say no to such a humble request? She put her bag down and placed her hands on Kyrie's face. The kiss was exactly what Elle needed. It reminded her that Kyrie had put herself into Elle's hands. She had to take care of them now. She had to take care of both of them. Kyrie was young and she needed Elle to be strong for her. Strong and in charge. Elle could do that.

When Elle pulled back, Kyrie had tears on her face.

"Don't be scared," Elle whispered. "I've got this. You believe me, right?"

"I believe in you. You're going to do amazing things out there in the world."

"We both are."

"I wanted to tell you…" Kyrie began. "I figured out how your book ends. I know what Daphne did when the light turned green."

"You did?" Elle asked. "What do you think Daphne did?"

"I think she went out on her own and had an amazing life. And I think John Apollo had a good life too, even without her."

Elle grinned. "I think you're right. More than one kind of happy ending."

She kissed Kyrie quickly on the lips again and picked up her bag. Elle took a deep calming breath and walked to the back door of the oratory. Kyrie unlocked it and opened it for her.

Elle looked over her shoulder and smiled at Kyrie. Elle stepped out of the chapel and into the real world again.

The night was cool but not cold, and the moon was high and full and bright. She could see everything—the cluster of white oak trees and the silver maples that stretched along the edge of the worn dirt path, the abbey glowing gray in the moonlight, and the road in the distance lit by a single streetlight.

She took a deep breath and inhaled. Of course the air smelled the same out here as it did behind the fence, behind the gates, but she didn't care. She breathed it in again. It was almost summer. That's what she smelled—the coming of a new season. Everything smelled alive. And the world was alive. She heard owls and crickets, a car on the gravel far away, the wind sweeping over the farmland behind her.

She turned around and held out her hand for Kyrie.

"Green light," Kyrie said. Then she shut the door to the oratory.

"Kyrie?" Elle knocked on the door. No answer. She knocked again, harder and louder, called Kyrie's name again. Still no answer.

Panicked, heart racing and sweating, Elle pounded even harder on the door. She ran to the side of the oratory and peered through the wrought-iron fence.

There she was, a dove in her white feathers gliding across the dewy nighttime grass on her way back to the abbey.

"Kyrie!" Elle called out her name once more. In her voice Elle could hear desperation, anguish, sorrow, the sound of her own heart breaking. Kyrie paused in her steps but didn't look back at her. Elle reached through the fence and waited, holding her breath, hoping against hope. "Come back," she said, willing Kyrie to change her mind, to come back.

Kyrie started walking again and Elle's legs gave out on her. She crumpled to her knees and rested her head against the iron bars. For the first time since coming here...for the first time in months...for the first time since she left home, Elle cried.

She wept deep, hard, copious tears that left her back shaking and her body trembling. All this time, Kyrie never planned on leaving with her. It had all been a ruse to get Elle to go back into the world where she belonged. That's why Kyrie had begged for the kiss—her last kiss.

Elle grabbed her duffel bag and wrapped her arms around it. She was that desperate for something to hold. She cried for three reasons.

She cried because she was scared.

She cried because she was alone.

And she cried because...

"Søren," she whispered into the cold dark night.

She missed him; she missed him so fucking much. She'd missed him from the second she walked away from him until this moment when she still missed him. She missed him and she loved him and she'd give anything right now for him to pull up on his Ducati and take her in his arms and drive her back to the city and put her in his bed and beat her and fuck her and forgive her for leaving him.

But she was alone. Søren wasn't here. And even if he forgave her for leaving him, she couldn't forgive him yet for what he'd said and what he'd done. If she went back to him it would be just as it was before. She would be his property and his possession. He would leave the priesthood and make her marry him. And that would be that. Her freedom would be gone, vanished. He would never let her top Kingsley again, or anyone for that matter. He'd made that abundantly clear.

Alone and with only five hundred dollars to her name, she had to make a decision. She couldn't sit on her ass and cry all night. Although it was certainly tempting.

Once upon a time she'd been happy. Truly happy. Somehow she'd lost that somewhere along the way. Whenever she'd lost anything—her car keys, her driver's license—Søren would take her by the shoulders and tell her to retrace her steps. Walk backward from now to the moment she last had it.

When was she last happy—truly happy—out in the world?

Elle walked backward in her mind, back past the fight she'd

had with Søren, past the day at the doctor's office, past the morning she'd woken up nauseous and had thrown up so hard both she and Kingsley had known immediately what had happened...

With her sleeve, Elle wiped her face and looked up at the moon and the stars. For so long she'd lived among city lights she'd forgotten that the moon wasn't all there was in the night sky. And although a riot of stars danced across the heavens, it was the moon that drew her gaze. Kingsley had a conservatory on the roof of his Manhattan town house filled with tropical plants and rare flowers in a glass box the size of a large bedroom. She loved the scent of hothouse flowers in bloom and spent lots of time up there reading and watching the city go by her. She'd often wait for Søren there, staring out the glass walls onto Riverside Drive. She'd watch for Søren and smile when she heard his Ducati's engine and saw him roll up in front of the house.

The last time she and Kingsley had had sex, it had been on the fainting couch in his conservatory. Earlier that night he'd beaten her brutally in his bedroom and fucked her raw. But a few hours later, they'd taken wine up to the conservatory and she'd ordered him to strip naked. With so many plants around them no one could see into the conservatory unless they looked in from the roof, which meant that maybe God was watching. She liked that idea. That night she'd doused King with scalding candle wax until he was so hard and turned on he begged her to fuck him. She straddled his hips, took him inside her. While he was in her and she on top of him, she'd looked up at the moon high overhead and had a moment of purest happiness. Søren would be home soon, she remembered thinking. And until then she had Kingsley to keep her company. Søren never left her alone when he was gone. He was always with her in one way or another.

Elle wanted that again, that happiness she'd lost along the

way. And the last place she'd had it was in Manhattan with Kingsley in his town house.

Maybe it was still there.

Slowly she got to her feet and shouldered her bag. She brushed the dirt off the ass of her pants and headed toward the road. It took two hours to reach the city of Guilford. She didn't bother getting a hotel room. She found the one bus station in the city and sat in the lobby waiting for the first worker to arrive. While she waited for someone to show up, Elle pulled out her book and stared at it. The pages were crinkled and bent, thick with ink. *The Virgin*. She wasn't sure about the title anymore. Daphne was only a virgin for about the first fifty pages. And being a virgin was a negative state. Nothing to brag about. Those years Elle had been a virgin, the lack of sex she was having was the least interesting thing about her. Who was Daphne really? Daphne was a runner. That's who she was. She ran track and cross-country, she ran when John chased her, and at the end she ran again, she ran away. *The Runner* didn't sound very romantic. Maybe something else…maybe…

Elle crossed out the words *The Virgin* on the front page and wrote a new title.

The Runaway.

There. That was better.

At 6:00 a.m., a boy who didn't even look old enough to drive, much less work at a bus station, arrived for his shift. She was in no mood to talk so of course he asked her how she was, where she was from, why she was here so early.

When he asked her where she was headed she answered with one word.

"Home."

35

FREEDOM IS OVERRATED.

It was all Juliette said and all she had to say. Kingsley had her in his arms in an instant, kissing her as if the world would end if he didn't. And of course, he had to save the world.

"Are you sure you want to be mine?" he asked between breathless kisses.

"Yes," she said. "Absolutely."

"There are things you need to know."

"Fuck me first. Then tell me."

Kingsley laughed in purest joy. He swept Juliette up in his arms and started up the stairs.

"Put me down," she ordered. "I can walk."

"I've always wanted to carry a woman up the stairs and ravish her."

"I won't stand in the way of your dreams then," she said, putting her arms around his neck as he mounted the stairs. He carried her straight to his bedroom, kicked the door shut behind him and pushed her onto her back on his bed. It took only seconds to strip her naked and to cover her body in kisses. He kissed her from the graceful turn of her ankle, up her muscular calves, over the soft flesh at the inside of her knees, the long line of smooth skin on her thighs, until he buried his tongue inside her and made her moan for him. His blood was pumping, pounding in his veins. He could feel every muscle in his lower back and stomach tightening with need for her. He licked her clitoris until she shuddered, coming hard with a hoarse cry. He'd missed that sound, the sound of her climax, the taste of her in his mouth, the sight of her on his sheets. For two months he'd convinced himself he'd never see her again, never have her again. He cupped her breasts and pinched her nipples—hard.

"That hurt," she said, laughing and recoiling at the same time.

"I had to make sure you were real."

"You're supposed to pinch yourself," she told him.

"Where's the fun in that?"

"You don't have to pinch me. This is real," she said. "I lived without you as long as I could stand. I couldn't wait another day to see you."

He kissed her breasts gently now, sucking her nipples until they hardened in his mouth.

"Come inside me," she said. "Please."

He straddled her thighs and pushed her wrists down deep into the bed, holding her there.

"What are you asking me?" he asked.

"No condoms," she said. Kingsley froze. He wanted to be inside her bare so much it hurt. And he could. He was clean. And he knew she was, too. But still…

"You know what happened the last time I fluid-bonded with someone…"

"I won't get pregnant. And if I did…I would keep it."

Kingsley felt something open up inside him, like a safe that had been cracked and everything that had been hidden, everything valuable was there for the taking. It terrified him to be this vulnerable.

"You can have my cum when you earn it," he said.

"Tell me how to earn it and I will."

"Stay," he said in his most commanding tone. She stayed.

He went to his closet, found a black briefcase and brought it to the bed.

"What is that?" Juliette asked.

"Something I've wanted to use for a very long time." Kingsley flipped the combination—2663—and opened the case. From it he pulled a long thin metal chain with a cuff on the end. He bent and locked one end of the chain to the bedpost at the foot of his bed. He took the cuff at the other end of the chain and held it in his hand for Juliette to see it.

"Pick a number between one and ten," he said.

"What am I choosing?"

"I'm not telling you until you've chosen."

Juliette answered quickly. "Seven."

"Perfect," he said. He grabbed her leg, put her foot on the center of his chest and locked the cuff around her ankle. "Seven days."

"What?"

"You picked seven days to stay in my bedroom chained naked to my bed."

"What?" Juliette demanded.

"Don't worry," he said in a paternalistic tone. "This chain is long enough so you can reach anywhere in my bedroom and my bathroom. You stay here seven days, locked in. I'll bring you food and water and anything else you need. You don't put on clothes. I'll touch you when I want to touch you, beat you when I want to beat you and fuck you when I want to fuck you. And in seven days, if you're still here and haven't asked me to unlock you, then you get what you want from me. Are these terms acceptable to you?"

"You chained me to your bed."

"Are you complaining?"

"Not at all."

"You said freedom was overrated. Let's see how you like being my property and my prisoner."

"I love it already. But I'd love it more if you were inside me," she said, sitting up on her elbows. She spread her legs for him by way of invitation, an invitation he eagerly accepted. He rolled on a condom and entered her hard and swift and she arched beneath him, taking him deeper. The thin metal chain hissed softly as he fucked Juliette as hard as he could. Chaining her to his bed wasn't enough. He had to hold her arms down by her wrists, push her legs open with his knees and impale her against the bed with his cock so deep inside her he might not ever get it back out again. If he died inside her, so be it. He'd die happy.

"I love you," he said, kissing her face.

"I love you, too. I didn't want to."

"Get used to it."

"Loving you?"

"Yes. And doing things you don't want to do." He gave her a devilish grin and she laughed, a joyful laugh.

"There's nothing you could make me do that I wouldn't want to do," she whispered, pressing her breasts against his chest.

"I accept that challenge."

Juliette loved rough and brutal sex, so he gave it to her as hard as he could. And then after he held her and kissed her and when the desire for her had grown to a fever pitch again, he took off all his clothes, pulled the covers down and made love to her until she couldn't take anymore.

He wrapped her in his arms and rolled her on top of him. She rested her head on his chest and they lay there together in his bed for a long time doing nothing but being.

Being still. Being loved. Being together.

"Tell me what I need to know," Juliette said at last as she lifted her elegant head and looked him in the eyes.

"I can't be faithful to you," Kingsley said. "And it's not for the reason you think."

"Not because your libido is stronger than your common sense?"

"That might be part of it," he admitted. "Also, I love having sex with men as much as women."

"I would never keep you from that part of yourself. I might ask to watch sometimes."

Kingsley smiled but only for a moment. Then the smile was gone.

"Do you know what the word *Switch* means?" he asked.

She shook her head.

"You like being hurt in bed, being dominated." Kingsley tapped the bruise on her bottom lip that his too-eager teeth had given her.

"Very much. I need it," she said.

"And I love hurting you and dominating you. But there are times when I want to be dominated myself, when I need to be hurt. I don't want that to be part of us. I want to keep that part of me separate from you. From us."

She nodded. "I can accept that."

"Please don't tell anyone. It's not something I want advertised."

"Your secrets are my secrets," she said. "I'll protect them with my life. There's something you should know about me, too."

"Tell me," he said.

"I do want children and I'll have yours for you. But my mother's doctor said her condition can run in families. Can you wait a few years until I'm certain it won't pass to me?"

"I can wait," Kingsley said, almost relieved. After all he'd been through with Elle, and failing her like he had, he wasn't ready to even think about being a father yet. "We should wait."

"My mother's symptoms started when she was a teenager, and I haven't had any. The doctor says I shouldn't be afraid to have children. He gave me his blessing. But still, you should know the possibility is there."

"I'm not scared," Kingsley said. "My parents were perfect. My childhood was perfect. And my sister still committed suicide. There are no guarantees in life. But you're worth taking the risk for."

"If we have a child, it might look like me."

"You mean a girl?"

"You know what I mean." Juliette laid her arm across his chest displaying the contrast in their skin color. He kissed her arm.

"I hope our children look like you. They would be beautiful then. I don't want ugly children. I'm very shallow."

She laughed to cover her tears, but Kingsley saw them anyway.

"Something else," she said. "I don't think I want to get married. I've been trapped in something too much like a bad marriage."

"You never have to worry that I'll force you to marry me," Kingsley said, laughing. "Not my style."

"And I want to work," Juliette said. "A real job where I'm paid. I need to have my own money."

"You can work for me. Calliope starts Columbia this fall. I'll need a new assistant."

"Work for you?"

"I pay very well. And it will be your money. If that doesn't convince you…maybe the fringe benefits will."

"I like the sound of that," she said with a seductive smile. "I handled all of Gérard's files in his home office. I did half his work for him. If something happened to him, I could have taken over as ambassador without missing a step."

"You should have let me assassinate him."

"No," she said, tapping him on the end of the nose. "No murders. It's a—what did you call it? Hard limit?"

"I suppose I have to respect it then."

She kissed him on the lips, on the neck, on the chest, on the old scar that had faded along with the pain it had once given him. "One more thing, *mon roi*."

"Name it," he said.

"I want a collar," she said.

"Why?" he asked, surprised by her request.

"You told me you'd never collared a woman. Or man. I'll let you have your freedom to be with whomever you want to be with. But I want something in return, something you haven't given anyone else. I need that for us."

Kingsley bent his head and kissed her. Then he slid out from under her and grabbed his pants off the floor and pulled them on. Somewhere in this bedroom…

He went back into his closet and found the bag he'd taken with him to Haiti. He hadn't unpacked it. And it was still there.

From a locked box on the highest shelf he pulled out a knife he'd carried on many of his missions when he was still ostensibly in La Legion.

When he returned to the bed, Juliette sat up. Even naked she looked elegant and regal, powerful, graceful. She was everything he'd ever wanted in a woman right here. And he would never let her go.

He set the bag on the bed and opened it. From it he took the black belt that had been his own souvenir from his nights with Søren back in their school days. Søren had beaten Kingsley with the belt and Kingsley had beaten Juliette with it. It had wounded them both so it would do for a collar. He wrapped it around her neck and with the tip of the knife put a hole where the buckle would fit. After measuring her neck, he sawed through the leather with the blade cutting off the excess. He wrapped it around her neck again and this time, he buckled it.

"There," he said, admiring her graceful neck now adorned by the black leather collar. "Perfect."

He slipped his finger between the leather of the collar and her skin. Tugging it, he brought her forward, closer…closer…

She took the hint, slid out of bed onto her knees and took him into her mouth.

It was going to be a good week.

At midnight, after he and Juliette had surrendered to sleep at last, Kingsley awoke from his sex- and kink-induced stupor and had the shockingly pleasant sensation of being happy to be awake. Juliette was sound asleep next to him in his bed, the chain around her ankle dangling out from under the sheets and onto the floor. She was his. Tied to him, chained to him, collared to him…all his. And she'd promised to have his children someday when she was ready.

He touched Juliette's face and she stirred in her sleep and smiled. There…if he could keep his eyes on her and what they could have together, maybe in time the emptiness he felt in Elle's absence would scab over and heal and she would be one more scar in a long line of scars he bore on his body and in his heart.

But Kingsley didn't want her to be a scar. A scar was a memory of pain. He wanted the pain.

To sleeping Juliette he whispered a promise. "My Jewel, I can't give you my whole heart. But the part of it I can give you is the part that isn't scarred and isn't broken. I'll give you the best of me and protect you from the worst for the rest of my life."

He moved to kiss her. He wanted to wake her with kisses and fuck her again. He'd warned her he'd take her whenever he felt like it, and he was determined to keep that promise.

Before his lips could touch hers, he heard something.

His doorbell.

Kingsley rolled onto his back and groaned.

Who the fuck was at his door in the middle of the night?

And when had he turned into the sort of man who asked himself who the fuck was at his door in the middle of the night?

Calliope was right. It was too quiet around the town house. He should change that.

Kingsley dragged himself reluctantly away from Juliette's body. He pulled on his pants and his shirt and left his bedroom. On his way to the stairs, he glanced left at a closed bedroom door. Behind the door sat an empty room that had once been Elle's. It had been Søren's idea for her to move in, not that Søren had told her that. He wanted her protected, watched, wanted her somewhere safe. A fool's quest, and Søren should have known that better than anyone. Safety was an illusion. One moment you were having some of the best sex of your life on the roof of a luxurious Riverside Drive town house. The next moment you're throwing your guts up in a toilet and facing the scariest decision of your life. He would do better with Juliette. He'd take better care of her. No one knew how much she meant to him, and so no one would be tempted to take him from her.

On his way down the stairs he saw Calliope in her bathrobe walking to the door.

"I got it," she said, calling up to him. "You can go back to bed."

"Best idea I've heard all night," he said, glad to see Calliope was safe at home from her date already. He turned around and started up the stairs again.

Then he heard a laugh, and such a laugh it was. A laugh that turned the lights back on.

"Good to see you again, too, kid," Elle said. Kingsley slowly turned around and saw Elle wrapped in Calliope's arms being hugged half to death.

His stomach dropped and he had to grab the stair railing for support. Behind him he heard Calliope talking in rapid, breathless tones. Her voice had gone up an entire octave. She'd wake the dogs if she didn't calm down.

He stood on the first-floor landing and looked down on the sight of Elle in his house. Right there. Before his eyes. She looked up at him and gave him a smile.

"Hi," she said to him.

"My office," he said. "Now."

Her smile disappeared and the mask of obedience she wore when submitting came down over her face. She started up the stairs following behind him, not speaking.

Once in his office he turned on a small Tiffany lamp. He pointed at the chair in front of his desk.

"Sit," he ordered. He wasn't sure why he was being so imperious and dictatorial except that he couldn't bear the thought of her running away again.

Elle sat in the chair. He sat on the edge of the desk in front of her. He wanted to tower over her, and he did.

"Why are you back?" he asked.

"I need a job."

"You're here asking for a job?"

"King, I—"

"You don't get to leave and then show up almost a year later and call me King. Call me 'sir' or don't call me anything."

He saw her clench her jaw tight.

"Yes, sir," she said, and he heard her struggle to say the words.

"You have no idea how angry at you I am," Kingsley said, realizing his anger at the moment he admitted it. She'd disappeared and hadn't written, hadn't called, hadn't told him she was alive. "After everything we went through—"

"We?" She looked up at him and met his eyes, a clear violation of every protocol a submissive was supposed to follow. "What did *we* go through? Sir."

There it was. She'd asked the question. They could talk about it, the pregnancy, the decision she'd made, and the mistake he'd made letting her go through with it alone.

Or he could let it go, drop it. It was in the past and they should leave it there.

"How are you?" he asked instead.

"Surviving. You?"

"The same."

He waited for her to ask about Søren. She didn't. Either she already knew or she didn't want to know. He'd put his money on the latter. He wished he didn't know.

"Where did you go?"

"My mother's."

"You were at her convent the whole time?" he asked.

"I was. I left."

"Did you—"

"I don't want to talk about the convent."

He raised his hands in surrender.

"What do you want to talk about?"

"I told you. I need a job. I'm doing something with my life. I think. Maybe." She laughed to herself. "But I'm broke and I'm homeless and I need help."

"It must have hurt to admit that."

"Look at me. You think I have any pride left at this point?" she asked him. He looked at her as ordered. She looked thin and tired and very pale. But the beauty was still there, and her eyes burned with a new light he'd never seen before. She had walked through Hell these past months and had survived the flames but carried the fire out with her.

"I think you have nothing left but pride."

She looked him in the eyes, a cold and penetrating stare that bore into him. If he had words written on his soul, her eyes could read them.

"I wrote a book," she finally said. "Someone is interested in it. But I need a job. Got any openings at Cuffs?" she asked. Cufflinks, Kingsley's private bondage parlor he'd opened three years ago.

"I sold Cuffs for ten million dollars while you were gone. Very valuable real estate."

"Fine. What about Le Cirque?"

"Sold. Twenty million."

"Your empire is shrinking."

"*Au contraire.* Merely reinventing itself."

"Can I help?"

"Perhaps you can. But first…tell me exactly what you need."

"Money."

"I could give you money."

"I don't want you to give it to me. I want to earn it. It's not really mine unless I earn it."

"And she says she has no pride." Kingsley laughed but Elle didn't. She glared, a cold and cruel sort of glare as merciless as any Søren had ever used on him.

"I'll go," Elle said, moving to stand. Kingsley put his foot on her thigh.

"Stay," he ordered. He knew if he let her walk out of his home tonight, he would never see her again.

"Staying, sir," she said. Every time she said "sir" it felt as if she was mocking him. She was mocking him and he liked it.

"Tell me this…what do you want to do?"

"Anything that'll pay the bills," she said.

"Anything, *chérie*? Anything at all?"

She winced at the *chérie*. Clearly she was in no mood to be charmed.

"Just a job, King. I'll cocktail waitress at the club, I'll scrub floors—I don't care."

He bent and took her chin in his hands. For a second she looked afraid. But then the fear was gone again.

"*Non.* Not a waitress, not a maid."

"Then what?"

"You want money. You're already worth a fortune," he said. With her face, her body, her reputation and with the right training she was sitting on a gold mine and didn't even know it. Men would give their right arm to kiss this woman's feet. And even better, they'd give over their entire wallets. Everyone in their world knew of her as Søren's submissive. Which meant everyone in their world knew of her. The curiosity factor alone would have them lining up around the block.

"What do you mean?"

"Kink is a kind of currency. You'd be surprised what it can buy you."

"You want me to sub for money? Fine. Like you say, if you're willing to get beat up for free, you might as well get paid for it."

He shook his head, tsk-tsked with his finger right in her face.

"No subbing. Not if we both want to live," he said, and Elle smiled knowingly. Søren would kill them both with his bare hands before he let his Little One submit to other men for money. He might kill them both with his bare hands anyway, so if they were going to die, might as well go out with a whip *and* a bang.

Kingsley had a vision then, a vision of this woman in front of him standing tall in a pair of knee-high black leather boots laced all the way to her thighs, a riding crop in her hand and a sadistic gleam in her eyes. He'd never known a sadist more vicious than Søren, but had never seen a Dominant more beautiful than Elle.

Elle was vicious too in her own laughing way. Søren took pain seriously. Elle didn't. He'd hurt you because he had to. She'd hurt you because she wanted to. And when she wanted to hurt you, you wanted to be hurt.

"Elle…*chérie*…*Maîtresse*," he said, tilting up her chin to meet her eyes. "No more serving for you."

"Then what the fuck am I doing?"

Kingsley bent low as if he was about to kiss her. Instead, he put his mouth at her ear and whispered.

"I have a much better idea."

36

"AND THE REST IS HISTORY," KINGSLEY SAID.

Nora reached out, and she and Kingsley clinked their glasses in a toast.

"One more toast," Nora said. Kingsley held out his glass again.

"To what?" Kingsley asked.

"You punching the shit out of him." She laughed and looked at Søren over her shoulder. He glared at her.

"That hurt," Søren said. "I couldn't take a full breath for two weeks."

"You get no sympathy from me, blondie," Nora said. "I couldn't masturbate for two weeks after you sprained my wrist that one time in your dungeon."

"You sprained your own wrist."

"Because you were tickling me."

"If you had taken it like a good girl and hadn't thrashed so much…"

"How have I put up with him for twenty-two years?" she asked Kingsley.

"A divine mystery," Kingsley said. Still laughing, he looked at Søren. "Now you know. That was the year I met Juliette, almost killed a man over her, came home and got everything back I'd lost and then some."

"Good year for you," Søren said.

"Hard year." Kingsley met Nora's eyes.

"Very hard year," she agreed.

"Did you ever speak to Kyrie again?" Søren asked.

"No." Nora drank the last drops of her wine and gazed into the bottom of the now-empty glass. "I was angry with her for a long time for letting me go without her. Then angry at myself for being stupid enough for expecting her to leave with me. I'd let the Church have you. Maybe I thought God owed me one."

"Did she remain in the order?"

"As far as I know, she did. When she finished her novitiate she was going back to the Monican abbey in Northern California. She might still be there. She might have left. I asked my agent about her once, but they're not in touch anymore."

"Do you ever think about her?" Kingsley asked.

"Sometimes. Not often. It was what it was while it lasted. Then it was gone. As soon as I was back with you at the town house...it all felt like another dream. Honestly I don't think Kyrie was even kinky. She just wanted to be with someone before she took her final vows and when I decided to leave, she knew she had to lie to get me to go without her. Tonight was the first time in years I've thought about her. The castle reminds me of the abbey. Although—" she smiled at her surroundings "—the beds are much bigger."

"Thank God for that," Kingsley said. "I can't fuck in a twin bed. I'm not a kid anymore." Kingsley glanced at Søren, who only shook his head in playful disgust.

"Do you two need some alone time?" Nora asked. "I could go check on the cake. And taste-test it. All of it."

"Stay," Søren said. "If he's too tired for Juliette, he's too tired for me."

"Not true," Kingsley said. "I don't have to get it up to bottom."

Nora groaned, collapsed on her side and covered her head with a pillow.

"I didn't need to hear that," she said from underneath her pillow.

Søren pulled it off her face and looked down at her.

"Grow up," he said.

"Do I have to?"

She sat back up again and started to say something along the lines of "Please don't make my life any weirder than it is" when a knock came on the door.

"I know he's in there." Juliette's voice came through the door. "You can't hide forever, you French coward."

"Come in!" Nora called out before Kingsley could stop her. Juliette came in with Céleste in her arms.

"I wasn't hiding," Kingsley said. "We were reminiscing. It's what you do before a wedding. And what is she doing up?" he asked, taking Céleste from Juliette's arms. "What are you doing still awake, young lady?" he asked in French.

"Your daughter needs her good-night kiss," Juliette said. "And so do I."

"I wasn't tired," Céleste said, wrapping her arms around his neck. She was a beautiful little girl who did take after her mother, especially in her personality. She certainly had her father wrapped around her tiny fingers, as her mother did. "And I can't sleep until you kiss me."

Kingsley kissed her on the end of her nose. "Better?" he asked.

"One more."

He kissed her again. "Now you sleep."

"Not yet," Nora said. "She has to kiss me good-night, too."

"Kiss your aunt and uncle," Kingsley said, patting her on the bottom of her little pink nightgown. Nora held out her hand

and helped Céleste navigate her way across the rumpled sheets and piles of pillows on the bed.

"Are you ready for the big day tomorrow?" Nora asked, looking deep into her dark brown eyes. "You have your petals all ready to throw?"

"I'm ready," she said, nodding solemnly. She reached out with her small hand and laid her palm on Nora's neck. *"Qu'est-ce que c'est?"*

"You know the rule," Nora reminded her in a faux stern voice. Céleste was being raised bilingual, and teaching her that not everyone spoke French had been the hardest part of the process. "French with Maman and Papa, and English with everyone else."

Céleste groaned.

"Ask your question again," Nora said.

"What is that?" Céleste tapped Nora's collar. "That thing on your neck."

Kingsley chuckled and Juliette sighed. Any child growing up in the home of Kingsley Edge was sure to receive an interesting and thorough education in alternative lifestyles.

"What do you think it is?" Nora asked her.

"It looks like a dog collar."

"That's exactly what it is. Didn't you know I was a dog?" Nora growled and barked, and Céleste exploded into giggles. Nora gave her a play bite on the neck.

"Don't get her wound up before bed," Kingsley said to Nora.

"She does the same thing to me," Søren said. Nora couldn't decide who to glare at—Kingsley or Søren—so she glared at them both.

"Go kiss your uncle good-night," she told Céleste. "And then go to sleep so I don't get in trouble with your papa."

Céleste kissed Søren on the cheek and he kissed her back. Juliette swept her daughter off the bed and into her arms again.

"I heard the good news, by the way," Nora said. Juliette grinned at her. "I'm thrilled for you both."

"Thank you," she said. She nodded down at Céleste. "Someone doesn't know yet."

"Know what?" Céleste asked.

"That it's your bedtime," Juliette said.

"I knew that." Céleste rolled her eyes, a know-it-all at age three.

"Are you coming to bed?" Juliette asked Kingsley.

"Is it safe?" he asked.

"I make no promises. But you should leave them alone." Juliette glanced at Søren and Nora. "They haven't seen each other in weeks."

"Fine. I'm coming," Kingsley said.

"That's right—you are." Juliette pointed her finger at the center of his chest. "It's a good thing I'm already expecting or that kilt would get me in trouble."

"You are trouble," Kingsley said to her. "I'll be there soon. Stay awake."

Juliette bent and kissed him before bidding them all a good-night and leaving with Céleste. She threw one last "You better behave" look at Kingsley over her shoulder before departing.

"God, I am a lucky man," Kingsley said. "What did I ever do to deserve her?"

"Chained her to a bed for a week?" Nora asked. "That's one way to get a girl."

"That was a good week." Kingsley stood up. "I should see if she packed the ankle chains."

"Good night, King," Nora said. "Try to survive the night. We need all our groomsmen in one piece."

Kingsley looked at her, at Søren, and laughed.

"It's a miracle, isn't it?" Kingsley said. "After all we put each other through that we're still together. All of us. A fucking miracle."

Nora laughed. "*Miracle* is the word for it."

"In the New Testament," Søren said, putting on his most priestly voice, "the word *miracle* isn't used in most translations. The phrase *signs and wonders* appears instead. I prefer that terminology. A miracle is a discrete act, special in and of itself but with no greater meaning to it. A sign, however, is trying to tell us something."

"What do you think it's a sign of?" Kingsley asked. "That we're all still together after everything?"

"I know," Nora said.

"What is it then?" Kingsley crossed his arms and leaned against the bedpost.

Nora unclasped the necklace she always wore that held the two engraved bands Søren had given her two Christmases ago and the little silver locket Nico had asked her to wear while they were apart.

"Your son gave this to me," she said, opening the locket. "Nico said my naughty stories remind him of *The Canterbury Tales*. So he gave me this."

She held it out to Kingsley.

"*Amor vincit omnia*," Kingsley read. He looked at Søren for the translation.

"Love conquers all," Søren said.

"That's what we're a sign of," Nora said. "The three of us. This wedding. Everything. *Amor vincit omnia*."

"Amen," Søren said.

"That," Kingsley said, "even I can say amen to." He gave Nora her silver locket back. She slipped it onto the chain and clasped it back around her neck where it belonged.

"I'll walk you out," Søren said to Kingsley, and Nora bit back a smile. They left the room together and she crawled into bed and curled up on Søren's pillow. He was a right side of the bed sleeper and would no doubt take issue with her stealing his side. Good.

She feigned sleep and kept on feigning it even when she heard the door open, close and lock. It wasn't easy to keep the ruse up when she felt Søren's mouth on her shoulder.

"Did you kiss Kingsley good-night?" she asked, trying not to smile.

"An entire castle full of people who've signed confidentiality agreements? Of course I did."

She giggled and squirmed deeper under the covers. Søren's kisses followed.

"He's happy," she said. "I've never seen Kingsley so happy as I have the past two years."

"He has Juliette, Nico, Céleste—"

"You," Nora said. "He has you. And even better, he has you to himself when I'm in France with Nico."

"I promise, by the time you come home from Nico, he's more than happy to give me back."

"And I'm more than happy to take you back." She rolled over and smiled up at him. "What about you? Are you happy?"

He nodded slowly. "Happier than I've ever been in my life. Getting older has its advantages. The past feels like ancient history now, gathering dust on the bookshelf. The ghosts have finally moved on to the other side."

"And you're turning into a silver fox," she said, running her fingers through his hair, the blond and the gray. "Another advantage of getting older."

He smiled and took her hand in his, kissed it. "Perspective. That's the greatest advantage. I can look back and see my life from far off and at a great height. And looking back on that year in particular I see that I owe you something. A long overdue apology. And your prize, of course."

"Prize?" She sat up in bed and batted her eyelashes at him. "I'd almost forgotten my prize."

"Close your eyes and hold out your hands."

She reluctantly obeyed. "The last time I played this game with Griffin," she said, "I did not get the prize I wanted."

"You'll want this prize," Søren said. He pressed something into her palms, something thin and smooth. "Open your eyes."

She opened them as ordered and saw that she held a riding crop in her hands. Thin black polished wood with a white carved bone handle.

"Is this—?"

"It's the same handle," Søren said. "We had to replace the actual crop, however."

Nora looked at it in awe. It wasn't quite the same as the one Kingsley had given her all those years ago, the one Søren had broken into three pieces. But it was close enough it gave her chills to look at it.

"Where did you get it?" she asked, looking up at him.

"Juliette helped with the restoration. She knows where Kingsley gets all his toys."

"You know I have dozens of riding crops."

"You should have dozens plus one," he said. "It was wrong of me to break it, and I should have replaced it years ago."

"Is this why you wanted to know about that year?" she asked, running her hand along the wood shaft to the leather triangle tip. A wooden riding crop could inflict the kind of pain a rattan cane could. It could even split the skin. A vicious devilish little weapon—she couldn't wait to use it on someone.

"Recent events have brought that year back to mind."

"What recent events? Me and Nico?"

"Yes," he said, tucking a strand of hair behind her ear. "Kingsley warned me when you were sixteen years old that you weren't the submissive that I thought I wanted you to be. I ignored his warnings, smug in my certainty that you would always obey me no matter what you were in your heart."

"I did promise I would obey you forever. I tried for a long time, as long as I could."

"And I promised you everything. Part of that everything should have been letting you be who you are and not trying to force you to be who I wanted. And now that you and Nico are together, and you and I have never been happier, I realize how foolish I was to be afraid."

It was true. They had never been happier together or during their four months a year apart. Søren had her and Kingsley and she had Søren and Nico. They both were living the life God had created them for and that, she'd found, was the key to happiness.

"I would have been afraid, too. If you'd come home from Rome and told me you'd decided you were a submissive now and not a Dominant anymore, I don't think I would have taken it any better than you took my news." She laughed at the very thought. "You're two people to me—Father Marcus Stearns and Søren—and I love both of you. I'm Eleanor and Nora. I was angry at you for so long because I loved both of you, and you weren't willing to love both of me."

"I tried to protect you, and I made it worse."

"Worse? No. Harder? Yes, but not worse. I might never have started writing novels if I hadn't left you. And if I hadn't started writing, I would never have met Zach. And...you know." She grinned. He tapped her under the chin in that fatherly way he had with her.

"All things work together for the good for those who love God and are called according to his purpose," Søren said.

"I think I heard that somewhere," she said.

"You should know that as much as I love my Eleanor, my Little One, I do love Mistress Nora, too. It took me longer to fall in love with her, but now I love her as deeply as I love my Eleanor."

"And as deeply as your Eleanor loves you."

She traced the carvings on the handle and remembered the rush of power she'd felt when Kingsley first put it in her hand.

She still felt that rush every time she held a crop in her hand. Where was Nico and his beautiful back when she needed it?

She raised the crop to her lips and kissed it.

"Thank you for this. It's beautiful. And I can't tell you what it means to have my first riding crop back. At least part of it."

"Use it wisely and well."

"I'll use it to beat the shit out of the first person I can until he screams like a little bitch."

"As God intended."

Nora laughed and kissed Søren.

"I love you, Søren," she said. "And I love you, Father Stearns."

"And?" he prompted.

"And I love you, my sir. Now and always."

She pulled back from the kiss and took his wrist in her hand. She laid the crop on his palm.

"Would you do me the honor of christening my crop for me?" she asked.

"You aren't ready to sleep yet?" he asked.

"I will always pick kink with you over sleep. Sir," she added at the end.

"You have a busy day tomorrow. Are you sure you want bruises?"

"Black and blue goes with everything. Especially white," she said. "Please, sir?"

"Well…" Søren said with a long-suffering and therefore entirely fake sigh. "Since you asked so nicely…"

He dug his fingers into her collar and pulled her off the bed and onto her feet. She stood still while he undressed her, moving only to cooperate with him taking her camisole off and stepping out of her pajama bottoms. He left her standing naked by the bed as he went to her toy bag. From it he pulled out her rope cuffs, which he brought over to the bed. He turned her to face the bedpost and lifted her arms. She let him move her, manipulate her body any way he wanted. Happiness was giving herself to him, putting her body and her life into his hands, knowing that when he was done, he would give her back, and she would belong to herself again.

He knotted the rope cuffs around the top of the bedpost and slipped her hands through the loops, pulling them taut around her wrists.

Nora waited for the first blow of the riding crop. But it remained on the bed. Instead, Søren stepped directly behind her and brought his hands around her head and rested them on her face. Slowly and gently he ran his hands over her hair and her ears, her neck and shoulders. He slid them up and down her back, up and down her arms. It had been years since he'd done this, since he'd reclaimed her body by touching every inch of it. He passed his hands down her inner thighs and over her calves. She shivered as his fingers caressed the soles of her bare feet. He worked his way back up her body, touching her stomach, her hips, her breasts and all the way back to her neck. There was no part of her he didn't touch.

With his hand flat against her throat he tilted her head back so that it rested against his chest.

"Why are you crying, Little One?" he asked.

"Because I love you, sir."

"Are you scared?"

"Not anymore."

Søren brought his hands to her face again and touched her tears.

He kissed her neck where the collar met her flesh. When he pulled away, she immediately missed the heat of his body against hers. He took the crop off the bed and Nora braced herself. The first strike hit her a few inches above the back of her knee. A red line of fire burst across her skin. The second strike landed on the middle of her thigh. She let out a gasp of pain. That was going to leave a bruise.

The sound wasn't the worst part although that whipping

noise as it cut the air certainly added to the agony of antici-
pation. Once she heard that sound, it was too late. No stopping it. He struck her a dozen more times at least, although the
pain had gone to her brain and she'd lost her ability to count.
A dozen times. A hundred times. What did it matter? Søren
would hurt her until she couldn't take anymore, and then he'd
take her until she didn't hurt anymore.

When the beating ended, Søren brought the crop around
her body.

"Kiss," he ordered, and she kissed the leather tip. "What do
we say?"

"Thank you for my beating, sir."

He didn't untie her immediately. Instead, he left her there
while he wiped the crop with a soft cloth to clean it, wrapped
it in the black felt it had come in and put it away in her toy
bag. Twelve years ago the thought of her exploring her Dominant side had made him so furious he'd broken her riding crop
into three pieces. Now he treated it with the same respect he
treated his own implements of sadism. She almost wept again
watching him wrap up her riding crop and put it away for her.
They had come so far together. She couldn't wait to see where
they went next.

Søren returned to her and pressed his hand into the welts
on the back of her body. She flinched and winced as his every
touch renewed her pain.

"Are you mine?" he asked her.

"I am yours. Forever."

And she was hers. But she was his too, and always would be.

At last Søren released her wrists from the rope cuffs. He
turned her and bent her over the bed, pushing her feet wide.
She heard him removing his clothes and grew wet with the an-
ticipation of having him inside her. From behind her he opened
her up with his fingers, and she exhaled in pleasure, her hands
digging into the sheets.

He was opening her up and she couldn't bear the wait and she made that clear with her pleas for mercy. And at last he took pity on her. With one hard thrust the full length of him was inside her where she wanted him, where he belonged. With his hands on her hips he worked her back and forth until every breath she took came out as a moan. The intensity of the thrusts left her reeling. She could feel him in her stomach. His fingers spread the lips of her vagina wider, then found her clitoris and stroked it, setting off small explosions of ecstasy all through her. She arched her back, parted her legs and raised her hips to offer even more of herself to him. His free hand grasped the back of her neck to the point of pain as he pounded into her. And when she couldn't take it anymore—the pain or the pleasure—he pulled out of her, pushed her onto the bed, and forced her onto her back.

Their mouths met in a hungry kiss. She was greedy for him and pulled him to her, on top of her, and he entered her again.

He devoured her mouth while he fucked her and she lifted her hips eagerly into his. They became nothing but bodies, nothing but burning flesh and need for each other. Søren slammed her hands down onto the bed, pinning her down so hard she cried out. Her renewed pain renewed his pleasure and he lowered his head to suck her nipples. It was what she needed to send her right to the edge, and there at the edge she hovered as the pressure built, every nerve in her hips tingling and thrumming, vibrating with bliss. Nora dug her heels into the bed and tilted her hips. The base of his cock grazed her clitoris and she came with a silent gasp, her hands clutching empty air as his fingers tightened on her wrists.

As she came, Søren moved into her with quick hard thrusts that ended with a final push. His body went taut and still against her as he came, pouring his semen inside her, filling her and fulfilling her. When it was over and done, he rolled onto his back and brought her with him. She luxuriated on top of his body, relishing his skin against her skin, his heart against her heart.

"I'm not sorry I left you that year," Nora said, lifting her head to kiss him. "But I am sorry it took me so long to come back."

"Don't be sorry. Go to sleep. We have a big day tomorrow."

"It'll be fine," she said, resting her head once more on his chest and settling into sleep. "After all, it's only a wedding."

"You know that's not what I'm talking about," he said, twining his hand in her hair and resting it on the back of her neck.

Nora closed her eyes and inhaled. Søren smelled like a winter's night, and though winter nights were cold and cruel, they were also clear. And Nora would happily sacrifice the heat of the nearest star to see the light of the farthest.

"I know."

37

IT WAS A BRIGHT AND SUNNY MORNING, AND NORA woke up alone. She looked around, called Søren's name and received no answer. Knowing Søren, he'd probably gone for a run to burn off his extra energy, his excess stress. Running for fun...proof Søren was as much masochist as he was sadist.

Nora dragged herself out of bed and touched her neck. Her collar was gone, locked up in the box where it would stay until Søren wanted to have his wicked way with her again. She pulled on her abandoned pajamas from last night and her black silk bathrobe and wrapped her hair up in a loose bun. When she was fit for human company, she left her room and went in search of breakfast.

The wedding wasn't until this evening at five but the castle already bustled with guests and workers and, of course, lawyers. Kingsley had imported three of them simply to handle all the nondisclosure agreements every guest and worker had to sign. Why couldn't they elope? Why go to all this trouble for something you could do in private in front of a justice of the peace? Then Nora saw a group of men walk past, all wearing kilts.

Oh yes, that's why they went to all this trouble.

Kilts.

In the castle kitchen she found coffee and chugged it. She met the castle's wedding coordinator and went over final details. She checked in with the caterers, the DJ, the florist and the photographer. By the time she was done Nora had decided she would rather fuck a haggis and eat it afterward than ever be part of another wedding again. Last time she ever agreed to play wedding planner.

Nora ate a pastry. Then a second one. She had a second cup of coffee and between sips went over the schedule with the waitstaff, who listened to her with impressive attentiveness. Someone had apparently told everyone working the wedding that Nora was a professional Dominatrix. Once she'd finished scaring the staff into submission, Nora headed back up the stairs, coffee cup in hand.

When she returned to her bedroom, she found the bathroom door closed and heard the sound of water running. Søren had returned from his run and hopped in the shower. She considered joining him but she heard him turning the water off. Damn. She'd missed her chance. No worries. Always tomorrow. She took off her pajamas and yanked on a pair of comfy jeans and a white T-shirt. While she finished her coffee she dug through her suitcase, pulling out her shoes and her stockings. Maybe she had underwear in here, too. Or had she not packed any? That might be a problem. No, probably not. Not with this crowd.

She had a shoe in one hand and her curling iron in the other when Søren emerged from the bathroom.

Both the shoe and the curling iron hit the floor at the same time. Galileo would have been pleased.

"Holy shit."

"Eleanor, behave."

"You're wearing a kilt."

"I realize this."

"You know I'm not capable of behaving under the best of circumstances. You are asking the impossible."

"Is this going to be a problem?"

"It is the opposite of a problem. It is the best thing that ever happened to me." Eleanor walked over to him and looked him up and down. He was in full Scottish regalia—black-and-blue plaid kilt, black socks, black shoes, blue sporran, black clerical shirt with his black jacket. He hadn't put on his collar yet so his shirt was open at the neck. His blond hair was wet and combed back and with the hint of his lean and muscular runner's legs peeking out from under the kilt, he looked as if he'd stepped out of a fever dream she'd had once and was apparently having again.

"Clergy in Scotland have their own tartan. I'm to wear it during the ceremony."

"I need your cock, not a lecture on Scottish fashion," Nora said. "Right now." She grabbed his hand and attempted to drag him toward the bed. He didn't budge.

"This is not happening, Little One."

"I'm going to violate you in so many ways you're going to have PTSD when I'm done with you."

"I already have PTSD from this conversation."

"Shut up, blondie, and get on the bed."

"Eleanor, no. Red. Stop. Safe word. We have work to do."

"Fucking first. Work after. You can slice me up like a Thanksgiving turkey if you want. Get hard and lie there. I'm getting under that kilt whether you like it or not."

"Rape-play is one of my hard limits."

"Who's playing?"

"Eleanor."

She looked at him and pouted. Really pouted. The pout to end all pouts.

Søren took a heavy breath.

"Fine. Best we get it out of your system now so I don't have to worry about being fondled during the ceremony. But make it quick. I'm supposed to meet with the wedding party in half an hour."

"You'll never know what hit you." Twenty-two years in love with this man and she still wanted him as much today as she did when she was a teenager. More even, but that was the kilt's

fault. She pushed him down onto his back on the bed and straddled his hips. She ripped off her shirt and threw it on the floor.
Pulling her down to him, he kissed her lips, then her neck.

"Are you a true Scotsman?" she asked, sliding her hand up
under the kilt. She encountered nothing but Søren.

In an instant he had her on her back, his hand pressing lightly
on her throat. He roughly yanked her bra down her arms to
bare her breasts. He lowered his head and bit her hard on the
shoulder. Søren needed to inflict pain to get aroused, and she
didn't mind at all. If he had to set the bed on fire and sacrifice
a virgin to get hard, Nora would hand over a lighter, a dagger
and every unsullied teenager in a ten-mile radius—that's how
much she wanted him right now.

So of course, right then, someone knocked on her goddamn door.

"Unless the castle is on fire and the British are invading, go
away," she yelled at the knocker.

"We have an emergency, Mrs. Sutherlin."

She looked up at Søren.

"If you're Mrs. Sutherlin, who's Mr. Sutherlin?" he asked
with his eyebrow cocked in suspicion.

"Vanillas." She sighed. To the girl at the door she yelled,
"What's the emergency? Somebody better be dead."

"We're missing the groom."

"Oh my God." She dropped her head back onto the bed.
"Next time I agree to plan a wedding, please tie me to the bed
until the fit of madness passes."

"I'll do that anyway. Go. Save the wedding. We'll play later."
He got off of her and straightened his clothes.

"You're in a kilt and you're not inside me. This is the worst
day of my life." She sighed. "And I've been kidnapped."

She grabbed her shirt off the floor and pulled it on more an-
grily than she'd ever put on a shirt in her life. That shirt was
lucky to survive.

"You." She pointed at Søren. "You guard that kilt with your life. I plan on violating the sanctity of it and you as soon as I can."

"The kilt is not going anywhere, and neither am I," he said. "Now go, before you assault me again."

"You're not out of the woods yet," she said. "Tonight you and your body and your kilt are mine."

"Have you forgotten who the Dominant is in this relationship, young lady?"

She exhaled heavily.

"Do I have your permission to violate you ten ways to Sunday tonight? Please and thank you, sir?"

"Yes, you may."

"Thank God."

She threw the door open and looked the interrupter in the face.

"Now tell me, please, what the fuck is happening?" Nora demanded of the girl. "I'm trying to fornicate with a priest in here."

Before the scared Scottish lass could speak, Juliette came running down the hall toward her looking both panicked and elegant which was a look only she could pull off.

"Nora, we need you," Juliette said. "He refuses to come out of his room."

"Which he?" she asked. "Groom A or Groom B?"

"Groom A," Juliette said.

"Thought so. Wait, which one did we decide was Groom A?" Nora asked.

"*A*," Juliette said, waving her hands like wings. "For *Angel*."

Nora sighed and rubbed her forehead. "I had a feeling this would happen. I'll be right there."

Groaning dramatically, she walked back into the room and slammed the door behind her. Søren was no longer on the bed, which meant this was shaping up to be the worst day ever.

"Michael won't come out of his room."

"Yes, I heard that," Søren said. "Whose idea was it to throw a million-dollar wedding for a groom with social anxiety disorder?"

"The other groom."

"Griffin should be flogged."

"He will be. By me. And hard. But after I go get Michael out of his room," she said, trying to figure out a plan of attack. "I'll see you at the wedding. And after the wedding. And all night tonight."

"Let me know if you need me."

"You're here," she said. "That's everything I need from you."

She kissed him, which was a mistake because now she was really furious about not getting to fuck Søren into the ground. *Later,* she reminded herself. Plenty of time to fuck him and be fucked by him tonight.

Nora started out the door again but stopped, turned around and walked back into the room. She grabbed her toy bag and slung it over her shoulder.

"Pray for me," she said.

"Always, mistress," Søren said. "And God speed." She made it to Michael's room and a small crowd that included his mother, his sister Erin, two of Griffin's sisters-in-law, his cousin Claudia, and Juliette. They were pleading at the door, begging him to open it.

"Out of the way," Nora said, snapping her fingers. The crowd parted like the Red Sea for her.

"We've been trying for an hour. He won't come out," Juliette said.

"Then I'll go in." Nora took a deep breath and slammed the side of her fist against the door so hard it shook on its hinges. "Michael Dimir, open this door for your mistress right now, or so help me God, I will pick the lock and use my entire shiny new set of scalpels on you, and there won't be a safe word in the world that will save you."

She paused. Everyone was silent. Then she heard soft footsteps. The door clicked open an inch.

Nora looked at the crowd gathered around the door and rolled her eyes.

Amateurs.

She slipped through the door, shutting and locking it behind her. She looked at Michael standing with his back to the wall, his arms crossed over his chest. He wore flannel pajama pants and a blue-and-white Yorke College T-shirt. His hair was shaggy and touched his ears and his silver eyes were shadowed by the dark circles from a night of no sleep. Six weeks ago he'd turned twenty-one and ten days ago he'd graduated from college with honors. But right now he looked as young and as scared as he did the day she'd met him when he was a few days shy of sixteen with still-healing scars on his wrists.

"I can't do it, Nora. I can't handle all those people staring at me. Please don't make me go out there."

"My Angel." Nora sighed. She took his handsome face in her hands and kissed him. Michael could do it and would do it. He was one of the bravest young men she'd ever known and loved. She simply needed to remind him of that. With her new riding crop, if necessary. Something told her it might be necessary.

She glanced at the clock. Griffin and Michael's wedding was T-minus six hours and fifteen minutes. She had to get Groom A calmed down, bathed and dressed, herself bathed and dressed and an entire wedding party corralled.

But Michael was her top priority at the moment. Even higher than getting under Søren's kilt, which was a close second.

Busy day ahead. Things to do. People to beat.

A Dominatrix's work was never done.

★ ★ ★ ★ ★